FURNACE
CREEK

First published in 2022
by Black Spring Press Group
Grantully, Maida Vale,
London w9, England, UK
United Kingdom

Graphic design by Edwin Smet
Author photograph by Lara Porzak
Cover photograph by Getty Images

Editor's note: the author has requested that American spelling and grammar be used in this work.

Set in Arno 11 / 14 pt
ISBN 978-1-913606-35-0

FURNACE CREEK

A NOVEL

Joseph Allen Boone

THE **BLACK SPRING**
PRESS GROUP

dedicated to my father

Harry Vester Boone Jr.

*who paved the way for all his sons' great expectations
and, filled with a vitality that belies his 96 years,
still champions our dreams*

Pause, you who read this, and think for a moment of the long chain of iron or gold, of thorns or flower, that would never have bound you, but for the formation of the first link on one memorable day.

Charles Dickens, *Great Expectations*

PART ONE

1

BAD DAY AT FURNACE CREEK

For years I didn't realize why it was called Furnace Creek, even though I'd been uncovering bullets in the vicinity ever since I was old enough to explore the creek on my own. The bullets in question were misshapen slugs of Confederate vintage, buried in the flinty soil, scattered in the underbrush, and sometimes wedged between the rough-hewn slabs that made up the sides of that rocky mound built on the steep embankment overlooking the creek. Decades of creeping ivy and a skein of Virginia honeysuckle held the mound in place, frustrating any temptation that its roughened walls might harbor to tumble earthwards.

That was the "furnace"—a towering outdoor stone oven in which molten lead had once been shaped into the slugs we kids showed off whenever we unearthed them from their recesses one hundred years later. It was one of the countless Civil War relics that haunted the mountains and valleys of Franklin County, reminders of a cause that, long since vanquished, stubbornly refused to vanish. But to my young fancy, the blackened furnace, hidden in the woods on the edge of town, looked more Egyptian than Confederate: it loomed in my childish imagination as a four-sided pyramid whose top had been whacked off twelve feet above the ground.

And whacking off was the fine art I learned there the summer of 1965, lying prone on those grim stones as Furnace Creek—taking its name from this landmark—churned and chortled through the forested landscape surrounding my perch.

In that initial onslaught of adolescence, as I was coming into my first and most vivid impressions of a wider world lying in wait just beyond the horizons of my vision, stealthy as a bobcat readying to pounce, I had found a haven for my solitary vice, so recently learned and so eagerly cultivated, on the top of that old relic. Stretched out on its summit and hidden by a shroud of greenery, visible only to unquiet jays hopping from branch to branch overhead, I found a refuge from the domestic surveillance that attended every creaking bedspring or locked bathroom door in my parents' well-regulated house. Here, dappled in sunlight that purified the act whose pleasure even then was obscurely related to the guilty suspicion that I ought not be doing what I so obviously wanted to do, I learned to bring myself to delirium with strokes as sensuous as those summer hours of daylight were long. That was the summer when semen still smelled astonishingly fresh, an elixir of unfathomed potency. That was the season of unmediated expectation, when the simple ecstasy of touch was all that was needed to bring me off again and again up in my leafy eyrie, my hideout from the world, ten-bike-minutes away from the chores I was avoiding at home.

How vividly I still remember the day I first came into a sense of my place in the world—that is, my place as something more culpable than a thirteen-year-old boy whose greatest misdeeds to date had been bullying his younger brother, tracking muddy prints across the newly waxed kitchen floor, neglecting his prayers. I was lying atop the furnace on that particularly blazing and humid July afternoon, shirtless and the elastic waistband of my shorts pushed to my knees. It was that kind of hazy day when the air conspired to look as thick as it felt, so that the sweat generated by the humidity and compounded by my handy exertions swamped me in a lubricant as much a deterrent as a stimulus to satisfaction. My vision had gone white from staring at the sun straight overhead, and just as my pent-up labors verged on completion, a dark fist bore down on my chest, a rasping voice demanded—

"GIVE ME YOUR NAME, BOY, QUICK!"

—and my world turned upside down.

I levitated in shock, the very instant a loop of liquid unspooled from deep in my gut and splattered the hand clamped down so fiercely on my chest. Sheer mortification joined company with the terror I felt.

Before I had time to react to the strong fingers pinioning me in place, the interloper had climbed higher up the mound, till she—for

I now saw it *was* a she, a powerfully built woman sweating even more mightily than myself as she gasped for breath—loomed over me, eclipsing the overhead sun. So intent was she on fixing me with her stare that she didn't notice, or at least notice enough to care, the milky ribbon clouding her walnut-brown fingers and spectacularly shaped, vermillion-painted nails.

"You're the Seward boy, I know *you*!"

At the instant that she identified me, I recognized her: Zithra Jackson Brown, the next-door maid till last year. I'd observed her across the laurel hedge separating our backyard from the Leroys, dressed in the gray uniform favored for the hired help in our neighborhood as she hung out the wash to dry, shook clouds of fluff from the dust mop, emptied the trash.

"Well I'll be, by bejesus," she said, and I didn't think I was imagining the gloating sound in her voice, broken by wheezing gasps as she tried to catch her breath. "Here I am lookin' for a place to squirrel away and what do I find? Newt Seward the Deacon's boy, abusin' hisself like he ain't never heard tell of the wages of sin. It'd be a pity, Lord save your soul, if word got out on how you been *wastin'* your seed..."—at which point she registered, too graphically for my adolescent taste, the inopportune moment at which she had interrupted my raptures by wiping her soiled hand on the shapeless blue smock she wore.

I was too terrified to reply. As her free hand ground my shoulder blade into the sharp rock surface, Zithra Jackson Brown smiled a gold-capped smile that was anything but friendly.

Uneasily I watched a beam of calculation light her knowing eyes.

"An' it would be a cryin' shame if folks was to hear how you forced poor ole Zithra to partake of your bad habits, wouldn't it now?"

"You daren't!"

"Oh yes I dare say I would, and it ain't the only shameful thing ole Zithra knows about you. Oh yes, Mr. Goody-Two-Shoes, I done seen into your bedroom window when you and your friends—" whereupon she leaned forward and hissed into my ear her version of the despicable acts that she'd espied from her observation post on the second floor of the Leroy house, on an afternoon I'd conveniently erased from memory. "I swear to God the world is about to learn *all* the evils you been up to, unless you do 'xactly as I tell you."

The fruits of her surveillance petrified me. All I could do was blurt out, "What do you want from *me*?"

She smiled her unfriendly smile, breathing heavily as she glanced at my now limp manhood, shriveling in the puddled residue of my ill-spent pleasure.

"I wants you to pull your pants up over your butt crack and high-tail it home like the Devil is riding your back. I know all you white folks is leaving for the fireworks soon, and when your family takes off you gotta find a reason to stay behind or else there'll be your Life to pay..."

I'd forgotten that this memorable day in my dawning awareness of my beleaguered place in the universe was the Fourth of July. Within the hour the whole neighborhood would load picnic hampers, lawn chairs, and swim gear into their station wagons and head to Bonner Lake for the Independence Day festivities repeated annually: kids cooling off in the murky water while the non-abstemious among the adults mixed Gin Fizzes and Old Fashioneds, a forgettable speech by the head of the VFW followed by an earnestly off-key chorus of "God Bless America," the firing of charcoal grills and spreading of checkered tablecloths to receive the fried, pickled, and jellied feast for which we gave ample thanks, and then—twilight turned ultramarine—the fireworks display set off from the diving platform bobbing in the middle of the lake.

I realized, with a jolt of dismay, how late I was in returning home: I'd lost track of time in service to my solitary vices. But the trouble I was going to be in for being late was nothing, I sensed, to the trouble presently looming over my head in the form of Zithra Jackson Brown. Who continued to hold me down with preternaturally strong hands until she had finished relaying the criminal deeds I must execute once I was alone at home.

"I'll be waiting here till you get back, and, remember, my friends'll be watching to make sure you done just like I said. They'll know the second you git to Taliaferro Lane. Swear on your life you won't tell a soul. Swear!"

With lighting speed she grabbed my tender gonads, squeezing to this side of acute pain. I gasped for breath. "I won't I swear I won't!"

"Cause if you don't follow my instructions to a Tee, honey-chile," she continued, not yet relinquishing her hold, "Zithra Jackson Brown will proclaim to the wide world how you, the Deacon's Son, had your wicked ways with me and the good Lord knows how many others. Trust me, your friends will laugh you out of town when they hear where your precious pud's been a-pokin'!"

At which point she gave the offending member a condescending shake, hot palm glued to sticky skin as she laughed, the rasp in her voice as discouraging as a mockingbird's jest. "Lil tadpole, all tuckered out and gone to waste."

"Just let me go," I croaked. "I promise I'll be back by dark."

"Then skedaddle." With unearthly calm, Zithra let go of my privates and settled her substantial bottom on the edge of the furnace's top as she crossed her legs and pulled a strange object that glinted with a metallic flash out of her shock of hair.

I saw that it was an extremely long and sharp-looking fingernail file, and for a crazy instant I thought she meant to slit my throat with it then and there. My dark thoughts weren't appeased as she proceeded to wipe a substance looking suspiciously like dried blood from the file onto the hem of her smock. That's when I noticed the words stamped above the breast pocket of her garment: County Correctional Center for Women. My heart leapt like a frog that's landed on a hot skillet instead of a lily pad.

"Damn rocks near wrecked my pretty nails," she muttered to herself. Then she turned back to me as she filed her glistening talons. They flashed with a life of their own. "I'll be waiting right here, Mr. Newt Seward the Deacon's Son, and I give you till sunset to get yourself back here. You figure out how to do what I told you by then, or my Spies will let me know. If you let me down, just watch me scream bloody murder to the world." Whereupon she wheezed a diabolical laugh whose low registers seemed designed to call the high heavens into doubt. "Don't I know something about *that*, Mister Newt. Things you never want to know, if you mean to save your soul from the Boogeyman!" She laughed again, rasping for breath. "Lord-a-mercy, *what a day!*"

I could hardly agree more as I took my departure, scrambling down the mound and tearing my way through the thorny foliage that surrounded that crumbling monument to a failed cause. Not too soon, the sound of her heavy breathing was lost in the slurps and trills of Furnace Creek as it coursed down its rocky bed, singing the same greedy song to which my forebears had cast unfriendly bullets in another world, another time.

*

Now why, you might well ask, didn't I hightail it to the police station, housed with City Hall in a tawdry brick Victorian extravaganza dominating the intersection of Rocky Hill's two main streets? Or, if that seemed too daunting, why didn't I immediately seek out my father—a forgiving soul if ever there were one—to report the crime I'd been commissioned to do? It was 1965, after all, and who would believe the ravings of a crazy black woman over an honor-roll student who (so I assumed) beamed innocence and truth? Put yourself in my place, try to remember what it felt like to be thirteen years old, literally caught with your pants down in a time and place where *sex* wasn't uttered, where the parental gift of *For Boys Only* would not mysteriously appear on my nightstand for another year, where my best friends and I had yet to fess up to our guilty self-discoveries. Think back to that time in your life, and you'll understand, perhaps, why it didn't occur to me to attempt to turn the tables on my persecutor. As I furiously pedaled up and coasted down the hilly slopes that led from Furnace Creek to Willow Woods, the residential subdivision where Rocky Hill's most upstanding citizens had built new split-level homes, all I could think of were the dark eyes peeking out from behind the sheers of every picture window and over the evenly trimmed boxwoods of every lawn I passed—the conspiratorial eyes of a network of maids and gardeners, handymen and deliverymen, working in league with Zithra, each of whom had the miraculous means of letting her know the minute I failed to make good on the promise she'd extracted from me.

Thus my panicked state of mind as I skidded to a stop in our driveway. As I feared, there awaited my mother, dressed to the nines, loading picnic paraphernalia into the back of our station-wagon like a fury, assisted by my prim older sister Katie and my hapless younger brother Jubal, as I—sweaty, shirtless renegade—hopped off my bike. It took one second to see Mother was on a rampage of the first order.

"New-TON Horatio Seward!!" she screeched, shaking me by the shoulders in a manner sorely bringing to mind Zithra's vice-like grip minutes before. "Where've you BEEN? You were due home an hour ago. An hour ago, and LOOK at you!" As her volume rose, my heart sank. "Covered in dirt and sweat, head to toe. What's come over you, boy?"

Let me be frank: the dizzying pace of the last hour of my small existence, from orgasm to terror, from threats against my being to this mad charge home, all helped me accomplish what I determined my only recourse as 326 Taliaferro Lane spun into view. I heaved the remains of my lunch at Mother's feet.

What followed, after her shrieks and my siblings' elated ejaculations of horror, were my contrite apologies but oh I felt so sick; Dad's appearance, freshly showered, shaved, and Brilliantined, giving me the benefit of the doubt; Mother's grudging acquiescence (having made sure her open-toed canvas pumps had escaped my graceless splatter); and, after a whispered parental consultation that bespoke years of tense negotiation, I was dosed with Pepto Bismol, ordered to bed, and forbidden to sneak out of my room to watch television. At which point the rest of the Sewards departed to partake of the celebration of our country's founding on the southwestern outskirts of town.

And so I found myself alone, left to my own wicked devices for the second time in as many hours, all on that fateful Fourth of July when I stumbled into a threatening world beyond my control—a boy blackmailed into committing an offense against family and community, a pip of a lad whose most recent deceit (declaring myself sick) was only one in the expanding list of crimes I was doomed to commit in a single day.

Which, half an hour later, after I was sure the neighborhood had emptied, I set out to execute in earnest. Zithra's instructions drumming in my ears with a beat whose insistence drowned the surrounding silence, I surveyed our house for loose cash, taking amounts whose absence I prayed would escape observation: some of the pin-money Mother kept in the jelly jar beside the potted African violets on the window sill over the kitchen sink; four crisp notes from the stash of half-C bills I'd espied my father secreting between the pages of his high school yearbook when he thought no one was watching; and, with a sigh of regret, the thirteen silver dollars in my desktop savings bank shaped like the Empire State Building, each coin a birthday tribute from Uncle Rafe in Waynesboro. Rummaging in the storage closet, I chose a shapeless skirt Mom might not miss, along with a pink button-down sweater top that had seen better days, both of which I stuffed into my school satchel. Next, maps of Franklin County and the State of Virginia pirated from Dad's Fairlaine and a flashlight. Zithra had grumbled that she hadn't eaten in ages, so I grabbed a jar of Skippy's and some Sara Lee rolls from the tin breadbox, on whose lid was painted a rooster crowing lustily amidst his covey of adoring hens.

It wasn't twilight, not quite yet, but the sky had turned that deadening shade of white that precedes sunset and the crickets were singing full chorus as I slipped out the sliding glass door into our backyard. A school of starlings dipped from the woods behind our house, settled down in the oak tree by the patio, then lifted off on their way to other limbs of repose.

I made my move.

It was wrong, in my heart I knew I was proceeding down a criminal path of no return, but there was no turning back. I gingerly turned the knob of the rear door to the Leroy residence—and as Zithra predicted, it opened like a dream. Holding my breath, I glided down the shag carpeting of the long hall into Judge Leroy's paneled study. There, I saw the black marble bust Zithra had said would be on his massive walnut desk—a likeness of George Washington—and when I moved the weighty stone aside, I saw the button worked into the pattern of the wood veneer, a disc I would never have discovered had I not been told where to look.

I held my breath and pressed. When the compartment built into the side of the desk sprang open, I sighed in relief—I half suspected that a desk with a secret compartment might have its own alarm system. There, amid sheaves of legal-looking papers and three dog-eared issues of *Playboy* was the black ledger Zithra had instructed me to bring back to her. I lifted it out and tucked it into my satchel. I hesitated, cowed by the accusing glare of George's "I-Cannot-Tell-A-Lie" eyes, but then decided: if the Judge could spare his diary, he might also forfeit one of his dirty mags. Mission accomplished, I closed the secret compartment with a satisfied sigh and moved the bust back into place.

Any fear I'd felt now disappeared in a burst of elation. Thief that I had become with such ease, I deemed this the perfect opportunity to reconnoiter the house. I worked my way through the premises, picking up and setting down knick-knacks displayed in rooms as tidily ordered as a photo spread in *House Beautiful*, till I found myself upstairs in the gleaming master bath that opened off the frilly bedroom of the Judge and his wife. Brazenly I lowered the crusty waistband of my shorts and took a leak, neither raising cushioned toilet seat nor flushing—let them wonder which Leroy had defiled this antiseptic sanctuary of wan tile and flickering fluorescent lights. As I shook myself dry, I noticed Mrs. Leroy's collection of fingernail polishes lining the countertop—hues from lightest rose to deepest burgundy. The image of Zithra filing her impressive talons flashed to mind. Without a second thought I reached for a fuchsia shade and added it to my horde of stolen goods.

I looked into the mirror over the double sink and smiled.

*

At Furnace Creek, the sun was lowering in the western sky and the air was growing heavy as I pushed through the prickly underbrush into the copse of pines, sumac, and oak saplings that separated the road where I'd left my bike and the creek gurgling downhill and out of sight. As I ventured forward into the darkness of the woods, the swagger that had come over me at the Leroys abruptly drained away. Every unsuspected tree limb that jabbed me in the ribs, every unfamiliar nocturnal noise, set my heart thumping, and the lightning bugs blinking in the dark looked like alien eyes spying on me. By the time

I reached the stone heap, I could barely make out its black silhouette, and the horizon beyond the treetops had turned lurid orange.

"Zithra?" I called in a whisper. "You up there?"

Two hands clamped down on my shoulders from behind, and Zithra stepped out of the shadow of a giant oak tree. Her face inches from my own as she spun me around, she glared intently into my eyes, fiery pupils tunneling deep into my own.

"You promise you ain't brought no one with you?"

"I promise! It's just me... Ma'am." A little politeness, I felt, was due an escapee from the County Correctional Center who'd so recently prisoned my privates in her palm.

"You got everything like I told you?"

"Yes Ma'am," I said, sighing with relief as she released my shoulders. They were aching mightily from the way they'd been set upon, first by Zithra, then Mother, now Zithra again. "Here, I'll show you." I reached in my pockets and pulled out a fistful of cash—the most money I'd ever held in my thirteen years—as I detailed the yields of my foraging raid.

Zithra chuckled gleefully, humming "Go Tell It on the Mountain" as she took the bills and coins in hand. I divested myself of the remaining fruits of my labor. First, Judge Leroy's black book, which she grabbed with a whoop of satisfaction.

"My ticket outta here!" She fanned me with the book, nodding her head as if I knew everything about it there was to know. "It's payback time for all the troubles that's done been heaped on my back. What else you got for me?"

I handed over Mother's skirt and sweater, which Zithra donned then and there, stepping out of her prison garb with nary an iota of self-consciousness. The sight of the ample curves of her dark flesh, offset by white brassiere and panties, temporarily made me forget my precarious situation. Zithra caught me staring as she buttoned the sweater over her commanding bosom and wiggled her way into the elastic-waisted skirt. Her swaying hips resembled, surreally, the hula dancers backing up Don Ho on the Ed Sullivan show.

"Don't tell me you're ready to wank that weeny thing all over again!"

I blushed furiously. But I needn't have worried, as Zithra changed topics without missing a beat. "Take these ole rags and burn 'em. High time Miss Zithra wore herself a new look! Am I a lady now or what?"

She spun in a circle, laughing with the delight of a child, or perhaps a lunatic. I gaped. Finally she stopped, wheezing at her exertions as she brandished the jar of Skippy's.

"Now, soon's as I serve myself a little dinner, I'll disappear. And, you *do* understand, Mister Newt Seward, you never saw me. Whether I make it out of this god-forsaken place alive or not, you don't know *a thing*. Breathe a word and your life ain't worth a dang-long diddle. My friends'll be watching you!"

I solemnly promised I'd never seen her, and could I go now?

"Wait a minute, chile." Zithra used her fingernail file to spread the chunky peanut butter onto the burnt bottom of a dinner roll. She munched, while I waited at attention, one roll, then another, till she reached the bottom of the jar. Licking the file clean and inserting it back into her hair, she flipped the flashlight on, letting it play over the surrounding trees till the beam picked out the animal trail that followed the creek upstream.

"Time I git going."

The exuberance lifting her spirits mere seconds ago had vanished faster than summer breath on a windowpane, and she heaved a deep sigh as she faced the last gleams of sunset filtering through the trees, looking for all the world as if she had just caught glimpse of a future that held no rosy endings for her kind. Out of nowhere, I found myself feeling sorry for the convict, and a warning sprang to my lips.

"Not that way. You have to cross too many roads and might get caught." I had not spent years roaming these backwoods for nothing. "Go downstream, and just before you get to Route 7"—I paused, pondering the enormity of the iniquity I was about to propose—"you'll come up on the old Johnson place, it's the only house in sight." Randy Johnson had been my best friend since the third grade, and I knew, as I now told Zithra, that the family was out of town. "Their second car is parked in back. A black Chevy. They always leave the keys behind the driver's visor."

Zithra thrust the rim of her flashlight flush to my chin, so that the light shone up into my face. All I could see was the translucent pink of my eyelids as my eyelashes danced in my line of vision like an albino centipede's flailing legs.

"You be meanin' what I *think*, Newt Seward?"

I nodded, solemnly, and she lowered the lamp as she straightened up. Its beam caught the glint of an object shining in the gloom of the needle-crusted ground near my satchel.

"What's that?"

I picked up Mrs. Leroy's nail-polish bottle and pressed it into Zithra's warm palm. "It's for you."

Total darkness had now overtaken the woods, and all of a sudden the air filled with popping sounds, first faint, then louder: firecrackers. Half-veiled by the branches overhead, distant bursts of red white blue began to light the sky—the fireworks display at the lake had commenced. I envisioned my family and their friends gasping in delight as they settled onto woolen blankets spread over the dewy grass, the unfurling explosions of beauty above suffusing them with a glow of belonging and community, an insidership from which my recent deeds had exiled me forever.

"Well me-oh-my, a gift for Zithra..."

It was of course now too dark to see the expression in her eyes, but in later years, as my imagination revisited and embellished that eventful day, I liked to think they had watered up and, perhaps, shed one tear for the boy whose life she had precipitously enmeshed in her own. All I know for sure is that Zithra soon walked away, flicking the flashlight on and off as she followed the faint path that led downhill along the edge of the creek. I watched until she disappeared into the darkness before I turned to walk in the opposite direction. A curtain seemed to rise before me as I stepped free of the saplings and briars by the roadside and looked up at the kaleidoscopic colors that traversed the sky; and, as I mounted my bike for the dark ride home, I felt as though I had crossed an invisible barrier and entered a new world, one in which a reborn Newton Seward harbored a secret past and, for the first time in his life, faced the immense melancholy of an unknown and terrifying future.

2

TABLE MANNERS

Contrary to popular impression, gossip—no matter how salacious—doesn't always travel like wildfire in the lazy South. To be sure, the urge to transform your neighbors' woes into juicy tidbits that improve with each titillated retelling is part of the charm—and bane—of small-town southern life. Once eavesdropping on party phone lines became a thing of the past, the housewives of Willow Woods made zealous use of their new multicolored wall phones to give notice of infractions in the codes of morality and decorum governing our quaint universe. But in the punishing heat of summer, the plain truth is that news slowed to a trickle, like molasses that's seen better days.

So it wasn't until suppertime two days later that the events of the Fourth began to catch up with me.

We were sitting at the yellow-topped, chrome-legged kitchen table, making half-hearted conversation as Dad flipped open the local paper, whose early evening arrival provided him the perfect excuse to read it over dinner. To Mother's chagrin, I might add: no one in her family, the Freelands, would have *ever* been so disrespectful of table etiquette. It was one of many small humiliations that she'd learned to swallow in marrying a man who was her social inferior, the truth of which she periodically reminded me and my siblings—we to whom she entrusted the task of rising above our unfortunate happenstance of birth. "I do love your father—but let's admit the obvious: his people lacked the breeding to instill proper manners in the poor man." Of course she never alluded to the fact that her grandfather had made the Freeland fortune by means of a less than proper moonshine and bootleg operation.

Forty years later, the mountainous terrain of Franklin County, Virginia, remained legendary for its wealth of hidden stills; but during Prohibition Freeland contraband outgunned and outsold all competitors. Conveniently forgetting that aspect of family history, Mother tried to mitigate our father's unbreakable habit of reading the paper at dinner by asking him to discuss the edifying tidbits that, along with oversized mouthfuls of lukewarm fried chicken, three-bean casserole, and red-mayonnaise coleslaw, he was ingesting.

Tonight he had just finished his summary of the national news—in which a pending Voting Rights Act led both parents to agree, for once, on the dangers of the illiterate masses flooding the ballot boxes—and had turned to the local items when he let out a whistle.

"Well, look it here, Jeanlyn, ain't that the Leroys' maid?" He passed the paper in Mother's direction. Discreetly, I raised myself from the sticky plastic seat of my chair—as dandelion yellow as the table's chipped top—to peer over her shoulder and see for myself: and, there, under the headline

FELONS' ESCAPE ENDS
IN NEAR FATAL STABBING

I spied two grainy mugshots displayed side-by-side, one of which was, oh so unmistakably, my Zithra.

Mother exclaimed her dismay that a convict had once been employed next door, while Dad, in his sweet-dispositioned way that sometimes drove Mother out of her mind and made her wonder out loud if he were plain dim-witted, remarked that he'd never observed anything untoward about the gal and that, despite her admittedly unfriendly scowl, innocent-until-proved-guilty was as American as apple pie. As Dad reclaimed the paper to give us digests of the article, I inched back down onto my seat. Before my eyes rose visions of the incriminating evidence stashed in the back of my closet—Zithra's uniform, along with the May issue of the Judge's *Playboy*.

"They broke out of the Women's Correction Center south of Old Fort Road," Dad paraphrased. "Not together, though. Says here they were arrested on the same insurance fraud scheme, but Miss Sherlene Williams received a lesser term by turning informer on Miss Zithra Jackson Brown. Sunday the Fourth, most of the staff had the day off, and that's when Miss Williams lifted a guard's keys and stole off. But looks like Zithra was keeping an eye on her turncoat friend and lit out soon after. Instead of just running, she tracked down her rival, so she did, and when she found her, she gave her the—" Dad paused dramatically and jabbed my sister in the ribs, as she shrieked on cue— "blade! Stabbed her with An Undetermined Weapon and left her in a ditch on the side of the back road where the state troopers found her, hanging to life by a hair. This Zithra's still on the loose, but the sheriff says his men are hot on her trail."

The bloodstained file brandished by Zithra danced before my eyes. I tried to distract myself by thinking how best to dispose of the evidence in my possession. Dad's next words, however, jolted me out of my reverie. "There's more, something about a Third Party being involved."

With a sinking heart I toyed with a kidney bean on my plate.

"Gimme the chicken," Jubal demanded before my complicity could be announced to the world. Mother hissed, "Say please. Manners!"

Dad chuckled. "Seems Miss Williams had initiated a relationship of a compromising nature—ain't that a fine way of putting it!—with the guard whose keys she stole when his clothes were—"

"Harold, the children!"

"—and then left him locked up buck-nekked in her cell!"

"Harold!"

Jubal chimed in. "What happened to his clothes?"

Katie rolled her eyes. "Don't be so square!"

"See?" Mother arched her lovely if threatening eyebrows. "Is this fit conversation for dinner?"

The butterflies in my stomach, meanwhile, were dancing up and down. "Son?" Dad put down his paper to look at me. "You look a mite green about the gills."

"Harold, you aren't listening to *me*!"

That was how it always played between my parents, back and forth between us kids, first one then the other using us to mediate their conflicts and silent wars; and because I was the child Dad appeared to favor, I was the one, more often than not, who seemed to aggravate Mom the most. In retrospect it seems perverse, since of us three siblings it was I who harbored ambitions of the sort that Mother's upwardly mobile desires would have approved, and since Dad's placid acceptance of his place in the grand order of things was worlds removed from the inner discontent that I hid behind a mask of filial obedience.

"May I be excused?"

A little more parental negotiation, and I escaped, forgoing banana pudding in order to dash straight to my room and ensure that my contraband remained undiscovered. Satisfied on that count, I curled up on my bed with the latest Archie comics, only to drift off into uneasy dreams in which the scowling mug shots in the *Daily Chronicle* included not only Zithra and her foe Sherlene but, wedged between the two of them, a school photograph from which one Newton Seward smiled with cunning innocence.

*

Poor Jubal. It was noon, and we siblings were gathered around the kitchen table while Mother toasted grilled cheese sandwiches in the waffle iron. I'd been up since early morning, claiming a return of good health, and as soon as possible I'd headed to the grove behind the back fence, where I pulled Zithra's uniform from under my shirt and used the matchbook snitched from Dad's ashtray to set it on fire. Cheap fabric, I then and there realized, doesn't burn like other things; the dress sizzled, frayed, resisted before yielding to the heat, at which point it flared into a puny conflagration that, eventually, left a small pile of charred textile that I poked and prodded with a stick. The last part of the uniform to burn was the stamped cloth above the breast pocket, so, to the very end, I had to watch the word "Correction" glaring out at me, a talismanic message warning me to change my ways before it was too late. Finally, all that was left was "Correct" (I felt temporarily vindicated) and then only the disconcertingly ambiguous "or"—at which point Jubal happened upon me. Sometimes my kid brother reminded me of a bumbling but ever-faithful hound dog, sniffing out my trail no matter how hard I tried to shake him or how long it took him, no matter the brush-offs or abuse I ratcheted his way.

"Watcha doing?" were his inevitable words as he grabbed for the stick in my hand. "Lemme try!"

Of course I resisted and tried to shove him away.

"We ain't allowed to make fires, you're in big trouble if Mom finds out!"

"I didn't make it," I lied, as if explaining the obvious to a simpleton. "I just found it, and I'm making sure it's out. Some hobo must have been camping here last night."

"This close to our house?" Jubal peered at the thicket of trees surrounding us with a tremor of frightened delight. "What if he's a robber? Or murderer? Let's call the police!"

Last thing we needed were more stories about criminals in the neighborhood. Zithra was one too many already. "Don't be silly," I said in a tone of brotherly superiority as I stomped on the remaining embers. "You want people to think you're a scaredy-cat? They will, you know. Besides, don't you know the Number One Rule in the Hobo Code of Allegiance? Never camp in the same place twice when you're on the move." Our hobo, I asserted with manufactured glibness, was halfway to Burnett's Bridge by now.

Jubal acquiesced when I promised not only to play catch with him but reveal all Six Rules of the Hobo Brotherhood as long as he didn't tell Mother about the fire and bring on one of her migraines— the likelihood of which, I warned, would keep her from driving us to the pool at the local rec center that afternoon.

But an eight-year-old kid brother's memory leaves much to be desired. Here we were getting ready to eat our grilled cheeses when Jubal piped up to anyone who'd listen: "Newt says there's Six Rules every hobo swears to obey. If I ran away from home, even for one night, would that make me a hobo?"

"Mind your manners!" Mother said as we grabbed at the sandwiches. "And don't bolt your food!"

"You think our hobo ran away from home?" my brother doggedly continued. His brow wrinkled as if he were parsing a mathematical equation. "If he has a real home somewhere besides his campsite in our woods, does that mean he really isn't a..."

Jubal realized his gaffe at the same moment I kicked him underneath the table. But before he could finish saying "Ou—ch!" his sand-wich suffered an unintended compression, shooting a hot drool of cheese onto his bare leg that made him yelp full-throttle.

"How many times do I have to tell you boys to behave at the ta-ble?" Mother scolded as she swooped to swipe Jubal's leg clean, then turned a steely eye my way. "New-TON Horatio Seward, I *saw* that." Whereupon she decreed I stay home and wash out the trashcans while she took Katie and Jubal to the pool.

Then, never one to miss a beat, her thoughts backtracked and she turned to Jubal.

"What were you saying about a hobo camp in our woods?"

Her mind could be a steel trap sometimes. I glared at Jubal, chal-lenging him to utter another incriminating word. "Just some non-sense I was making up. Right, Brother?"

"Some make-believe stories," Jubal echoed.

"Newt, I don't know what gets into you these days. Filling your little brother's head with nonsense when there's more than enough crime to worry about happening before our very eyes!"

Contemplating my exile from the Olympic-sized pool and glimpses of bathing-suit beauties sunning around its periphery, I sulked through the rest of lunch. Scrubbing the aluminum trashcans mid-summer was an especially noxious punishment. Then the perfect revenge for Jubal's loose lips dawned on me. I'd slip the Judge's maga-zine under Jubal's mattress. If Mother found the May centerfold while changing sheets, let *him* explain it away; I knew from experience that the more he protested the guiltier he sounded. And until she hap-pened upon the contraband—well, it was there for me to borrow as needed. I felt so satisfied with my scheme that I smiled forgivingly at Jube, who flashed a gap-toothed smile of pure gratitude, hopelessly unaware of the duplicities spreading like kudzu in my crafty brain.

*

The events of the next day seemed destined to keep my sins in front of me. Maybe I'd forgotten, or more likely I wasn't listening when Mother announced it a week ago, but this evening we were invited to dinner at none other than the Leroys, as Mother reminded us over breakfast. Zithra's former employers were going to show slides from their Niagara Falls vacation, and Mother was hoping the images would inspire Dad to undertake a similarly edifying family trip—foolish notion, given that he'd as soon spend his vacation rearranging the tools in the shed out back as trekking to any resort more distant than Ferrystone Beach one county over. The thought of returning to the scene of my robbery made me wish I could plead sick—but I'd milked that excuse dry by now. Besides, I knew there was no backing out: Mother's ambition was to have us all there, spruced up and on best behavior (Dad included), examples of the good breeding that connected her, a former Freeland, to the distinguished judge and his blue-blooded wife, whose Copeland stock went back to the plantations of Tidewater Virginia and, so Mrs. Leroy liked to hint, to the Santa Maria itself.

From the moment we arrived at the Leroys' door—the broad-paneled front door with stained glass squares lining its sides, not the back entrance that had yielded so effortlessly to my touch three nights before—the adults' conversation was all about Zithra Jackson Brown, fueled by the *Chronicle*'s continuing headlines and the fact that a year ago she had been in the Leroys' employ. I could not help but feel that, among such fine company, I was in a false position. Their point of interest—and my source of shame—was difficult to ignore since I'd been abandoned by both my siblings: Katie was best friends with the Leroy daughter, Annabelle, and the two of them had retired to the privacy of the Annabelle's bedroom to debate the swoon appeal of "Michelle" versus "Yesterday." Jubal, meanwhile, found in Annabelle's seven-year-old brother Charlie a willing disciple he could boss around in older-brother fashion, a role, obviously, he never got to play in our household. My adolescent pride kept me from following the boys to the basement rec room to share their childish amusements.

So I was left sitting with the adults, sipping my cherry Coke with shaved ice and pretending to study the view from the picture window while the adults talked Zithra-this and Zithra-that over gin and tonics. At least the topic at hand rescued me from the unwelcome attention the Judge usually heaped on me in front of my parents.

Jowly, garrulous, and much too fond of hearing himself pontificate, his white flattop standing on end as if he'd just seen a ghost, he had developed the bad habit (so I thought) of slapping me repeatedly on the back while intoning how lucky I was to be doing so well in school (as if my grades had nothing to do with my abilities), how fortunate to be the scion of such upright Christian parents, how he had been raised by hand (here, another hearty slap on my sunburned back) and thereby knew the importance of discipline in becoming successful. So I too might become when I took over my father's dealership—or, if I choose to study law at the Judge's alma mater, the University of the South, when I returned to Rocky Hill to join its team of God-fearing civil servants.

So, at least tonight I was spared the Judge's slaps, indeed virtually ignored as the conversation feasted on Zithra as greedily as if she were a rack of hickory-smoked ribs. According to everyone but my Dad, her behavior was an ominous sign of the coming race wars. She'd been a sullen gal from the get-go, Mrs. Leroy declared, did her work but let you know she considered herself above such tasks, and the straw that broke the camel's back occurred last Thanksgiving, when she carelessly let drop a serving platter that had been in the Copeland family for over a century. But no, in response to Mother's query, Mrs. Leroy had never caught Zithra stealing, not even toting groceries, though the two women agreed that most surely she did, since it was common knowledge that *all* the help considered toting—a few cans of string beans, a bag of sugar—an unspoken perk of the job. Meanwhile, Judge Leroy ventured that the woman must be touched in the head, seeing that she'd had the perfect opportunity to make a clean get-away but instead wasted time tracking down Sherlene Williams and picking the fight that had left the latter woman in critical condition but not so critical that she couldn't give the police the particulars on her assailant. (No doubt cat-fighting over a married man, Mrs. Leroy interjected.) Well, the two of 'em were sure fighting like mountain bobcats, the Judge chuckled, you should have seen the police photos of the cuts and scratches Miss Sherlene Williams sustained—even skin as coal-black as hers couldn't hide the damage her foe had wreaked! Dad's mild interjection, hoping that she would recover, was ignored, so he philosophically settled into his drink, contenting himself with the prospect of one of the Judge's pre-embargo Cuban cigars after dinner.

Meanwhile the Judge assured his captive audience that, according to his Inside Sources, the police anticipated apprehending the miscreant any hour. A negro woman on the lam couldn't get far on foot in Franklin County without making herself known—or, if Zithra chose to hide out in the surrounding mountains, without running into a white moonshiner staring her down the barrel of his shotgun. Listening to the Judge's bluster, I couldn't help but feel a bit of satisfaction imagining Zithra zipping down some road hundreds of miles away in the Johnsons' beat-up Chevy, the AM radio blasting Ray Charles. But as the Judge started in on the highway patrol alerts sent to all neighboring states, I felt my smugness yielding to old trepidations like a kite buffeted to smithereens in a tunnel of merciless wind.

The topic of discussion shifted to the security lapses in the detention facility, and the way Sherlene had managed to use her low-life charms to bamboozle a smitten prison guard (one of those white-trashy Akers boys)—the details of which were conveyed increasingly *sotto voce* till Jeanlyn, by repeated nods in my direction, made it clear that the topic was too risqué to carry on, even in fervid whispers, with a Youth present. On cue Mrs. Leroy sent me to round up the other children for the pre-dinner slide show. So I missed the rest of the tawdry tale, left to ponder the consequences should the police indeed apprehend Zithra. Not only wearing Mother's clothes and driving a stolen car, but with the Judge's personal property on her. How long before I'd be implicated in her crimes?

Thus preoccupied, I found it impossible to lose myself in the polychromatic wonders of the Kodak slide show that commenced in the living room once the shades were drawn, and the dinner that followed promised to be as dismal an ordeal. I'd been sentenced to the *children's* table—a card table set up in the den, just off the formal dining room—with Jubal and Charlie. The fact that Katie and Annabelle got to sit with the adults at the gleaming cherry table to which our scruffed dining room set paled in comparison seemed a serious slight to my coming manhood. My resentment carried me through the tomato-shrimp aspic, which we boys did little more than jiggle with our forks, and the pork chops with an applesauce glaze, when the telephone rang. Mrs. Leroy answered the call, cupping her hand over the receiver to summon her husband.

"Dear, it's Tom Allbright, he says it's urgent."

Tom Allbright was our town's most sought-after lawyer. He attended First Methodist, as did our family, and was revered far and wide in Franklin County as the right man to pull you out of a pinch. He was not only unflappable in the courtroom, but unreadable one-on-one; never a twitch crossed his face or a spark of acknowledgment lit his eyes to betray how he really felt about his client's situation—a trait that made him everyone's ideal confidant, particularly in those private matters of a slightly sordid character needing legal counsel and, most of all, discretion.

"It can't be *that* urgent!" the Judge huffed. "Tell him I'll call him back after dinner."

When Mrs. Leroy reported back that Mr. Allbright wouldn't take NO for an answer, the Judge sighed, took one more noisy bite of pork chop and heaved himself up to grab the receiver, turning his back to his guests while he leaned against the entrance to the telephone alcove next to the family room where I sat. Although I couldn't see the dining room table, I had a straight view of the Judge's face as he listened to his caller. His expression went from bored to belligerent, and from anxious to ashen, in as many seconds as it took him to say, "What the DEVIL? Hold on, I'll check now... "—at which point he asked his wife to hang up the receiver while he resumed the call in his office. Anticipating a momentous revelation at hand, I excused myself to go to the toilet and entered the hallway from the den. The shag carpeting absorbed the pad of my steps as I glided towards the Judge's half-open office door.

One peek inside revealed that George W. had been moved from his usual spot, and although I couldn't see the side of the desk with the hidden compartment, I could hear the Judge rustling through its contents, then picking up the desk phone and shouting a string of obscenities that would have resulted in mouths being washed out with Ivory soap in the Seward home. Without notice he strode towards the office door and slammed it shut.

Lucky for me he didn't pause to look into the hallway. Less luckily, I couldn't hear a word now. However, the Leroys were nothing if not contemporary, having installed extension phones—four to our two—throughout the premises. I made for the one in the upstairs master bedroom, lifting the turquoise receiver as quietly as I could.

"Damn it, Tom, it'll be the end of me if that book gets into the wrong hands! Not only me, but a lot of other good citizens... what's the sneaky bitch want?"

She wanted, Mr. Allbright calmly relayed, for the Judge to use his leverage to pull the police off the search for her. Create a cover story, call the testimony of the Williams woman into question, fish a body out of a lake and say it was Zithra. But do it *now*. Next, Mr. Allbright continued, the Judge was to deposit 2500 dollars into a secure bank account—Mr. Allbright would take care of the details. Another 2500 in September. Then, when Missus Brown was certain no one was looking for her—no Private Eyes either, the lawyer warned— the Judge would start receiving pages from the black book, one a month. If he failed to comply or tried to find her, he could guess what she would be doing with the information.

Five thousand and her freedom was all she wanted; give her that and she'd remain silent.

"Impossible! This is an outrage, Tom! If she can get away with this, who's to say what comes next?" I imagined puffs of angry smoke issuing from the Judge's flat-top as he fumed. "It's up to you to stop her now!"

"Now Jack," Tom Allbright said patiently, "I wouldn't say five thousand's so much, given what that information's worth. She's shared enough of the details with me. You and a whole bunch of your friends all the way from here to Richmond are sitting on a bombshell. Mind, I'm not passing judgment. But she knows what's she got, she's playing her cards right, and I'd wager there's nothing you're going to be able to do about it."

"It's goddam blackmail! What's to keep her from asking for more? Or never turning over my book? Or making copies?"

As if in response to the mounting panic in the Judge's voice, Mr Allbright assumed his most soothing of neutral tones. "She means what she's saying. She's authorized me to draw up a document you both will sign, then she'll give *me* the ledger for safekeeping, and I'll be responsible for releasing the pages to you, starting in October. Ten pages, it'll all be over by next August."

"So just hand it over to me and to hell with any documents!"

"Sorry, Jack, this is now an attorney-client matter, I've got to proceed by the books."

"What the fuck-all are you *saying*, Tom? You now a *nigger's* lawyer?"

Nothing got under Mr. Allbright's skin. "It's business, Jack, and I must do my job. I'd recommend you think about the best way of holding on to *yours*. Act sensibly and this will all go away. That's what a man of your standing should do. Think about your position, Jack."

The Judge hung up.

I dashed down the stairs, past the closed office door and back to the den, just in time to be served Mrs. Leroy's triumph: Dream Whip Strawberry Shortcake in a parfait glass. For the first time that evening, food tasted delicious. I suspected Judge Leroy, when he returned to his place at the head of dining room table, enjoyed his whipped confection considerably less.

The ghastly sheen on his face when he sat back down—which he attributed to a case of dyspepsia—was to grow over the months that followed and become part of the general pallor inhabiting his once florid features. I still remember the stricken expression on his face as he shook our hands goodbye, looking for all the world as if he were closing a door not just on us but on a vast segment of his life. The pall that had fallen over him slowly settled over the entire Leroy household in the days to come. Not because Zithra ever betrayed her word; the incriminating contents of his black book—a meticulous record of the paybacks and bribes he had used his position and influence to extort—would eventually reach the public without Zithra's intervention. No, as Mr. Allbright himself informed me as we sat in a Paris bistro, all of a decade later, the pages of the Judge's precious record were monthly returned as promised. But the very fact of being blackmailed fed a subterranean current of fear, one that led the man to drink more and more heavily—whether to allay his dread of exposure or dull his guilt, who is to say? One evening a few months after the Niagara Falls slide show I chanced upon him sitting in the dark on the wooden swing in our backyard, lost in an alcoholic haze. At the sight of him, I nearly jumped out of my skin and crept away without saying a word, as if the stale odor of his decrepitude might enter my lungs and infect me.

Little over a year later it was widely rumored that one of his major investments had failed; then, surprise of surprises, Mrs. Leroy filed for divorce, received a hefty settlement and with the kids in tow took off to live with an Italian-American race-car driver from Darlington, South Carolina. Mother's succinct verdict was widely quoted by the neighbors: "Well, she's kissed *her* Tidewater roots goodbye!" Drink and despair—or perhaps lassitude—made the Judge sloppy, and sloppiness eventually led to the exposure of his various wrong-doings by an enterprising cub reporter on the *Daily Chronicle* who knew that a story of courthouse corruption might be her ticket to the *Atlanta Journal*. None of the charges, finally, stuck; but disgrace had fallen upon the Judge, and he meekly retired from his courtroom and transformed into a persona non grata in our neighborhood; a solitary shade inhabiting the house next door, occasionally glimpsed walking stoop-shouldered to the curb to retrieve the mail, opening the front door to receive a home delivery from Winn-Dixie, returning from the ABC store with a brown bag tucked under his arm.

He had become the ghost, at that point, that I saw foreshadowed in the man who returned to the dining room table, ashen-faced and perspiring uncontrollably, that July evening when I was still a boy of thirteen and filled with the desperate hope that the taint of Zithra's intrusion into my existence might now fade away, once and for all, and leave me as untroubled as the boy I fondly believed I had been before our encounter by Furnace Creek. Little did I suspect that I already harbored my own ghosts, ones that had taken up residence in my being and weren't about to desist, now that they had found a kindred spirit in my inmost thoughts and desires.

3

MIXED MESSAGES

It was late October, and the acrid smell of burning leaves, meticulously raked into symmetrical mounds by the wizened gardeners of Taliaferro Lane, stung my nostrils as I bicycled home from Hill High. More than two decades later, October still catapults me down the tunnels of memory, the scent of change that hangs in the crisp air bringing all the autumns of my life tumbling down on me, and it was the same then as now. There I was, charging home on my Schwinn Sting Ray counting the days (forty-seven) till I turned fourteen, yet, as the tingling particulate of oak and sycamore penetrated to my brain, I was simultaneously the second-grade child allowed to walk home from school alone for the first time, kicking through the piles of leaves that lined every block in a world of golden light, coppery chrysanthemums, and frozen time; I was the ten-year-old who carefully ironed twenty varieties of leaves between sheets of waxed paper for my fourth-grade science project; and I was the preschooler who spent an October afternoon stapling feathers to a ribboned headband, the finishing touch to a Halloween costume that included a bow and sheath of suction-tipped arrows, dishrag loincloth draped over fringed buckskin leggings, and a pair of beaded moccasins Uncle Zeke had sent me from Cherokee, North Carolina.

That choice of costume expressed an inchoate feeling that stirred in me even at that precocious age; I instinctively identified with Indians over cowboys because in my secret reveries I fantasized that I was an anomaly in Rocky Hill, an outsider whose actual origins (and hence future) spoke of other worlds, of a life extending beyond the circle of mountain peaks that pinched Rocky Hill in a stony embrace. Precisely to hide this sting of inner discontent, I worked overtime to appear happy, polite, conscientious—a parents' dream.

Without exactly meaning to, I lived a double life. Little wonder, then, that my complicity in abetting Zithra's escape made me feel an impostor among good folk.

On this particular October afternoon I pedaled home with a sense of possibility that utterly transformed the subconscious growl of dissatisfaction that made me look back at my trespass into the Leroy house as one of the most exciting acts I'd ever committed. During math period, I had been summoned over the intercom to the guidance counselor's office. Hearing one's name reverberate in so disembodied a fashion was enough to cower the cockiest student, but even my guilt-prone conscience couldn't fathom an infraction of school rules for which I might be culpable. Still, my jitters weren't allayed until I entered Mr. Powell's office and saw the grin splitting his two-o'clock shadow. The conference that followed was a revelation. At the beginning of the term, we eighth graders had been subjected to a battery of intelligence tests, and Mr. Powell proceeded to tell me I'd scored, in his words, off the charts. Himself a transplant from New England by way of marriage, he spoke eagerly about my prospects— not just the future but what should be done *now*. His enthusiastic recommendation was that I look into private schools Up North, since in his frank opinion neither Franklin County nor the South's educational system could provide the education my talents warranted. He'd written a letter to this effect for me to give my parents.

I won't deny that his words went to my head; what child doesn't yearn to be told he is special? When Mr. Powell began to walk me through a series of catalogues for New England prep schools, I felt as if a dream that I had not even known I sheltered was being answered: my horizons expanded as I imagined a world in which I was no longer an anomaly for desiring all that I desired. A choir of possibilities sang in my head as I biked home.

The second I slammed open the kitchen door, Mother sensed I was withholding something, remarking that I was acting as skittish as a tomcat caught in a downpour. Much as I yearned to blurt out my news, even more I desired the attention of both parents as I parlayed this new epoch in my being. So I bit my tongue till Dad got home, at which point I solemnly invited them to join me in our rarely used living room, crowded with faux Colonial pieces upholstered in autumnal plaids. Once we settled onto the uncomfortable furniture, and once they learned that I wasn't in trouble at school, indeed quite the opposite, both were as excited as me—initially, at least.

"I *knew* you were keeping a secret," was Mother's first comment, keen to confirm her sixth sense. "Always thought you were a critter outter the ordinary, Newt!" were my father's first words. "Never was much of a learner myself, but you, you always had your nose in a book ever since the day we brought you home from the hospital."

"Newt did learn to read at four," Mother corrected him.

Father continued to beam at me, the sides of his mouth nearly tickling his large ears. "I never forgot the time your uncle Rafe looked at your report card and said to me, Brother, you got yourself a future Noble Prize winner right here in your own home!"

Mother's pride was of a different, self-reflexive sort. For her my scores confirmed the superiority of the Freeland genes. Plus they elevated her, as Mother of a Gifted Child, above all those other PTA moms whose offspring were mere middlings. But when we sat down to browse the glossy brochures Mr. Powell had sent home with me, reality began to take on a more sober face. It came down to dollars and cents. Not only the annual cost of tuition but also room, board, proper clothes, books, travel—especially at the distant Andovers and Exeters and Phippses on which Mr. Powell had trained my sights. As my parents tallied figures, the gulf between my dreams and the Seward coffers widened. I suggested that I take on an after-school job, as if flipping burgers at Hardees would rectify the numbers. The possibility of loans, a night job for Dad—all these options were aired, mulled over, and ultimately dismissed as impracticable in the larger scheme of things. All the money that Granddaddy Freeland had left Mother had gone into paying off the mortgage on the house. I grew despondent as my fantasy of a high-speed lane to the future dissolved into that of a rutted country path.

"I wish we could do more, but there's the reality of it, Newt. I'm doing the best I can for you kids, but I guess it just ain't good enough." The hangdog look in Dad's eyes, the awkward affection with which he reached forward to thump me on the back—these made me temper my disappointment.

As Dad grew lachrymose, my mother grew silent, hands clamped on the maple armrests of her chair as she attempted to control the tick at the edge of her lips. I noticed it then, but was too caught up in my own misery to ponder the emotions coursing through her mind: that this was her fate, not simply for "marrying down," as her two older sisters (one had married a Hot Springs attorney, the other a Richmond orthodontist) were always eager to remind her, but for casting her lot with a man who lacked the ambition to do more than "get along" in life. Make no mistake: ours was a thoroughly respectable small-town existence—Mother had made sure of that—but it would never be more. Early in the marriage, Dad had worked his way up to general manager of the downtown Ford dealership, but that was as high as he aspired. A natural-born tinkerer, he would have been more content working under the hood of automobiles than selling them. He'd grown up living and breathing the atmosphere of his father's auto repair shop, and when Grandpa Seward had died, he'd have been happy staying there. But by then he had met Jeanlyn and she was determined to wipe the auto grease off her beau before she presented him to the Freeland paterfamilias. And determined, as well, that her husband attain a level of respectability that, if not automatically conferred by a white-collar managerial position, was enhanced by the natural piety that led to his rise as Head Deacon at First Methodist—the same church where Mr. Freeland Senior piously thanked the Lord for the blessings that his illicit moonshine business had brought to him and his own. Father's lack of guile made him one of the more popular dealers in town, so business was steady, his income rose modestly, and, by getting his father-in-law to cosign a loan, he and Jeanlyn had been able to build in Willow Woods, where all the respectable townspeople who had tired of their tilting Federalists and drafty Victorians were erecting split levels and ranch houses; and he had bought good insurance policies and kept promising to begin college savings accounts for us kids. That spelled the limit of Father's horizons. He was pleased where life had brought him, and by all measure we ought to have been too. But there were moments, like today's conversation, that forced my mother to acknowledge that, if we were a model family for our circumstances and community, those circumstances were crushingly narrow.

So life continued as it had always continued, golden October days darkened into nippy November evenings, and I began to forget the sting that had brought an end to what had been a fantasy of a few hours' duration. Any disappointment I felt couldn't take away Mr. Powell's underlying message—that I had Potential—and I hoarded that message, a talisman summoned forth in the privacy of my thoughts to stoke ambitions that would not be stilled.

All the leaves had fallen, been raked and burnt or hauled away, and the grass lawns up and down Taliaferro Lane had transformed into shades of sere as my feet aimlessly dribbled a soccer ball down the street. School was out, Mother and Jubal had gone to the grocery store, Katie was at JV cheerleading practice, and I was trying to decide whether there was time to bolt over to Furnace Creek before dark. Now that the weather had changed, the furnace was a less welcoming haven than it had been during the warmer months; lying back on the cold rocks and looking upward at bare limbs quivering against a steel-gray sky made it too grim a spot on which to dwell, even for my private pleasures. Caught up in such musings, I heard a voice drawl my name—"Massa Newt"—from the Presley driveway. It was Littlejohn, a bent-over elder who did chores for several families in the neighborhood; this week he'd been repairing the Presleys' fence. He looked to be finishing up for the day, for he was loading a battered toolbox into the back of an equally battered Chevy pickup. I stopped the ball with my left heel and waited.

"Holt on, son, I've got something for you," he said, and opening the passenger door, he retrieved a manila envelope looking the worse for wear.

"What's this?"

"Can't say I know, I was jes told to pass it on to you. With some partic'lar instructions." He paused, plucking at the white hairs that soared from his dark nostrils like milkweed run amok in rich loam. "*Somebody* hopes you being good, boy, good and—" The old man lifted shaky fingers to his lips, made a motion as if zipping them shut, and winked a rheumy eye at me, before handing over the envelope. "That's the long and short of it. G'day to you, Massa Newt." Littlejohn got into his truck and carefully nursed the engine to life.

The unstamped envelope he left me holding as he tipped his battered straw hat and drove away was stiff, heavy, and smelled of strange places. I turned it over. It was addressed in block letters:

Deliv. By Hand
& IN PRIVAT to
Newton Seward
(DEACONS SON)

I prized the flap open, and extracted two pieces of flimsy cardboard—
the kind that newly bought shirts come wrapped around, white on
one side, gray on the other. Taped to one of the boards were thirteen
shiny silver dollars that I instantly recognized: one per year for the
dates running 1952-1964. On the other board, the last letter of the
alphabet, painted five inches tall, gleamed out at me with a fuchsia
sheen: an enameled Z. It glistened like blood but I knew very well it
was nail polish.

I have made it to the other side, don't mess it up for me now. That,
I intuited, was the message being conveyed by the communication
in my hand. That, and perhaps a hint of... gratitude? After all, she'd
seen fit to return the coins that I'd volunteered were birthday gifts.
Where Zithra had ended up, I had no idea, but she was telling me it
was someplace where she had begun life anew. One of us renegades
had made it out of Rocky Hill.

I slipped the pieces of cardboard back into the envelope and,
ball tucked under my arm, walked thoughtfully home. In the front
window of the Pettigrews' house, I could see their cleaning woman
spraying the plate glass with Windex, and she stared knowingly at me
as I passed by. At the Smythes' place, the maid was closing the side-
door, jacket on, paper-bag in hand. "Massa Newt," she murmured,
eyes narrowed. Across the street, I thought I caught the movement of
a person rattling tools in the shadowy interior of the Johnsons' garage.
The late November afternoon teemed with eyes, everywhere silently
watching and waiting, and I knew I did not have the desire to visit
Furnace Creek today.

4

THROUGH THE LOOKING GLASS

I was fifteen before I realized that my mother was dangerously attractive to many men. The day it dawned on me, she and I had stopped by Dad's dealership on the way home from taking our dog Buster to the vet for a case of worms. Dad didn't see us when we pushed open the double glass doors but we saw him, waxing poetic to a potential customer about the merits of the 1967 Thunderbird Landau, mint-green with white vinyl roof, prominently displayed in the showroom window that reflected the buoyant spring day back to strollers passing by.

"Nothing like last year's Bird, just look at these lines!" Dad's hands traced the curves of the car with a grace his gawky body rarely displayed at home, his toothy smile shining as brightly as the car's glistening hood. "And this radiator-grill design, have you ever seen anything like this?—the idea's inspired, pure jet aircraft, and man alive can this Bird Fly! Four doors, that's a first for the line. And watch this!" He proceeded to open the driver's door and demonstrate the automatically tilting steering wheel. "Instant leg room!"

Mother and I were so engrossed in this demonstration of Dad's expertise that we barely noted the new salesman, Hank Atwater, sidling up to us—or, more accurately, up to Mother—until he spoke. "Your man knows a beaut, *that's* for sure, Missus Seward. Course one look at you is enough to see he has a connoisseur's eye." Hank's voice was as smooth as the product he used to shape his thick dark hair into a rock 'n' roll wave that threatened to buckle in on itself, and its intonation was pitched just low enough to make my mother uncomfortably aware that his compliment was not intended for public consumption. "Just look at Mister Seward carryin' on about the *curves* of that Bird." Hank leaned forward, his voice a low purr. "Sure knows his business." I sensed Mother's disapproval in her icy reply, and I could feel, behind her coolness, feelings akin to perturbation.

"Tell Mr. Seward that we'll be waiting for him in his office." She turned her back on Hank, cutting short his offer to fetch us Cokes from the machine, and she marched me away at a brisk if measured pace.

I had always assumed, so accustomed I was to my mother's domineering ways around our household, that there was nothing in her demeanor to elicit desire. But for the first time I saw that Jeanlyn's ice-queen facade could not wholly erase the visceral effect of her presence on others, a presence that—as I now pictured her through Hank Atwater's eyes—was arresting in a Grace Kelly kind of way. Everything about her appearance was as proper and refined as debutante lessons in small-town comportment could produce; but while she revealed not a whit of untoward flesh for visual consumption, her belted dress flared from a waist that would have done a 21-year-old proud, her nyloned legs were perfectly shaped, and the coif that gathered her honeyed tresses into a French curl at the nape of her neck added regal allure to her profile. Even the proper way she had of walking on her high (but not too high) heels—hips resisting all but the slightest tendency to sway—accentuated what I'd never really registered before: Jeanlyn Seward, matron and mother of three, was a feast of feminine beauty that, however corseted by upbringing and personal choice, emanated a sexual appeal that put leery-lipped sensualists like Hank Atwater on red-alert.

"I've told your father a million times that man isn't worth half his salary," she grumbled once we were out of hearing distance. "But does he ever listen to me?"

We were sitting in the cracked green naugahyde armchairs in Dad's office when he joined us, bending to give Mother a chaste peck on the cheek and me a thump on the back when I rose to my feet. I was now almost as tall as he.

Mother immediately launched forth.

"I simply can't fathom why you employ that Hank Atwater. He'd cheat his grandmother out of her home. Mark my words, Harold, he'll bite the hand that feeds him."

"Jeanlyn, honey, don't fret your self 'bout business." Settling on the arm of the chair in which she sat, Dad fondled the faux pearl nesting in her right lobe with his thick fingers. Earnest lines furrowed his

brow as he fondly gazed at Mother. "Sure, he's slick, but some customers lap it up. You know I ain't one for sweet-talking folk just to
close a deal—so I reckon I'm darned lucky to have him to do it for me.
It don't harm nobody."

Mother changed the subject. "Why did you ask us to stop by,
Harold? You *know* it's my busy day." When Dad continued to stroke
her earring, she fretfully removed his hand. "I have to get home to fix
dinner early so that I can get to my class by four."

Three months ago Mother had surprised the family by announcing that she had signed up for art lessons in Ferrum, a half-hour drive
away, and thus we Sewards would just have to make do without her
every Wednesday afternoon. Her classes had blossomed into a passion; so consumed was she in her studio projects that sometimes
she called to tell us to proceed with dinner without her. Gradually,
we'd grown accustomed to this hiccup in our weekly routines and no
longer thought of it as odd.

Dad hemmed portentously—he wasn't about to let Jeanlyn's impatience rob him of the dramatic delivery it turned out he had been
rehearsing all day.

"I called you to stop by," he said, pausing to prolong the suspense
he was so clearly relishing, "because a Proposition's come my way
that might be of interest to our boy here. You listening, Newt?"

I turned from the one-way window that looked out into the
showroom. There, Hank was practicing his seductive arts on a young
couple that'd just strolled in. They had the glow of newlyweds still
disposed to believe the world a trustworthy place.

"Sure, Pops, what's up?"

"Tom Allbright dropped by this morning." The mention of Allbright's name set the hair on my arms tingling, a vestigial response to
a two-year-old secret almost but not entirely forgotten. "And he had
a MOST interesting proposition concerning you, son. Seems one of
his clients is looking for a smart lad, and a strong one at that, to do
chores for him this summer. Allbright thought you might be the man
for the job."

"Who's the client?" Mother asked before I could open my mouth.
One of the tacit understandings that had followed my parents' reali-

zation they could not afford to send me to boarding school had been to provide me with the local resources to keep my studies up. Last summer I'd started private French lessons, which I'd continued concurrent with third-year Latin this school year and planned on continuing this summer. I'd already begun accumulating the eclectic library I intended to tackle as soon as school ended—Wharton, Bergson, C. S. Lewis—and I was wary of relinquishing my studies without good reason.

"It's old Julian Brewster. Allbright says he's more an invalid than not these days, needs a boy to push his chair around, but most of all he wants a bright lad to help him organize his library, read to him, help him put his papers in order." Dad raised his eyebrows at me. "So Allbright thought our Newt here might fit the bill. It's only three days a week, son, leaves plenty of time for your studies. Plus you'll have free range of all the books in Mr. Brewster's library. Allbright says there's thousands."

I knew who Julian Armistead Brewster III was, all right, as did anyone who'd grown up in Rocky Hill. He was one of the stars (albeit a fading one) in our community's local cosmology, the scion of the family that owned the town's main industry, a furniture factory that had its humble beginnings as a sawmill on Furnace Creek and that specialized in high-end replicas of antique period pieces. When the manufacturing interest had been sold for a hefty profit, the remaining heirs had hunkered down in the family mansion on Honeysuckle Heights Road, where all but Julian died out over the years. By every account old Julian Brewster was an odd bird, though no more eccentric than the living waxworks that populated every Southern backwater hamlet in 1967: a patrician bachelor counting sixty-odd years who remained defiantly out of step with the times, a practitioner of the Catholic faith (as near as heresy as you could get in Rocky Hill), a fastidious dresser never seen in public except in the dapper whites, linen jacket, bow-tie, and fedora befitting Joel Chandler Harris's tales of plantation life. That was before Julian Brewster became a recluse. These days, he was more memory than dandy about town, infrequently spotted tottering across the grounds of his vast, unkempt property or shouting gentrified obscenities at the neighborhood boys who snuck over its walls to steal Muscat grapes from its once legendary arbor.

But I wasn't thinking of his decaying house, or his eccentricities, or his temper, at that moment: my imagination flared at the mention of what I imagined to be the cornucopia of books collected by generations of Brewsters, interspersed with mementos of the worldwide travel that family had been taking ever since transatlantic steamers made Europe a destination for the leisured class. Before I realized I was speaking I accepted the position— that is, should Mr. Brewster decide to take me under his wing after the interview Mr. Allbright had arranged for next Monday.

Dad was pleased as punch that he could give a positive report to Mr. Allbright; Mother was at once more skeptical—"How can he keep the boy busy enough to warrant paying him so much?"—*and* more ambitious regarding my prospects: "This could be the making of you, Newt. His connections, that family fortune—and no offspring!"

So there you have it: it was only mid-April, and, provided I passed muster with Mr. Brewster, my prospects for the summer were settled. The job beckoned as an entrance into a realm I only knew through books and innuendo: a world of inherited money and family trees with deep roots, a world of education and refined tastes, a world of contacts circumventing the globe. Such vistas seemed heaven-sent, a break from the humdrum regularity of life as I knew it in my fifteenth year, and they stoked my deepest desires.

I don't want to give a false impression of my fifteen-year-old self: I wasn't quite the snob I may be making myself sound. Yes, a part of me was driven by ambition, and Mr. Powell's words of counsel continued to stoke my daydreams. And, yes, no doubt I read more than most of my peers at Hill High, where I was now a ninth-grade honors student. But in the eyes of my classmates I didn't let myself appear all *that* different. I wasn't as outgoing as some but I was not an introvert nor a geek, either. My goal was to pass without attracting attention. So I read my Sartre in private, advertised my relative normality by joining the swim team, and cultivated a circle of friends to whom I never confessed the extent of my yearning for change. I watched and waited.

Meanwhile, I'd grown. At thirteen, I was the shortest boy in my class, with a cherubic mien that belied the hormonal turbulence firing my onanistic reveries. By fifteen, however, I was nearing six feet and lanky everywhere, from a lean torso that descended from newly broadened shoulders, to arms that seemed to dangle apishly low, to wispy blonde sideburns that occasioned Dad's amusement and Mother's disdain. I'd never been one for competitive sports but had joined the swim team to burn off the energy that was stretching my muscle and bone as I added inches to my frame by the month. I grew to look forward to arising an hour and a half early to execute drills in the school pool with my swim team buddies Dwayne Hickman and Billy Swearington. Skimming across that skin of chlorine, I could think more clearly, the rhythmic strokes and breath-counts disciplining not only my body but my mind as I organized ideas that teemed pell-mell until I hit the water and lapped them into coherence.

This, then, was the youth who rang the bell outside the wrought-iron gate at 5 Honeysuckle Heights Road a week later. Here, the houses were discretely set back from the street on large properties, their distinguished facades screened by venerable oaks, hickories, sycamores, and elms, their domains parsed off from the world of ordinary beings by high hedges, fences, walls. The air was heavy with the odor of lilacs in full bloom and honeysuckle careening over the gray stone wall that framed the gate to the immense Brewster property—stones of an identical shade and heft to those that made up the bullet refinery down by Furnace Creek, a lost paradise I'd ceased frequenting ages ago.

The gate swung open, electrically powered from an unseen source, and I stepped onto a graveled drive that curved between two rows of elms and culminated, at some distance, in an immense, weathered house whose mossy brick walls, stone coping, exposed timbers, and gabled appurtenances I glimpsed through the foliage. A dewy chillness pervaded the scene, and the breeze that wafted across me belied the afternoon heat and cloudless sky outside the gates. I leant my bike against the inside wall and looked around in wonder.

I still remember, distinctly, the first sight that caught my eye: the raised terrace that fronted the house, irradiated by a patch of dazzling sunlight that had broken through the foliage and made it the one warm spot in the melancholy landscape. Immediately after I became aware that I wasn't alone; there, camouflaged in the shadows cast by the elms bordering the drive, stood a black man in a worn butler's outfit who limped forward in the gloom while the gate behind me creaked shut. The next impression I took in was more ineffable—a sensation of loneliness and neglect, tangibly manifested in the uneven condition of the lawn, the overgrown shrubbery, the unkempt flowerbeds dotting the slopes and rises of the property, some of which flourished wildly, and some of which struggled to stay alive, even now at the height of spring blossoming. Who knows how much of this atmosphere of desolation I took in at once, and how much only subconsciously registered in my mind to reemerge and form a more complete picture through repeated visits and later remembrances? But at this moment some twenty years later I feel, as if it were yesterday, the sensation of standing on that graveled path, a stranger in a strange land taking in the quiet weight of decline and decay as it pressed down upon the fictions of generation and gentility embalming the Brewster mansion at the end of the lane.

In the few seconds it took me to get my bearings, the man on the drive reached me.

Stopping a few yards short, he made a curt bow. "George Geronimo Washington at your service, and YOU, I presume, are Mr. Newt." A tone of disapproval seemed to tinge his declaration. "Mr. Brewster's asked me to escort you in. Follow me."

So follow him in silence I did, there being no other option.

The slight bowing of his shoulders, the solidity of his frame, the pinch of extra flesh at the back of his neck where crinkled gray hair met the line of a starched but frayed shirt collar—all suggested to me that my taciturn guide was in his sixties; the limp in his right leg, I was afterwards told, was the result of polio contracted in boyhood. I could not imagine that he had ever worked anywhere but in the Brewster mansion.

Without speaking a word, he motioned me under a trellis of wisteria and climbing rose—the overgrown vine slowly strangling the thorn—that framed the elaborately carved, heavy front door, and led me through the entrance into a dark hall where the scent of rose was

displaced by odors more elaborately musty and worn. As my eyes adjusted, I saw a grand mahogany staircase leading to an overhanging
gallery that enwrapped the hexagonal entry. The floor was made of
glazed terra cotta tiles, also hexagonal in shape, the dark-paneled walls
hung with unlit portraits and landscapes, and a chandelier shrouded
in a dusty slipcover presided over this forlorn grandeur.

George Geronimo Washington tapped me on the shoulder and
pointed my way to a double door whose wooden panels he slid open.
He gestured for me to enter, and I stepped down into a drawing room
where faded Turkish carpets formed archipelagos anchoring islets of
sofas, chairs, and end-tables that I surmised were high-end replicas
of the sort in which the Brewster company had specialized. However
worn and faded they were, even the most scuffed pieces bespoke an
elegance to which none of the furnishings in the Seward household
even remotely compared.

The panels slid shut behind me, leaving me alone in the room.
A grandfather clock ticked off the seconds, though on second look I
realized the minute hand was stuck at the quarter-hour. Photographs
in silver frames, vases filled with bouquets of dead and dying flowers, and bric-a-brac that looked vaguely foreign crowded the tables
and cabinet tops. A wall of half-open French doors gave access to the
terrace and lawn in back of the house, and a faint breeze moved the
yellowed sheers that hung over the doors. A fly buzzed around my
face, and I had no idea what I was supposed to do.

The sound of a drawl that managed to sound refined and snappish
at the same time took me off-guard. It emanated from an adjoining
room whose entrance had been blocked from my vision by an ornate
highboy.

"Boy, here! This way!"

And thus I found myself, for the first time in my life, confronting Julian Armistead Brewster's strange and unforgettable presence.
He was sitting in a wheelchair in the middle of the cavernous library, behind a long, ancient-looking walnut table with squatting
griffins for legs, on whose surface books, magazines, clippings, and
files competed for space. More books rose on the floor around him
in perilously stacked towers, a storied metropolis awaiting the Great

Quake. Capped by a frescoed ceiling that soared twenty feet above, all four walls of the windowless room were lined with grand built-in bookshelves; and a wrought-iron gallery, accessible by a spiral staircase, wound around the upper echelons of the chamber. Books were crammed everywhere, lining the shelves, piled at their base, and they filled the close air with the odors of leather bindings, old paper, and mildew, odors intermingled with the faint aroma of tobacco, heavy damask, spilt drinks long since absorbed into the carpets, wax drippings from decades of candelabra lit and snuffed out, and—most redolent of all as the old man waved me to approach—the scents of French cologne, talcum powder, and lavender soap masking the whiff of slightly decaying flesh. A furry black and white cat, a grossly overweight Angora, rubbed herself against the wheels of his chair.

"It's overwhelming, just overwhelming! Each time I begin, my head starts spinning!" Mr. Brewster dropped a volume with a thud on the table and leaned forward to scrutinize me. "Come closer, boy. Let me have a look at you!"

He looked. So did I. Meeting the intense gaze of his watery sky-blue eyes catapulted me into places I'd never been, and then some. Those penetratingly sharp orbs triggered a myriad of contradictory memories: the admonishing blue gaze of the Virgin Mary in a portrait that had hung in my fourth-grade Sunday School room; the calculating stare of the fortune teller at the County Fair who wrongly informed me I was an orphan; the dead-blue irises of the psychopathic murderess in "You Shall Not Live," a Saturday matinee in Technicolor that gave me and Randy Johnson nightmares when we snuck into the Rialto Playhouse to see it years before.

"So you're Newton Seward," he said in an impatient drawl, eyeing me up and down over his thin, aquiline nose like a hawk casing out all-too-easy prey. "I see you favor one of those ridiculous Age of Aquarius haircuts, but at least you look fit enough to push my chair and help me about when I need an assist—not that I'm *that* heavy, mind you."

Nor did he appear to be. Looking to be sixty-going-on-eighty, Julian Brewster III was a trim bird-figure of a man, sitting ramrod stiff his chair, dressed in a maroon velvet smoking jacket, shiny black pants somewhere between slacks and pajama bottoms, and white suede loafers on sockless feet that revealed thin, blue-veined ankles. Almost as arresting as the pale eyes set above sunken cheeks in his long, angular face was the finely textured hair on his pate—too blonde to be natural and at surreal odds with the wrinkles that creased his pale skin, hair so feathery that his pink scalp showed through, palimpsest-like.

I'd never seen anyone, anything, quite like him before.

The obese cat jumped to his lap and hissed in my direction. "Temper, Mimi!" he chuckled. Mimi stared at me through slits in cornflower blue irises that were as shrewdly appraising as her master's eyes. Now I recognized another odor mingling with the fragrances in the room: the faint tang of cat urine.

"But can you *think*?" Mr. Brewster raised his quavering arms with a dramatic flair that, I was to discover, was part of his everyday means of expression. Mimi sprang from his lap as if struck by lightning. "I need a boy with brains, not just brawn! Look at this room. It wants a system, and I simply don't have the stamina to go it on my own!" Before I had time to comment, his mood swerved. "But what cares youth about such things? Books, they mean nothing to youngsters! *Plus ça change!*"

"*Quel dommage que vous pensiez cela, Monsieur! Parce que les livres, ils sont l'amour de ma vie.*" My French, however halting, seemed to do the trick, for Mr. Brewster looked at me anew, as if—beneath Aquarian hairstyle and rock-star sideburns—there might lurk a minimally intelligent being.

"Mercy me, don't tell me that Hill High has added French to the curriculum—miracles never cease. Sit!"

Lowering myself into the leather chair to which his bony finger regally pointed, I explained that I was tackling the language with the help of a tutor. That intrigued him, and led to more questions about my studies, my penmanship, my command of syntax—and, finally, back to the job at hand.

"Firstly, young man" (I was pleased to note I'd graduated from "boy" to "young man") "I am tired, and I am in dire want of diversion. I need someone to push my chair when I need a change of scene, help me with my correspondence and papers, but above and beyond all, I'm simply desperate, I emphasize *desperate*, to put this library in order! It's been dreadfully neglected—everything hopelessly jumbled together, from books I've purchased since I was your age to my grandfather's collection—some fine first editions, though Lord knows where to find them—plus all my art books and museum catalogues, heaps of periodicals, over there the design catalogues for Brewster Furniture, and, let's face it, hordes of trash in need of tossing—oh, it's just a mess, and I can't find anything when I want it anymore." He rolled his eyes in distress, and again threw his arms up to the high heavens as the dusky pink cherubs in the overhead fresco leered down at us. "And my infirmity hasn't helped, Heaven knows. As for those volumes"—he saw my eyes scanning the upper gallery—"I haven't attempted those stairs for years, who knows what naughty treasures lurk up there!"

At which point he launched into a further monologue about the various organizing schemes he'd considered—using simple alphabetical order, separating books by genre, classifying them by century and nation, even grouping them by priority so that the ones he'd be most likely to use would be within easiest reach: "Oh dear, I get this far, and then my head swirls and I throw up my hands. In. Despair!"

I assured him that the task wasn't impossible and that there was nothing I'd enjoy more than bringing some order to the collection, including making a catalogue of its contents and the location of each item. He seemed delighted with my ideas, so much so that he hoped I wouldn't wait till school was out to start. I volunteered to work Saturdays till the summer recess began.

The formal part of our interview over, Mr. Brewster summoned George Geronimo Washington over an antique intercom to bring in refreshments—to "sweeten the deal," as he put it. When Washington arrived balancing a crystal pitcher filled with lemonade, two etched tumblers that sparkled like diamonds, and a plate of cookies on a silver tray, Mr. Brewster could barely contain his excitement. "What a *find*, G.G., you can't imagine! This youth's actually *educated!* He'll start Saturday, and the library's our first priority. Of course we'll be calling on you to assist with the heavy labor when we reach that stage."

I might have been imagining things, but Washington's eyes

seemed to glower at me as he withdrew, with a curt bow, from the room. Given the tonnage of volumes to be moved from one shelf to another, I certainly understood the steel darts he'd shot at me. Curiosity compelled me to ask more about the man who, for better or worse, was going to be my co-worker.

"Ah, that G.G.!" Mr. Brewster pronounced the initials so that they almost sounded like "Gigi." I smiled at the sheer incongruity—Leslie Caron Mr. Washington was not. "*No*, take that biscuit, the ginger cream. He's worked for me for more years than I care to remember...." Mr. Brewster proceeded to inform me that "G.G." Washington was a bit of everything—manservant, butler, valet, gardener, and caretaker rolled into one. Mr. Brewster's only other regular employee was the cook Sassafras Beebe (known as "B.B." to complement "G.G.") who usually worked five days a week, and sometimes G.G.'s son Samson came over to assist with the more tasking chores. "Indispensable as G.G. thinks he is, he *can't* do everything, and he's absolutely *worthless* when it comes to arranging these books. No doubt he resents the fact"—Mr. Brewster's blue irises glistened with wicked delight—"that I've found a task to which he cannot lend an iota of service."

Our conversation lasted another ten minutes, at which point the old man announced that he needed to rest. So he summoned Washington to wheel him to his siesta. But when Washington arrived, Mr. Brewster perversely changed tune—I might as well get started, so *I* should push his chair from the library to the drawing room, after which Washington could settle him on the couch for *une petite sieste* before seeing me out. I dutifully complied, then respectfully stood back while his servant shifted his spindly limbs to a worn but elegant satinwood sofa upholstered in an art deco brocade shot through with gold and violet—a Duncan Phyfe knock-off, I later learned. Mimi, who'd trailed our expedition out of the library, leapt onto the shredded arm of the sofa before settling down on the old man's frail chest. I feared his heart might give out. Lying thus, Mr. Brewster faced an oil portrait on the opposite wall, emblazoned by a shaft of light from one of the open French doors. "Ah," he sighed, following my eye to the portrait. "*Oui, c'est bien moi...* an early Enzio Sorrento—he painted it my first visit to Florence back in, oh dear! The Thirties? Sotheby's says it's quite valuable, though in those days who'd have guessed Enzio would become such a commodity. Life's ironies!"

I moved closer to study the painting. Its slightly cubist planes of color captured Julian Brewster framed against a window that opened onto a view of terracotta rooftops hinting at a labyrinth of narrow streets below. He sat on the windowsill, arms crossed in all the imperious confidence of angularly handsome manhood, pompous and preening but not altogether as arrogant as the glinting rings on the right hand propping up his chin and the curl of his upper lip first made him seem. The youthful eyes in the portrait were exact mirrors of his eyes now, the same disturbingly cerulean hue, and he stared out at the viewer as if with bemused impatience for having interrupted his observation of the scene below. I stooped to make out the signature. "*Il miglior fabbro*, E.S., 1931," I read outloud.

"Ah, yes, thirty-three it was..." he murmured, eyes closing. "G.G., show the boy out"—I noticed, ruefully, that I was once again mere "boy"—"by the back way, why don't you, he might like to take in the gardens on his way out. And draw the shades."

Washington ushered me to one of the French doors, whose faded curtains he drew closed as he stepped out onto the back terrace with me.

"You really don't mind if I wander a bit?"

"Suit yourself, it's his idea. Take that path, I'll leave the front gate cracked open."

He started to walk away, stopped and turned back. "You know, you're not the first."

"Beg your pardon?"

"Ever so often he gets the same crazy notion—hiring a boy to help him out. Never works out. *None* of you work out."

He bowed and limped away.

Needless to say, that left me feeling low. To dispel the pall the manservant's words cast over the pleasantries of the past hour, I set off down the path, only gradually coming to a sense of my surroundings. The acreage behind the house was extensive. The terrace opened onto an overgrown lawn, down one long slope of which I spied a ruined tennis court. Beside a rush-filled creek, choked with yellow iris and shaded by a weeping willow whose branches supported a wooden swing, I made out the pointed roof of an ancient ice house, circular and half-buried in the slope. Closer at hand, an arch cut into a towering hedge led to what had once been a formal garden laid out in parterres. Straggling roses budded here and there amid the rank weeds, and in the center where the paths intersected rose a desiccated fountain—a scalloped seashell atop which a lithesome nymph bent forward, revealing curiously pointy breasts as she tipped an urn through which water had once splashed into the basin below. One quadrant of the garden had been cultivated and mulched, and here tendrils of squash, tomato, melon, and cucumber sprouted— Washington's handiwork, I surmised. To the garden's rear was the grape arbor of neighborhood legend, under which a corroded confederacy of broken lawn chairs had retreated.

I retraced my steps, walked through another arch in the unkempt hedge, went up some steps, turned a corner, and, passing through a gap in the greenery, found myself looking onto a swimming pool filled with turquoise water. Of art-deco vintage, the pool was lined with what I later learned were Malibu ceramic tiles, exquisitely patterned in vibrant shades of emerald, gold, and garnet. A perilously sagging pergola on the far side of the pool, opposite the entrance through the hedge, connected the Greek-styled porticos of two dressing rooms. A flagstone terrace ran between the two structures. It looked as if Washington, or his son, made a half-hearted effort to keep the pool area tidy. There was a long-handled leaf skimmer propped upright against the shrubbery, and only a few days' worth of leaves and dead insects floated on the surface of the water. The entire area was surrounded by towering hedges, giving the spot a feeling of privacy that struck my fifteen-year-old imagination as simultaneously melancholic and romantic. Looking at the diving board at the deep end of the pool, I found myself envisioning a younger Julian Brewster, the man of the Sorrento portrait, clad in outmoded bathing garment and jack-knifing into the water. So vivid was the scene my fancy created that I was hardly surprised when I looked again and saw immediately superimposed on that mental image another one, so vibrant as if to seem positively real: a young woman, a feminine counterpart of Julian Brewster, sitting in a white wicker chair by pool's edge and clapping with delight as his body sluiced the water. For a second I hallucinated the lilt of their voices calling back and forth to each other as he broke the blue surface. I blinked my eyes, and the strange vision disappeared. Chill-bumps prickled my arms as I turned to go.

Passing through yet another arch in the hedge, I came upon a brick carriage house converted into a garage, all four doors padlocked shut. Going around to its side, I tried without success to peer through the shuttered windows to see if any automobiles remained interred within. A narrow path led to the rear of the building, so I followed it, and there I stumbled onto the former horse stables: weather-worn, sun-bleached planks warped loose of their nailings, beams draped in cobwebs, and corroded tin roof collapsing inward. When I gingerly pushed open the upper half of one of the stall doors, the scamper of mice broke the silence. Here the ghosts of times past seemed more mournfully in attendance than anywhere else on the estate, dreaming dreams too dreary for me; so I returned to the carriage house, where I followed the drive as it gradually connected to the front lane.

The entrance gate, as Washington had promised, stood ajar. I retrieved my bike, and as I guided it out onto the street the gate automatically closed behind me. I had visions of Washington invisibly standing sentinel all this time, awaiting my departure. As I mounted the bike and began to pedal, the rush of daylight and the sounds of normal life—a car pulling into a driveway, a lawnmower whirring, a child laughing—quite confounded me; and I felt dazed, as if I just exited a stranger's dream and stepped back into time itself.

5

CUSTOMS OF THE COUNTRY

Rocky Hill was about as far as you could get, geographically or culturally speaking, from San Francisco. So there was no way to foresee that the first paying job of my life would coincide with the Summer of Love that drew tens of thousands of restive youth across America to Haight-Asbury. But even in Rocky Hill there were signs of the seismic revolution rocking the country, and its tremors reached all the way to 326 Taliaferro Lane. For while I was having my interview with Mr. Brewster, the very grounds on which Freeland-Seward values had stood firm for decades were being shaken by a clash of generations that threatened to bring the whole edifice crashing down.

The sight of Jubal flailing his arms in the driveway as I biked into view led me to suspect a rampage of the first order was underway. Inside the house Katie's angry protests and my parents' strident voices emanated from the living room. "Sis is in BIG trouble!" Jubal declared, bug-eyed with pleasure. In what seemed the wave of a tripped-out fairy godmother's wand, Katie had morphed from a pert junior varsity cheerleader who swooned to the Beatles, adored the color pink, and accepted Jesus Christ as her Personal Savior, to a seventeen-year-old flower-child who rocked to the Stones, festooned her room in Indian print fabrics, and championed Khalil Gibran over the Bible. Wholesome tresses that once flipped upwards from her shoulders now fell straight down her back to her waist, parted in the middle and crowned with a beaded headband. She had also taken to an excess of purple eyeshadow, minidresses she hoisted even higher once she left the house, and a morose boyfriend, Ronald to his parents but "Rat" to his friends. Rat wore an extraordinarily scruffy, fringed suede jacket, summer and winter, day and night, inside and outside, pretended to play electric guitar, and was growing a white-boy Afro. Mother saw in him portents of the Anti-Christ, and Dad—well, Dad, was so befuddled at the whole youth rebellion that he could only shake his head in wonder.

Whatever truce my parents had struck with Katie regarding her dubious object-choice had exploded sky-high during my absence. Mom and Dad had received a distraught phone call from Rat's parents, who'd found a "marijuana pipe" in his room—no weed, but the head-shop artifact carved from jade was sufficient evidence of criminal intent. Adding injury to insult, Mother had uncovered a pack of L&Ms in Katie's hand-crocheted bag, and since in Jeanlyn's mind one form of inhaled contraband implied another, that unfortunate discovery only deepened the air of urgent crisis and flying recriminations that assailed my ears as I trotted into the house.

Need I say, the moment was not propitious for the telling of *my* stories, although I'd been rehearsing them all the way home. Perhaps that's why, when over dinner my parents finally calmed down enough to query me about my visit, I couldn't help but embroider. My embellishments grew reckless. Father was so awed by my mention of a garage built to house four vehicles that I found myself extemporizing upon the phantom autos harbored inside: a black 1956 Mercedes-Benz 220S Cabriolet convertible, a late 1940s silver Cadillac Coupe, a burgundy 1952 Alfa Romeo. Dad's eyes bulged with amazement at the existence of such automotive royalty. To forestall his asking when he might see such splendor, I solemnly declared none had been operational for years.

For Mother's edification, I painted a portrait of Mr. Brewster as the frailest of invalids, a devout Catholic who might expire any moment and was in mortal terror for his soul. As evidence thereof, I casually mentioned the silver crucifix he wore around his neck (a gift from Pope Paul) that he habitually stroked as if doing so might heal his crippled limbs. Having riveted both parents' attention, I proceeded to describe the private chapel housed within the mansion, replete with altar, medieval triptych, jewel encrusted censors, and two reliquaries—one a vial of St. John the Baptist's chest hair (which Salome had shaved from his headless torso) and the other the iron tip of one of the arrows hastening Sebastian to sainthood. Raised Methodist in the God-fearing South, Jeanlyn was ready to believe the worst of Papist excess and shook her head in horror at such idolatry, while my father pondered the injustice of three vintage cars gone to waste, their neglect obscurely related in his thoughts to Mr. Brewster's misguided faith.

Why my parents didn't worry that such Popery might negatively influence an innocent youngster like myself, I don't know—perhaps they were simply grateful that Mr. Brewster wasn't a countercultural activist spouting quotations from Mao's *Little Red Book*. At any rate, the following Saturday found me at my new post with my parents' happy approval. After a week dominated by Katie's sullenness at being grounded and tedious homework assignments I could master with my eyes closed, escaping into the antiquated but weirdly fabulous world of Julian Armistead Brewster III and George Geronimo Washington seemed more glamorous than ever.

Over the week I'd devised a simple organizing schema appropriate to Mr. Brewster's collection. I now proposed it to him. Since his books fell into three categories—fiction, general nonfiction, and arts-related texts—I proposed dedicating one of each of three walls to these categories. The fourth wall, bisected by the entrance, could accommodate the collection's first editions, rare books, and folios of the Brewster furniture designs to the left, and quality periodicals like *National Geographic* and *Scientific American,* of which the family had amassed full runs, to the right. Further, we would subdivide the books into those most important to Mr. Brewster, which would be shelved on ground level, and those least likely to be consulted in that category to the gallery directly above. The clippings, files, and miscellaneous papers would need to be housed elsewhere, perhaps the basement; we could order file cabinets later. My proposals sent Mr. Brewster into raptures. I warned him, though, that the task would be immense and involve ruthless winnowing.

So I began, on that Saturday, and succeeding Saturdays, to separate the wheat from the chaff. Coupling an elderly person's impatience to see progress with a childlike eagerness for new diversions, Mr. Brewster wheeled himself into the room every chance he got, only retreating when the microscopic dust of crumbling bindings set afloat by my efforts occasioned a wheezing fit. But the old man's combination of curiosity, bossiness, and sadistic pleasure in having me for a captive audience kept him returning to the library for longer spates of time, till he seemed a permanent fixture of the room. All those initial Saturdays spent in that windowless chamber, shut off from the rest of the world, seemed to merge into a perpetual day interrupted, every so often, by George Geronimo's taciturn appearance: bearing snacks, or the mail, or his master's pills, quantities of which seemed necessary to sustain Mr. Julian—for so I will now start referring to my eccentric employer, as it was during this period of our acquaintance that he instructed me to begin addressing him as such.

And nearly every weekend throughout April and May, at least one of the invariably dusty, occasionally mildewing items in the library yielded a tantalizing glimpse into Mr. Julian's past, triggering memories that spilled out in histrionic asides and imperious monologues. Running across a 1937 playbill from the Mercury Theatre, I learned that he had been a costume consultant and set designer for the company until he had a falling out with "that egomaniacal Orson." The rupture happened soon after the opening of the infamous production of "Caesar" in which the actors had been outfitted to resemble Mussolini's Brownshirts. During one performance Welles, taking method acting to an extreme, stabbed a fellow actor with his sword. It was the fact that Orson hadn't even deigned to pay a hospital visit to the herniated actor—a close friend of Mr. Julian—that led to their split. Mr. Julian had moved to New York City in 1923 after finishing his bachelor's in art history at UVA in order to make a go of it in the world of theatre. His father, who had taken over the family business from his father and expected the same of Julian and his brother, had disapproved and threatened—ineffectually it seemed—to cut off his namesake's allowance. Ultimately, it seemed, Mr. Julian was more successful cultivating friends associated with the theatre—some whose homes he was hired to decorate—than in becoming a moving force within it himself. Elsa Lancaster, Katherine Cornell, Leslie Howard, Paul Robeson, Tallulah Bankhead: these numbered among the "amusing friends" he recalled as I set aside their biographies and memoirs—some of which volumes mentioned him by name—for shelving on the west wall.

Of course I was spellbound, I who had never imagined that anyone from Rocky Hill mingled with celebrities, and I couldn't fathom what would have finally drawn Mr. Julian away from the glamor of Manhattan and back to our close-minded mountain town—a fate that I vowed would never be mine. As we worked our way through the shelves, other volumes hinted at other emotions: Mr. Julian consigned most that bore his father's bookplate to the dustbin without comment; those belonging to his grandfather, he reviewed with sentimental affection and assigned places of privilege.

One Saturday I proposed discarding a series of novels by an author I'd never heard of, Ronald Firbank, upon which my employer gave a shudder as if I'd committed the most grievous of sins. He set out to correct the error of my ways by having me read several passages outloud till I too began to laugh. *Stones of Venice* made him gloomy, as he counted the decades since he'd set foot in Italy, where, he declared, he had passed "some of the happiest moments" of his life. When I admitted ignorance of Langston Hughes, he ordered me to read first editions of *The Ways of White Folk* and *The Weary Blues*.

"I met Langston around the time he'd published his first novel and was the talk of the town. But he was always a bit of a loner. We used to run into each other at Artie's on West 80th. He'd invariably be alone, savoring his Manhattan, and we'd always exchange a few words. He liked to scribble verse as it came to him on his napkin, and if I were lucky he might share a line or two."

The idea of black and whites patronizing the same establishment was novel to me, and I said as much. Mr. Julian rolled his eyes. "New York was *always* light years ahead of the rest of the country."

In my own quiet way I was sensitive to the racial inequities that striated the social terrain of my upbringing, but I'd never pondered the race question deeply till Mr. Julian began to lecture me on the subject; New York had changed his way of thinking, indeed made something of a progressive out of him. Now he was happy—in his typically scolding way—to educate me in turn. Not that his relatively enlightened views were without their glaring contradictions: his attitude to the household staff remained that of Master to Inferior, and his commands ranged, on a given day, from curt to plain bad-tempered.

So spring revolved into early summer, and the library began to take on a life of its own. But my days at the Brewster estate weren't always bound to books. Mr. Julian needed his diversions, and part of my job was to provide them. After so many hours sequestered in that windowless library, I was grateful for the change of pace. No doubt George Geronimo was, too, since it was he who otherwise had to keep Mr. Julian entertained. When I was busy, G.G. would be called upon to play endless games of double-solitaire and gin rummy at the felt-top card table (one of the Brewster firm's eighteenth-century replicas) that stood by the French doors—games G.G. stoically endured while no doubt worrying about the silver in need of polishing, the fertilizer to spread on the east slope, the cracked window pane on the second floor—too many tasks for one aging man to attend to, particularly when at the beck and call of so mercurial a taskmaster as Mr. Julian Brewster.

"What'd you do with the ten of diamonds?"

"I ain't played no ten o' diamonds, sir."

"Didn't say you had."

"Right, sir. You didn't say nothin'."

"You aren't paying attention. What the—?"

With nimble fingers that belied his slow-moving body, G.G. fanned out his cards in a winning hand. Mr. Julian exhaled a whine and accused G.G. of bamboozling him.

"Uh-huh," G.G. grunted. "Always do, sir."

One day I decided to ask Mr. Julian how George Geronimo had come by his odd name. "Ah, the vagaries of ancestry!" my employer clucked. "I like to remind him that while I'm merely Julian Brewster the Third, he's George Washington the Fourth. You see, there's been a George Washington in his family ever since the Emancipation. A patriotic whimsy on the part of his ancestors, who needed a surname when they stomped off the master's tobacco fields at the end of the War. Pity they didn't realize how many slaves the original George owned." For the fraction of a second, the marble bust of our first president—countenance every bit as sable as G.G.'s—that had sat on Judge Leroy's desk flashed across my thoughts. Mr. Julian's snort brought me back to reality. "As for *Geronimo*, he told me his grand-father spent some time cowboying out in Arizona, married one of Geronimo's cousins, that was back in the 1870s when the Apaches were doing their damnedest to decimate the U. S. cavalry. But *entre nous* I suspect our G.G.'s cheekbones are the result of inbreeding be-tween his forebears and the Cherokee in these regions—there was a lot of that, even before the Revolutionary War—and *Geronimo's* just a fancy signature put to the deed. But I do rather like the idea that a savage Apache heart beats beneath his livery, itching to relieve me of my scalp!"

G.G. limped into the room to fetch Mr. Julian for his bath just as the old man's inspired monologue was ending. "Hair you got left ain't worth the wampum it'd fetch."

Mr. Julian cackled and winked at me as G.G. rolled him away. I swore I heard G.G. muttering, under his breath, "Oh, yes, sir, we gon-na *shampoo* that paleface scalp of yours. Yessirree!"

Periodically, Mr. Julian called on me to help him "exercise." That meant easing him from wheelchair to walker, then following him as he pushed his way around the drawing room. Only the drawing room, since, as I learned early in my visits, library, kitchen, and drawing room were the sole chambers on the first floor in use. The remain-der had been shut up over the years, furniture draped, windows shut-tered, and cabinets locked against tides of dust and decay no belated housekeeping could hope to reverse. The upper stories were as yet off-limits to me. All I knew was that, once Mr. Julian's infirmities had made it impossible for him to climb stairs, an elevator whose blandly utilitarian design would have affronted the sensibility of the house's architect had been installed in the pantry off the kitchen, where it ascended directly to his second-story bedroom.

So the drawing room was the de facto scene of our "strolls" when Mr. Julian decided exercise was in order. Oh, the endless circles that we walked, around and around that room! The tedium of the task, of keeping a step behind Mr. Julian's shuffling progress forward, hands ready to support him should he wobble as Mimi weaved in and out of our path, was lightened by the narratives summoned forth by the ob-jects on display in the room—a sepia-tinted photograph of his grandparents surrounded by workers at the furniture plant, a pair of brass scimitars from Morocco, a one-of-a-kind glass vase from Tiffany's, a bronze Roman statuette of Adonis, the reading lamp whose base had been crafted from a Ming ceramic of a scowling Foo Dog. Each time we made the circuit of the drawing room, Mr. Julian pointed out one more artifact whose provenance he had not yet explained, whose history he fondly—or sardonically, depending on the object—imparted. In those slow perambulations, I reaped an unexpected education into a world of culture and art I'd only glimpsed in books and magazines, and it filled me with intimations of greatness and longing.

Other afternoons, Mr. Julian ordered me to wheel his chair to the flagstone terrace onto which the French doors of the drawing room opened. There we sat at a wrought iron table whose white paint was chipping off, waiting for the faint breeze that sometimes wafted up the hill from the creek and across the rectangle of lawn fronting the terrace—the one spot of green G.G. kept as immaculate as the increasingly warm weather would allow. While Mimi rubbed against our legs, begging for delicacies to add to her heft, Mr. Julian savored his afternoon tea and biscuits as I read him the *New York Times*—a few days old by the time it arrived, but, so Mr. Julian declaimed, better late than never.

Sometimes, as we sat on the terrace, he and I, he broke into French and demanded the same in return, making sure I was keeping up with my studies; later, he began to instruct me in the Italian he'd mastered on his trips to Italy. My studies preoccupied Mr. Julian a good deal. He listened sympathetically when I told him about my shattered hopes of going to boarding school up north, and almost daily he commanded me to report on my readings so he could quiz me. His teasing interest in my intellectual development fed my dreams. "Keep studying, Newt, what a disappointment you'll be to us all if you don't go far." Sometimes, too, we sat on the terrace playing Scrabble, at which he was ruthless in his misspellings and gleeful in his triumphs: the only time I was able to use double zz's, in the word "muzzle," he trumped me by spelling out "trapezoid," which simultaneously intersected with a preexisting "a" and an "x" on a triple-point square to form "tax," thereby winning the game by a landslide.

Then there were those lazy afternoons when, after a morning spent hunched over the library table, I was only too happy to accede to his request to wheel him around the vast property—his announced intention to see if G.G. had taken care of this or that repair and his sharp eyes always finding reason to complain in the harpy's drawl he'd perfected over the years of his invalidism. How G.G. bore those complaints, I couldn't fathom at first. Gradually it became clear that he and Mr. Julian, like many an old couple, were now playing parts whose roles had been fixed long ago—the querulous master who perpetually finds fault, the faithful servant who stoically endures because he knows he calls the shots.

I've noted that George Geronimo's son sometimes stopped by to help out on the more difficult handyman chores, and I met him unexpectedly the first Saturday of June. I'd finished for the day and, having left Mr. Julian napping in the drawing room, I fancied I'd wander around the grounds before returning home, looking for a quiet nook where I could chuckle at Undine Spragg's attempts to scale the heights of New York high society in a first edition of *The Custom of the Country*—gilt letters gleaming against its faded red cloth cover—I'd found in Mr. Julian's library. Storm clouds were gathering over the mountains on the northern horizon, bringing with them the scent of rain, but I wasn't too worried about a cloudburst. Halfway down the hill on my way to the swinging seat that hung from the weeping willow, I remembered G.G. telling Mr. Julian that a rotten arm had broken from its chain. That option foreclosed, it occurred to me to seek out the swimming pool hidden behind its leafy walls. As I trotted uphill, thunder growled in the distance.

Heading towards the break in the untrimmed shrubbery that led to the pool, I heard an unfamiliar racket. My first thought was that a stray dog had snuck onto the property and knocked something over. So I was taken back, when I stepped through the green arch, to see a strange fellow standing under the pergola at the opposite end of the shimmering rectangle of water. He was strapping in size, and his shirtless ebony-hued torso glistened with sweat under the many-pocketed blue overalls that he wore. Simultaneously, a waft of chlorine hit me, and I heard a closer rumble of thunder.

"What are you doing here?" I asked sharply. He stared at me across the distance, one hand on his hip, the other resting on a column supporting the pergola. Then, as if I hadn't spoken, he picked up a hammer from the table and recommenced his labors.

I realized my mistake as my eyes registered the fresh slats of wood stacked nearby and the tools lying about. Surely he was George Geronimo's son, repairing the elaborate frame structure that connected the two dressing rooms. I noticed, now, that the pool's circumference had been swept free of debris, the weeds between the flagstones neatly cropped, and the water recently skimmed. A major offensive against the estate's relentless entropy was underway, though the victor was yet to be declared.

"I'm sorry," I said. "You must be Mr. Washington's son."

He drove a nail into a beam.

"You must be Newt," he echoed back. "The Librarian."

My job description, coming from his mouth, sounded less elevated than I preferred.

"What are you up to?"

"My old man says I need to get all this mess fixed up before the summer guests arrive."

That was the first mention I'd heard of impending company. It unsettled me; I didn't ken to the idea of my summer idyll being disrupted by strangers monopolizing my employer's time and energy. I could already picture them: spoiled sophisticates, New Yorkers of a certain age, quaffing martinis by the pool as they made fun of the quaint customs of the South and belittled the earnestness of the country bumpkin hired to bring order to the hopeless library. What if, under their allure, Mr. Julian's enthusiasm for our project waned— or worse, altogether ceased?

To shake off such gloomy thoughts, I traversed the perimeter of the pool to inspect the work at hand. On closer view, G.G.'s son appeared not much older than me, though as finely muscled as a collegiate All-Star. I couldn't remember his name, so I asked.

"Samson," he responded. "Like in the Good Book." In light of his strength, that seemed a rather prophetic choice on the part of his parents.

An awkward silence followed as he put down his hammer, wiped his hands on his overalls, and hesitated. I hesitated, too, then extended my hand.

"Pleased to make your acquaintance." We high-fived each other's palms.

"Samson to the world, but the folks they call me Pockets."

At that strange proclamation I laughed, and the stiffness that had starched our attempts to strike up a conversation wilted away. "*Pockets?*"

"When I was a little kid, I'd collect anything and bring it home in my pockets. Folks never knew what I'd be pulling out next. And look at me now!"

He had a point. His overalls had cavities everywhere, from which screwdrivers, wrenches, a measuring tape, wipe-rags, and other devices protruded.

"I'll stick to Samson. Show me what you're up to."

Samson was pointing out the specific nature of the repairs the portico entailed when the sky suddenly cracked with lightning. Then, as we both stared, a solid wall of rain hit the end of the pool by the diving board. Magically, the downpour advanced in a perfectly straight line across the face of the water till the entire rectangle of turquoise churned with white froth. Samson and I stepped under the shelter of the door header of the nearest changing room, where, shoulder to shoulder, we watched the rain become pieces of hail the size of cherries, then golf balls, pinging the water and dancing on the flagstones.

Standing under that threshold, I grew conscious of the faint odor of dank concrete, tile, and mold that wafted from the dressing room behind me, enveloping me like a strange caress and mingling with the warm salty odor of Samson's skin and sweat closer at hand. In that millisecond, a thought flashed into my brain, mundane in its simplicity but for me as revelatory as the lightning zigzagging on the horizon: the knowledge that Samson was just another boy, a boy like myself, sheltering from a freak storm. Before my thoughts traveled further, the hail stopped as abruptly as it had begun. The thunderheads scudded out of sight, as if wiped off the face of the sky by an invisible hand, and sunlight immediately flooded the poolside. The ping-pong balls of hail littering the flagstone pathway melted into wet circles.

We looked at each other, Samson and I, stupidly grinning at the natural wonder we'd just witnessed.

"I better let you finish before the next shower surprises us," I said as we moved back out into the portico. Only then did I think to glance down at my hands to make sure *Custom of the Country* had escaped damage. In the spell of the past minutes I'd forgotten I was holding it.

"Well," Samson said. He picked up his hammer and tossed it from one hand to the other, a carpenter's juggling act that made his biceps pop like baseballs.

I wanted to say something, the occasion seemed to call for it, but words evaded me.

"Later," we both blurted out at once.

The vital smell of dampened earth mingled with the chastening scent of chlorine as I walked around the pool and exited through the green-fringed arch. The phantom sound of Samson's hammer rang in my ears long after I crossed the front lawn and mounted my bike to pedal home.

6

SWIMMING LESSONS

School was out at last, and it had been determined that I'd work for Mr. Brewster four days a week, Mondays, Wednesdays, Fridays, and Saturday mornings. Monday I woke up to discover my front bike tire was flat, so I decided to walk to the estate, a route that took in all five blocks of downtown Rocky Hill. Just as I passed Davis Drugs, debating whether to quiz Mr. Julian about the upcoming guests, a bright red factory-fresh Mustang slowed down and honked. Hank Atwater, Dad's salesman at the dealership, leaned across the white vinyl passenger seat and waved.

"Thought it was you, Junior. Hop in, Hotshot, I'll give you a lift."

I didn't like being called Junior—or Hotshot. I wasn't named after my father, and *hotshot* I was not.

"I'm only going a few more blocks."

"Aw, get in. I'll deliver you to your boss's door in style."

I couldn't think of a polite way to say no, so I slid into the passenger seat and Hank accelerated.

"What's this?" He thumped the top of my head. I'd gotten my hair cut a week ago and shaved off my sideburns. "Cleaning up your act for the Man?"

Hank was hitting close to home. I'd gotten so tired of Mr. Julian's witticisms at the expense of my shaggy locks that I asked the barber to neaten me up. Mr. Julian had been quite approving, and I hadn't minded the praise.

Hank continued his annoying monologue. "We all gotta please our betters, don't we? Your pa's doing right by me; make sure that old Brewster bird does right by you! They say he's worth a few mill easy. Too bad the miser doesn't have a pretty gal like your ma to take the flint outta him, might make him more generous. Speakin' of which, buddy"—he craned over his shoulder to ogle a girl we'd just passed on the sidewalk—"look at those Hooters!" So it went till we pulled up to the gates of the Brewster estate. I let myself out and Hank screeched off.

If Mother found out that Dad was letting Hank drive one of the new models for his personal use, she'd read him the riot act. I can't say I disagreed.

That morning, Mr. Julian was in a particularly foul mood, chiding G.G. for a dozen perceived oversights, summoning B.B.—that is, Sassafras Beebe—out of the kitchen to scold her for the abomination of a breakfast she'd sent up on his tray, propelling Mimi from his lap with a firm whack on her rump that sent feline fur flying, and lambasting me for proposing to shelve Jean Renoir's biography of his father under nonfiction—as if that were the crime of the century—instead of with the other books and catalogues on Impressionism.

Later, when I mentioned that I'd run into G.G.'s son repairing the swimming pool pergola Mr. Julian arched an eyebrow. "What of it?" When I pressed further, noting that Samson seemed to be working on a tight deadline, Mr. Julian glared at me with his unsettling blue gaze.

"Leave that boy alone, or he'll never get the job done," he snapped acidly. "And neither will you, Newt Seward, if you keep dilly-dallying with these books like you have a thousand years and I have all the money in the world to waste on your salary!"

Now my pride really *was* wounded, since two walls of the library shelves were nearly filled in perfect alphabetical order—an effort that had taken six Saturdays of intensive labor. Determined to meet sullenness with sullenness, I worked away in silence for the rest of the day as Mr. Julian aggrievedly rolled in and out of the room.

Around three o'clock, the buzzer for the front gate sounded, reverberating past closed doors and empty rooms into the recesses of the library. George Geronimo was down in the basement sorting laundry, and Sassafras, having set out a cold dinner for the master in the Frigidaire, had gladly absconded for the day.

"Don't sit like a bump on a log, open the gate and wait by the door!" Mr. Julian ordered. It dawned on me, with dismay, that the mysterious guests had arrived and that I was being sent to admit them like a common servant.

Hence my surprise to see a familiar face emerge from the car that stopped in front of the terrace.

"Well, it's *you*, boy!" Tom Allbright said as he entered, smiling a smile that could signify anything from good fortune to impending catastrophe as he doffed his panama hat. "Job going well, eh?"

"Yes, of course, sir," I ventured.

"Keep hard at it, Newt Seward!" He hesitated, then looked me in the eyes. His voice was suddenly serious. "But don't be duped by this grandeur, such as it is. Trappings, it's all trappings. Nothing is exactly what it seems; remember that!" I didn't understand but I nodded gamely. "Take me. I dare say you consider me the most unexciting of souls—but are you *sure*?" Mr. Allbright suddenly stopped, as if he had startled himself by saying too much, and dabbed the sweat beading on his nose with a fine linen handkerchief that smelled faintly of carbolic soap. "Mr. Brewster is expecting me, I believe. If you'd show the way."

I led him through the drawing room into the library, where he greeted his client in the same neutral cadences I vividly remembered hearing two years ago, when I eavesdropped on the extension line in Judge Leroy's bedroom.

"So it comes along, Julian?" Mr. Allbright took in the room. "Step at a time does it!"

"Step at a time, and I'll be two feet in the grave before I see results!" Mr. Julian snorted. "Newt, skedaddle downstairs and tell G.G. to bring us gentlemen some iced teas. We've private business to discuss, so you're dismissed for the day. Close the library door on your way out, will you?"

It was all very mysterious. Something was brewing in Brewster-land, and I was being left in the dark. I delivered the message to George Geronimo and skulked out the back door. Earlier Mr. Julian had all but forbidden me to fraternize with the help, so naturally I headed towards the swimming pool to see if Samson was working today.

I didn't hear any hammering as I approached the surrounding hedge, but when I stepped within its parameters, I saw him standing halfway up a stepladder as he dabbed white paint on the newly replaced overhead beams that crossed the space separating the two dressing rooms.

"Looks like it's coming along."

"Finishing touch for the day, as a matter of fact."

Samson stepped down as I skirted the circumference of the pool. He was wearing his overalls rolled down and bunched around his waist. White paint speckled the burnished skin of his shoulders, chest, and arms like a shower of stars against a night sky.

"I'm done, too, and not soon enough. Mr. Brewster is in a *mean* mood today."

Samson chuckled. "Heard as much from my old man. He knows when to make it a laundry day!"

As I watched Samson squat on his toes to clean the brushes in turpentine, it occurred to me to ask where he and his dad lived. I assumed they resided in the enclave of Rocky Hill dubbed Browntown by the locals. Browntown lay ten minutes to the west of Honeysuckle Heights, where the old elite of our citizenry had built their dignified homes four and five decades ago. In some warped variation of plantation logic, the rich liked to have their supply of servants within calling distance, close but not too close.

Samson punctured my conjecture by replying that they lived out in the county, off Route 3 past Dillard Crick and the McGregor farm. I knew both Dillard and McGregor landmarks, quite a hike away, so I was curious how George Geronimo made it to work.

Their pickup truck had died two years ago, Samson explained, so when his dad wasn't able to hitch a ride with neighbors, he walked into town despite his gimp leg, declaring a little shoe leather was as trusty as patched truck tires. The image of the old man making the hour-long trek made me frown. It wasn't so bad, Samson said, since his father often stayed at the Brewster mansion overnight, especially if the master was ailing. All this was news, reminding me of how little I knew of my taciturn co-worker, much less our employer, after hours. George Geronimo slept in a room on the third floor, where Mr. Julian could summon him by intercom if necessary.

Having tapped the lids of the paint cans shut and stored the supplies behind the dressing rooms, Samson knelt at the water spigot to rinse off. While he was thus occupied I wandered into the men's changing room. What a revelation! However decayed and grimy, however pervaded by a damp odor of age and rot, however rendered macabre by spirals of plaster unfurling from the mildewed ceiling, the dim room vibrated with beauty.

I stood still, taking it all in. Light filtered through the wooden louvered shades of a skylight overhead, faintly illuminating the deep green tiles that lined the walls. Inset at vertical intervals were tiled lotus patterns, lavender and pale yellow. A large mirror, speckled gray over time and etched with deco flourishes in its corners, hung over two milky green pedestal sinks. A toilet of the same hue stood nearby. Idly I pulled the rusted chain that dangled above it; out of order. Opposite the sinks and separated from them by a worn slatted bench, two open shower stalls were lined in tiles of a dusky cornelian hue. I reached into one stall and turned the cracked porcelain knob; after a few fits and starts, water shot forth from the copper head suspended from the ceiling, first cold and brown, then warm and clear.

"Samson!" I called, walking to the door of the changing room and looking out. "You should use the showers in here, they work—there's even hot water."

He looked up from the spigot where he was dashing water, by the fistful, over his shoulders.

"Didn't you read the sign over the door?"

I looked up; there was no sign except for the three lettered tiles that spelt M-E-N. "Huh?"

"Smart guy like you can't read?" He made a face. "Dis Negro ain't about to be caught using de White Man's facilities."

I countered, rebelliously, "Who's to know?" In the same instant I flashed on the segregated water fountains at Woolworths, one noticeably cleaner than the other, and recalled an evening when Dad had taken us to dinner at the new café attached to the local Greyhound Bus station. An elegantly dressed black woman travelling with her four-year old son had gotten off the Richmond bus and asked for a table. She had been turned away. My parents were sitting with their backs to the entrance, so only Jubal and I had noticed the incident.

Samson looked at me. "Whatever you're imagining, I've seen worse. Believe me, it doesn't pay to be caught on the wrong side of that door." Then he added, impishly, "But don't worry, I won't hold it against *you*," and splashed a handful of cold water at me. We both laughed. He stood, pulled a bit of towel from one of his many pockets, wiped his torso dry, rolled up and refastened his overalls, then dared to poke a little more fun at me. "So how come I don't see any books on you today, Scholar?"

"I don't *just* read. I do other things, too."

We began to walk around the pool. "Like what? Got a sport?"

I told him that I swam for the school team.

"Too bad the old man doesn't let you practice here, seeing he's having it cleaned up for the summer guests and all."

I figured I knew my place as well Samson did his. "Last I heard I'm not getting paid to dawdle in the water."

As we continued to make small talk, something between us clicked into place. Samson told me he was going to be a junior at the all-black high school in the fall. He played all the school sports but his passion was boxing—he trained at a club in Browntown—and he was hoping to get his first exhibition match, up in Roanoke, next year. His dream was to turn pro once he graduated, using his talent to punch his way out of Rocky Hill—the alternative being a tour of Nam. Better a fist in the face than a landmine busting my nuts, he quipped—a jest more prescient than either of us could have guessed.

"And in case you think I'm just a dumb jock," he said, cocking an eye at me and breaking into an irresistible grin, "I like to read a book, too, when I'm in the mood."

We reached the entrance cut into the hedge.

"Maybe one of these Sundays we could meet up out at Dillard Crick, away from things, and I could show you some good fishing."

"Sure thing," I said as we turned to head back to our separate worlds.

His phrase, "away from things," hung pendant in my mind, a slowly swelling drop of water that you fear will fall before you can cup your palm to catch it.

*

Thankfully Mr. Julian was in a less fretful mood on Wednesday, and we spent several profitable hours sorting through an avalanche of books. Maybe he had just been suffering from a bad night's sleep two days before. I never quite understood the actual state of Mr. Julian's health, what lay at the bottom of his invalidism or how his condition affected his moods; asking about his infirmities seemed too indelicate a subject to raise to a Southern gentleman of uncertain if certainly advanced years. Besides, Mr. Julian's personality was so mercurial that it was impossible to distinguish what might be illness from ill temper. He could exude childlike delight one moment, transform the next into a wasp with a nasty sting. Sometimes I suspected these fitful shifts of mood were performances, trying out contrary personae on George Geronimo and me to pass the time.

Today my sense of Mr. Julian's chameleon personality hit a new high. Around two o'clock he declared he was tired tired tired of books and needed a distraction. G.G. had informed him that the repairs to the pool house were done, so he wanted to inspect the work first-hand. Thence I was instructed to wheel his chair, a truly Herculean labor given that the path to the pool sloped uphill and involved negotiating some steps—and wheelchairs in those days were more cumbersome than now. But push I did, since push I must—although I admit I did so with a reluctance that, however absurd, stemmed from the fact I considered the pool area my private discovery—the one place on the Brewster estate where I was the adventurer, not the employee.

The surface of the pool was rippling with sunlight, a thousand bright mirrors, when I finally eased Mr. Julian's chair through the gap in the hedge. The freshly painted pergola gleamed across the water, the vivid whiteness of its posts, beams, and fancy latticework beckoning the wayfarer to enter its checkered shade. Even Mr. Julian, I believe, appreciated the dazzling play of light and shadow, and he was silent so long that I fancied that he was seeing in his mind's eye, as I had seen on my first visit here, ghosts of times long past: friends and family lounging about the watery perimeter, colorful floats bobbing, divers jack-knifing off the springboard.

"Yes, this will do quite nicely," Mr. Julian finally said, and directed me to wheel his chair around the pool to the pergola.

Once there, he caught me offguard with a statement that could have been a question but was uttered like a command. "You swim. On the school team."

"Yes, sir," I said, wondering at the network of informants who might have shared this obscure fact with my employer. I had only revealed my bookish tendencies to Mr. Julian, as I surmised he judged all sports—except, perhaps, something as aristocratic as polo—as manifestations of a lower aspect of human nature.

"Allbright said he thought so. Never cared a fig for athletics in my day, still don't. *Mens sana in corpore sano*—bunch of baloney if you ask me. But Allbright hit the mark when he said lettering in a sport could make all the difference for a smart boy from the South getting admitted to the Ivy Leagues, what with their quotas—all the A pluses in the world won't cut the mustard for those of us born beneath the Mason-Dixon line, no sirree. No time like now to practice—are you ready?"

"Excuse me?"

"To swim!"

Baffled and not a little weirded-out, I blurted out, "What?"

"Don't make me testy, there are trunks in the dressing room. Humor me!"

So I disappeared into the men's dressing room, newly swept, mopped, and disinfected, and surely enough on the counter rose a stack of men's vintage swim trunks—relics of yesteryear—and freshly folded towels. But, more conspicuously, laid out on the changing bench was a racer's Speedo—blue with white stars, sales tag still attached—along with swim goggles and stopwatch. These had been set out, so it appeared, with me in mind.

Was Mr. Julian turning softhearted, making me these gifts? Or was I being turned into an object of amusement, my duty to perform at his command?

"Give it to me!" he barked, as soon I emerged from the dressing room. My perplexity must have been apparent.

"The watch! You swim, I keep time!"

So began a bizarre new ritual in my working hours at the Brewster estate, swimming an hour every afternoon as my employer presided over my exertions, barking out times as he tilted precariously forward in his chair. He had become the presiding genius of the swimming pool, both evil sorcerer and fairy godfather, to whose eccentric whims I bent.

Sluicing through the aquamarine water, under a relentless gaze even more translucently blue than the pool, I couldn't rid myself of the strangeness of it all. What was it about being watched that left such an odd feeling in my gut? As I executed a flip-turn at the end of the pool, it came to me: my unease was obscurely linked to the sensation I'd experienced back on Taliaferro Lane two weeks before, late one torpid evening when everyone else had gone to bed. Because my floor fan was broken, I was lying restless and sweaty on top of my sheets, unable to fall asleep. Facing the window to catch any breeze that might wander in, I could just make out, whenever I opened my eyes, the far edge of backyard below. All of a sudden, I heard the crack of a branch being stepped on and a muffled giggle. Buster, our old hound who slept at the foot of my bed, snorted as he chased squirrels in his sleep. I raised myself on my elbow to scan the darkness outside.

There I spied my sister Katie, creeping across the lawn in short-shorts and halter top, making for the corner where storage shed met back fence. Out of the shadows Rat materialized, wearing his fringed leather jacket despite the sultry temperature. I watched as Katie reached his arms. My eyes adjusting to the dark, I realized that my big sis had developed talents that went well beyond first and second base. I saw her halter top disappear and her small pale breasts emerge out of the darkness; I saw Rat lean her against the shed; I felt the force of his rising desire as he (jacket still on) moved against her; and I saw, with a thrill of disbelief, Katie drop to her knees in front of him as he lowered his jeans even further. I couldn't stop watching, even though I knew I shouldn't, and I couldn't control my own excitement, even though it was my sister I was watching as I began to stroke myself.

Now, as my strokes sliced the water's skin, leaving trails of froth in their wake, I reached deeper into my mind, layer beneath layer until I touched the memory that had been lapping at the edges of consciousness all along. I was eleven, our neighbors the Ledbedders were moving away, and one afternoon the entire family arrived to say their goodbyes. Somehow, I'd ended up in my bedroom with the two Ledbedder siblings, Mac and Lindy, when the former knowingly locked the door and suggested we play doctor with his younger sister. Lindy was probably ten, Mac thirteen. As if this were a game with which she was familiar, Lindy shed her underpants and Mac invited me to join him in touching, ever so softly, her pink, dimpled, mysterious cleft, all three of us caught up in the illicit thrill. Soon enough, Mac unzipped his trousers, proudly displaying an adolescent's erection rising from a puff of red pubic hair, and challenged me to compare. I hadn't reached puberty, so there was no comparison as he measured the length of his boner along my smaller but no less rigid one. Left out of our game, Lindy pulled up her panties and demanded to be let out of the room. Mac obliged, relocked the door, and turned to me.

When he announced, "Let's play like we're making babies," I had no idea what he meant but, instinctively, as he tried to turn me around, I felt something was badly wrong and pushed him away. One avenue closed, Mac turned to another, dropping to his knees before I could react and taking me in his mouth. I swooned at the alien sensation, shuddering in ecstasy and dismay—and the image, as it now reformed in my mind, superimposed itself on that of Rat and my sister. Their oral tryst had suffered no interruptions, whereas the exploration that Mac had launched ended abruptly with his father calling up the stairs that it was time to go. We guiltily pulled apart. Nonetheless Mac left grinning like a Cheshire cat who didn't care who delivered his saucer of cream, so long as he got his share. But I felt obscurely dirty—excited, yes, but deeply ashamed. This was the event that Zithra witnessed from an upper-story window in the Leroy home; these were the details she had whispered in my ears at Furnace Creek. She had *seen* us, she whispered. She *knew*.

Propelling myself forward through the cool water in the old Brewster pool, I realized that I was again being watched, no longer the onlooker as I had been two weeks ago when my excitement had overridden my guilt in getting off at the sight of my sister with Rat. I wasn't at all sure I liked the feeling of the tables being turned and increased the swiftness of my strokes as if to escape Mr. Julian's gaze. But when I surfaced for air, and saw him looking happy, gleeful as a child as he leaned forward in his chair and marked my times, I thought: this is his offering, be grateful and better things may follow.

7

UNDERCOVER ACTS

When Mr. Julian had told me, with a wry chuckle, "These apertures were the secret weapon of the mistress of the house," I little suspected the use to which I would one day put the very spy-holes he was revealing to me on a whim.

"Enough of books!" So he had once again declared that morning, interrupting our labor with a command that I lever his walker up to the gloomy entrance hall and into the powder room located under the winding stairs. "Something here a boy like you will get a kick out of!" That's when he showed me the three peepholes: one behind a mirror that swung back on silent hinges, one concealed by a framed sampler of Robert Louis Stevenson's "Auntie's Skirts," and the other hidden in full view in the peeling wallpaper's florid design. The first looked into the kitchen; the second into the pantry; the third into the servants' hall. "A Southern Lady," Mr. Julian drawled with relish, "needed every resource at hand to ensure her household ran efficiently. My dear Mama was most expert in using the information she gathered here—as well as in a few other locations I shall keep to myself!" He heaved a dramatic sigh. "I, however, was an utter failure at keeping the staff in line, even before my poor legs gave out. Ah well, now it's only me, G.G., and B.B., so it hardly matters."

I, who had never imagined a world where one maintained a retinue of domestics, much less spied on them, found myself disturbed and tantalized in equal portions. As a boy, I'd devoured mystery novels where houses abounded in secret rooms; the reality, I now perceived, was rather different, especially when such devices might be deployed to put my own movements under surveillance.

Just how many secrets Mr. Julian kept up his sleeve was driven home a few days later. In the library I'd come across a smartly produced catalogue, twenty-five years old but its slick pages still redolent of printer's ink and filled with shiny color images of the Brewster furniture line: reproductions from a range of historical periods that once shipped to high-end retailers across the States and, according to Mr. Julian, graced a few rooms in the White House. Under Mr. Julian's tutelage I had become fascinated in learning to spot the difference between Queen Anne and Empire, between Jacobean and American Colonial. It now occurred to me to take the booklet into the drawing room and see if I could match any of the illustrations with the room's furnishings. Yes, here was the reproduction of the Duncan Phyfe sofa, upholstered in the same glamorous brocade; here, the felt-topped card table, modeled on a mid-eighteenth-century Italian original; and here, the wingback armchair in the Louis XV style featured on page 15.

"What in heaven's name are you up to?" Mr. Julian drawled as George Geronimo pushed his chair into the room. Waving G.G. away, he greedily reached for the catalogue in my hands once I explained what I'd been doing and cackled.

"Planning an auction behind my back? You'd better call in Sotheby's!"

He proceeded to confide, in a histrionic whisper, what he claimed to be his "greatest secret" of all. Yes, several of the pieces in this and adjoining rooms were indeed Brewster reproductions. But were I to examine the furnishings with an expert's eye, I would know better than assume they were all copies of originals.

"Take that highboy!" Mr. Julian pointed with pride to the massive chest of drawers in figured mahogany that stood sentinel by the entry to the library. "That's an original Heppelwhite, worth its weight in gold!"

His greedy, grasping relatives, he proceeded to explain, assumed that all the finer-looking furnishings in the house were Brewster reproductions. But, in fact, over the decades he had been smuggling into their midst the real thing, antiques in pristine shape that were worth more than all the mansion's other valuables. "Let this be our little secret!" He winked at me. "If I choose to leave choice pieces to persons I care about in my will, I'm commissioning *you*, here and now, to inform them they're treasures any museum would fight to possess!"

He pointed to a Sheraton satinwood sideboard, circa 1790, with subtle curves in its drawers, tapering bellflower figures running down its legs to its brass claw feet, worth tens of thousands of dollars, and to a Federalist bookcase with glass doors and carved mahogany facing inlaid with iridescent trim—"a signed Lannuier no less!"—and he alerted me to a few more choice pieces in rooms I had not yet seen, which, all told, were worth at least half of what the property itself would bring in. "I intend to keep those appalling relatives guessing and gaping to the bitter end!" he gloated with not altogether becoming gusto.

Over the next month Mr. Julian had me pulling out drawers and turning over chairs as he taught me how to distinguish the antique from the clever reproduction: looking for hairline cracks and warping, tell-tale signs of handcut dovetailing, types of mortise and tenon joinery, discolorations around the mounted hardware. And he taught me how to read with the stroke of my fingers the surface of polished wood veneer for signs of aging and shrinkage, the braille of dimpled pegs and sandburnt inlay, and the grain of saw cuts on the blindspots behind the cabinetry and on the underside of chair leg braces.

I was hooked.

"Remember, our little secret!" He clucked with mordant delight.

That Mr. Julian's mansion also harbored secrets he did *not* choose to share with me revealed itself one afternoon when I'd left him dosing in his chair on the back terrace while I continued my labors in the library. The task at hand involved sorting through the sundry items stashed pell-mell on the upper gallery of the library. The dog-eared paperbacks relegated to these shelves, crammed between stacks of random papers and buttressed by bundles of decayed receipts, business ledgers, and tattered magazines, were among the collection's least interesting, so Mr. Julian had left me to make my own judgments. I filled cardboard boxes with the obvious discards, setting aside items potentially worth Mr. Julian's scrutiny—a few scrapbooks of clippings, folders of correspondence written in spidery handwriting, a set of Mr. Julian's high school essays bearing titles like "Iago the Super-Villain," "The Threat of Global Apocalypse," and "Famous Tidewater Plantations."

Tired of squatting on the narrow catwalk, I stood up, the top of my head inches away from the saucy cherubs fringing the ceiling fresco. Leaning my shoulder against the built-in bookshelving, I was thumbing through a copy of Forster's *Life of Charles Dickens* when, all of a sudden, a section of shelf behind me gave way, swinging back before my amazed eyes to reveal a hidden passageway five feet high and perhaps ten feet deep.

Peering into its depths, I made out a faint line of light at the bottom of the back wall of the empty space and moved towards it. When I pressed the wall in front of me, it sprang open on silent hinges—and I found myself staring into the shimmering gloom of Mr. Julian's bedchamber.

Or so I intuited, since my nostrils immediately registered the commingled odor of aging flesh and Chanel cologne that belonged to my employer. Other telltale signs of Mr. Julian's habitation came into focus as my eyes adjusted to the room's dimness: a phalanx of familiar pharmaceuticals on a silver tray; a walker parked beside a high-canopied bed; a well-known smoking jacket; an elevator door that must lead to the pantry below. The walls of the room were covered in crimson fabric decorated with an Oriental design sewn in gold thread that faintly glimmered in the dim light; shrouding the long windows were heavy red and black striped draperies matching the fabric of the bed coverings and canopy; Louis XIV-styled furniture and Chinoiserie filled the chamber. As my eyes canvassed the space, I couldn't help but think that such a darkly shimmering decor, flushed with vibrant shades of red and gold, was the worst possible backdrop for a man of Mr. Julian's wan appearance, his papery skin and bleached-out hair ghastly pale in contrast. Perhap, I whimsically mused, that was why the room's mirror, on a far wall, was draped with a silken black shawl.

Ignoring the voice of conscience urging me to return to the library before my absence was noted, I stepped further into the faded glamour of Mr. Julian's room and tiptoed across the grinning dragon faces worked into the worn Chinese carpet to the long windows. Peering through the curtains, I spied my employer asleep on the terrace below as Mimi rubbed her considerable heft against the wheels of his chair, impatient for his awakening. I stood there for longer than

I knew, trying to reconcile the image before me with all the blank spaces in his life that I might never fathom. These gloomy thoughts filled me, irrationally, with the need to see my own reflection in the mirror on the far wall—perhaps to assure myself that I was a living being and not a ghost trapped in an old man's warped dream. I walked to the gilt frame and, when I touched the black shawl, the silky fabric slid to the floor. But instead of my own reflection, I found myself starting, with something akin to terror, before a visage that I had already dreamed into existence.

In front of me hung an oil painting uncannily similar to the portrait of Mr. Julian in the drawing room downstairs—except that the subject of this painting was a beautiful young woman in her twenties, blonde hair bobbed around a face that was a dead ringer of Mr. Julian's. She also stood in a similar pose by an open window, as if she too had been caught in the instant of turning from its view—but this time the vista that opened beyond the window was, instead of the terracotta rooftops in Mr. Julian's Italian portrait, a cubist rendition of the blue-green Virginian mountains outside the bedroom window from which I'd just been looking. The painting bore Enzio Sorrento's initials.

Eerie enough: but the uncanny feeling engulfing me went further. For the face of the woman staring at me with a patrician gesture of genial disregard was identical to the one my overactive imagination had conjured into being my first day on the Brewster estate, when I'd discovered the deserted swimming pool. Impossible as it seemed, I was gazing at an image of the phantom who had perched on the edge of a white wicker chaise lounge and applauded as Mr. Julian jack-knifed into the pool.

Before I had time to ponder this mystery, the door to the bedroom swung open and I jumped in fright for the second time in as many minutes. There stood George Geronimo Washington, holding a stack of folded clothing. I blushed to my roots.

"I didn't mean—that door just... " My voice faltered and I nodded my head at the secret passage connecting library and bedchamber.

George Geronimo registered surprise neither at my presence nor at the door leading to the library's gallery. In fact, he hardly seemed to deign my intrusion worthy of comment as he deposited the items he was carrying inside an immense wardrobe that smelled of cedar.

"Then I—" I nodded at the portrait, feeling worse by the minute.

Picking up the black shawl from the floor, G. G. stood on his tiptoes to drape it over the frame.

"That," he said, breaking the silence, "would be Miss Julia. The master's sister." He exhaled what I might have mistaken for a wistful sigh had he not been George Geronimo. "He had her portrait moved up here after she passed away, all those years ago. But sometimes a dark mood comes over him and he can't bear the memory, that's when he asks me to drape the portrait."

During all the weeks we'd spent in each other's company, despite all the family tales he'd related, Mr. Julian never mentioned a beloved sister. Again I felt cheated.

"It's by the same artist who painted the portrait downstairs, isn't it?"

G.G. scratched his head as if contemplating the risks of a prolonged conversation with the likes of myself. Yielding to the moment, he proved surprisingly loquacious.

"One and the same. Julia was so taken with the likeness of her brother that Mr. Brewster promised he'd bring the artist to the States so she could sit for him. Before my time, the two portraits used to hang side by side in the drawing room. Sorrento posed her right there, back in—what's the date, '33 is it?" G.G. indicated the window where I'd stood minutes before. "My guess is the master should've known better than introduce Julia to his friend. Things might have gone far better, for all concerned, if the two of 'em hadn't fallen in love. That's my guess."

He limped midway across the room before turning to face me again.

"You best get back to work. I'll push this shut after you"—he gestured to the concealed door covered in wall fabric. "Don't want the master to note anything amiss, do we?"

So I disappeared into the hidden passageway, with the oddest feeling that George Geronimo wasn't going to reveal my misdemeanor. Such unexpected discretion, combined with his confidences, was yet another mystery in this strange house for which I had no key. Emerging onto the gallery, I pulled the bookcase door closed. I looked, and looked again; no one would ever guess the shelving concealed an entrance.

I peered down into the library, at the table in the center of the room where I had so often sat, head bent over books, pen filling out the color-coded note cards that I would type up for the final library index. As I contemplated all the occasions I'd sat there assuming I was alone, it dawned on me that I could have been under covert observation by anyone who knew of this hidden entry. The idea was disconcerting, even though I told myself I had nothing to hide, even though I was sure Mr. Julian could never have made it through the closet space without chair or walker, either of which would have betrayed his presence. Nonetheless I couldn't shake myself of an old feeling—one that had first come over me two summers ago at Furnace Creek and one that now reemerged in all its former power—that my life had been stripped of its privacy and that a thousand eyes lay in wait, ready to report my every move.

8

DEGREES OF KINSHIP

Sunday, true to the pagan origins of its name, was glorious—brilliant sunshine and healing warmth; Monday, when I was due back at my post, drenching rain and unseasonably cold. Since the downpour ruled out walking or biking to work, Mother drove me to the Brewster estate, but not before giving me an earful about Dad's ineptitude in managing his staff, her suspicions that Katie was seeing Rat on the sly (I kept my lips sealed), and her worries that Jubal was going to balloon like Cousin Chester if he didn't curb his adolescent addiction to MoonPies and Cracker Jacks.

Entering the mansion from the rear in order to shed my dripping slicker in the mudroom, I came upon a tempest of human activity that made the storm outside pale in comparison. G.G. sat at the kitchen table furiously polishing an avalanche of silver, brass, and copper—flatware, candlesticks, coffee urns and tea pots, punch bowl, platters, figurines—that spilled across the white-painted oak surface and onto the surrounding chairs, as if an overflow from Ali Baba's cave. Not only had Sassafras been pulled off kitchen duty, her sister Lupita and Lupita's daughter had been summoned to air out all the first- and second-floor rooms (including ones whose existence I hadn't even suspected), remove the sheets off furniture, beat the faded carpets, polish the warped floors, uncover the entry hall chandelier—anything to diminish the aura of decay and the odors of age that had settled on the house long ago.

Before I could ask what was going on, Mr. Julian wheeled himself into view and answered for his servants. "Wouldn't you know, our houseguests have advanced their arrival an entire week. Lord-a-Mercy, they're descending on us this very Sabbath!"

The secret was out. Having been kept in the dark so long, I felt it fully within my rights to ask *who* these expected guests were.

"My wards!" Mr. Julian snapped, as if I should know what he was talking about. "My departed cousin Wilfred Sumner's children, Mary Jo and Marky Joe. It's been two years since they spent school vacation with me, and I *hate* to think of them telling the relatives how woefully I've neglected the property! And, oh they would, those two. They may be trust-fund babies, but it'd behoove their Royal Be-Highnesses to remember *I'm* the one who administers their allowance!"

I don't believe I'd ever seen Mr. Julian in such a twitter. He was wound like a spring, all nervous energy, flamboyant gestures, and facial ticks. I was nonplussed as well; Mr. Julian's family tree seemed to be sprouting new limbs by the day, and with each branch I felt all the more an outsider. First, a dearly beloved sister, deceased; now, two stuck-up second cousins, very much alive; beyond them, how many others?

I ventured a question. "Your wards—how old are they?"

"Oh, let me think, sixteen or seventeen, the two of them; they're twins, you know." No, I didn't know, but I could only assume my lack of knowledge was irrelevant. "Not sixteen, seventeen. You'll meet them soon enough, and I suppose you're near enough their age to do."

Small comfort, that. I really wasn't sure I wanted "to do" at all.

"Does their arrival mean, sir," I asked, determined to press the issue, "that my duties are going to change?"

"Of course not! Oh, I may ask you to stop by on your off-days— there's just so much a man my age has to say to two saucy-tongued youngsters! I'll have Allbright iron out the details with your parents."

All fine and good, but I still needed a better understanding of these interlopers before I faced them. "Where do they live, your wards?"

"Boarding school. Abroad, if you must know. Don't be tedious, Newt. You can ask them all the questions you want when they arrive. *Your* concern is doing something with these hideous piles of paper..."

I learnt, in short order, that filing cabinets were being delivered this afternoon, and that G.G. had arranged for Samson to help me set them up in a spare room in the basement. After the most unleisurely lunch I'd ever seen Mr. Julian inhale, Samson made his presence known, Murphy's Office Systems delivered the four-drawer units, and, after 40 minutes of heaving and grunting, Samson and I finished helping the delivery man—all of us soaked through and through by the continuing storm outside—wrestle the metal beasts down the back hall, around two sharp turns, and into the cellar without too badly wounding the wainscotting.

"Well, Librarian." Samson winked at me. I was resting my hands on my knees, catching my breath, while he made a feeble attempt to wring out his tee shirt. "Guess the boss never told you your job included time on the chain gang."

I warned Samson we hadn't finished our servitude; I showed him the crates bursting with clippings and files that I'd been gathering in the library, all of which Mr. Julian had banished to the basement. Soon enough I suspected I'd undergo a similar exile, doomed to toil in the bowels of the house while the guests loitered above ground.

Beset by such thoughts, it dawned on me that once the pool became the playground of our guests, I'd lose the privilege of my afternoon swim practices. That realization struck me hard. Mr. Julian had come to relish his self-appointed role as surrogate coach, I'd sensed, rasping out my drills as I surfaced for air, and in spite of my initial misgivings I found myself looking forward to his tinny cackles of approval when I hoisted my body, dripping and heaving for breath, from the water, having bested my own time on a particular interval. Now I foresaw that all too soon Mr. Julian would be too preoccupied with his own flesh-and-blood to indulge his whim of overseeing the physical and intellectual betterment of the local boy. And despite what Mr. Julian had said about enlisting me to "entertain" the twins, I also foresaw their disdainful responses to any such proposal.

"They get here Sunday, *whoever* they are," I said to Samson. Sweating, begrimed, and our clothes clammy from the rain, we'd just lugged the last crates to the cellar.

"So I've heard. My old man's been called in to work on his one day off, and he ain't none too happy about giving up his Sabbath. I'm thinking maybe you could use some distraction yourself, come Sunday. How about joining me up at Dillard Crick if the weather's good? We'll lay back, catch some fish, shoot the breeze."

I admitted I'd be glad to get away on this of all days. The word *usurpers* sprang to mind whenever I thought about the twins, which was pretty constantly. Samson and I made a plan to meet. While Mr. Julian and his wards reacquainted themselves over pallid sherry and crustless finger sandwiches, I pictured myself roaming free in the countryside and, Samson by my side, striking one small blow for the common brotherhood of man.

*

Reverend Jenkyns, having announced his text for the day, began to hold forth on the Sin of Prevarication as the congregation of First Methodist shifted and resettled on the uncomfortable wooden pews: with the sermon underway, we all knew only thirty minutes remained, countdown to benediction and our collective release. The offertory hymn had been sung, the collection plates had made their rounds, and the Deacons (Father at their helm) had retired to the church office to count the tithes. It had always struck me as highly unfair that the Church Deacons had a ready-made excuse to miss the sermon the rest of us congregants were forced to withstand.

I glanced sideways at Jubal on my left, whose glassy-eyed look and slightly vibrating elbow betrayed the fact that, hand in pocket, he was furtively diddling himself under the navy blazer draped across his lap—a ruse I remembered from my own younger years. It was a not-ineffective way to ride out the tedium of the sermon. To my right, Katie looked positively beatific, radiant as the multiple Virgin Marys in the stained-glass windows bathing us in a prism of rainbow shades. Her contentment no doubt owed to the fact that late last night, as I'd again espied from my bedroom window, she'd reconnoitered with Rat in the shadows of the back yard, demonstrating skills sufficient to make Rat lose discretion and yelp "That-a-way-baby!" in an orgasmic frenzy fortunately brief enough to disturb none of the human sleepers in the house—although Buster, lying at the foot of my bed, emitted a disapproving moan from the depths of his old-dog slumbers. On the other side of Katie, Mother sat upright, immaculate in a crisp navy-blue dress with shiny white belt and starched white collar, her gloved hands gracefully folded atop the white Bible in her lap. A half-smile played across her carefully painted lips as she listened, in all apparent sincerity, to the Lord's message.

For me, the lesson of the sermon was somewhat more ironic. As Rev. Jenkyns thundered on about Falsehood as the Fountain of Satan's Truth, I contemplated the bald-faced lie I'd told my parents over breakfast: that Mr. Brewster needed me to come over after Sunday dinner—the noon meal—to assist with the arriving guests. By that time I intended to be halfway to Dillard Crick.

Two o'clock found me waiting as planned at the spot where the creek crossed Route 3.

When I say *crossed*, I speak literally: there was no bridge to span the shallow expanse of creek—a foot of water submerged the tarmac in the summer, more in the winter. If you were driving down the backroad, you just revved the car and sped through, trusting you didn't stall midstream. As for *crick*, well, that's what the sign posted by the crossing declared. So had Dillard Crick been known, and so had it been misspelt, for one hundred years.

"Hey Scholar!"

Samson, outfitted in his trademark overalls, materialized in the flesh from the shadowy woods on the north side of the stream.

"Howdy, Pockets."

"Ready for some country-boy fun?"

"I'm here, aren't I?"

"Cross over, Sir."

I waded through the water in my Ked high tops. Samson pointed out our trail, snaking away from the creek and into the woods. Fifteen minutes later we reencountered the meandering stream, which had widened and deepened considerably, fed along the way by invisible tributaries. The forested bank sloped down to the water, where it terminated in an outcropping of mossy granite that overhung the water by several feet. Unlike the sparkling froth of Furnace Creek, Dillard meandered at a lazy pace, pea-green and prone to washing back on itself, dragonflies and darters skittering across its sluggish surface in drunken abandon. Downstream, out of sight, I caught the sound of falling water.

"That's a right nice waterfall you hear singin' to us," Samson explained. "We'll trek down later. See how the current slows down?" He pointed directly below the outcropping on which we stood. "Back-flow makes this the perfect fishing spot—the stripers and catfish get plain lazy grubbing off the river-bugs here."

"Then why'll they bother with us?"

"Because of this!" From one of his many pockets Samson produced a jelly jar writhing with fleshy worms and tossed it to me. I grimaced. Next he extracted two homemade fishing rods cleverly stashed in the hollow of a felled tree trunk, and with admirable patience he showed me—a novice who might have learned such skills had I been inclined to join the Boy Scouts—how to bait the hook, where to cast the line, when to give it play. Soon enough we'd kicked off our shoes, pulled our tee-shirts over our heads the better to enjoy the sun, and found comfortable spots to settle down while we watched and waited: me, damp trouser bottoms rolled to my kneecaps, dangling my feet over the rock ledge while Samson reclined against a lichen-covered stump, pink soles pointing my direction. More items magically appeared from his pockets: glittering fishing flies ("just in case"); fatback biscuits his mom had secured in a checked napkin; and a pouch of tobacco and rolling papers. The latter he immediately put to use.

"Here you go, I'll roll another for myself." He lit the makeshift cigarette and, as he passed it to me, a bit of ash fell on my calf. Samson flecked it from the curly blonde hairs of my leg with a deft tap of his finger.

"Smoking can't be good for a boxer."

"Don't care. Smokes, waiting for the fish to bite, this nice heat. Just what the good Lord made Sunday afternoon for."

He parted his full lips and exhaled a perfect ring my way. As it dissolved into my face I found myself recalling a favorite Whitman verse. *The atmosphere is not a perfume, it has no taste of the distillation, it is odorless, it is for my mouth forever, I am in love with it.* I took the first drag of my lifetime. Sooner than I expected I was able to blow a wobbly ring back at Samson. I sank into the languid rhythm of the afternoon.

All of a sudden, Samson felt his line go taut but his fish got away with two-thirds of his nightcrawler; a few minutes later it was my turn to get excited, even though the trout I pulled in was so small Samson made me toss it back. The new wriggler he helped me thread onto my hook, however, did the trick, for I pulled in a fine-sized smallmouth bass. "It's the biting hour," Samson whispered, and within seconds he'd hooked another bass, a fighter that gave him a nice workout as he coaxed it to shore. It looked twice the size of mine.

Now we were fishing in earnest, and we brought in two more, a trout for Samson and a catfish for myself. A pleasurable lull followed, during which we recast our rods, sat back and waited, listening to the birdsong, watching the cloud of black gnats hovering over a mossy rock jutting up midstream, and chewing over the topics that came most naturally to us: sports, girls, school, music, family. At one point I shared Mr. Julian's theory of the origins of the Washington surname. Giving lie to the myth that it had been adopted post-emancipation in honor of the Founding Father, Samson explained his family were descendants of the same line as Booker T. Washington. The latter figure, I learned for the first time, had been born in Franklin County, and his birthplace, a few miles to the north, had been designated a national landmark a decade before: facts absent my school curriculum.

As for "Geronimo"—Samson swore it was just a playful nickname his grandmother had affixed to her son because of his expressive cheekbones, and that his old man had made up the story of the grandfather who'd intermarried with the Apaches to pull Mr. Julian's leg. The idea of G. G. solemnly telling Mr. Julian an outright fabrication added a new wrinkle to their relationship—unless, perversely, Mr. Julian was participating in G.G.'s odd humor by passing off the lie onto me. In turn Samson was happily entertained by the bits of lore I extracted from the Seward and Freeland family closets—from my otherwise sweet Nana Seward's attempt to stab her husband during a fit of rage brought on by menopause to the recent turmoil wrought by sister Katie's dual embrace of Flower Power and Free Love.

About the time I landed a second catfish, Samson declared we'd done well enough for one afternoon. We picked out a trout and a bass to gut for cooking; the rest of the catch he'd promised his ma he'd bring home. Soon the fish were roasting on hickory spits, sending up an aroma only surpassed by my first bite of their sweet, moist flesh.

"Fish sticks be damned!"

Reclining with a contented stomach in the warm sunlight that filtered through the tree limbs overhanging the riverbank, savoring the breeze that wafted out of nowhere and cooled the sweat trickling down my sides and beading on my nose, I decided, then and there, that my exclusion from the social niceties unfolding in the Brewster mansion were more than amply recompensed. As we lay back and wiped our mouths clean, our conversation wound around to the person we knew best in common: Julian Armistead Brewster III. I asked whether his dad had known Mr. Julian's sister and if Samson knew what had happened to her. He tried to piece together the tidbits he'd heard since childhood. His old man started working for Mr. Julian in the early 1950s when the latter returned from New York. The story went that Julia had died "tragically" in the forties—a boating accident that involved her fiancé. Samson's recollection was that Julia and Julian had been moving in different directions for some time.

"What I don't understand," I said, "is why Mr. Julian came back to Rocky Hill, when he claims those years in New York were heaven on earth."

"Temporary, at first, to nurse his sick mother. Mr. Brewster, Senior, had already passed, Mr. Julian's brother had been shot down over the Pacific, there was a sister living in California who'd broken off from the family a long time ago." More and more Brewsters whose particulars I was unaware of. "So it was just him. But his mother took half a decade to die. That's when my old man started working for him—back when they still had a houseful of servants."

By the time Mrs. Evelina Sumner Brewster, Julian's mother, crossed to the other side, the estate had begun its decline, and the servants had dropped off like flies. During those years Adelaide, the sister who'd renounced the family to move to California, also died. Eventually, there was just Mr. Julian, George Geronimo, and a succession of short-lived cooks, of whom Sassafras Beebe was the latest and, thankfully, most talented incarnation.

"Something happened," Samson said, "back around the time we were born. Somebody, or something, got to him, made his return to Rocky Hill a one-way stop. He hasn't traveled further'n Richmond since he settled back here, growing more ornery by the year. But Pop's always stood by Mr. Brewster. Won't let us speak bad of him to this day."

I mulled over Samson's brief history lesson, which hinted at a sadder past than I'd suspected. Bereft of his sister Julia, outliving the rest of his family, exiled from his Manhattan life, Mr. Julian had closed himself up in his decaying mansion, and closed in on himself. Using the remnants of the Brewster fortune and memories of better days to feed his eccentricities—which, with George Geronimo as his sole remaining audience, deepened and festered—he had become the quixotic gnome, shrill and commanding, acerbic and droll, frightening and alluring, who ruled over a dwindling domain from a wheel-chair throne, his diadem the pale hair that topped his pate and framed his watery stare.

Before I quite knew what was happening, Samson was shaking me out of a deep slumber. The shadows cast by the trees had deepened, and the late afternoon sun was glinting on the stream.

"Time to wash off," Samson announced. He'd already stored away the fishing gear.

"This way. Watch your step." As he led me on a narrow path that skirted the bank of the creek, the sound of falling water became louder; the path veered into a thicket of gnarly pines, and I found myself inching down an incline whose toeholds had been created by the exposed roots of the descending trees. There, at the bottom, over Samson's sculpted shoulders I spied the waterfall. In the grand scheme of things it was modest; but to a fifteen-year-old still hoping for a family vacation to Niagara Falls, that twelve-foot drop, issuing between two boulders that narrowed the stream above so that it thundered down in a solid sheet of glistening pea green, was awesome. The constant motion of the falls had hollowed out a circular basin at its base, deep enough to dive into from above. In an instant we stripped to our skivvies and waded, laughing and shouting, into the water. At the pool's center I couldn't touch bottom, but beneath the cascade, submerged under a few feet of water, rose a flat, slimy boulder on which, after much practice, we both managed to rise to standing positions. We teetered there precariously, catching the sheet of water thundering down on our heads and shoulders, when something hard hit me on the head, and it wasn't water. It was a fat grouper, which ricocheted off my scalp before disappearing into the churning froth. I lost my balance and slipped off the boulder. Samson was howling mightily as I bobbed to the surface, and I had to laugh too.

So we floated, suspended in that fluid medium, detached from our usual orbits of contact, till it was time to pack up and leave. Even as one race riot after another broke out across the nation that summer of 1967, I dared hope that the bond that had sprung up between Samson and me on this June day was something beyond the ordinary, talisman of a perhaps better future.

9

SAVOIR-FAIRE AND THEN SOME

The following Wednesday opened a new chapter in my life. In my imagination I'd of course painted an unflattering picture of Mr. Julian's niece and nephew, and I fully expected to find them haughty, sophisticated, and aloof. With my impressions so adamantly formed in advance, the fact that I needed to go through the motions of welcoming the Sumner twins filled me with distaste. Haughty, sophisticated, aloof they proved to be; but what I hadn't expected was that they would also turn out to be irresistibly alluring, witty, and attractive, forcing me against every fiber of my being to take note of their presence.

Not that I caught a glimpse of either immediately. I had reported to work on Monday expecting to lay eyes on the ballyhooed twins, only to have my curiosity thwarted by a larger force of nature: the fatigue of overseas travel that kept them upstairs, in bed, and out of sight.

"Do NOT disturb," G.G. relayed with an emphatic tongue clack as I checked into the kitchen that morning and B.B. mixed me a glass of chocolate milk. "The two of 'em were quite clear that they need their beauty rest and please Keep all Noise to a Minimum. Lord and Lady of the Manor already!"

Sassafras harrumphed in turn. "And I'm supposed to send fresh-squeezed orange juice, *no* pulp, and hot *Crescents* up to their rooms at noon, tap on their doors twice and leave the trays outside!"

Before I had the chance to ask for more details, Mr. Julian summoned me over the intercom to the library, eager that we make the most of this respite to continue our work. Not that there was so very much left to do—the sorting and shelving was nearing an end, the cataloguing and labeling nearly completed, and, with most of the loose papers moved to the cellar, the library was beginning to look the impressive chamber it had been designed to be. Monday ended without laying eyes on the twins. Given the fact that I had supposedly spent the prior afternoon in their company, I was forced to respond to my parents' queries for the second day in a row with a litany of fabricated descriptions. I just hoped my imaginary portraits would approach reality when the twins presented their actual faces in Rocky Hill.

It wasn't until Wednesday that our meeting took place, and of course it came when I was least ready for it. I'd been sorting papers in the basement since early morning, and, when I came upstairs for more file folders, I was beginning to feel as smudged and earmarked as the duplicates I'd been filing away.

"Newton!"

Mr. Julian's voice arrested me on the threshold to the drawing room. First I took in the flowery scent of Oolong tea that hung in the air—a departure from Mr. Julian's Earl Grey—and then I saw *them*, silhouetted by the light streaming in from the French doors. To the right of Mr. Julian's wheelchair, by the tea caddy, I registered the outline of a lithe girl, a young woman really, seated on the Duncan Phyfe. She was dressed in a sleeveless sheath of a black dress with white panels running down the sides, very chic, very Mod. My initial impression was that she was very pretty and very proud. One shapely leg in a black mesh stocking was drawn up gracefully beneath her, her posture mirroring that of Mimi, regally purring at the opposite end of the sofa. To Mr. Julian's left, sprawled in an overstuffed chair, I made out the form of a young man, legs in finely tapered European trousers splayed before him with insouciance. Both lounged as if the room had been summoned into existence to gratify their wishes. Even though I could see the steam rising from the cups of tea they held—that is, *she* held hers; *his* nestled on the flat of his stomach, saucer teetering on the arm of his chair in a violation of etiquette Mr. Julian would never have allowed me—and even though the heat of the day was beginning to permeate the chamber through the open doors, they looked as if the air immediately surrounding them were ten degrees cooler than anywhere else in all of Virginia. They were just that cool.

"My great-niece, Mary Josephine, and my great-nephew, Markus Joseph. Mary Jo and Marky Joe to their familiars. This is Newton

Seward, the local boy I was telling you about."

I hovered, self-consciously, on the brink between rooms, aware of their eyes appraising me. I was just apologizing that I needed to cut through to the library when Mr. Julian stopped me short.

"Don't be daft. Come introduce yourself, like any civilized being. They won't bite."

I stepped down and moved forward, feeling impossibly awkward. Extending my hand to Mary Jo, I murmured a welcome that became progressively less coherent as her face came into focus. Darkly lashed, sapphire-blue eyes—the most seductively beautiful eyes I'd ever seen—looked into mine with a hint of amusement, and I saw the slightest curl form at the edges of her lips. As I touched her cool palm, I noticed her eyes travel down to my dusty fingers and bitten nails. I had never felt more common in my entire life. To mask my confused feelings I turned to Marky Joe.

"Drop the Joe, for God's sake, just call me Marky," he said, drawling out his words in a tone more patrician than Southern as he gazed up at me with eyes as darkly fringed as his sister's, except that they were cat-green. His full lips curled as he appraised me, head to toe, and I was suddenly aware of my dime-store jeans, wrinkled tee-shirt, and mud-stained high-tops. His leather espadrilles positively shouted their Italian provenance.

I have to state the obvious fact now, at this place in my narrative, because, even if I were too dazed to articulate it at the time, I know I *felt* the truth of what I have to say, and I know I felt it from that very first moment that I laid eyes on the two of them: the Sumner twins were the most handsome creatures I had ever seen or imagined could exist. The imprint of their beauty existed not only in their stunning eyes—so nearly identical but for the color; not only in their perfectly straight noses and full lips; not only in the sheen, when they moved their heads, of their nearly identical dark manes of hair, or in their perfect complexions; not only in the casual assurance with which their shapely bodies occupied space: it was not any of these things, alone, that constituted their beauty. It was the aura of self-possession and breeding that emanated from their good looks and filled the physical space between us with inevitability and impossibility: the two qualities most guaranteed to kindle my innermost desires.

"Yes," said Mr. Julian, watching me watch and speaking as if his wards weren't present. "Aren't they *fine*? Spectacularly transformed since I saw them last. What credit they bring to the family!"

Mary Jo deftly turned Mr. Julian's unsubtle compliment into light banter. "Uncle Julian, you're too kind. We're only what you've helped make us." Technically, of course, he was the twins' uncle once removed, since they were the children of his cousin, but, as I soon learned, they nominated him "Uncle" nevertheless.

"Nothing like education abroad to take off the rough edges," Marky said. "Nice *finish*, that's what finishing school's given us."

"Well, you're showing it beautifully," Mr. Julian replied.

Mary Jo turned to me. "Uncle Julian says you're a marvel at organization, besides being the brightest teen in Franklin County."

Of course I couldn't think of a "bright" response. "I like to read, that's all."

"The perfect candidate, then, to set Uncle Julian's library to rights," Marky said with a carelessness that threw the compliment into instant doubt. "No wonder he's taken to you so quickly. From what he tells us, it sounds like you've taken up residence for all practical purposes." He leaned to Mary Jo, murmuring sotto voce, "*Un garçon de la campagne aux les ongles sales, exactement ce qu'il faut pour cette tâche!*," and they exchanged smiles. Only the fact that Marky didn't realize that I knew what he was saying kept me from feeling entirely mortified; to them I might be a "country bumpkin with dirty nails," but that wasn't going to stop me from firing back a reply.

"It's not like I've moved into the servants' quarters." I paused before launching into French. "*En fait, je suis juste sous contrat avec M. Brewster trois jours et demi par semaine. Ce travail, il ne nécessite pas un énorme degré d'engagement, certainement pas.*"

Marky blushed, to my immense satisfaction.

Mary Jo graciously intervened, as she had done a few minutes before. "Three and a half days. Well, that's brilliant! All the more opportunities for us to get to know each other. I'm sure my brother will appreciate that as much as myself, won't you, Marky Joe?"

I noted that *she* still called him by both names.

The blush on his cheeks gradually faded, and his full lips parted in a seductive smile. "*Mais oui*, you'll have to show us how you have fun in Rocky Hill."

"Yes yes yes, you children *must* have fun!" Mr. Julian broke in, clapping his hands gleefully. "It's been preying on my mind ever since you announced your visit. An old man like me isn't entertainment enough to keep you occupied, not for long. I release Newton into your hands whenever you want, so that you three can play—I insist on it!"

"Uncle Julian," Marky said in a droll voice, "We're too old to *play*."

"But not too old to have fun," Mary Jo added with spirit. Clearly diplomacy was her forté. "And we'll find so many ways to amuse ourselves in this wonderful house—and outside of it too, if Newt has the time to spare to squire us around." She mouthed *Please!* in my direction, a mute show that escaped Mr. Julian's eye as he merrily prattled on.

"Washington should know where all the board games are stored and he'll set up the badminton net tomorrow, the croquet set is by the terrace, there's the Hi-Fi in the parlor on the attic floor, with all the recordings you two had so much fun listening to the last time you stayed here—"

"Some of those 78s are classics," Marky gallantly noted.

"If you like music," I timidly interjected, "Rocky Hill has a really cool used record store."

Mr. Julian galloped right over my comment before Marky could respond, intent on reaching his climax.

"But for *real* fun, I've got a special treat to share with you... " Mr. Julian raised his hoary eyebrows and looked from one twin to the other. "I suspect, with good reason, that you'll find what I have to say pleasing enough to compensate for our poor town's deficiencies!" He paused again, clearly enjoying his moment of suspense. The two waited, in polite anticipation. "I remember how disappointed, I mean absolutely crest-fallen, you both looked two years ago, when you discovered the pool had fallen into disrepair. Well, I've gussied it up just for you, and it's yours for the whole summer, good as new!"

"Superior!" Enthusiasm fired Marky's voice for the first time since we'd begun talking. He must have noticed the odd look on my face, because he turned to me to explain. "Let's just say there was more debris than water filling its bottom when we saw it last. I swear I spotted frogs, a snake or two, and other nameless deformities of the deep slithering in its muck, right, Uncle?"

Mr. Julian fluttered his hands up and down as he chortled, seeming to find Marky's description extraordinarily humorous. In the interim, I attempted to regain my composure. Truth is, the look that Marky had caught on my face had less to do with the pool's murky history than with the sinking feeling that what I'd suspected was now a certainty: swimming practice with the old man was a thing of the past.

"I still remember how put out you were," Mr. Julian chuckled. "The water pump had been broken for Lord knows how long, the weeds were waist-high, and the smell was—well, primeval! Your aunts had been feeding you too many tales about the grandeur that was once Brewster Manse. Fret no more, my dearies. You'll see at one o'clock—Washington is serving us luncheon poolside."

That invitation further reminded me that my place was, literally and figuratively, downstairs, so I took the first opportunity to excuse myself and retrieve the file folders I needed from the library. I was on my way back through the drawing room when Mr. Julian drawled to the twins, "But I *do* warn you. There is one restriction regarding your use of the pool. A hard and fast rule. It's off-limits before lunch." He waved an imperial hand at me. "Newton—*wait* a minute! I'm changing your schedule. Starting Friday we'll be holding your swim practice in the mornings, quarter till eleven pronto. And I'm expecting you to join us for lunch in an hour. So look smart and make the most of the next sixty minutes!"

"Swim practice?" Marky's eyes flitted my direction with look of cool reappraisal, even though he was nominally speaking to his uncle. "We can't come and watch?"

"Not until I say so!" the old man cackled happily.

Mary Jo spoke. "Don't worry. During summer recess my dear brother is rarely out of bed before lunchtime—and, even during school term, well...!" She pursed her lips as if to suggest tales of delinquency unfit for polite company.

"Not that you haven't tried to rouse me at unconscionably inappropriate times," her brother retorted with a sly, lazy grin.

As Mary Jo remonstrated, I exited into the back hallway, trailed by the sound of their playful banter—I could no longer hear the words, but words didn't matter: they were performing a skit, call it "Sibling Love," for Mr. Julian's benefit, and he was enjoying the show with the relish of one quite ready to be so entertained.

10

THE SUMMER OF LOVE

So began a new phase of the summer, one that I would never have predicted in my wildest dreams. Perhaps it was a foregone conclusion, given our strange surroundings and the dreamlike spell that the Brewster estate cast over the three of us, that we would cleave together. To an outsider peeking in we must have seemed glowing fireflies, particles of charged electricity, flitting against the darkened backdrop of age and decay, moldy memories, and stoppered time that imparted to Mr. Julian's mansion its aura of enthrallment and utter ennui.

Yet if the three of us were drawn together, it was by no means because we had discovered a host of shared affinities. No, from that first poolside lunch during which we began to form our alliance while we sat in the filtered shade of the pergola and watched the sun creating mirages above the water's surface, I remained keenly aware of the differences—of birth, of upbringing, of age, of worldliness—that separated us, and nearly every day that I spent with the twins something would be said, or intimated, or left unspoken, that reminded me of the gulf dividing us. But in spite of these differences—perhaps because of them—we were increasingly drawn to each other, first under Mr. Julian's calculating eye, and soon enough of our own volition and in our own time. I came to desire nothing more.

Within the week I found myself invited by the twins to return to the estate on my days off. That was a relief since, separately and in tandem, the two of them cultivated the bad habit of interrupting whatever task I was about and, when I demurred, wheedling Mr. Julian to release me to their amusements. The upshot, ironically, was to make Mr. Julian realize that he'd come to depend on me for more of his creature comforts than he liked to admit. So he solved the problem by commissioning Tom Allbright to strike a new arrangement with my parents, whereby I would additionally be paid to come to the house on Tuesdays and Thursdays for the express purpose of providing the twins a companion. Soon enough I was spending more and more of my free time with them, lingering after work, returning after dinner, dropping by on Sundays, finding excuses to turn down my local friends' invitations to hang out were there any chance the twins might be soliciting my company. In spite of my awareness of our differences, in spite of my fear of appearing woefully unsophisticated, I couldn't keep away, I didn't *want* to keep away; I looked forward to nothing more, when I woke those balmy summer mornings and again when I went to bed those sultry summer evenings, than returning to the enticing world that opened to my vision whenever the twins admitted me to their presence. The Sumners' savoir faire, their sense of entitlement, was so strong that it became infectious, and I caught it.

Even as we were increasingly drawn into a circle of intimacy, I learned that getting along with either was an exercise guaranteed to keep me on my toes. Given the diplomacy she'd demonstrated during our initial meeting, I assumed Mary Jo would be the warmer and more outgoing of the pair, her brother more aloof and elite. But almost immediately, Marky began treating me like his best pal, cajoling me to share confidences, as Mary Jo grew comparatively distant. Next encounter the roles would reverse, pendulum-like, Mary Jo warm effervescence and Marky offputtingly temperamental. The tease of proffered intimacy that seduced me into believing I was special, unexplained withholdings that made me feel inadequate: these were rhythms that I knew all too well, for they were the ones to which Mr. Julian had so habituated me that, confounded as they often left me feeling, they lured me on, deeper and deeper into a labyrinth of all our makings.

One halcyon afternoon blurred into the next as we whiled away the hours behind the towering wall of shrubbery that enclosed Mr. Julian's pool. Mary Jo's portable radio provided the soundtrack to our sun-dazed reveries as we baked under a remorseless sun, floating in the water or lounging poolside. Of course I had the head start on a tan, given my hours of swim practice. But Mary Jo boasted naturally olive skin that took to the sun and, as if determined to catch up with me, she'd lathe her body in baby oil and lie back on the chaise lounge in French-designer two-pieces more daring than any swimwear Rocky

Hill had yet seen or would ever live to see, dark hair pulled back in a high pony-tail and cigarette dangling from her lips, painting her toe-nails crimson, reading a dog-eared NRF Edition of *Les faux monna-yeurs* through white-rimmed sunglasses right out (as Marky was quick to note) of Godard's "Contempt." Lacking the voluptuous curves of a Bardot, Mary Jo was nonetheless blessed with a body that was simul-taneously taut and shapely, its lines and sinewy strength balanced in a teenaged harmony that utterly enchanted me.

In contrast, Marky—whose fairer skin was always burning, then peeling, till his freckled shoulders became a cubist palette of shades—had a physique that was both more solid and, dare I say, soft-er-looking than Mary Jo's, though those features did not render him any the less attractive. He was at once unapologetically non-athletic (like his uncle, he lost no time pronouncing sports a bore) and sen-sually voluptuous, for he was completely comfortable in his skin in a way, I suspected, that Mary Jo was not. Once Marky discovered the vintage bathing suits stored in the men's changing room, he reveled in making dramatic entrances into the sunlight attired in one outfit after another: a Buster Keaton one-piece, Clark Gable belted knit trunks, Frankie Avalon surfing shorts, each costume change accompanied by a facetious imitation of the film star being channeled—for, as I quick-ly learned, Marky was nothing if not a living archive of film history and cinematic citations, and a more than adequate mime. Paradoxi-cally, the more he played the buffoon, the more appealing he became, a pagan faun cavorting for our enjoyment.

It was at poolside that I felt less subject to the twins' aura of in-born superiority, more their equal. The first afternoon we spent alone there, the twins unabashedly complimented me on the physique that two years on the swim team had honed. In my mind's eye, I was an overgrown and ungainly scarecrow, pimply skin just disguised by my tan; but they whistled when I emerged from the dressing room for the first time. "Who knew, Adonis in our midst!" Marky declared, applauding. To which Mary Jo responded, "Darling brother, he's what we girls call a *hunk*!" I blushed crimson, but I also temporarily for-got my self-consciousness about my complexion, my unruly hair, my thick hands and big feet, as they poked fingers into and poked fun at my washboard belly, till I squirmed away in pleased embarrassment and dove into the pool.

In time, Mary Jo and Marky cajoled Mr. Julian into letting them sit in on our swim practice, and the consequence was that, occasionally, one or the other would saunter out to the pool before lunch. They'd open their book or magazine, but as Mr. Julian barked his orders and timed my drills, they gradually ceased reading and joined the old man in cheering me on as I plowed through the water. There were also late afternoons when Mr. Julian asked us to wheel his chair out to the pergola while we frolicked in the pool under his gaze. But those interruptions were relatively infrequent; on most afternoons when I was off-duty, the pool was our private sanctuary, awash in unacknowledged, triangulated imaginings.

The pool wasn't the only site of our growing companionship. With the twins' arrival, I gained access to the vast upstairs of the mansion. Their quarters, located in a wing opposite to that housing Mr. Julian's room, became familiar to me, as did the low-ceilinged, gabled parlor on the third floor where Mr. Julian's vintage records and Hi-Fi were housed, and this room quickly became our indoors enclave. Not that the twins had any compunction, when Mr. Julian was napping or otherwise occupied, about exploring all the second and third floor rooms whose doors weren't locked (and clever Mary Jo soon located a ring of master keys). My curiosity meant I was usually only a few steps behind them, even though I was always anxious that G.G. might catch us in the act, just as he had surprised me in Mr. Julian's room. Such twinges of compunction never seemed to bother the twins—they assumed that any Bluebeardian secrets lying behind those locked doors were theirs by right to discover.

Rainy days and evenings when I showed up after dinner usually found us in the third-floor music room, sprawled on overstuffed chairs with broken springs and soiled slipcovers that had been exiled to the mansion's upper regions decades ago. We played records—everything from scratched 78 rpms of Bessie Smith and the soundtrack of "Meet Me in Saint Louis" to contemporary grooves that our forays into Leopold's Record Emporium, Used and New, in downtown Rocky Hill had brought to light.

It was in this attic eyrie, listening to music late one June evening, that the twins got me stoned for the first time. I was a willing victim. Marky rolled the joints from the remains of a stash he'd purchased in Amsterdam, Mary Jo wedged a damp towel against the bottom of the door (George Geronimo's room was just around the landing), and, to the reverberations of Crimson King, I learned what it meant to get high. The twins delighted in facilitating my corruption, instructing me to lie down on the pillows they'd piled on the floor and ride the waves of music. We rolled on and off the cushions and laughed because everything we said seemed hysterically funny as we passed the jay back and forth; and each time that their saliva-moistened fingertips brushed against mine, I felt my nerve endings on the verge of exploding in sensual ecstasy.

We were buzzed the evening I learned about the accident that killed their parents.

We were listening to an old Elvis Presley album when Marky remarked, out of nowhere, that "Good Luck Charm" had been playing on the car radio the afternoon Mr. Sumner, driving the family car to their summer home on the Cape, slammed the brakes to avoid a jeep that had charged through an approaching intersection. The surfboard resting on top of the luggage in the rear of the station wagon had shot forward with the ferocity of an Olympian's javelin, hitting Mr. Sumner in the small of the neck and snapping his spinal cord instantly. Marky, who'd been seated behind his dad, had just lowered his head to Mary Jo's lap to doze—else the board might have bludgeoned the top of his head instead of lodging in his father's nape. The car careened into a telephone pole, and Mrs. Sumner's body had sailed through the shattered windshield like a frightened pigeon taking flight. Unlike her husband, who died instantly, she lingered three weeks, a glass shard having pierced her frontal lobe, before she gave up the ghost and left the twins orphans. They'd been eleven when the world they'd hitherto known ended in a second.

"Shit," I said, with a virgin pothead's acuity.

"Shit happens," Marky replied. "Who says any of us are long for this world?" He inhaled another toke. "Live for the moment, dudes."

Mary Jo reached across me to hug her brother, which soon became a group hug. We lapsed into silence, listening to the music.

A few evenings later, long after the lights on the first two floors had dimmed, the twins spoke again of their parents. The odor of the scented candles Mary Jo had shoplifted from Woolworth on a dare from Marky mingled in rich confusion while the wail of Chet Baker's trumpet shivered across our skin. We lay on the unbraiding oval rug, propped against cushions and each other. I reclined against a battered Ottoman footrest opposite Mary Jo, lazily gazing on as she slipped her arms up the back of Marky's polo shirt and massaged his shoulders. I imagined him purring, content as cat, under Mary Jo's feathery touch.

"Light against dark," she murmured, looking across his shoulders and pointing at my darkly tanned, outstretched legs, covered with fine curly hair that, bleached blonde by months of sun and chlorine, shimmered in the golden candlelight.

"Turning our Newt into a Manichean allegory?" Mark rolled up his trouser legs knee-high and, without ceremony, draped his bare left knee across my allegorical limb.

"Perhaps I should have said dark against light." It was obvious to our stoned collective consciousness that Mary Jo was now marking the contrast between the silky black hair and much paler skin of her brother's leg. The warmth of his bare calf was palpable. Eventually, the twins changed positions, so that now she lay on her side in front of him; it was his turn to reach under her darkly shimmering hair and caress her neck. I continued to watch.

A question spontaneously spilled from my lips. "Who do you miss most, your mother or father?"

"Let Mary Jo tell you." The note of harshness in Marky's voice surprised me. He bent forward to peck Mary Jo's cheek. "*She* was Daddy's little girl."

"I worshipped him, like all good little girls do. Even after he let me down time after time. But now?" Closing her dark-fringed eyelashes, Mary Jo leaned into Marky's chest as his fingers traced small circles on her temples. "Now, I'm all yours."

Marky was more blunt. "He was a bully. Mom was as scared of him as me, only I didn't have her recourse to chain-smoking to calm me down. It was shit when they died, but you know what? We got over it. The one good thing Father ever did was make Julian Brewster our guardian. And thank God the old man took me out of that awful military school and shipped us off to France instead of sending us to live with our Connecticut relatives." He draped his arm around Mary Jo's waist and squeezed her tight.

Mr. Sumner had expected Marky to follow in his footsteps and demonstrate the skills of a CEO by the time he was nine and, when Marky acted out, packed him off to a military academy in western Pennsylvania. Back then the Sumners lived in Hartford. Mr. Sumner had indeed doted on his only daughter when he deigned to take the time, doing so in an ersatz fashion that left Mary Jo feeling she'd done something wrong when he disappeared into his work—or, as the twins later learned, into the series of extramarital affairs with under-qualified secretaries that fed their mother's increasingly shrill admonitions to her uncomprehending daughter to beware the evils of men.

"They'll bring you down," she repeated between drags on her cigarette, swallowing barbitols with her Chablis. "Unless you control them first. Pity I didn't learn in time."

While Marky underwent the humiliations and hazing rituals of his academy, Mary Jo, separated from her twin brother for the first time, rebelled against her mother's warnings by turning with ever greater allegiance to her father, as if to prove "Daddy's little girl" knew the worth of the love that her mother had so carelessly forfeited. But her adoration proved no better an anchor for her father's erratic attentions than the eclipsed charms of her mother. He failed Mary Jo again and again, in little ways, until he failed her in a very big way indeed. The November before the car accident, he'd promised to pick Mary Jo up from ballet lessons on his way home from the office. The girl had waited on the curb in front of the shuttered studio one hour, then two, as the evening cold penetrated her plaid woolen jacket and lavender leotard. When a shiny black car had finally approached—so much like her father's Lincoln that she yearned with all her heart to believe it was—she disobeyed the one instruction drilled into every child since infancy: don't talk to strangers. Yes, he was a stranger but he said that he'd been sent to fetch her home, and she was so very cold. His voice was kind, as were his eyes.

Mary Jo explained all this, and more, in a quiet monotone as we lay on the worn rug.

The man had taken her to a motel on the outskirts of West Haven, where he forced her to touch his genitals—threatening worse if she didn't—until his semen spilled over her face and matted down her hair. Later, in the middle of the night, while he snored in the one double bed in the overheated room, she disentangled herself from his grip and slipped out undetected.

He'd been arrested, justice was done, but the trauma traveled so deeply into Mary Jo's soul that she became old overnight. Mr. Sumner had forgotten to pick Mary Jo up because he'd been with one of his mistresses, as Mrs. Sumner never failed to remind the girl.

"He's as much a monster as that pervert," she seethed. "*All* men are nasty monsters."

The warfare that now erupted between the parents made Mary Jo even more miserable, and only the knowledge that she and her twin brother would be reunited in June kept her sane. Marky, meanwhile, had suffered his own version of abuse at the hands of his proctors—roused at three in the morning to do pushups, forced to grip a toilet brush between his teeth to clean the bowl on hands and knees, for imagined truancies. Confiding these torments to each other when their school terms ended only strengthened their fierce desire to protect each other from a terrible world. The Cape Cod vacation was a last-ditch effort by their parents to repair, or at least put a good face on, their rotten marriage; the twins were so happy to be together that they temporarily forgave both parents' trespasses. Then Marky had grown sleepy in the back seat, put his head in Mary Jo's lap, and, as Elvis sang his charmed heart to pieces, luck ran out for the Sumner parents.

In an instant, I forgave them their snobberies, their pride, their ability to make me feel unworthy. My heart flowed out toward the twins in a wave of compassion, and, like the banks of the Nile when the spring floods recede, love blossomed in the fertile loam that filled the space between.

11

REPETITION WITH A DIFFERENCE

Before I knew it, the Fourth of July was upon us—a celebration that, as I've already related, entailed certain prescribed rituals in our community. It didn't matter that our family was fraying at the edges—Katie grooving in her hippie persona, jolly Jubal growing overweight, me playing a moody Hamlet—this was one occasion where we were expected to present a united face to the world, and I resigned myself to spending the entire day with kith and kin. But once Marky and Mary Jo learned about the fireworks at Bonner Lake, they took it into their heads that they *must* sample the festivities, as if our town were a box of dimestore chocolates whose pieces, however unexceptional, must be tasted before they were thrown away. Since there was no convincing their reclusive guardian to escort them to this display of plebeian humanity, they started in on me, insisting they join the Seward party. There was no event I wished less to witness than a meeting of the two opposed realms composing my daily existence, so I flatly said no.

Mark and Mary Jo took the matter out of my hands, however, by appealing directly to Mr. Julian over lunch. Their stealth attack caught me unprepared.

"We want," Mary Jo said in her sweetest voice, placing a shapely hand on the man's liver-spotted arm and caressing it ever so gently, "to know our country better. Off in Europe, we feel so—so alienated from what it means to be Americans. We want to feel like we *belong*."

I couldn't imagine a cynic like Mr. Julian would fall for such nonsense.

"You needn't come, Uncle Jules. Just see to it that Newt's parents ask him to bring us along."

I objected vociferously.

"We promise to be on our best behavior, Uncle." Mary Jo smiled her most fetching smile at Mr. Julian, ignoring me entirely.

"I *have* to be there." It was Marky's turn to take up the offensive, revealing he'd agreed to contribute photos to a feature on American holidays a friend was writing for *Paris Match*. "Your quaint habits are very fashionable in Europe these days, you know!" It was the first I'd heard of *ami* or project, but it was true that Marky, in addition to being a film buff, was a photography fiend. For two weeks he'd been training his Leicaflex on Mary Jo and me in various poses, sunny and sultry, throughout the rank grounds of the walled-in estate.

I tried my best to convince the twins that the celebration would be a total bore—bad food, bratty children, bloodthirsty mosquitoes, banal fireworks. But to no avail. They were fox hounds on the scent: in want of a new object on which to sharpen their barbed wit, they rightly sensed that our town's most risible rusticities would be on abundant display on the Fourth.

Evidently Mr. Julian sided with the twins, because without consulting me he talked to Mr. Allbright, who in turn conferred with my parents. They signaled their delight at including my "new friends," who were having "such a positive influence" on me. Dad threw in an added incentive, announcing that he'd send a car over to the Brewster estate for our transport. Long ago, I'd managed to convince him that none of the vintage autos I'd fictitiously placed in Mr. Julian's carriage house were in working order. Since Marky had a driver's license, we could use the loaner to travel to Bonner Lake on our own—and, what the heck, Dad added, confident that automobility was the solution to the world's ills, we could keep the vehicle a couple days. When I learned that, as a gesture of parental détente, the once-banished Rat was joining the Sewards for the festivities, I groaned. No end of mortifications loomed ahead, as my family exposed their follies to the twins' titillated eyes.

Nothing, of course, plays out exactly as you imagine. The fates are much cleverer than that. On Tuesday, one of Dad's assistants dropped off, as promised, a beautiful tan and cream convertible. Filled with not a little pride at supplying such fancy wheels for our use, I proposed to the twins that we take an afternoon spin in the country before heading to Bonner Lake. The day was hot and humid, the Mennen deodorant I'd plastered under my arms was dribbling down my sides as I waited in the driveway for Mary Jo and Marky. The vain creatures were still primping and preening in front of their bathroom mirrors while I dissolved, like the Wicked Witch of the West, into a puddle of sweat.

At that moment Samson appeared around the side of the carriage house, slats of wood hoisted to one shoulder. I hadn't seen him since we carried the file cabinets to the basement in preparation for the twins' visit. Well, that's not entirely true: once I'd caught him out of the corner of my eye, at a distance, but we hadn't spoken, as I'd been with the twins. The hours the two of us had spent at Dillard Crick seemed months rather than weeks ago, and I felt a twinge of guilt.

Samson's face immediately riveted my attention. His left ear was grotesquely swollen, three times its normal size, and his left eye and cheek, too, had taken a battering. He shrugged as he took in my gaze.

"Boxing. My trainer put me in the ring with a pro on Saturday. Toughening me up for a demonstration match. Shoulda seen me three days ago if you think *this* looks bad."

"So what's with these planks? Don't tell me the old man's got you working on holidays."

"No rest for the wicked. I'm fixing the swing down by the creek. How are you doing, Scholar? I hear those twins have taken quite a shine to you."

"They're okay." For some reason I felt the need to hedge. "But it's work too. I mean, I'm getting *paid* to hang out with them."

Samson snorted. "Hell, I get paid to work. But not to play!"

I wanted to explain that, snooty as they looked, the twins were amazingly interesting—that everything they had to say, everything they'd seen, every place they'd been, dazzled me—but I stopped, not quite sure how to put my feelings into words, and especially to Samson.

"Hey, nice wheels." Samson acknowledged the convertible with a nod.

"Dad's loan. I'm off for a spin now."

Samson lifted his unswollen eyebrow. "Since when did the DMV start handing out licenses to minors?"

"I'm going *along* for a drive I meant. Marky has a permit. We're leaving any minute."

"Won't hold you up any longer. Arms gonna break if I stand here jawing." To the contrary, the muscles popping in his arms looked ready to shoulder a few more tons. He winked. "Don't let the fancy car go to your head."

"I'll try not."

"How bout we meet up at Dillard Crick this Sunday? Our own little Independence Day celebration?"

"Maybe... I could get into that."

"That a yes?"

I racked my brains, trying to recall whether the twins had mentioned plans for Sunday. I didn't think so.

"Sure, it's a deal."

Samson grinned and turned to the break in the shrubbery that opened onto the back lawn. Simultaneously the twins appeared, arm in arm, more appropriately dressed for the country club than a county celebration. Samson stepped aside to let them through and departed without a further word.

"Did you see that boy's face?" Mary Jo gestured in Samson's direction.

"I *thought* I heard you talking to someone," Marky interrupted, curiosity lighting his eyes as he turned to look back through the shrubbery at Samson's receding form. "I just didn't expect it to be a Browntown Bruiser!"

"Smart-ass. That's Washington's son. He does odd jobs here. He's training to be a boxer, he took one in the face the other day."

"Our misanthropic G.G.'s the progenitor of a prizefighter with the physique of Hercules?" Marky whistled. "I figured the old geezer was as impotent an old bachelor as our uncle!"

"Don't be so cruel." Mary Jo flicked Marky's face with the back of her hand. "What will Newt think?"

"All I care," Marky theatrically intoned, "is what Newt thinks of my driving abilities."

Making a mock sign of the cross over Dad's vehicle, I tossed Marky the car keys, and the silver link bracelet on his wrist—definitively marking him more Euro than local—glinted in the sunlight. I took

the passenger's seat to navigate while Mary Jo sat in the rear, leaning forward with her brown arms resting on the backs of both bucket
seats. Watching her fluff the nape of Marky's dark mane of hair, I was
beginning to feel something like envy when her right fingers brushed
the curls at the back of my neck. My skin tingled, and I forgot the
image of Samson's battered face.

*

Some hours later, we arrived at Bonner Lake, and I braced myself for
the gaffes I anticipated my family committing. That my parents would
be cordial to my companions, earnestly welcoming them to the point
of embarrassment, was a given. But I was thrown off-guard by how
exceptionally attentive Mary Jo and Marky were to the Seward con-
clave. Not that their well-mannered solicitousness fooled me for a
second—Mary Jo was surely egging Mother on when she confessed
her regret that dear Uncle Julian was a Catholic and then spoke of the
difficulty of maintaining her Protestant faith in so Papist a country
as France. Equally suspect were Marky's leading questions about the
latest in Ford technology, which soon had Father taking Marky for an
extended below-the-hood tour.

Marky, when not appropriated by either parent, quizzed by Jubal,
or fawned on by Katie (quite taken with his breezy charms, so unlike
Rat's taciturnity), roamed the picnic area with his Leicaflex, brazenly
introducing himself to Rocky Hill's more colorful citizenry: each potential fodder for *Paris Match*. Old Miss Avery, who always brought
her songbirds to the picnic in their cage, built to resemble a Tidewater plantation, easily yielded to Marky's sweet-talk and posed for
several portraits as chirpily as if she were a debutante at her first cotil-
lion. Equally susceptible was my high school principal, Mr. Cornell
Negroponte, a rotund, uneducated fool whose last name was the inspiration for countless racist jokes lobbed across the football field by
our cross-county rivals. Stopping by our table just as Mother pried
the Tupperware lid off the fried chicken, Mr. Negroponte wasted no
time in spearing the very piece I was eyeing as he introduced himself
to our distinguished visitors.

"Newt here, ain't he jest the cat's meow?" Mr. Negroponte paused between chews of chicken. "He's a quiet un, but that never fooled none of us teachers at Hill High. Son, don't never forget who gave you your first step up in the world!" Then, in response to Marky's request: "A picture of me with our prodigy? Why of course Young Sir"—he licked his fingers clean before throwing a heavy arm around my shoulders—"click away!" While my parents looked on with pride at their son being so singled out, I aimed thunderbolts at Marky and Mary Jo. They maintained perfectly straight faces.

Marky's lens uncovered countless other subjects likely to confirm the world's opinion of Southern deformity, both in its figurative and all-too-literal manifestations. The four Wade children, all with six toes on the left foot, proudly displayed their extra digits for Marky (each was also rumored to have a third nipple tucked under the right armpit, information I refrained from passing along to our intrepid photographer). Equally willing to preen for Marky's camera was Beau Billingsly, a town fixture nearing ninety who always dressed for the Fourth in a moth-eaten army tunic, sleeves pinned together behind his back for the simple reason he'd lost both arms (as well as most of his hearing) in the Great War. He proudly posed with his new bride (and third wife), a girl my age for whom missing limbs, defective eardrums, and failing memory were preferable to her widowed Pa, a mean-spirited drunk whose abuse of his children was the subject of many a prayer circle at First Methodist. The photo that finally made it into *Le Match* captured our high school bandleader leading the crowd in the national anthem as the first fireworks lit the indigo sky. In the right foreground Rat's hazy face leers into the frame, middle finger shooting Marky a bird (probably because of Katie's unsubtle interest in Marky)—a gesture nicely repeated by the bandmeister's uplifted baton on the left side of the composition. Bearing the title "American In(ter)dependence," the image garnered second-place in a contest for young photographers in 1968, two months after the eruption of the student riots that rocked Paris to its core and, as I shall have occasion to relate, profoundly altered Marky's life and ultimately my own.

After dinner, the three of us managed to sneak off long enough to get high, and by the time we gathered at the edge of the lake to watch the fireworks display the Seward and Rocky Hill quirks that earlier made me squirm with embarrassment now seemed more comic than appalling. As the black sky ripened with explosions of color and a cloud of acrid-smelling smoke thickened over the lake like swamp miasma, I no longer felt, as I had two summers ago when I'd stumbled from the woods surrounding Furnace Creek, that those distant bursts of color were omens of my alienation from all that I had known. No: the starry exfoliations now streaking the darkness seemed the sign of my good fortune in simply being here, high, with these unexpected and improbable friends.

It was the memory of that prior Fourth of July that led to my spontaneous proposal on the drive home that we three take a detour by the old shot tower at Furnace Creek. The twins were up for any adventure, especially when I explained that this bit of Americana, one hundred years old and buried in the woods, was once a favored retreat for the self-gratifying exercises of yours truly. A screech owl heralded our intrusion into the dark woods separating the road from the creek embankment on which the furnace was built. "Too spooky!" Marky whispered, grabbing hold of us both. Mary Jo giggled and nudged her brother forward, who in turn held on the back of my shirt as I threaded a path through the underbrush. Every unseen rustle had us jumping, and I suddenly recalled, as if it were yesterday, the way my heart lurched when Zithra had clamped her hand down on my unsuspecting chest and I'd feared for my life.

"There," I announced.

The furnace rose dimly before us, its black outline more evocative of a foreboding prison than an adolescent's autoerotic refuge. The twins, however, were most impressed, so I showed them the footholds on the mound's shortest side and, cautiously, we hoisted ourselves to its top. Marky lit our last jay, which we passed back and forth as we lay on our backs and gazed at the moon and the stars.

As the eerie magic of the spot began to work its spell, I found myself yearning to unburden what had happened to me here. The twins had revealed their childhood traumas and I craved to seal our intimacy by sharing my own secrets. And, so, as the chill of the lichen-covered stones penetrated the backs of our shirts, as the night breeze rustled the hickory and oak canopy above us, and as the drone of invisible insects twined with the ghostly burble of the stream twenty yards away, I closed my eyes and blurted out, in fits and starts, that series of strange events—the shock of Zithra's sudden appearance, my raid into Judge Leroy's study, the overheard telephone conversation, Zithra's mysterious letter—events that, spoken outloud, made me relive my childish terror, my guilt and shame, all over again. I censored nothing, from the hair-raising shock of Zithra's hand squeezing my genitals to the theft of the Johnson's car I'd set into motion.

When I opened my eyes, I made out the silhouettes of both twins, one on each side, peering down at me. Marky spoke first. His face was invisible but his whisper filled with awe.

"Who knew you had it in you, Newton Seward! Under that squeaky-clean facade you're a rebel. Man, we've got to keep our eyes on *you.*"

"I would have been terrified." Mary Jo shivered beside me. "For all you knew, she might have hurt you." Perhaps she was recalling the pervert who had terrorized her, half a life ago.

"That's not the point: the point is that in spite of everything Newt's been raised to believe, he *acted.*" Marky rested on his side, facing me. "It's not a question of right or wrong. That's bullshit. For just a minute you followed your heart"—his fingers thrummed my chest, then rested there, lightly caressing the cleft between my pectorals—"and let yourself live dangerously."

I felt immeasurably sad, and yet somehow relieved, as I looked up at the stars, raised my arm, traced the outlines of the Big Dipper with my fingertips, and listened to the sounds of Furnace Creek churning over the rocks in its stream. "But I sometimes still feel guilty—even now."

Marky reached his free hand to my own, still pointing overhead, brought it down to a resting place on his ribs, where, through the gap in his shirt, the beating of his heart coursed through my fingers. So alive, so vibrant; that the world might one day go on without him seemed impossible.

"*Il est interdit d'interdire,*" he said. "We've got to learn to live outside the rules. Nothing forbidden. Fuck the consequences. Live for now."

Mary Jo joined her hand with ours. "If we're going to live at all." In the distance, a night bird began to sing a solitary melody. "*Tous pour un—*" Marky began.

"—and one for all," I finished, grateful for the quirk of fortune that had provided me companions with whom to share this darkness.

12

WHITE LIES

Two events occurred to disturb the lazy harmony of the July days that followed.

Due to the fine impression that the twins had created, Dad arranged to make a car available to us on a regular basis—all we had to do was stop in the dealership and sign out a loaner. Our geographic horizons expanded exponentially. Instead of relying on strolls downtown when the Brewster estate became too small for our restless energy, we drove wherever, within reason, we desired: Buck Run, Powder Mill, Burnett's Bridge, Mad Cap Creek, we explored them all. Twice we even took Mr. Julian out for a spin—despite G. G. looking on disapprovingly from the front terrace, shaking his head as if three of the Four Horsemen of the Apocalypse were spiriting his master away in a chariot of fire.

The weekend after the Fourth, we ventured to Roanoke, the only metropolis within an hour's drive, to see the film, *To Sir with Love*, whose title song the radio had drummed into our brains, and afterwards we used fake IDs to get into the jazz club in the cellar of the grand old Roanoke Hotel. Experiencing on my own, without the supervision of parents, the brave new world of a bustling city whose downtown came alive in the evening, whose four-story office buildings and glass-fronted banks formed corridors trapping exhaust fumes whose sting I perversely found intoxicating, whose shop windows reflected back to us a hundred times our images gliding down sidewalks, I felt more awe than Nick Carraway upon his first venture onto Gatsby's lavish grounds. The ribbing I took from the twins for mistaking sleepy Roanoke for a pinnacle of urbanity could not dissipate the rush of excitement that filled me; my dream of one day escaping small town life seemed tantalizingly within reach.

Perhaps that was one reason why, the next day, I couldn't prevent a vague discontent intruding on my spirits as I set out to meet Samson at Dillard Crick. True, I was suffering from the noxious throb of a hangover serrating the edges of my skull, a fact I did my somber best to disguise over breakfast and during Sunday service, and I was also feeling guilty at having told my parents I was spending the afternoon with the twins—or, to be honest, less guilty than anxious I might be caught out in my falsehood. To compound my worries, last night on the return trip from Roanoke the twins insisted that I join *them* after Sunday lunch.

"I can't, I'm really sorry, I *can't*. I promised the folks I'd spend the day at home," I said, trapping myself in yet another lie.

"*That's* your excuse? Sis, can you believe Newt would neglect *us* just to stay at *home*?" Once on a riff Marky rarely stopped; he relished annoying me with vaguely lewd insinuations. "What wanton are you sneaking off to see, Romeo? Don't think I won't find out!"

At last their clamor—mostly Marky's—subsided when I agreed that I'd *try* to join them late afternoon or early evening.

"We'll be ringing your folks to plead for your early release if we start going stir-crazy," Mary Jo laughed, adding to my fear of being caught out in my white lie.

Thus my mood as I set off to Dillard Crick. The obvious solution would have been to tell parents and twins alike my intentions. But in my gut I knew that attempting to explain my friendship with Samson was fraught with landmines. For my parents, having a "colored friend" was as unimaginable as dating a Jewish girl. And I feared that the twins, with their sense of entitlement, would scoff at such a low companion. Above all else, I wanted to avoid their judgment.

Samson and I were approaching the rock outcropping overhanging the creek when a branch whipped back and stung the bad side of his face. He yelped.

"And I was just getting ready to say your ugly mug was looking a tad better."

Samson's lips curled: his signature grin. "And I've been holding back from saying it's *you* who's looking worse for wear today, Scholar. I take it you weren't up *reading* all night?"

I admitted to the folly of last night's libations in Roanoke.

"Our lazy country ways can't compete with the fast life you're living now."

Evidently, the fish were in agreement, because we waited for an hour before getting a bite, a puny catfish that Samson tossed back into the water. We talked, desultorily, about life, about the future, about our dreams of leaving Franklin County behind in quest of a wider world. That's why I box, Samson said; that's why I study, I echoed. Schooling made me think of Sidney Poitier's inspirational influence on his East End working-class students in the film I'd seen the night before.

"If only I had one teacher that cared about me that much."

Samson leveled his gaze at me. "If you ever see a teacher as black as Sidney Poitier at Hill High *please* let me know."

We'd both stretched out our bare legs on the ledge. Samson waved the pink bottoms of his feet at me. "When I was a kid, I puzzled over why God didn't make white folks with brown palms and soles, like us in reverse. My mom said it was a courtesy, so you wouldn't always be reminded who you were stepping on."

I had no witty comeback. As the minutes passed I increasingly worried about the Sumner twins ringing me at home and finding out I wasn't there. By three o'clock, our fishing lines still slack, I suggested we call it a day.

"No time for the waterfall?"

Samson sounded rueful. Another day, I promised, so we stored our gear and trudged back through the woods to Route 3. Now that it was time to part, I felt just as unhappy and discontent as when we'd met up.

We lingered by the edge of the road, where the creek coursed over the submerged, cracked asphalt. Impulsively I reached out and grabbed Samson's broad palm, squeezing hard. "I'm sorry I've seemed out of sorts today. I *do* like hanging out with you."

Samson grinned. "Even if I'm not as dashing as Sidney Poitier?"

*

When I arrived at the Brewster house, Marky was brimming over with excitement, and I was its immediate target. Not because my cover had been blown, no, but because he'd just discovered that the

Roxy in downtown Roanoke was hosting a foreign film series on Saturday nights. "Jules and Jim" was screening in two weeks: we *had* to be there. Marky swore that he needed to save me from my provincial self before it was too late and that, next to his idol Godard, Truffaut was guaranteed to blast open a window in my imagination.

The consummate cinephile, Marky had already decided that he wanted to study film at the Institut des hautes études cinématographiques and eventually direct films that Andrew Sarris would champion in the *Times*. Nothing roused his passion more than talking about movies, or rather, the *art* of movies. He'd arrived in Rocky Hill full of "Belle de Jour," which had opened in Paris shortly before his departure, and he'd asked me to proofread an essay on the paranoiac achievement of "Blow-Up" slated to appear in an upstart film journal. From Marky I learned as much about the history of European film— the work of Ophuls, Cocteau, Carné, Melville, Godard, Rohmer—as I'd learned about high culture from Mr. Julian.

His enthusiasm was contagious, and the three of us spent the next several days planning our second excursion to Roanoke, which, lo and behold, Marky no longer belittled as a backwater outpost. Nothing interfered to spoil our excitement until I arrived at the house the Wednesday before the big event. As I entered the kitchen George Geronimo surprised me with a note from Samson. I had no idea his father was aware of our acquaintance. "Don't know what that boy sees in you," the old man groused. "And for sure I don't know what he sees in that damn sport of his!"

The note, it turned out, was a disarming appeal to attend a demonstration match at Samson's boxing club Saturday evening. It was a preliminary for his first semi-professional bout, and he proposed to meet me at the carriage house and walk me to the site in Browntown. He added that he'd warned his fellow pugilists that a Scholar might be in attendance, and in turn everybody promised to mind their grammar.

Suddenly I was faced with a choice for Saturday night: movie or boxing match? Much as I wanted to cheer Samson on, I reasoned that a film that Marky claimed would change my life was more vital to my education. Lurking behind that self-justification was the suspicion that, had I told the twins of Samson's invitation, they would have either laughed at me, or, worse, changed plans and insisted on tagging along. I wrote Samson a note of apology.

This prick to conscience was followed by a second incident, one that disquieted me far more. It occurred on the way home from Roanoke that contested Saturday evening. Till that moment, our outing had been euphoric. We three had dressed up for the occasion in outfits that combined our notions of contemporary chic and the slightly outrageous. Marky wore low-slung black velvet bell-bottoms, and I'd purchased my first paisley shirt. From a vintage-era champagne-colored nightgown she'd unearthed in one of the Brewster armoires, Mary Jo had crafted a lacy concoction that floated sylph-like around her slim figure, scandalously diaphanous in certain lights, and she'd pinned her dark upswept hair with a camilla blossom whose waxy scent lingered about her temples.

Best, though, was Mary Jo's surprise gift to us: handmade love beads she presented once we loaded into Dad's car. "For my dashing escorts," she said. Where Marky's was a strand of mixed colors, mine had been designed with extra care: polished beads of quartz and amethyst alternating with oblongs of obsidian. "For my special friend," she whispered as she pulled it over my head and kissed me, French-style, on each cheek. With less self-restraint, I might have found myself growing hard at the brush of her pink lips against my skin. Mary Jo smiled at Marky, and Marky smiled at me.

"Jules and Jim" was pure adrenalin, I'd never experienced anything quite like the rush of its camera work, or the sexual charge that bound its three Bohemian protagonists in their doomed love triangle, or the alternation between attraction and ambivalence, desire and self-destruction that, despite the turn-of-the-century setting, seemed of our moment. We were giddy afterwards, the three of us, as we strolled down the sidewalk arm in arm, lighting the Galois cigarettes that Marky provided for the occasion. When we came to an alley bisecting the block, Mary Jo halted, and Marky and I watched in curious suspense as she rubbed her finger into the soot accumulated between the bricks making up the wall and passed it over her upper lip.

"Ah!" Marky immediately recognized the allusion to the film.

"But in that dress you hardly make as convincing a boy as Moreau!"

"I'll show you!" Peeling laughter, Mary Jo knelt facing the alley in runner's position: Marky and I followed suit, intuiting the scene we were about to reenact. And, like Catherine in the film, Mary Jo dashed away before I finished our countdown, lifting her whispery gown waist-high and calling "Catch me!" as she led the way. We emerged, breathless and laughing deliriously, on the adjacent thoroughfare, where passersby jumped aside as if we were alien creatures escaped from an otherworldly zoo.

We stopped for late dinner at the Conga Room, filling the volcano-shaped ashtray with cigarette butts while sipping cocktails topped with diminutive paper umbrellas. Over charred steak and cheap Chianti we dissected Truffaut's masterpiece, Marky explaining the film's cinematic references with the passion of a master. I happily played the role of acolyte; Mary Jo steered a course between, returning us every now and then to the film's subject matter. So while Marky waxed poetic about camera angles, Mary Jo interrupted to say it was unfair of Truffaut to turn Catherine into a love-crazed, suicidal murderer simply because she doesn't choose to be understood.

"You're missing the point," Marky countered. "She's pure libidinal energy, keeping Jules and Jim yearning for more. And no one could have played her better than Moreau!"

"Except Mary Jo," I added, gallantly, fingering my love beads.

We were halfway through a second carafe when Mary Jo excused herself to go to the ladies' room. Marky and I watched her weave, tipsily, through the tables.

"So if Mary Jo is our Catherine, who are *you*, Newt? Hopeless Jules or handsome Jim? Jules, I think, since I'm obviously Jim. Unless"—Marky's eyes narrowed, holding my gaze—"you'd rather play Catherine. You do like playing the cock tease, don't you?"

For a brief moment the thought crossed my mind that I might grow to dislike this Marky —especially when he chose to needle me like this. But the feeling dissipated when he clapped me on the shoulder, declaring me a good sport. He refilled my glass and raised his own.

"To comrades in art, crime, and love!"

By the time Mary Jo returned to the table, Marky and I had resumed our discussion of New Wave cinema with such fervor that it took us several minutes to realize that our companion had gone silent. Marky turned to his sister.

"Something wrong?"

"How unlike you to worry about *me*."

"What is it, *ma petite*?"

"Don't *ma petite* me." She paused, then spoke with slow determination. "I'm not like your precious Catherine, I just need to know."

"What on earth are you talking about?"

"I just need to know," she repeated, stubbornly.

"*As-tu perdu la tête?*" Exasperation rose in Marky's voice.

Mary Jo shot back, looking at Marky as if I weren't there. "You think I'm a fool?"

"*Je ne le crois pas...* no more wine for you."

"*Casse-toi.* Don't you tell me what I can't have."

"Don't make a scene," Marky hissed.

I tried to turn the conversation, get us back on track, recapture the magic we'd shared exiting the theatre, but my efforts fell as flat as the taste of a bottle of Tab opened days before. I wanted to disappear, so much did I feel like an intruder in a private argument to which I feared finding the key. After we paid our bill and walked in awkward silence back to the car, I claimed the back seat, where I curled up and pretended to sleep. Of course I couldn't; my heart was pounding too rapidly. Once or twice the twins exchanged nonsensical, terse words. "How dare you?" from Mary Jo. "*Nothing's* happened," Marky's reply. And later, from Marky, "You and I are okay, Mary Jo, I swear." Her words were slurred. "Why should I believe you?" I pretended to wake up just as we approached Taliaferro Lane at 2 am.

Watching as they drove away, I felt bewildered and confused, as if I had entered an overgrown labyrinth and, like the ill-fated child of a dark fairytale, forgotten to leave a trail of breadcrumbs to retrace my path.

13

BIRTHDAY BLESSINGS

Whatever sibling misunderstanding had marred our excursion seemed to have resolved itself by the time I returned to Mr. Julian's house at the beginning of the week. The twins were back to their normal selves, laughing in unison, completing each other's sentences as they so often did, teasing each other with an easy repartee, and, thankfully, treating me no differently than before. It was almost as if nothing had happened—though, unless I was delusional, I knew *something* had. But since they said nothing about the ugly way that evening had ended, I followed their lead and set about erasing it from the oft-cleansed slate of my conscience.

Soon enough there were other matters to think about. Mr. Julian had asked George Geronimo to set out lunch by the pool after my swimming practice, where Mary Jo joined us. G.G. stood by on duty. Marky was unaccountably missing.

"The sloth can't still be sleeping!" I said to Mary Jo, wringing the last of the water from my hair before I sat down at the table smartly laid out for four.

"He was roaming downstairs like a caged tiger an hour ago, then disappeared. I assumed I'd find him here cheering you on."

"Poof on Marky!" Mr. Julian interrupted. "Eat. We have more important matters to worry about." His voice dropped a stentorian octave. "Something dreadful has occurred!"

Beneath the white fedora Mr. Julian wore to shade his sun-sensitive skin, his countenance verged on the tragic—a look that alarmed me until he informed us of the "dread" at hand: three of his Brewster cousins had decided, with neither provocation nor invitation, to descend on the house to celebrate his birthday this coming weekend, a week in advance of the actual date. On August third Mr. Julian turned sixty-eight. We must brace ourselves, he warned, to withstand this pack of jackals, each waiting to pick his bones the second his corpse was laid to rest.

"That is, if they don't slash each other to death first, trying to claw their way into my good graces." He emitted a chortle that hovered between delighted and malicious. "Oh you'll see. Well, one can't close one's door to Family, but—no, G.G., don't even think of asking B.B. to bake a cake; we'll order one of those nasty concoctions Jenkyns Bakery churns out, Crisco frosting and all." He turned to Mary Jo. "Thank God you and your miscreant brother are staying here—it gives me a *perfect* excuse for putting the lot of 'em up at the Tiptop."

Now, I knew that Rocky Hill didn't have much to offer in the way of classy accommodations for the wayward traveler, but I also knew that the Tiptop Motel, on the rowdiest thoroughfare leading out of town, had been at the bottom of the list ever since Bubba Russell's salvage yard had gone up next door and the no-name tavern across the street had become Franklin County's biker bar of choice. My thoughts were interrupted as Marky dashed through the gap in the hedge and hurried to take his place, wiping beads of sweat from his face as he made his excuses. For once, Mr. Julian was too thrilled plotting his cousins' misery to reprimand Marky for his tardiness.

"And don't you know it'll stick in their craw when they find you Sumners here!" Mr. Julian hooted. "We'll *endure* their humbug for twenty-four hours, then send 'em on their merry way."

Saturday arrived, as did the cousins. I thought that by now I knew everything there was to know about my employer's capacity for withering sarcasm, but witnessing Mr. Julian in action as he entertained his relatives—if "entertain" is the word for such unsubtle torture—was a revelation. Then again, so were his relations, whose behaviors made me think more forgivingly of the foibles of my own kin.

First to rumble up the gravel driveway was a two-car caravan from Newport News bearing the weight of two cousins, Letitia Brewster Maddox and her brother Mason Dixon Brewster, along with all their assorted progeny and grandchildren. Alarmingly vigorous for a short, stout woman, Letitia had the legs and lungs of an Alpine hiker and immediately panted her way into our faces, bearing heavily down on my poor employer—whom G.G. had wheeled to the front terrace to greet the arriving guests—in order to set lipstick roses blossoming on his sere cheeks. All the while she proceeded to remind him of the personages in her all-important entourage: her blandly vicious (so Mr. Julian had forewarned me) husband Rafe, their grown son Willy and his wife Penny, and Willy and Penny's three noisy small children. Willy had a complexion the color and texture of a brick wall, into which had been set the ice-blue Brewster eyes—the difference being that his were as dull as Mr. Julian's were penetrating. Penny, I knew at a glance, was as greedy as her name was impecunious, and their three children were bouncing balls of sugarcoated hyperactivity. I pitied the tired-looking station wagon whose bumpy journey had commenced five hours ago.

Letitia's brother, Mason Dixon Brewster had followed Letitia's clan in his Chevy sedan ("That *can't* be his real name," Mary Jo whispered. "Only in the South," Marky whispered back.) A good old Southern boy who lived in Norfolk where he supervised a naval shipyard, Mason Dixon was a long-time widower and accompanied by his painfully awkward adult daughter Maybelle. What he lacked in his sister Letitia's aggressive push, Mason Dixon recompensed in unctuous sociability. He was so *very* glad to see all of us—though, like Letitia, he too was nonplussed to learn the celebration had been infiltrated by Sumners—nothing made him happier than taking joy in the good health of dear cousin Julian, whose improvement turned Mason Dixon pink as a haunch of ham with delight. While her father purred and praised, Maybelle clung to her black patent leather purse and stared through horn-rimmed glasses at her blunt-toed shoes. I dare say she wished she were anywhere else on earth, and I felt sorry for her. Under more favorable circumstances she might have been the one Brewster arrival worth getting to know.

We were sitting on the gray flagstone terrace off the drawing room, cooling off with iced teas and making small talk when Mr. Julian's third out-of-breath cousin, Wanda Wilmot, arrived in the company of her toady of a husband Wilbur and two of their four children: CindyLou, who smiled sappily as she nursed a croupy six-month old, and SheriAnn, who frowned sullenly and, unlike her sister, sported no wedding band despite the fact she was seven months pregnant and counting. Wanda was clearly flummoxed to discover that Mason Dixon and Letitia had already arrived ("The i-*de*-a! You swore y'all wouldn't git here till two o'clock!" she blurted out before even saying hello—and as it was barely noon, I could only surmise she'd meant to arrive first to cozy up to Cousin Julian). The twins and I quickly nicknamed Wanda *La méchante sorcière* behind her back—and for reasons not only connected to the fact that she dyed her white hair raven black, had a conspicuous wart on her angular nose, and displayed sharp, yellowed eyeteeth when she smiled—if smile is what you call the parting of her pursed lips when she turned her countenance your way. Mr. Julian had alerted us to beware the rivalry between the siblings; though the three pretended to share an equally loving concern in dear Cousin Julian's welfare, Wanda was convinced (apparently not without reason) that Letitia and Mason Dixon had leagued together to convince Mr. Julian their interests outweighed her own. And Wanda was having none of that.

If Wanda the Witch was thrown off stride by her rival-siblings' early arrival, she was even less happy to espy Mary Jo and Marky among the gathered company. "Well, who woulda thought!" she hissed. "I had no i-*de*-a that there was anything, or *anyone*, in our deah state of Virginia of sufficient interest to lure you Sumners *here*, when you could be gallivantin' round Europe on somebody else's dime. I fear poor Rocky Hill don't have much in the way of style to offer up to *your* tastes."

"Speaking of style, aren't they something?" Mr. Julian cooed. "Just look at what their education's done for them! The four of us have been having a *grand* time."

The mention of "four" turned everyone's attention, alas, from the twins to Yours Truly, thwarting my attempt to fade into the furniture.

Wanda the Witch's eagle eye bore down on me. "I suppose you're one of *their* school friends?"

When she found out otherwise—for Mr. Julian lost no time waxing rhapsodic about his discovery of a local "diamond in the rough" who, with a little polishing, might amount to something and who, in the meantime, was proving a *most* invaluable employee—Wanda fixed me with a glare that might have turned me to stone on the spot had I not already seen how hopeless her game was.

"Why Cousin," she protested, "you know that my teenagahs

would have been as happy as the summer is sizzlin' to lend a helpin' hand had you but *asked*!" She exhaled her disappointment noisily. "Poor Dewitt and Little Wanda, they wanted terrible to join us but can't *afford* to take time off from their jobs. So smart, the deah hearts, but Wilbur and I'll count ourselves lucky if we can afford to send 'em to a decent junior college—"

Mr. Julian tittered. "No junior college for Newt here! With a little luck and the right backing, I can see him going Ivy League, all the way to the top!"

Wanda glared at me again. "No handouts for my deah Dewitt and Wanda—every penny they earn they save! CindyLou and SheriAnn" (she nodded at her daughters) "bless their souls, had to work twenty hours a week on their student-aid packages, that is till the Good Lord saw fit to bring CindyLou a fine husband and before SheriAnn" (killing glare) "sinned in the Lord's eye. It's a shame, when you think how far such brilliant children could go if *they* had the opportunity!"

She paused to scowl at me a third time and sighed deeply, an unwise move because it allowed Letitia the opportunity to champion the travails of *her* offspring and the potential of her even more gifted grandchildren. That opened the floodgates, and the conversation that had been struggling to find pleasantries sufficient to keep afloat became a free-for-all, every Brewster jockeying to make sure Cousin Julian comprehended the needy merits of his or her own—merits, it went without saying, that would be enhanced to no end by the security of knowing that their future needs had been assured.

Julian played them like a maestro, all the while provoking their worst fears by showering undue attention on the twins and myself. "No, no, Rafe, don't bother yourself, Newt will wheel my chair into the shade; stand here, Newt, right behind me... why Cousin Letitia, you mixed that drink all wrong, let Mary Jo do it, *that's* a dear!" and even more maliciously, "Maybelle, honey, you look downright pathetic, let handsome Marky take you for a little stroll in the garden, now *that* will lift your spirits!"

The cacophony of competing family claims carried over into the birthday dinner that followed, which I helped G.G. and Sassafras set out buffet-style on the back terrace (no poolside dining for these

Brewsters, I noted with satisfaction). Those claims rose to a fevered pitch as the lightning bugs appeared and G.G. popped the bottles of prosecco that were the one indulgence Mr. Julian had approved for the occasion. And the bubbly uncorked an overflow of birthday toasts—each a more flagrant attempt to outdo the previous encomium—that followed the cutting of the tiered monstrosity of a cake delivered earlier in the day by Jenkyns Bakery, a cake whose ratio of sugar to other ingredients left the Maddox children screaming like banshees as they raced in and out of the house. Shortly after ten o'clock, the relatives, driven quite maudlin by the occasion and even more exhausted by vigorous displays of loving affection for their aging relative, were finally coaxed, not-too-subtly, to take their leave.

"Enough feasting! And enough feasting on *me*, my dearies!" Mr. Julian announced. "My health demands I retire. Now scoot!"

Which reference to "health" would have set off another round of expostulations, had not G.G. immediately rolled Mr. Julian's chair out of the drawing room—where we gathered around the toppled remains of birthday cake—and into the back elevator without further ado. Finding themselves left to the twins and myself, the Brewster clan suddenly discovered the fatigue they shared in common and wasted little time piling into their autos and making their way to the forlorn rooms awaiting them at the Tiptop.

The next morning, when they returned to bid their farewells, Brewsters young and old looked and sounded a little less exuberant than the day before—the dual effect, I surmised, of the Tiptop's notoriously overused bedsprings and the roar of motorbikes being revved all night across the street. A palpable feeling of having been sorely mistreated hung in the air, and it hovered over the pitcher of fresh orange juice Sassafras had prepared and the jelly donuts I'd fetched from Krispy Kreme. In contrast Mr. Julian was positively vivacious, taking miserly relish in his relatives' downcast mood by dispensing an endless stream of advice and well wishes.

I overheard Letitia murmuring, "Poor soul... nobody's enemy but his own," and Mason Dixon's respondent sigh seemed to sum up the general consensus that an elderly relative with a fortune at his fingertips ought not so abuse those very persons who held his best interests foremost in their hearts.

"Poor soul's never been the same since his sister died," Mason Dixon added, sotto voce. "They were so close, ever'body said."

"Too close, if you askin' me," Penny replied. "Plain perverse, the way their mother used to dress 'em up like twins."

"Couldn't a been healthy," Willy, red-faced paragon of good health, sagely agreed.

All the while Wanda the Witch kept shooting particularly steely glances my way, as if I were the upstart inheritor of Mr. Julian's fabled riches. Such thoughts, however, didn't inhibit the bleary-eyed Brewsters' outpouring of affectionate farewells and parting tears once the coffee had been drained to its bitter dregs and the glazed donuts demolished, one and all.

And then they were gone, the three carloads disappearing in a cloud of dust.

14

THE END OF THE SUMMER OF LOVE

In the lull that followed Mr. Julian's birthday, the dog days of summer set upon us with a ferocity unmatched in the annals of Franklin County history. The August sun seemed to have stalled in the listless sky overhead, as if determined to pummel us into utter lassitude. The twins and I lived at the swimming pool. The library project was finished, every book claiming its rightful place in my ordering system; the filing in the basement had been completed. So my duties with Mr. Julian reverted to the simpler tasks of conveying him from room to room, listening to his stories, helping with his correspondence, reading to him when his eyes tired. Since I'd become adept in intuiting his needs in advance, I ended up with even more free time to spend with the twins as we worked to outwit the punishing heat. In the back of my mind lurked the unwelcome knowledge that the twins would be departing in a few weeks. The prospect of returning to my former life filled me with dread.

On Tuesday Mary Jo got it in her head she wanted to have a picnic, somewhere in the country so long as water was nearby. First I thought of Ferry Stone Lake, the resort in Patrick County our family sometimes visited, but the likelihood of its small beach being overrun by sand-kicking toddlers and cranky parents squelched that idea. Then it occurred to me we should take our picnic and swim by the waterfall at Dillard's Crick. The twins would like that—a taste of real Franklin County countryside—though I couldn't picture them fishing for their banquet as Samson and I had done. Then again, they probably couldn't imagine me doing the same either.

Mary Jo joined forces with Sassafras to pack us lunch while Marky and I set off to borrow a car. We entered Dad's dealership just in time to witness the end of an ugly row: a belligerent Hank Atwater hurtling out of the showroom like a human cannonball, screaming

"I QUIT!"

as Dad watched flushed and flummoxed. It turned out that Hank had gotten fresh with a customer; she'd complained to her father, and he'd spoken to Dad.

So Dad had had it out with Hank, not that a confrontation had been his intention. "Me? I wasn't trying to pick a fight, no sir," Dad told us with childlike incredulity. "I just wanted to warn him gentle, like I'd do you boys, about behavin' on the job. Sure, he's the type to take a little license with the gals what take a shine to his kind of charm. What he does on his own is his business. But this here's *my* business, you know, and I can't have him crossing the line with Mr. Syke's daughter." Dad's eyes filled with wonder that anyone would react to his mild remonstrances so vehemently. "But he lashed out like a fury, he did, near to knocked me off my feet! Said some right unkind words about Miss Sykes, then told me he'd been wasting his talents here long enough."

Hank had charged out of Dad's private office, where the two had been talking, into the showroom, and when Dad followed in an attempt to calm him down, Hank tried to pick a fight, swatting away the hand that Dad had extended in a conciliatory gesture and raising his fists, daring Dad to see who the "real man" was. Fortunately, a couple of other employees intervened. Marky and I arrived just after Dad told Hank to take a few days off to cool down, at which point Hank had shot out of the showroom declaring he'd rather quit.

"Just goes to show, boys," Dad said, his mind working overtime to turn this perplexing display of human nature into an edifying moral. "You Never Know!"

With this sage advice ringing in our ears, we left Dad still shaking his head and recanvassing the event with the other employees—who, now that their co-worker fallen from grace, were all too eager to tell the boss what they'd thought all along of that good-for-nothing piece of white trash. As they shared the tales of trespasses they'd hoarded for such an occasion, Marky and I left in a Mustang trade-in to pick up Mary Jo.

A half hour later found the three of us taking a respite from the sun in the limpid green shade dappling the banks of Dillard Crick. Once we finished our lunch—pimento egg salad and pickle relish sandwiches made with thick slices of Sassafras's homemade rye— on the rock overhang where Samson and I had fished, we climbed down to the swimming hole hollowed out by the waterfall. Marky produced the inevitable joint, we got high, and then we took to the water like frisky otters. Marky figured out how to scramble up one of the big boulders to the top of the falls, from which he executed a se- ries of comic dives and cannon balls. Mary Jo paddled to the edge of the bank where footpath met water and reclined in its oozy shallows, dribbling fine bronze-colored silt onto her legs. I zoned out floating on my back. The beat wafting from Mary Jo's transistor radio mingled with the hum of forest insects coming at us from both sides of the stream.

"Look at sis," Marky called, bringing me out of my reverie.

I looked. Mary Jo was now standing on the edge of the bank, her bikini so plastered with silt that she almost looked naked, since its color blended with the rest of her tanned body. She held her hands aloft, and I applauded and whistled at this New Eve, created, I joked, from the good dirt of Franklin County.

"Didn't Eve require Adam's rib?"

So Marky retorted as he dog-paddled towards his sister.

"As if either of you boys is man enough to supply the rib—or should I say bone!"

Marky stepped out of the water, flinging water from his body like a wet mongrel, and joined his sister on the bank. Whispering into her ear with a devilish twinkle in his eye as he moved behind her, he unfastened the top piece of her suit, slipped it off her arms, and tossed it aside. She quickly stooped to the water's edge where, kneeling, she smeared two handfuls of dripping silt onto her otherwise radiantly white breasts, till they too approximated the earthy hue of her bur- nished skin. I floated closer to the bank, shocked and fascinated, and when my butt scraped bottom, I stood up to watch, mere yards away.

Mary Jo had also risen to her feet, hands no longer hiding her breasts. Haughty, proud, she turned her erect body to meet my gaze, looked at me with preternatural calm in the deafening heat.

"Sis *is* beautiful, isn't she?" Marky remained behind Mary Jo, his hands stroking her bare shoulders and arms as he spoke.

"Yes," I answered, wishing I dared to move closer. "You *are.*"

"You may kiss her, if you like," Marky said.

"You may kiss me, if you like," Mary Jo echoed, archly. She paused. "But be forewarned—I have no heart."

"Then I'll save my kisses," I responded, after a beat, though in my thudding heart of hearts kissing her was the least of the things I wanted to do right now. Instead, I flopped back in the water with a noisy splash that broke the tension and hid the excitement that had inflated the front of my surfer shorts.

"Our earnest Newt," Marky said, laughing as he stepped out from behind his sister. "Who's the heartless one now?" Then he and Mary Jo ran, splashing, back into the water to join me in its deeper center.

"Not fair that I'm the only naked one!" Treading water to keep her head above its green surface, Mary Jo held one hand up to display her bikini bottom.

Marky briefly disappeared underwater to wrestle off his trunks, which he threw onto the bank. "Your turn, Newt, or we'll rip 'em off you! *Tous pour un—*"

"—and one for all!" I finished, tossing my suit on shore, as well, and the sexual heat of the moment seemed, if not dissolve, to shift into a more mellow, even chaste, sensuousness. Or so I thought, as we swam naked as jays, flashing white butts as we dove beneath the surface and chased each others' indistinct images, pale yellow in the murky water. Before the long, lazy afternoon was over, filled with the vanity of youth that blinds the soul, we swore to each other that we'd always remain children of nature.

*

We talked about romance, too. Beyond the superficial "Have you had a boyfriend or girlfriend?" questions, and the "Not at the moment" answers that had been sufficient at the beginning of our acquaintance, we now talked, with teenaged profundity, about Love.

Marky—no surprise—took the cynical view.

"One and only one true love? Bullshit. There's no perfect half out there waiting to complete me—or either of you!"

Mary Jo pouted. "Being your twin, I thought I *was* your other half."

We were eating burgers at the Hub when Mary Jo interrupted Marky's diatribe in which he was busily proclaiming "love" nothing but an excuse to cover over the human race's animal urges and curtail his own randy behavior. "As if anyone's stopping you! Newt, you can't imagine the number of girls whose hearts if not hymens my feckless brother has broken."

"You're one to talk!" Marky reminded Mary Jo that she'd wasted six months of the past school year dating the captain of his school's soccer team simply because all the other girls wanted him.

"What happened?" I asked.

"What always happens," Mary Jo said. "He bored me. Brrrr! He left me cold."

Marky turned the spotlight my way. "What about *you*, Naughty-Newtie? Don't you dare try to convince me that Rocky Hill has left you pure of heart!"

I attempted to plead the Fifth rather than confess that my adolescence had thus far been bereft of romance—or sex. We were all virgins—technically, that is, since Marky had done "everything but" with a good half-dozen of his conquests.

We talked, too, about Mr. Julian's romantic past. Family legend was that he'd come back from Manhattan, those many years ago, with a "broken heart," though no one was ever clear who had broken it, or why. He'd led a private life, Mr. Julian, and although the Sumner side of the family assumed it encompassed "irregularities," they never probed. Marky was less circumspect, and less kind. "We can see how *terribly* fond he is of *you*, Newtie-boy!" he minced.

"That's so not funny," I said, annoyed.

Mary Jo, as usual, intervened. "Don't be jealous, brother, just because Uncle prefers Newt's sweet temper to your foul mouth and fouler mind!"

Clearly, the one sustained love in Mr. Julian's life had been his sister Julia, who, to those Sumners old enough to remember, had been a radiant woman with a wit as sharp as her brother's, an independent streak challenged at her opponent's risk, and a passionate devotion to Mr. Julian equaling his own to her. Julia's engagement had crushed her brother, so family lore had it, nearly as much as her tragic death shortly after. Of Mr. Julian's surviving relations, no doubt he favored the Sumner twins because in them he saw a reflection of his sibling bond with Julia.

Musing about love, joking about sex, pondering romance: all these elements added to the August heat a warm sensuality that acted on us like an aphrodisiac. Even unspoken, it was everywhere, hanging in the air we imbibed, in the rays of sun that browned our bodies, in the late-night sessions we spent recumbent on the floor of the third-floor den listening to sultry jazz—an easy-going Eros that was as yet without the urgency that might have broken its spell; instead, fluid, unthreatening, slowly ripening within us so that we shone with an unconscious vitality that made these last weeks together precious.

Sometimes, though, the whisper of discord broke through the Elysian harmony in which we hung suspended.

There was the afternoon Marky joined me as I was reading under the shade of the weeping willow, down by the rush-filled creek at the bottom of the back lawn. I was sitting in the same swing that Samson had repaired mid-summer when Marky appeared at the top of the summit. He caught sight of me, half-shrouded by the drooping branches that swept the ground, and loped down the embankment, hands in his pressed khakis. Always pressed slacks, never jeans and hardly ever shorts, not even on the hottest of days: it was one of his European affectations. "So here's where you've been hiding—*lisez moins, vivez plus!*" Parting the branches, he entered the penumbra of shadow, grabbed Henry Miller from my hand, and gave the swing a vigorous push.

"Careful now, it's broken once this summer already," I grumbled, grabbing the volume back.

"You want to be alone?"

"Nah, it's okay. You bored?"

"Out of my *mind.*"

He wandered out of the tree's protective shade and over to the abandoned icehouse half-buried in the embankment. "Ever been in here?"

"G.G. keeps it locked."

"So the neighborhood kids don't fall down the well? How kind of him." Marky pretended to tug at the entrance. "Why, look what I just happen to have!" He pulled a skeleton key out of his pocket, and, sure enough, it fit the bolt perfectly. The door swung open, revealing the dim gloom of the low stone interior. He motioned to me. "Come take a look."

Curious, I joined him inside, pausing to let my eyes adjust to the dimness. The space seemed miraculously clear of the cobwebs and vermin scuttling out of sight that my fancy expected. A clammy stone floor surrounded the central well, over whose mouth a rusty iron grating had been screwed, and a raised stone ledge, damp with mold, traced the inner circumference of the circular walls. A bucket and pulley contraption dangled over the well, and several iron posts had been drilled into stone walls from which pails of fresh milk and other perishables once hung. I marveled at the coolness.

"Make a wish."

Marky handed me a penny to drop between the iron latticework into the well. His dark bangs brushed against my forehead as we tried to peer down that dark hole. We saw nothing, heard nothing.

Lifting my eyes, I surveyed the low space, its conical ceiling, as one fanciful image after another filled my mind. "Maybe this is what it looks like inside of a prehistoric tumulus. Or a Pueblo spirit house." We sat down on the rim of the well, side by side, hugging our arms against our chests, not ready to abandon the shadowy quiet for the hum of life emanating from the rushy rill beyond the willow tree. "Imagine the elders grouped around these walls, chanting hymns to the dead..."

"Morbid! Let's imagine their lusty rites."

In the dim light filtering through the open door, I could make out the smirk crossing Marky's lips. "You've always got sex on the brain," I accused him.

"Just like any normal American guy."

"*You're* the typical American? Tell me."

Marky tapped a cigarette from the pack in his shirt pocket, offered me one. I declined.

"No, you tell *me*. I can't believe that you've never had a girlfriend.
What's that about?"

"There's nothing to tell. When it happens, it'll happen."

"I don't believe you, Mister Slyboots! You always keep something
to yourself."

"Do not."

"Do so. The quiet ones are the dangerous ones."

I didn't reply.

Marky leaned towards me, opened his mouth, and lazily exhaled
a cloud of smoke that tickled my cheeks like feathers. He drawled, his
patrician voice at once teasing and taunting, "Sure you aren't one of
those fags who gets off"—he blew more smoke into my face—"blowing cock? That what you wished for, when you dropped your penny
in the well?"

Shocked, I took a deep breath and waved the smoke away. Then I
rebounded with the only weapon I had. "Get *those* fags out of my face,
or I'll blow you right out of here."

Marky laughed. "*Touché!* Too smart for your britches, and a smart
aleck on top of it." Even if he was just pulling my leg, it rattled me to
be the butt of his provocations, and it was a relief, when we stepped
outside, to inhale the clean air. "Come on, perv, let's see what Mary
Jo's up to." Marky stepped on his cigarette and carelessly draped his
arm across my shoulders as we ambled up the slope of lawn. Here, in
the sunshine, everything seemed almost normal again.

*

"That's it, one step closer... tilt your hat to the right, Sis. Newt, focus
on the water."

It was late afternoon, the heat wave had not broken, and Marky
was practicing the art of fashion photography poolside, having cajoled Mary Jo and me into serving as his models. I was dressed in a
pair of Marky's immaculately pressed linen trousers and one of his
white shirts, unbuttoned and untucked. Mary Jo wore a strapless sil-

ver sheath, a strand of black pearls, a glamorous broad-brimmed hat, and her trademark Bardot sunglasses. Was it our eighth or ninth costume change? I'd lost count.

"Think of me as David Hemming and cross your arms under your magnificent bosoms á la Redgrave, thaaat's right... Newt, step behind Mary Jo, put your hands on her waist."

"Ooh, Newt, you're *ripe*!"

"I can't help it, it's been hours."

"It's my shirt, and if I don't care, then Miss Prissy-Pants doesn't have any reason to complain. Give me one last sexy pose."

So Marky commanded, and so we obeyed. Unbeknownst to G.G., who was having a laundry day in the basement, Marky had filched three bottles of prosecco left over from Mr. Julian's birthday and a bucket of ice from the kitchen, and we'd just popped the cork on the last bottle. Needless to say, the more we slaked our thirst the more we'd become compliant to Marky's commands. So what if icy bubbly and overexposure to the sun was a sure recipe for a disastrous hangover? At the moment I cared not a whit.

"It's a wrap! Time for the last dregs."

We gathered under the checkered shade of the pergola, where Marky filled our glasses. Mary Jo unzipped her dress and threw it on top of our other discarded outfits. She was wearing her white bikini beneath. Against it, her skin gleamed like polished bronze. We clinked our glasses.

"To the perfect summer!" I saluted the twins.

Marky lifted his glass in the direction of the mansion. "To Uncle Jules for having the foresight to procure your services, thereby making our visit bearable!"

"We couldn't have asked Uncle to provide us a better playmate," Mary Jo teased.

"I'm not your little pet," I protested a bit weakly.

"Yes you are!" Mary Jo leaned in to tickle me in the ribs. "You're the cute baby brother we never had."

"Our cute little sib," Marky echoed.

Putting down his glass, he moved in behind me and joined Mary Jo in tickling me, going for my sweaty armpits.

"Very fragrant, baby brother!" he teased. "Take my shirt off before it disintegrates!"

"Baby? I'll be sixteen in a couple months."

I shucked Marky's shirt, with a pout.

"Little Newt doesn't like being teased." Mary Jo stopped tickling me and reached her hands to my cheeks, pulling my face downward to meet the sparkle in her eyes.

"We stand corrected, there is nothing little about you. In fact you better stop growing before you turn into a giant. Our giant pet!"

So saying, Marky extended his arms around me and towards Mary Jo, drawing the three of us into a hug. Wedged between the two siblings, I closed my eyes and willed myself not to think. We swayed in position, one warm mass.

Then, somehow, our hug became an embrace—or, rather, a series of interlacing embraces as time shuddered to a stop. I opened my eyes and saw Mary Jo gazing up at me, a new look in her sapphire eyes— not quite quizzical, not quite earnest, not quite determined, but part of all of those things as she reached her hands upward and pulled my head down until my lips brushed hers, and then I closed my eyes again, savoring the touch of lip against lip and warm breath commingling and my tongue melting into the moistness of her mouth.

Leaning into the small of my back, exhaling deeply into the damp space between my shoulder blades, Marky whispered, "It's all good."

Mary Jo's fingers were playing up and down my chest, touching my nipples, as her open lips cradled my tongue. Marky's hands closed over mine and carried them to his sister's breasts.

"Touch her," he whispered as he pressed in behind me and reached around to unsnap her top. "Touch her, like this." Marky lips grazed the hairline of my neck. "Isn't she beautiful?"

I was fully erect as my fingers cupped the unexpectedly fulsome softness and felt her nipples come to life under my caress, and as I felt my hardness graze her pelvis, I felt Marky rub his body into mine, his hardness a mirror of my own.

And, then, my tongue and my thoughts lost in the touch of Mary Jo's lips and in the warmth of Marky's body rocking against my own, I felt his hands lower themselves to my waist, wedge themselves between my navel and his sister's bare stomach, and undo my belt buckle. "It's all right," he whispered again, unzipping the linen trousers and freeing my hard-on, "Let sis touch you, too. Like this," and then someone's hand was stroking me.

I shivered, in a torment of ecstasy and half-formed thoughts that ricocheted against the underside of my closed eyelids, when a familiar voice broke the silence.

"Hey, Newt! You back here?"

We looked up, the three of us, frozen in our ecstasy and guilt.

Panting, Samson appeared in the leafy arch cut into the towering hedges that cordoned off the pool from the rest of the gardens. "Mr. Julian says it's an emergenc—"

He stopped, seeing us: stopped as dead in his tracks as we were frozen in our compromising embrace on the opposite side of the pool. Irrationally, I remembered the first time I'd dashed through that hedge and happened on Samson mending the pergola.

His eyes widened, and, swallowing his breath, he forced out his words. "It's really serious, Newt, there's something wrong at your place, you've got to come now." He turned on his heel and disappeared.

15

NEWS BAD AND GOOD

If Samson's sudden appearance at the pool slammed me with a tidal wave of horror and shame, my feelings of guilt only increased when, dashing into the drawing room, I saw a police officer blocking my path. As Mr. Julian and George Geronimo solemnly looked on, Sgt. Collins—the sole female member of Rocky Hill's police force—tersely directed me to the squad car that she'd left running in the driveway, deferring my frantic questions with the minimalist maxim that time would tell.

Looking over my shoulder as I slid into the passenger seat, I saw that Mr. Julian, with the help of his walker and George Geronimo, had miraculously hobbled all the way to the front door in what, for the old man, was record time. The sunlight filtering through the rose and wisteria lattice surreally fractured the bodies of the two men into so many disconnected parts. I thought I caught a glimpse of Mary Jo and Marky's faces floating in the shadowy foyer behind them. Samson was nowhere to be seen, but George Geronimo's grim eyes, to my agitated state of mind, glowered like crimson coals, burning with the same dismay that had lit his son's incredulous stare moments before. That's when I realized that Sgt. Collins had switched on the red strobe light atop the car's roof.

In my dazed state, I wasn't even aware that she had also activated the siren until, turning onto Taliaferro Lane, the sound of our transport was engulfed by the ear-splitting alarm of an ambulance shooting past us. It had just pulled out of our driveway, where two squad cars had screeched to a stop at acute angles. Bizarrely, the blue hood of one jutted onto the lawn, where it had toppled a decorative urn and spilled its magenta petunias onto the grass. A crowd milled in the carport: more officers, my sobbing sister Katie, neighbors. Mrs. Washburn, who lived two doors down, latched onto me as I bounded from the car, tugging me in Katie's direction and enveloping us both in fleshy arms that smelled of Yardley's powder—a group hug that made the one in which I'd just been apprehended seem all the more criminal.

"Your daddy's riding in the ambulance with your mama," she whispered in piteous tones. "Another officer's gone to fetch Jubal, and when he gets here I'll be taking all three of you to the hospital."

Soon enough, I learned what had happened. Mother had been sexually assaulted in our home while we were all away—Katie ringing up groceries at Winn-Dixie, Jubal on an outing with his Scout troop, Dad at work. The crime had occurred little more than an hour before. Struggling to the carport door she had fallen sideways and split her head on the concrete surface. Wedged between side door and automobile, her unconscious body had been spied by a neighbor twenty minutes ago.

Once Mrs. Washburn whisked us to Franklin General, we joined our distraught father watching Mother through a glass window. She was resting in a coma that was half-drug-induced, half-shock. No permanent brain damage, the doctors assured us—but for weeks afterwards Jeanlyn was unable or unwilling to speak more than a few words at a time. Mother stared ahead vacantly, lost in another world, as we sat by her bed and told her how much we loved her. The unspoken—the sheer horror of the rape—hung in the air like an annihilating shroud. "Honey, I love you more than ever," Dad whispered as he sat by her side, stroked her hand and kissed her brow, waiting for her to show any sign of response beyond the irregular tick that came and went at the corner of her lips. "We'll make it through all right, sweetie-pie, don't you worry."

Nothing will ever be right again, I bitterly thought to myself. While my siblings had been away engaged in honorable tasks, what had I been up to? I, who during past summers would have been at home, reading my book sprawled on the Ethan Allen sofa in the privacy of the living room and first in line to answer the doorbell? Suspended between Mary Jo and Marky in greedy spellbound rapture, while Mother—my train of thoughts refused to go further while my face burned with shame. Yet even as self-reproach and self-revulsion overwhelmed me, the nerve endings of my flesh thrilled to the memory of fingers stroking me, and I despised myself even more.

The nightmare continued for weeks. We returned home from the hospital to find our house turned upside down by the local police in search of clues, and we had to sit through interminable interviews with the members of the detective unit assigned to the case. I lost no time voicing my suspicions about Hank Atwater—from his leering comments about Mother to his fisticuffs with Father. But the scoundrel's alibi for his whereabouts the afternoon of the assault were rock-solid. Because the front door, which we usually kept locked, more as a formality than from any fear of robbery, had been open, the detectives speculated that the assailant had entered after ringing the bell; and because the door showed no signs of having been forced, they conjectured that Mother had no reason to fear when she admitted him. Inside, the upended coffee table, the bunched center rug that had skidded to one side of the room, the brass eagle lamp on the floor—all indicated that the living room had been the site of a primary struggle, which had then moved into the kitchen, where the glass storage jars lining the countertop had been swept to the linoleum. No doubt struggling to the side door to summon help, Mother had lacerated her bare feet on the glass shards before falling in the carport. Neither neighbors nor their hired help had noticed or heard anything amiss. The spies that Zithra had sworn, years ago, would be watching my every move had been spectacularly inattentive when Mother's assailant entered and exited the house.

And Mother was no help. She said she couldn't recollect any detail of what had happened, beyond the vaguest memory of walking into the living room to answer the front door—the whole vicious event seemingly cleansed from memory. More disturbingly, her former sense of self had vanished with her memory. The Jeanlyn we all knew—a demon of energy driven by propriety, morality, frustrated ambition, a sharp tongue, and an eagle eye—had disappeared, replaced by a vacant being who, as she physically recovered, went through the motions of daily life, but just barely. At any time of the day we might find her staring blankly into space, and have to remind her that it was time to dress for church, or that it was her usual market day (one of us always accompanied her now), or which brands of cereal to buy. "Yes, of course!" she'd say, giddily, as if surfacing for air, "so silly of me to forget!" before relapsing into distant silence. One afternoon, I came upon her at the kitchen table, going through her art portfolio. Her red eyes brimmed as she shredded the drawings and sketches, one by one. That depressed me most of all.

In the following days I dedicated as much time as possible to staying by Mother's side—taking care of my parents had replaced my job of taking care of Mr. Julian. You see, immediately after the assault, Dad asked me to take a week off from Mr. Brewster's to stay home, ostensibly to look after Jubal but, in reality, to tend to him as well when he wasn't at the hospital and to help prepare the house for Mother's return. Mr. Julian, of course, was obliging. Dad was a wreck, falling apart at the seams, eyes watering at the slightest comment. There's something about your father putting his arms around you and sobbing like a helpless child that's too unnerving for words. Before the week was out, Dad brought Mother home, so I focused my attention on anticipating her needs. In the past, my presence was often apt to irk her more than that of my siblings. It was heartwrenching to see how she now passively suffered my ministrations, acquiescing in a voice almost entirely without affect. "Oh, Newt, sweetie, that's not really necessary," she would say, when I attempted to distract her by placing a family photo album in her lap or by recalling favorite anecdotes. Again she'd lapse into silence, her face impenetrable, except for the way her mouth sometimes curved in a wan smile, a rote but meaningless reflex from a past life as automatic as had once been the carmine lipstick that we now had to remind her to apply.

Toward the end of the week that Mother came home, I received more bad news: this time in the form of a phone call from Mary Jo and Marky. As much as my mind refused to dwell on the last time we were together, as much as I tried to repress the surges of guilt that overcame me when images of our fevered gropings towards an end that I should have anticipated flashed into my brain, I also, perversely, couldn't stop thinking of the twins. For two magical months, they had been my entire world—the closest friends I had ever had, living embodiments of the sophistication and worldliness that I desired for myself—and on some level I still idealized them. Without their daily contact, I felt shorn of part of my self. And, yet, when I tried to imagine facing them in person, I faltered, unable to conceive looking either in the eye without utter shame. How to pick up where we'd left off, when I didn't know whether that meant resuming our intimacy as if *nothing* had happened, or as if *everything* had happened, to change the nature of our friendship since we had last clung together?

The twins' news solved the problem for all of us. Their departure date had been moved up, and they were leaving Virginia by way of Connecticut in three days in order to pay their respects to their Sumner relatives before returning to France. So on the afternoon of the day before their departure, I left Mother in the care of Katie and Dad and traced my path back to the Brewster house. It seemed months, not mere days, since I had buzzed open the gates of the estate, and I again felt myself a stranger entering an unknown land as I walked down the graveled pathway through the elms, as I knocked on the carved front door. Over tea, with Mr. Julian looking on, the three of us said our goodbyes. To be constrained by formalities after so many weeks of intimacy was surreal. Part of me despaired: despite our vows to correspond regularly, despite their promise to return to Virginia next summer, despite talk of my visiting them in Paris someday, the twins sitting before me seemed as distant as a dream within seconds of waking from its seemingly imperishable reality. So part of me despaired; another part of me felt a reprieve at this pending separation.

The week after they left an onslaught of truly disturbing dreams began pervading my sleep, reminding me of the horrors of Mother's rape that, in waking life, I worked overtime to suppress. They occurred randomly but with variations on the same theme: I was at the scene of the crime, in the living room, or the carport, or more bizarre locations, as Mother's assailant fiercely wrestled her to the ground, and sometimes the assailant bore the face of Hank Atwater, once he was a male version of Zithra Jackson Brown, and, once, most terrible of all, he was myself—and when I woke up in a cold sweat the side of my head ached as if I, not Mother, were the one who had crashed onto the concrete pavement. The frequency of the dreams tapered off as the season changed, but their haunting returns always left me feeling debilitated, bereft, and criminally culpable. The detectives' trail of clues ran dry, and the longer the case remained unsolved, the more the authorities lost hope of an arrest and a conviction.

August simmered into September, the school year began, Mr. Julian requested that I come by his house one or two afternoons a week, to keep him company and do whatever tasks he conjured up to make my presence worthwhile. Much as I was reluctant to leave Mother in my after-school hours—for I couldn't rid myself of the insane fear that she might be beset by another assailant the instant I let her out of my sight—those respites were a life-line from my existence at Taliaferro Lane.

Again, I shadowed Mr. Julian's walker, round and round the drawing room, and pushed his chair across the lawn, as the autumn days shortened and the smell of burning leaves again catapulted me down the lanes of memory, some distant but many much more recent. I narrated to him my days at school; reported my independent readings; relayed my progress on the swim team; and—spurred on by him—talked, gingerly at first, then more and more unguardedly, about his wards. All the while, I steeled myself against the embarrassment of running into Samson doing chores on the premises. But it never happened. And much as I was tempted to ask G.G. about his son, I held back—I shuddered to think what Samson might have revealed to his father about that August afternoon he'd appeared through the gap in the shrubbery to summon me home.

Then, in late November, as families across Rocky Hill prepared for Thanksgiving, G.G. rang to say that Mr. Julian had suffered a stroke. Hearing the news, I experienced something akin to the unnerving shock I'd experienced upon learning of Mother's assault, again rendering the world I'd known unfamiliar and myself a cypher.

I visited Mr. Julian in the hospital; I visited him at his home when he returned, half-paralyzed and confined to bed. He cackled his inimitable cackle; drawled out pithy witticisms when he could muster the strength; but his vitality was much diminished, and I was very sad to see it. My services were no longer needed; there was now a full-time nurse who lived in, and between her medical expertise, G.G.'s intimacy with my patron's basic needs, and a physical therapist who visited several mornings a week, Mr. Julian was as well taken care of as could be expected. The twins wired him extravagant flowers and wrote me expressing their dismay, hoping he would be well enough for them to visit next summer—but that, from all I could see, appeared unlikely. Another chapter in my life was slowly but irretrievably closing.

*

When one door closes, however, another sometimes unexpectedly blows open.

The evening of December 8 a cold blast of air swooped down the surrounding mountains and gave Rocky Hill its first real taste of winter, frosting the dining room windows where (this being no ordinary occasion) I sat with my family and Rat, gathered over an overcooked roast of beef, lumpily mashed potatoes, and burnt creamed spinach—my favorite dishes marred by Dad's supervision in the kitchen, which had largely fallen to his command since Mother's trauma. We were celebrating my sixteenth birthday. All in all, it was a dismal affair, despite Dad's heroic attempts to make us laugh and compensate for Mother's disengagement. "You're a Man, now, Son!" Dad declared in tones of surprise, as if I'd somehow left *him* stranded in infancy. "A Man, now, jiminy-jumping-junipers!" He proceeded to entertain us with every coming-of-age joke he could muster before presenting me with a set of keys to the two family cars—I'd passed my driver's licensing test earlier that day. I blew out my sixteen candles, and we had begun slicing the chocolate cake—chocolate had been my birthday preference for as long as I could remember, though this cake, sad to say, came from Jenkyn's Bakery—when the front doorbell rang. We all jumped; it was a vestigial reaction we shared, ever since the determination that Mother's assailant had entered the house through the front entrance when she had answered its bell.

Dad made fun of our jitters, roughing Jubal's towhead and pinching Katie's cheeks as he stood to go and see who waiting outside. "Why, how do ye do, Tom!" we heard his voice boom out moments later. "Step on in! You're just in time for a piece of our Newt's birthday cake. Sixteen candles, yessiree, he's growed up right fast he has."

Dad reappeared, Tom Allbright by his side. The lawyer, briefcase in hand, looked as blandly neutral as ever. "Look what the cat drug in, Jeanlyn, children!"

Tom Allbright paid his respects round the table, with a nod of courtly deference to Mother, who silently accepted his tribute. As always, the appearance of Mr. Allbright stirred old associations. He ceremoniously wished me a happy birthday, which, he hoped, would prove to be a very memorable turning point in my career. I squirmed restlessly, wondering what business had brought him here this evening of all evenings.

Dad must have been wondering the same, for he asked as much once he'd seated Mr. Allbright in front of a thick wedge of cake and glass of cold milk. "So, Tom, what brings you out on a night like this?"

Mr. Allbright put down his fork and looked around the table till his eyes rested on me. "Well, Harold, I've come of a purpose, I have, and coming tonight, on Newt's birthday, is no accident."

My siblings and Rat stared at me, wondering what trouble I'd gotten myself into. I felt guilty as charged without cause. Mother's eyes fixed on the remnants of my birthday cake. Only Dad remained looking at Mr. Allbright, waiting to see what else he had to say.

"In fact, I was commissioned to come on Newt's sixteenth birthday, not a day sooner or a day less. You see, I have some unusual business to transact with the boy." Mr. Allbright paused, delicately, to pat his lips with his napkin. "I should commence, I reckon, by explaining that what I have to say is not of my originating. I merely represent the interests of another party."

"So what's the dude like saying, man, this legal shit makes no sense at all," Rat muttered. Dad scowled as much as he was capable. Rat shrank into his leather jacket. "Sorry dude, I was just asking for some clarity, like turn on the lightbulb!"

Mr. Allbright, model of discretion that he was and years of practice to prove it, ignored the interruption and proceeded in his magisterial monotone. "What I have to say is particularly addressed to Newt and his parents, though I see no reason the rest of you shouldn't be privy to these comments, considering I wasn't explicitly instructed to exclude you. The long and short of it is that I'm the bearer of a communication, a communication of good tidings relative to this boy's future."

Dad turned from Mr. Allbright to peer at me. "What's this about our boy here?"

I blushed to my roots.

"Well you may ask, Harold. Namely this. An anonymous donor has decided the boy deserves a chance—a chance, you see, to realize his potential—and to facilitate that hope, has bestowed on Newt a handsome bit of property, in the form of a trust to be used expressly as follows: to remove the boy from his present circumstances as soon as possible by providing the capital to fund his education in a private academy Up North; upon his successful completion of said academy and acceptance into a top-rung college (mind it must be top-rung), to provide the means to pay all expenses involved in that pursuit; and, finally, upon completing university, to make available a living allowance for six years while the lad sees a bit of the world and determines his future course. This largesse, as you see, great as it may be, has an end, roughly twelve years from the date it commences, and the administering of said trust—left to my supervision—is contingent on Newt's successful completion of each stage of his progress. There it is, in brief: a plan that guarantees your boy a future well beyond any ambitions he might have anticipated by remaining here in Rocky Hill." Having kept to his usual business-like monotone, Mr. Allbright allowed himself the uncharacteristic flourish of a final exclamation. "Yes, There It Is!"

As the meaning of his words dawned on me, I rose from my seat, I vividly remember standing up, and I remember looking around wildly, feeling for all the world like I'd just dismounted from the Tilt-a-Whirl at the county fair and stumbled into the nearby freak show, so dreamlike and distorted did everyone staring at me appear. I caught Mother looking in my direction, a flash of recognition lighting those muted eyes for the first time in four months.

That's when I realized what I'd heard was true, and elation coursed through my veins. My dream was out: my wildest fantasies had become reality, and my heart warmed in gratitude towards Mr. Julian, my poor, crippled, bed-ridden benefactor, for making this momentous turn in my life possible.

As if reading my thoughts, Mr. Allbright continued. "Listen up,

Newt. There are a few conditions you need to attend to, should you accept this offer. The name of the person funding your education remains a strict secret until such time as that person chooses to reveal said identity to you. That could be years, or never, for aught I know. Further, Newt, you are expressly forbidden from making *any* inquiries into, *or* speculating about, *or* in any other way attempting to address that person's identity, at the risk of losing said prospects altogether. If you have suspicions as to the identity of your benefactor, you are to keep your speculations entirely to yourself." Having delivered these admonitions, Mr. Allbright again allowed himself a mild rhetorical flourish. "Discretion, my boy, discretion! Discretion is the key to the making of you!"

"This news is—I can't believe—and on your birthday, too! Let's toast our dear—!!" Dad sputtered, awe in his voice as he grabbed me in a bear hug. My siblings and Rat sat stock still in their seats, watching as intently as if they were witnessing a live broadcast of "Let's Make a Deal" with Tom Allbright filling in for Monty Hall.

"Time enough for congratulations in a moment," Mr. Allbright said. "First, I need to hear from the boy. Listen to me, Newton Seward. I need an answer on three points. One, do you wish to be advanced in life such as your anonymous patron desires? Two, do you accept without question the conditions as I have laid them before you? Three, are you up to the challenge? Take a minute, and think carefully before answering."

I took no time at all. "Yes, sir, I've always dreamt of such a chance, and yes sir, I will abide by Mr.... by his conditions, and, yes, I will make him—*whoever* he is— proud."

The table heaved a collective sigh of relief, and Rat, surprisingly, led the way in a robust cheer of "Hurrah for Newt!" picked up by everyone around the table but Mother as they raised glasses of milk in my direction. Yet even she lifted her glass, a smile on her lips.

Mr. Allbright, meanwhile, continued to hold forth as jovially as his matter-of-fact manner would allow. "Well, now that that's settled, I have some practical matters we need to go over, given my position as administrator of your prospects." Dad suggested we continue the conversation in the living room, its uncomfortable formality being entirely suited to such lofty proceedings. The two men led the way, Katie and Rat trailed after. Jubal openly gaped at me as I made my way around the table and passed Mother, who hadn't taken her eyes off me.

I felt a wave of guilt—what a cad I was, thinking of leaving my mother behind in her condition.

"Come, Mother, join us," I said, reaching forward to help her rise from her chair.

Instead of taking my hands, she grasped one arm with such ferocity that her nails imprinted themselves in my flesh. Pulling me down to her level, she fiercely hissed in my ear "Go!" She looked intently into my eyes. "Don't you dare think of *not* going!"

In the living room, Mr. Allbright removed a sheath of documents from his briefcase, passing identically paper-clipped stacks to Dad and myself. Over the next half hour, we learned that my patron had very definite ideas about the direction my education should take; indeed, a most generous gift had already been proposed to the oldest and best preparatory school in New England, Phipps Academy located north of Boston in Andover, should I meet their criteria for a special-case, mid-year admission. So motivated, the august institution had immediately signaled their willingness to entertain my application at this late date. For reasons I was not to question, I would not live on campus but reside with a local couple, a Mr. and Mrs. Fortinbras whose qualifications to serve *in loco parentis* Mr. Allbright had investigated in depth and which information he would gladly communicate to my parents later. Hearty, and heartfelt, exclamations of relief from Dad signaled that he found this domestic plan quite sane. The hint of a smile continued to dance at the corners of Mother's lips.

There were more details, covering items like clothing, travel allowance, future yields, stipulations on the trust, and the like, but I stopped listening. On the verge of realizing my fondest dreams, I had a short attention span for the financial details that formed the base of my good fortune, nor had I the decency to appreciate the labor of those like Mr. Allbright whose job it was to worry such facts and figures into sufficient ballast to keep my prospects afloat. No, my head was already in the clouds, sailing into imagined futures that all seemed to find harbor, at some indefinite point, in a resplendent Paris flat in the company of those two other beneficiaries of Mr. Julian's care, Mary Jo and Marky Sumner, who returned to their full ideality in my newly vested visions of the years to come. Given his interest in all of us—as their legal guardian and, now, as patron of my advancement—it only made sense that our futures were truly destined to intertwine. The feelings of shame I associated with our poolside tryst had dissolved, at least temporarily, in the heady swell of my good fortunes.

The days that followed passed in a whirlwind: I was indeed admitted to Phipps, and suddenly there was a flurry of activity focused on equipping me properly for my new surrounds; there were visits to be paid to all in Rocky Hill who had watched me grow up over the years and, most especially, to Mr. Julian, with whom I shared my news as if I weren't a word the wiser regarding the identity of the unnamed person for whom I declared I felt the deepest gratitude. I pretended to ignore the telltale twitch of his hoary eyebrows as I conveyed my news, and I pretended not to understand the approving glint in the watery-blue gaze turned on me as he knowingly winked and drawled, "Do well, Newt, do very well, and make us all proud."

Then Christmas was upon us, occasioning a dramatic increase in Dad's declarations of rue at our pending separation, an event that was, for me, far outweighed by the potential that lay at hand; and before I had time to feel proper trepidation about the new realm that I was about to enter and the difficulties that might confront a waif from the backwoods of Virginia, January arrived; and just after sunrise on a wintry, snowy morning two weeks later, I was hugging my parents and siblings goodbye and suddenly feeling unsure of myself, annoyed at the tears welling in my eyes, and I was stepping into Mr. Allbright's cadillac for the long drive north that was to remove me, once and for all, from the past I both loved and resented; and through the rear window I watched the only world I'd ever known disappear into a white haze of thickening snowfall; and so I turned around to face forward, flush with fear and joy, and prepare for the new lands that lay spread before me, as yet unseen and waiting to be discovered, but palpable behind the blanket of still-falling snow and the silence of the stillborn new year.

PART TWO

16

TUMBLING UP AND DOWN

The chill of the stone balustrade had penetrated my thick corduroys and, tingling its way up my spine, made good company with my wintry spirits, long overdue for a thaw. For three months, I had shivered my way through life at Phipps Academy. Today's fitfully gray day carried the palest hint of better weather to come but did little to dissolve the flurry of anxieties that had become a daily part of my prep school existence.

I was waiting in the cemetery behind Samuel Phipps Hall for Miranda Fortinbras, the daughter of my parental surrogates and my best friend in this unfamiliar world. Along with the lunch counter at Doc's, Chapel cemetery was one of our favored rendezvous sites after classes ended and before I had swim-team practice. In the gloomy shadows of its unpatrolled circumference we felt free to share a contraband cigarette, bemoan life in general, and satirize our peers in particular.

Little had I anticipated, heading out the door this morning, the fresh arsenal of humiliations that the hours would lobby my way. En route to campus, I'd had the misfortune of stepping on a frozen pile of dog shit nearing the end of its earthward descent as the layers of snow receded. I thought I'd successfully prized the dung from my boot treads before entering Grant Hall, but the steaming radiators in the long corridor stirred the offending material still attached to my soles to life. Jeers that "Johnny Reb" was bringing in cow paddies from the pasture greeted me as I walked into Mr. Saunders' history class.

As if that weren't enough, after third period I discovered that my locker had been decorated with the centerfold from the "Naked Fat Ladies" calendar. A half-dozen suspiciously nonchalant classmates lingered nearby, offering commentary on my tastes. The hazing of campus greenhorns was both commonplace and unrelenting, but seriously my persecutors took it too far when, in English class, I retrieved my essay from my bag only to discover that someone had glued its pages together. Released from my last class, I mentally rehearsed the tales of woe I would share with Miranda. Three months into my dream of elite education, I still felt an outsider, a misfit, and—more often than not—a failure.

However frosty my mood, in point of fact the last snowfall of March had almost disappeared—only discolored lumps of slush lingered in the shadows of those tombstones unlucky enough to tilt north. When I entered the graveyard, the earth between the haphazard rows of grave markers, frozen solid days before, gave way and emitted soft crunching sounds as the ground-frost caved in on itself. Miranda and I had agreed to rendezvous by Mrs. E.D.E.N. Southworth's tomb. An imposing Victorian edifice erected in memory of the prolific novelist, the tomb was necklaced by the cold balustrade to which my rear was beginning to freeze. Given the gloomy setting and my defeatist mood, I had no idea that, within moments, a piece of heaven would drop into my lap.

"Newt! Guess what arrived in today's mail!"

I looked up. Miranda, cheeks flushed and parka zipped to her chin, crinkly red hair floating behind her like a fiery swarm of bees, stood mere yards away, waving a light blue envelope.

"*Par Avion*—I *knew* you'd strangle me if I didn't bring it with!"

She danced back, an impish smile on her lips and dark eyes sparkling.

I played along by feigning utter disinterest.

"I know how *much* they mean to you, those Fabulous Twins." She pretended to scrutinize the return address. "Who has written this time? Could it be *she*?"

Miranda, who liked me too much to torture me too long and who had every intention of vaulting her way onto the U.S. Women's gymnastics team, backed up a few steps, executed a handspring in my direction, and rising from her landing crouch—perfectly nailed—deposited the coveted envelope in my lap.

And that's how I learned Mary Jo had been admitted to Radcliffe come this fall.

*

If Mary Jo's news planted something like hope in my breast for the first time in a very long time, it also reminded me of how hopeless—how endless—those first months at Phipps had seemed, when humiliations lurked like assassins on the far side of every classroom door. I sometimes think the only thing that saved me from giving up entirely was the knowledge that my roommate "Charleyhorse" Snodgrass had it even worse than me. Despite the shock my poor system underwent as I discovered that the world of education to which I aspired was more intellectually and socially combative than I'd ever dreamt, I could always tell myself that, even at my most pathetic, I wasn't as bad off as Snodgrass, whose habit of bed-wetting on the eve of any test (and there seemed to be one a week) was so inevitable that he took to spending those nights in the claw-footed tub of our cramped third-floor bathroom. Yet even more fearful to Snodgrass was the conviction he'd sleep right through his exams; hence the five clocks with alarms of varying degrees of nerve-racking shrillness distributed throughout our quarters, in the hopes that at least one would jolt him from his damp bower of repose. Too many chill dawns I was the one who, tumbling bleary-eyed from my bed, silenced the cacophony of rings that had failed, after all, to rouse Snodgrass. He certainly wasn't going to get a helping hand from our third roommate, Alexander "Sandy" Dewey III, who'd at most toss a pillow at the nearest alarm and burrow, with bestial growl, more deeply under his bed-covers.

"Easy does it," I'd say as I knelt by the tub and prodded Snodgrass into consciousness, doing my best to ignore the fusty aroma of his sodden wool blankets. "No use cracking your head open." And, really, I didn't mind being Snodgrass's sentinel, since my actions made me feel useful to at least one person in the daunting universe I now inhabited.

Snodgrass's quirks didn't stop here. If he could be counted on to wet himself every night before a test, he could as reliably anticipate being assailed by a scream-inducing charleyhorse in one or the other calf during the actual exam—hence the nickname by which he was known amongst his peers. Sandy's nickname, on the other hand, was "Dewey-Do-It," a moniker based on his purported prowess with the female denizens of the Abigail Adams Academy for Girls, four blocks from Phipps. The active resonances of "Do-It" certainly didn't refer to Dewey's leadership abilities, as he was the most slothful hulk of a human being I'd ever encountered. Yet if many of his male peers at Phipps shared my low opinion of him, a number of Adams girls susceptible to his louche charms seemed of another mind. I cringed pondering the nicknames classmates were inventing for me: "Johnny Reb" sounded in my wake more than once, a reminder of my lowly Southern origins; others, demonstrating the scatological humor endemic to sixteen-year-olds, altered my surname to "Sewer"; but the elongation of "Newt" to "Neuter," uttered by one wit, was worst of all, a mark of distinction I had no wish to bear.

All three of us roomies were special cases, less politely known as Misfits, within the hallowed halls of Phipps Academy. Which is why we lived together under the watch and care of Wim and Mick Fortinbras in their rambling clapboard Victorian house on Walnut Street, a stone's throw from campus. The majority of Phipps students were boarders, housed in ivy-covered dorms named after famous donors, although a minority of day students went home in the evenings. Unlike either of these groups, we three were a category unto ourselves. My placement with the Fortinbrases was one of my benefactor's stipulations, as it appeared that Said Person had determined it would be emotionally healthier and socially easier for me to adjust to my new surroundings living with a surrogate family. Snodgrass had been placed with the Fortinbrases for the obvious reason: his persistent bedwetting would have made him an object of ridicule in a dorm setting, shattering the little self-esteem he had left. Despite his assorted ticks, which were legion, he was as smart as they came. Moreover—guaranteeing his admission to Phipps—he was the grandson of one of the Academy's most beloved former headmasters.

Dewey-Do-It arrived at Phipps the prior year under a special dispensation. He had already been ejected from two boarding schools because of violent behavior, as well as a pyromaniacal streak: a mysterious fire at the home of a teacher who had caught him plagiarizing an essay on "Our Town" had precipitated his departure from his last school. Much as I hate to admit it, he didn't copy the essay because he was dumb but because he could give a shit. He wasn't as whipsmart as

Snodgrass but beneath his apeish habits lurked a frighteningly cool, calculating brain. His wealthy family used every bit of leverage they had remaining to have Dewey admitted to Phipps on a probationary basis. One of the administration's stipulations was that he board off-campus in a "nurturing" situation where his fiery tendencies could be closely monitored—and where the school's residence halls wouldn't be subject to increased fire insurance premiums. Having (so to speak) burnt his bridges behind him, Dewey's violent streak seemed to diminish under the watch of the Fortinbrases, aggression against classmates and teachers replaced by his determination to conquer as many of the female sex as possible.

The Fortinbrases were nothing if not nurturing, albeit haphazardly so, happy to make room in their lively, noisy household for Phippsian strays who didn't otherwise fit the institutional model; so they'd been doing for years, merrily integrating into their family up to three boarders who resided in the drafty attic bedroom on the third floor, its three dormered windows outfitted with identically battered desks. The fourth, north-facing dormer—iciest of all—accommodated the bathroom where Snodgrass all too often spent the night.

It quickly became apparent I'd merely traded the neurotic repressions of my birth family for the more outgoing eccentricities of the Fortinbras clan. Mr. Wim Fortinbras, whose stock hailed from Denmark, was a hoary-headed legend at Phipps, where he'd taught World History to generations of students in an oratory style at once garrulous and visionary. Under his wing, we three Misfits gained a certain, albeit incomplete, immunity from the worst taunts of our peers "up the hill," as the locals called the campus. Mr. Fortinbras was in his mid-sixties when I arrived in Andover; Mick, his second wife, twenty years younger. When his first wife died on the eve of Eisenhower's inauguration, Wim had confounded campus wisdom—which forecast the widower's remarriage to a certain Miss Peggy Sprinkle who'd worked in the President's office as long as Wim had taught at Phipps—with a double whammy: first by taking a teaching leave and departing to Jamaica; second, by returning with a new bride, Mick, clearly younger than he and just as clearly a woman of mixed race (her mother was Afro-Jamaican, her father Scottish).

If anyone in the tight-lipped but liberal-minded town of Andover was flummoxed by this new faculty wife's difference, they were
forced to hold their tongue. "Forced" was the operative term, because
the new Mrs. Fortinbras was an enthusiast of multiple causes and a
dervish of aggressively friendly energy who refused to be taken on
anything but her own terms. She soon ensconced herself in so many
community activities and causes—tutoring wayward children in art
appreciation, inaugurating the town's first Scoop That Poop campaign
(which, obviously, hadn't prevented my clumsy feet from stepping in
same), championing a shelter for battered women—that she became
as hallowed a fixture in Andover's civic life as her husband was in the
classroom up the hill. All the while she managed to fulfill the duties
of faculty wife, appearing at Wim's side at the appropriate assemblies
and award ceremonies, entertaining faculty, and haphazardly dispensing maternal warmth to the boys who wandered within her sphere.

Wim had two sons by his first marriage. The elder, clean-cut Larry,
had won the declamation prize in Latin during his student days at
Phipps, a feat inscribed on a plaque hanging in the stairwell; now in
his late thirties, he worked for an international finance corporation in
France. Early on Larry's younger brother, dopehead Andy, had manifested a willfully non-Phippsian aptitude, barely squeaking through
Andover High. Affable and unflappable, Andy still lived at home
but kept his own hours and company, alternating shifts at Littleton's
Hardware and a clerking job at the Andover Spa. Remarrying, Wim
became a father once more. Betwixt and between all her charitable
causes, Mick carried four children to term, to whose needs she attended in the scattershot way she juggled her multiple good works:
one project left unfinished as a new cause was taken up, chaos forever
on the brink of upending progress. But plowing forward with the best
of intentions and an ability to laugh merrily when matters got too far
out of hand, Mick pulled through with the sheer force of good will
and unending drive.

Of Mick and Wim's four progeny, two were truly precocious.
Fifteen-year-old Miranda—who quickly became my best friend and
confidant—wore her mother's Afro-Scots ancestry in a fierce mane of
kinky red hair and a confidence that encompassed all the brave new

worlds of her Shakespearean namesake. A first-year student at Abigail Adams, she'd read Mary Wollstonecraft's *The Vindication of Women* as a pre-teen, devoured the essay version of Kate Millett's "Sexual Politics" before it appeared in book form, and deeply felt the inequity of her exclusion from all-male Phipps.

"Sure, we take *Classes*," she'd hiss when we'd meet at the soda fountain at Doc's for shaved vanilla cokes. She flipped through my notebooks with envy. "Abby Adams's all about *Class*, if you hadn't noticed, training us to be *Ladies*."

When she wasn't busy reading the lives of famous women, Miranda practiced gymnastics for hours on end, as she was determined to tumble her five-foot frame to Olympian glory, after which she envisioned a B.A. in political science at the University of Pennsylvania, a law degree from Georgetown, and a run for the State Legislature. The other frighteningly precocious Fortinbras was Kirby, a ten-year-old rocket scientist-in-the-making whose chemistry lab in the basement exerted, I feared, an alarming fascination on Dewey, whose propensity for combustibles was perhaps not entirely quelled by his prior evictions.

Rounding out Mick and Wim's brood were two urchins, one five (Daisy) and one just out of diapers (Lee), whose boisterous screams augured oratorical skills of bellicose intensity. You'd think a house filled with so many people would be enough, but "too much" wasn't a concept Wim or Mick understood, and in addition to their progeny, their third-floor boarders, and a series of live-in nannies (at present Britney from Britain, whose bedroom in the basement stood perilously close to Kirby's lab), the house was always packed with houseguests and droppers-by: eager acolytes swallowing words of wisdom at Wim's feet; battered wives from Mick's halfway house; Andy's townie friends (who tended to congregate, weather permitting, on a screened side porch hidden by overgrown boxwoods, where they felt most comfortable chugging their brews); chatty colleagues and nosey neighbors; and, not least, the ever-rotating crew of hired help and repairmen, from maids and cooks to gardeners and plumbers, who kept the old house groaning along.

Everyone tumbled over everyone else, bounding upstairs and

downstairs, slamming in and out of doors, dodging Frisbees and fretful dogs in the front yard and overturned trikes and wet diapers flapping on the clothesline in the back. Yet, miracle of miracles, in the midst of this mayhem the Fortinbrases enforced quiet times when the paterfamilias would retreat to his office to prepare class and Miranda, Kirby, and we three boarders would curl up with our books to do our homework. And the third floor, off-limits to everyone else, was a haven for us Phipps Misfits as we crammed into the wee hours.

Sunrise followed those late-night study sessions all too quickly, for, with or without the benefit of Snodgrass's five alarm clocks, we had to rise at the crack of dawn to attend compulsory chapel. From which, spiritually fortified, I'd step out into another stressful day filled with expectations that weighed on my shoulders like a ticking time bomb. For Phipps Academy exuded ungodly achievement to a fault. You couldn't avoid it, it was part of the burnished atmosphere we lived and breathed, inseparable from the patina of tradition, history, and privilege warming the Colonial and Georgian brick facades that rose proudly on the hill above town. So I felt, from the moment Mr. Allbright walked me through the wrought-iron gates of the campus's entrance and across the snow-covered Great Lawn for my initiatory interview with the Headmaster, in whose antechamber I found myself stared down upon by an original Stuart Gilbert: a purse-lipped George Washington who eyed me with a disdain that overlooked the fact that he was every bit as much a displaced Virginian in these environs as myself. So I felt, during our First Assembly when I learned that two of the legacy boarders in my class were sons of U.S. senators, their dads rumored to be contenders for the vice-presidential nomination in the not too distant future. So I felt, time and again, till I began to suspect that that the school's motto, *Non sibi* ("not for thyself"), might hold a secret message: Phipps was not for me, I was shamefully out of my league and would never measure up, either in status or in brains.

If this aura of privilege and history weren't enough to shake the confidence of a raw sixteen-year-old newly arrived from the Virginian backwoods, the overwhelming aura of academic intensity tipped the scales my agonizing first month in residence. As a "lower" entering mid-year, I had to play catch-up in classes that had been ongoing since September, and I felt stupid for the first time in my life. At such moments I'd recall Mr. Allbright's parting words, as he reminded me that my benefactor would be querying him for reports of my progress. "Of course you'll go wrong somehow, but that's no fault of mine," he proclaimed jovially as he slapped me, man to man, on the back; and within weeks I felt I'd gone wrong with depressing rapidity. The pressure to succeed that hung in the air as densely as an arctic blizzard seemed to turn my peers—even the lazy ones—into formidable competitors. No wonder I found myself ready to pack my bags after many a torturous winter's day, floundering through snowdrifts of despair from which only the worse woes of Snodgrass lifted me.

To make matters even more trying, my benefactor had decided, for the good of my soul, or to remind me that nothing in this world comes free, that I be admitted on a work-study basis, just like the scholarship boys whose parents couldn't afford to pay full tuition. I dutifully filled out forms at the Office of Self-Help (so it was euphemistically called), hoping my experience organizing Mr. Julian's book collection would recommend me for a library position, where between stamping date-due slips and shelving books I might chip away at my daily assignments. Wrong. I groaned when I learned I'd been assigned to serve at the senior teas and Saturday socials that followed sporting events. I couldn't imagine anything more demeaning, till I learned about the even less fortunate scholarship boys who reported to kitchen duty at six in the morning. At least I got to wear a tie and jacket and stand at attention in mahogany-paneled rooms filled with the aroma of freshly baked sugar cookies decorated with sprinkles in the school's colors, instead of fishing grease-covered dishes from vats of tepid gray water. Unless I committed an egregious faux pas, a plebe like me remained as invisible as the worn designs in the Turkish carpets on which the seniors unthinkingly trod as they congratulated each other on their self-importance.

Of course, the occasional faux pas occurred, making me feel as unsophisticated as the small-town boy I was. At the Dennings' senior tea I was peremptorily summoned by the housekeeper—a post-war Austrian immigrant in whose presence even her employers cow-ered—to fetch more plates for the overflow crowd wolfing down the cook's savories.

"Sandwich plates!" she hissed. "Off with you! *Beeile dich!*"

Dashing to the pantry, I found myself standing in a panic before multiple sets of fine china in the glass-faced cabinetry. Yes, I remembered the correct china pattern, but how was I to distinguish sandwich from luncheon, dessert, fruit, and bread plates—all of which seemed to differ in size by such miniscule degrees that none seemed identical to those onto which I'd just been plunking mini quiches and finger sandwiches. Nothing in Mr. Julian's lessons in etiquette had prepared me for this crisis.

At that moment Mrs. Denning popped her head into the pantry. She was one of the younger faculty wives, almost as new at this game as myself, and she looked at me conspiratorially. "Do you even *know* what are you looking for?"

I explained my dilemma, and as Mrs. Denning had lately committed her place settings to memory—fearful of otherwise dismaying the housekeeper, who had been attached to the house for as many decades as Mrs. Denning was old—the matter was soon remedied. Over the course of the semester, I came to feel a kinship with the faculty wives who, like Mrs. Denning, found it part of their prescribed duty to host weekly teas. Mick was one of the few exempt from this servitude. When I innocently asked her how she'd escaped this duty, her face brightened with an arch smile.

"Oh, Newt, honey. Just how unenlightened would it look to have the single biracial faculty wife dispensing tea to snotty-nosed white boys! Phipps is smarter than that!" Camaraderie with faculty wives notwithstanding, the upshot of being a lowly work-study boy meant six less hours a week to burrow into my books—and in those first months, panicking at my unspectacular marks, every hour counted. But panic and despair weren't all I experienced that first frozen winter up north. Not even the trauma of flailing in the academic sphere that had hitherto been my one sure area of competence could blot out those moments when I lifted my head from my books, and, with a rush of adrenalin, registered the wonder of my new environs. After all, I was living out a dream that had occupied me for as long as

I could remember, and it was a dream so filled with vivid first impressions and piercing sensations that I knew it wasn't a dream at all: the savory smell of Yankee pot-roast simmering in steamy kitchens; the low stone walls surrounding white clapboard houses; the morning my hair, damp from the shower, hardened into icicles that threatened to break off, follicles and all, when I left the house hatless; the discovery of the Edward Hoppers in the Bullhorn Gallery on campus, whose calm helped me forget the red ink bleeding from the margins of my English compositions; the staccato rhythm of New England accents, so different from the syrupy diphthongs of the South; the white fog that descended over campus at night and clung to the tree branches till late morning, as if trying to lift the Academy to its proper home in the heavens.

And, of course, Chapel cemetery behind Samuel Phipps, conjoining the youthful living and the long dead in ironic proximity, where Mrs. E.D.E.N. Southworth's ghost became the unlikely witness to the revelation of Mary Jo Sumner's imminent arrival.

*

"So is your heart leaping in ecstasy?" Miranda raised her eyebrows as she sat down beside me. "I trust this means I'll get a glimpse of the Princess herself. I promise I won't hold it against her when she joins a sorority, gets pinned by a Crimson Cabot, and breaks your tender heart!"

To tell the truth, Miranda wasn't so very far off. My tender heart *was* throbbing, in a strange elixir of trepidation and ecstasy. Time and distance—to say nothing of loneliness—had worked miracles in displacing my guilty recollections of that unguarded moment by Mr. Julian's pool, restoring Mary Jo and Marky to their former status as near-perfect beings in my imagination. Over the past months Miranda had listened patiently to my earnest attempts to explain how I felt that I had come to life in the presence of the twins, how deeply my aspirations responded to their savoir faire, their cool cosmopolitanism, their aura of privilege.

So, yes, my heart leapt in joy to learn Mary Jo would soon be living a heart's beat away. But with the knowledge of such proximity returned those other, less easily classified sensations that filled me with shudders of fear and excitement: memories of Mary Jo's lips brushing my own, the pressure of our tongues parting each others' lips, the sudden swell of her nipples in my hands, the electric jolt as Marky reached around me, my erection straining toward the fingers that stroked me—sensations that collapsed before the sting of recalling that they had occurred at the very moment my mother was being assailed.

"What are you thinking?" Miranda gazed at me. As close as we were, these were not thoughts I was ready to share. "I thought you'd be overjoyed!"

"Believe me, I am."

Yet as I spoke, my mind's eye froze upon that moment at the pool. If only we could begin again, as if it had never happened. But that was impossible, and if I had to confront one of the twins in the flesh first, I was obscurely glad that it was Mary Jo.

17

EXTRACURRICULAR

It's a truth well acknowledged that New Englanders are more proudly reserved than the garrulous Virginians among whom I'd spent my childhood, wasting no time in small talk for its own sake. But beneath the thin-lipped faces of the adults I daily encountered dwelt Yankee souls steeped in passionate convictions that, once agitated, ran as deep and fierce as any emotions I'd known down South.

This I learned first-hand from living with the Fortinbrases, for passionate convictions—especially beliefs espousing "the common good"—were a way of life for the family and their friends. That long first winter, as I struggled with my contradictory feelings of yearning to belong but feeling myself an interloper, the family's profound engagement with world events occasionally pierced my cocoon of misery and opened me to realms outside my petty concerns. Watching the evening news with the Fortinbrases, then watching them seriously discuss what we'd seen, and I mean really *talk* about it, was an education as transformative as the one I was receiving up the hill. The world was shifting in 1968, old paradigms falling by the minute as Wim—ever the history teacher—was fond of proclaiming.

"Newt, do you realize how fortunate you are to be a young person *right now?*"

We'd been discussing the sit-in by black students at a Woolworth lunch counter in North Carolina—an event I would never have imagined transpiring in the South I knew even a year ago. What did G.G. think of these events? Was Samson cheering these youth on?

Again Wim reminded me to read Thomas Kuhn. "We're living through a genuine paradigm shift: history at a fork. Which road will we take? Multiple outcomes are possible—and it's up to kids like you to create the right one."

Miranda torpedoed past us. "Earth to Dad, Earth to Dad!"

I'd barely settled into Andover when the Tet Offensive began. I wasn't sure what Mick and Wim meant when they darkly pronounced a new horror had been born. Despite its ubiquity in the headlines, Vietnam had existed as an abstraction to me. But Wim pulled out old maps, patiently explained the history of Indochina and the onus of French colonialism, showed me it was in my interest to care. So I was ready to pay attention when our religion teacher, Mr. Witherspoon (religion being a required course at Phipps), put aside the day's assignment and asked us to react to Eddie Adams' notorious photograph of an SVA officer pulling the trigger against the head of a VC suspect—a man whose slightly askew face captured the very instant of life-terminating impact, gun recoiling and captive's eyes saying, in the last millisecond in which they could express anything, a mute *I am I am I was.*

I remember, too, the chill that traveled down my spine that late February evening when Walter Cronkite ended his newscast with the declaration that the war was no longer winnable. Someone in the room added, "the war at home's just beginning." I remember listening one night as Andy's townie friends argued with moral probity what to do if a lottery were instated ("Not if," Andy interjected. "*When*"). And I remember Mick breaking down in tears at the news of Martin Luther King's assassination, then channeling her grief and rage into a memorial tribute held on Andover Commons that combined the choirs of five local churches. That spring was the season of assassinations and would-be assassinations—King, Bobby Kennedy, Andy Warhol—and it was a semester filled with news of student uprisings, such that it sometimes seemed, when I emerged from my self-involved worries and looked outside of myself, that the world was teetering on a precipice.

The most visceral incursion of politics into my consciousness arrived from abroad. Shortly after I received Mary Jo's news that she couldn't wait to meet me on Harvard Square in the fall, Marky wrote to say that he'd been admitted to the Institut des hautes études cinématographiques. But that was two weeks before the events that came to be known as the French May occurred, events that radically transformed Marky and his ambitions. Marky kept me apprised of the growing tumult in Paris with a series of cryptic messages scribbled on postcards that inevitably arrived after the fact. Thus I learned, long after reading about the event in the papers, that he had been present on May 6 when 20,000 students and professors marched to protest the police invasion of the Sorbonne:

I'VE BEEN GASSED, NEWTIE,
DO YOU BELIEVE IT, **GASSED**!
BY THOSE **FASCIST** PIGS!

Another card, with a black-and-white long shot of the Champs-Élysées, dated May 7, telegraphed in shorthand:

BANNER AT TRIOMPHE TODAY:
La poésie est dans la rue.

And another card, featuring Catherine Deneuve in guerilla uniform:

REVOLUTION IS UNBELIEVABLE
BECAUSE IT'S **REAL**!

The Marky I'd known last summer would have been thoroughly scandalized that the Cannes Film Festival had been cancelled because of the events of May; the reborn Marky of the Student Spring said it served the Establishment right. That, alone, spoke worlds of the changes besetting Marky.

Initially Marky skipped school to be part of the mobs amassing on the Left Bank that May. A few days later, as workers across the nation went on strike, the school administration called for a week's hiatus from classes as a million strong amassed on May 13. Mary Jo chose to travel to London with some girlfriends to visit museums and shop at Harrods. Marky, *au contraire*, marched and ended up in the emergency room at Hospital Hôtel Dieu with a broken leg. Not, to his chagrin, because he'd been brutalized by *les flics*, but because he'd taken a hard fall from a window ledge onto which he'd hoisted himself to photograph the crowds surging through Rue Jacob. Being fettered by a plaster cast for six weeks curbed Marky's participation in the heady events unfolding on the streets, but his outward immobility didn't quell the political and moral transformation occurring within.

Bits I heard from Marky, albeit never too coherently given the exclamatory nature of his postcards, and bits I gleaned from Mary Jo, exasperated by her sibling's revolutionary fervor: the gist was that he had fallen in with new friends—one a disillusioned ex-doctoral student in philosophy who invited him to join a Maoist study group, another the founder of a Leftist film collective who, as Marky wrote me, "actually *met* Godard!!!"—and under their influence he had come to believe that enrolling in the Institute, or any other fascist educational system, was unconscionable.

"Especially when the SYSTEM's getting ready to explode!" Marky scribbled in one of his posted notes. He wanted to be making a difference, he wanted to engage first-hand in the sphere where art and activism were allies; it was his duty, his life's calling, to learn to "unmake" cinema, to free it from the shackles of tradition, so that it might speak in new idioms and new images to the political exigencies of the moment.

"He acts like they're gods," Mary Jo wrote me of his newfound friends. "I beg you to talk some sense into our dear Marky Joe. He'll listen to *you.*"

My attempt to oblige Mary Jo didn't have the desired effect, however, beyond the teasing postcard (image: a communist flag hoisted in front of the Panthéon) that Marky fired back.

DEAR MISTER-INTELLECTUAL-WHO-THINKS
HE'S-**HOT-SHITE**-NOW-THAT-HE'S
PHIBBING-HIS-WAY-THRO-LIFE:
**FUCKETH
OFF!**

While Marky's political conversion increasingly distanced him from the academic world that I had entered, I found myself undergoing my own modest sea-change: contrary to the despair that had colored my first three months at Phipps, I was beginning at last to feel, ever so tentatively, that I might emerge to see the light of day.

Was there one turning point? Probably not, but the first time I caught myself thinking "you might just pull through" occurred in early April, after a home swim meet and owing to a conversation with my coach Pastor Pete (so he encouraged us to call him, for in this world where our instructors wore multiple caps, he also served as associate chaplain). I'd been sitting on the sidelines with the other lowers on the team, cheering on our squad as the over-chlorinated water slapped the cracked blue tiles of the pool in the old Brent Peterson building. I hadn't been slated for any individual events or relays beyond the exhibition runs, nor had I expected to be as rookie member of the squad.

So I was surprised when Pastor Pete waved me over to tell me I was substituting in the 200 butterfly and the 400 mixed medley because Jacob Mendelsohn had a leg cramp, and besides it was time for me to show my stuff. I don't know what got into me as I parted the waves with a burst of pent-up energy that surprised me as much as it did my teammates, placing first in the butterfly and pushing the medley to its best time all season. Post-game, as we boys were filing out of the locker room that no amount of scrubbing could make smell less of sweat and piss, Pastor Pete motioned me into his cubby hole of an office next to the Cage where we tossed our sodden towels. Pastor Pete sported a legendary white beard whose lower fringe he'd just caught in the zipper of his winter parka. Finally liberating his whiskers, he looked up, cheeks ruddy as Santa Claus. "Those were the races I was hoping to see. Had a hunch that catching you off-guard might do the trick. You've been holding back, but I knew you had it in you."

I shrugged, embarrassed yet pleased.

"I can only imagine how tough it's been starting midyear. You can always talk to me if you need a friendly ear. You've got potential, son."

Pastor Pete acted as unofficial mentor to half the boys on campus, and when he leaned forward to squeeze my shoulders, I realized why—all of a sudden I wanted nothing more than to confess every misery, every mishap, I'd undergone since arriving in Andover. I settled for nodding appreciatively.

"What happened out there today?" He motioned me to walk with him as we followed the last stragglers out of the locker room. "Aside from the fact I gave you a chance to race, what made the difference?"

As he paused to turn off the lights and lock the door, I realized that I *was* feeling differently, and all because the day before in Latin III Dr. Vance singled out an assignment I'd written, declaring to the class that my translation was the only one to respond to the poetry of the language, not just the grammar and mechanics. After class he'd encouraged me to look more deeply into Classics, mentioned that I might want to start Greek in the fall. That was all I needed, one positive stroke. In the pool I hadn't been desperately swimming for my survival; I had been swimming, only I hadn't realized it, with ambition.

However small the precipitating cause, I turned a corner. The news that Mary Jo was bound for New England filled my lungs with a buoyancy that vied with the spring breezes warming the quad as the hours of daylight grew longer. Grades of C were becoming Bs, then B pluses. I began to master the art of sines and cosines, rather than allow them to master me. I once again dared to entertain hopes of a respectable future at Phipps and beyond, and I confided some of my aspirations to Miranda. Although the pranks played on me didn't cease altogether, I at least felt included in the mischief when I was invited to join a half dozen other boys rolling the English tutor's front yard with toilet paper. Tim Brotherson asked if I were interested in signing up for Drama Club. When finals period arrived, Snodgrass and I toted our books outdoors, apple blossom petals dancing across our notes as we worked out mathematical formulas.

I was, in a word, beginning to tumble up in the world, and my change of attitude was enough to make Mick announce one May afternoon, "Well now, Newt! I'm going to miss you this summer if I may say so!" We were seated at the dining room table, where I was helping address invitations to the Andover Citizens for McCarthy Political Action Group. Mick, of course, was its founder.

"You've become quite a member of the family, you have. What are we going to do without you this summer?"

And what am I going to do in Rocky Hill except go stir-crazy, I was asking myself when Mick piped up again. "Maybe we can find a way to keep you here—provided you'd like to."

I was, to say the least, thrilled with the possibility. Mick continued to think outloud. "You know, Britney" (that was the younger childrens' nanny) "is planning a month's vacation in August. And dear oh me I've too much on my plate this summer to *begin* to think of getting on without some help with the toddlers, and they rather seem to like you already, and Andy might put in a word for you for some part-time hours at the Spa..."

Without any effort on my part, my next three months were thus arranged quite to my liking. Once exams ended, I'd travel home for a two-week visit—where my biggest hurdle would be to convince the family that it was to my educational advantage to spend the summer in New England—and upon my return, I would begin clerking at the Andover Spa, working the early evening to one a.m. shift three or four times a week; come late July, I'd add to these duties the daytime job of caretaking the younger Fortinbrases. I wasn't convinced that ministering to the needs of a sniveling two-year-old and a sassy five-year-old was my forte. But then again I'd gotten in some good practice at the opposing end of the age spectrum with Mr. Julian, so perhaps my new employment would be a change in degree, not kind. Miranda, elated at the thought of keeping me in her orbit all summer, promised she'd help with the younger siblings when she wasn't busy tumbling through gymnastics practice, and she vowed she'd show me wicked good times on my days off.

18

A SERIES OF SURPRISES

Sun-dappled New England farms giving way to Manhattan sky-scrapers, then the industrial suburbs of the mid-Atlantic corridor yielding to the rolling blue hills of Virginia as evening descended: the shifting landscapes reeling past the smudged windows of the trains that bore me home put me in the mood to ponder the transitions that I, too, had undergone since January. When I arrived at the Roanoke terminal where Dad and Jubal were meeting me for the final hour's drive home, I couldn't help but feel as if I had re-entered a backwater where time, like the train screeching to a standstill, had stopped. At least I was moving forward, I congratulated myself.

Naive me for presuming I was the only person capable of undergoing change.

Stepping onto the passenger platform, smartly dressed in school blazer with Naugahyde suitcase in hand, I scarcely recognized the tall doppelganger approaching me with a gawky gait and gawkier grin. Jubal had grown a half-foot in my absence, the baby fat that had so fretted Mother melting away in the process. It was a shock to see my own features reflected in his face—resemblances I'd never noticed before. Then my dad—emerging from the men's john—trotted forward with a broad grin on his guileless face, still damp from the water he'd just splashed on it, outstretched hands transforming into a bear hug, and I was relieved that he, at least, looked and sounded the same as ever.

That was before we'd loaded my suitcase in the trunk of the new Fairlaine he'd driven off the lot. On the misty ridge rising beyond the train depot, the spotlit façade of the Roanoke Hotel floated suspended in the night sky. Thoughts of last summer's foray into the jazz club on its basement floor surfaced, only to be disrupted by noisy throat-clearings from Dad, his usual signal that he had something important to impart but didn't know how or where to begin.

"You okay, Dad?"

Just a tickle in his throat, he explained. Jubal took up the slack by entertaining me with gossip about the group of Hill High seniors who'd been caught smuggling a bottle of Boone's Farm into Christ+Cross+Crest, a Baptist family retreat in the mountains. But when Dad started clearing his throat yet again, Jubal and I knew well enough to stop yakking and wait.

"Mother," he said, fixing his eyes on the road ahead. "We should talk about Mother."

I looked at him in concern. During my most recent Sunday night calls home, Mother seemed magically to have returned to the world of the living.

"What's wrong, Dad?"

Dad cleared his throat again. "It ain't exactly what's *wrong*," he said with a sigh, "but what's *right*." Jeanlyn, he agreed, was nearly back to normal. Although she still didn't recollect a thing that had happened to her that dreadful day last August, she was once again as sharp as tacks, as busy as a hornet, and as fit to fly off in high-velocity rampages against any offending Seward as ever.

"Home Sweet Home," Jubal said from the back seat. His irony was new to me.

"Well," Dad said slowly, "by all rights it *should* be the best news in the world." He cleared his throat again, fiddled with the windshield wipers on the pretense of cleansing the glass of invisible insect splatter. "But the problem is, she's got some newfangled ideas about things. Strange ideas." He glanced at me.

"Aw, Dad, it's not *that* bad!" Jubal said.

Dad's head furrowed—the pained look he always wore when he was trying to be fair and impartial.

"Is anybody going to tell me what's going on?"

Mother, it turned out, had announced that she was tired of being a domestic drudge every born minute of her remaining existence. Housework bored her. So did the idea of helping Dad balance his books in her spare time, hitherto his nod at letting her do wage-worthy "work." She wanted to go into her own line, whatever that might be, and had already made inquiries into acquiring a real estate license, with an eye to showing and selling houses, perhaps taking up interior design as well. Dad looked at me balefully, as if sorry to be the one to impart his next bit of dire news. "You'll be sharing a room with Jubal. She's taken over your room as her... Office." A euphemism that, I was to learn, meant it had also become her bedroom; for in her revitalized state of being, she declared that Harold's snores and tendency to hog the sheets had been driving her crazy these past twenty years and it was time to do something about it.

"That's not all," Jubal broke in, showing a great deal more enthusiasm for Mother's transformation than our aggrieved father. "Katie and Mom are talking about going into business *together*." Now *that* was news. When I'd sent Katie a graduation card two weeks ago, I assumed she was still ringing up groceries at Winn-Dixie and, stoned and clueless as to her future, would command that register to infinity unless she and Rat actually made good on their threat to join a hippie commune Out West.

"No joke, it's like Mom and Katie are best girlfriends now, and did I say Sis's ditched Rat *and* bought a pantsuit? She thinks it's cool that Mom's striking out on her own, and I do too."

So feminism, admittedly of a garden variety, had entered the Seward household like the wily serpent of old, and poor Dad—ever patient and long-suffering—had no earthly idea how to respond to this disruption to his peace of mind. Domestic order, albeit fearfully enforced, had been Jeanlyn's point of pride, the one thing Dad could count on. All he'd prayed for, when Jeanlyn snapped out of her lethargy, was a return to some semblance of the known and familiar. But now that succor was being taken away from him. He didn't say all this on that midnight drive home, but I could read it in the distracted look on his face as he left the house in the mornings that followed and as he returned in the evenings in time to help prepare the dinners that Mother now declared a shared task: she and Katie commanded, Dad chopped and stirred and sweated, Jubal set the table, I washed the dishes.

The surprises continued.

I'd written in advance to Mr. Julian to alert him of my pending visit, and he'd responded with an invitation to tea at four on Tuesday afternoon. So on my third day home, I made the trek out to Honeysuckle Heights, but not without a touch of perturbation, since I wanted so much for Mr. Julian to be *proud* of me—which is to say, to be proud of the person his unacknowledged generosity was allowing me to become. The iron front gate swung open when I sounded the buzzer, and, as of old, the grand avenue of elms beckoned wonderfully, a tunnel of mysterious shade that led to the pool of sunlight bathing the raised front terrace and the carved entry where the wisteria, now past bloom, continued to vie with the climbing rose. And where, as of old, George Geronimo stood watching my approach. Happy is too strong a word, but the stooped old man didn't look entirely displeased as he nodded for me to enter the old house. G.G.'s grizzled gray hair seemed a bit thinner, and, dark as his skin was, I detected darker semicircles beneath his eyes that made me wonder whether Mr. Julian was "in a mood" and wearing out his faithful assistant's patience.

In a mood Mr. Julian was, though not the one I anticipated. I was ushered out to the back terrace, but instead of finding the wizened invalid whose stroke had left him more incapacitated than ever waiting in his wheelchair, I espied, rounding the left corner of the house, three unrecognizable figures.

As I tried to make sense of the scene, my brain could only stupidly register the still-life arranged on the wrought iron table directly in front of me, where a crystal pitcher of iced lemonade caught the sun like diamonds, a bit of lace draped over its mouth to ward off the lazily droning flies and occasional buzzing wasp. There was a plate of wafer-thin cookies dipped in chocolate and decorated with filigrees of candied orange rind, one of B.B.'s specialties and one of my favorites, and an arrangement of overblown peonies and wildflowers. Polished apples gleamed as brightly as the silver bowl in which they rested.

As if in a daze I watched the three figures amble forward and, before I quite knew what to think, I intuited that the fellow on the left, dressed in hospital green, must be Mr. Julian's new physical therapist, and that the elderly gentleman who walked carefully by his side, a hand resting on the therapist's muscular forearm to steady himself, was Mr. Julian. No wheelchair; no walker; not even a cane. The smirking youth with flaxen blonde hair on Mr. Julian's right drew a blank. Then, as the group got closer, I realized: he's my replacement.

I didn't know which struck me more, in those first slow-motion moments of perception—the shocking transformation in Mr. Julian's mobility or the fact that he had already found someone to take my place.

"Newton Horatio Seward!" Mr. Julian crowed, and I quickly stepped forward to grip his offered hand as he broadly winked for everyone's benefit. "Turned Yank already?"

Before I quite came out of my daze, introductions had been made and I found myself seated with Mr. Julian and Bruno Epps, who indeed was his physical therapist, while Scotty McDougall—now I vaguely recalled him from Hill High—obsequiously poured our drinks and handed round the sweets.

I couldn't get over my amazement at Mr. Julian's genuine improvement of health, nor could he restrain his own delight.

"Frankly, boy, I feel fifteen years younger!" Bruno had worked wonders, simply wonders; he had taken the place of Miss Pettigrew, the dour-faced therapist the hospital had assigned Mr. Julian. And Bruno had cracked the whip, indeed he had, Mr. Julian tittered, new sets of exercises and a regime of special vitamins and supplements, and before you could say jackrabbit he'd "forced—yes, forced!—me out of bed and onto my poor feet, willing or not!" and then the real work of rehabilitation had begun. It appeared that Mr. Julian had submitted with delight to exertions of which I in my wildest dreams would never have thought the self-involved invalid capable; he had even been coaxed into doing water exercises in the pool. Next Bruno—who'd taken up residence in the mansion, a perk of the job— banished the wheelchair; and tentatively Mr. Julian had graduated from walker to the silver-headed cane I now noted leaning against the brick wall. And lately even that prop was becoming more accessory than necessity. Mr. Julian added that he'd saved this good news for me to witness in person, rather than spoil the fun by revealing all in a letter.

It would have been mean of me not to salute Bruno for the achievement he had wrought. His ability to discipline so inveterate a hypochondriac as Mr. Julian into relative fitness was as close to a miracle as the Brewster estate had witnessed in a half century. But, congratulate Bruno as I did, I couldn't warm to the man or puzzle him out. Somewhere in his mid-thirties, he was a man's man, able-bodied, muscular, sporting a five o'clock shadow several hours ahead of five o'clock—a not-altogether-unhandsome cross between William Holden and a younger Mario Lanza. He sat too complaisantly in his chair, tilting it onto its back legs as he stretched his powerful arms over his head. He seemed happily aware of his hypnotic power over Mr. Julian.

As for Scotty, I felt no ambivalence whatsoever. I disliked him immediately. If Bruno were too complaisant, this pink-cheeked cherub was too solicitous to be believed— surely I hadn't grovelled so to win Mr. Julian's approval! I gradually observed that Mr. Julian's health wasn't all that had transformed. A new degree of maliciousness soon surfaced in his barbed wit, as if it had strengthened along with his body. True, he had always been snippy, but I discerned a more gloating gleam in his eye than ever as he began to pit the three of us current and former employees against one another.

We were still chatting about his surprising return to health when he mentioned that, if his improvements kept up at this rate, he just might start planning his first trip to Europe in decades. "And, of course," he added with a warning sparkle in those liquid blue eyes that hadn't changed a whit, indulging in his habit of talking about people in the third person as if they weren't present, "I'll need a traveling companion, an aide de camp, and I've promised Bruno that if I go to Italy—Bruno's half-Italian you may have guessed!—he can accompany me. I know it will break Scotty's heart, the poor dear boy says he's *dying* to see Europe." He patted the blushing lad on his arm. "Aren't you? All things in good time for those who wait their turn— Newt can tell you!"

Bruno gave a deep laugh, and Scotty a nervous giggle. Revising my prior impressions, I decided I disliked Bruno even more than my replacement.

"Of course," Mr. Julian drawled, catching my eye, "*you've* always dreamed of traveling to Europe yourself, eh, Newton? You and the twins used to talk of nothing else. Should Bruno and I drop by Paris, pay Marky Joe a visit? Someone needs to rein in that boy before he ruins his life!"

Soon enough, Mr. Julian put me through a catechism about my first semester at Phipps. In my letters to Honeysuckle Heights, I'd accentuated the positive, not revealing the bouts of inferiority besetting me so much of the term; but Mr. Julian was too crafty a fox not to have picked up on the subtext of my occasional plaints, and these miseries he made me rehearse in uncomfortable detail for Bruno and Scotty before jumping forward to what he cast as my Triumph over Odds.

"I knew Newt would pull through!" he declared to his new employees. "I only bet on winners. Learn from Newt's example!"

An hour later, it was time to leave. Mr. Julian invited me to return on Sunday, when Bruno and Scotty had the day off. What imp of the perverse was it that made him ask Scotty see me to the door?

"It's been an honor to meet you," Scotty murmured with annoying insincerity as we passed through the dim and airless drawing room. "I've heard *so* much about you. I've only worked here since April, but Mr. Brewster tells me *everything*." He smiled as if we were best friends. "And of course *everybody* at school talks about That Kid who went Up North to boarding school. Boredom school, that's what we call it down here!"

I thanked him for his kind words.

"I can imagine how traumatic your adjustment's been." Scotty lowered his voice to a meaningful hush. Whereupon he elaborated upon the trials that a Southern boy of lesser means, dubious background, and hopeless accent must have suffered among the privileged sons of Phipps (he managed to interject the fact his father managed Cleveland Bank on Main Street). I gritted my teeth and engaged in fantasies of fleecing the angelic locks haloing his not-so-angelic face.

At the front door he wished me a safe return North. "I won't be here Sunday when you visit, so I doubt we'll see each other again. The three of us keep so busy I'm surprised he had time to squeeze in one last visit with you."

I answered in my nicest voice. "Oh, I'll be dropping more than once—I'm sure of it."

A flicker of vexation marred the pearly effect of Scotty's perfect teeth as he smilingly hissed good-bye. The massive door closed behind me loudly. I was strolling down the graveled driveway when

I noticed Geronimo weeding a scraggly flowerbed bordering the azaleas on the front lawn. He saw me, straightened, and dusted off his palms.

"That one?" he said, nodding his head towards the front door. "I give him two more months. *Tops.*"

I could swear he grinned as he returned to his task and I went my way.

*

No sooner had I gotten home and started rummaging through the refrigerator than I heard Mother's car screech to a stop in the carport. Seconds later, she sailed through the kitchen entrance, parking her purse and a new leather briefcase (briefcase!) on the Formica countertop.

Then it hit me, and I stood open-mouthed while the cold air from the Frigidaire rushed out around me. Jeanlyn's fabled French twist, the signature-swirl of Grace Kelly regality that had adorned the back of her head for as long as I could remember, had disappeared. While I'd been fantasizing taking revenge on Scotty McDougall's locks, Mother had been patronizing Lois's Beauty Parlor, exchanging her twist for a short, sassy bouffant in which one could easily to imagine her negotiating serious business deals.

"So?" she asked, taking a turn as Katie entered the kitchen.

"I told you it was time!" Katie cried.

It looked wickedly good, I had to admit, it just didn't look like the mother I'd always known. Nor did she, evidently, resemble the Jeanlyn Dad had wed. He kept gaping at her over dinner that evening as if she were an extraterrestrial on a temporary visa from a far galaxy. Meanwhile, she chatted on about the office rental spaces she'd spent the afternoon viewing, the one on New Loudon Street particularly tickling her fancy. Plus her real estate licensing course started on Monday. Not to be outdone, Katie announced that she'd given a month's notice at Winn-Dixie as she was enrolling at Roanoke Business College this fall—something to sink her teeth into, until she and Mother decided on their business plan. The Seward girls were charging into the future. We Seward guys listened, slack-jawed.

*

Before I knew it, Sunday arrived, and I found myself back at the Brewster estate. Sassafras, forearms dusted in flour, answered the door and announced that Mr. Julian was waiting for me at my old post in the library. Those talismanic words moved me strangely.

I found Mr. Julian seated at the long walnut table with the scowling griffins for legs, reading glasses perched on the bridge of his patrician nose as he leaned over the contents of a mottled pasteboard binder whose faded black satin ribbons had been untied. What appeared to be very old photo albums also lay open on the tabletop. When he motioned me over, I saw that the binder contained exquisite drawings of furniture designs on trace paper as fragile as butterfly wings.

"Just look! Found 'em upstairs. We'll file them over there." He gestured to the cabinetry by the library entrance, where we'd housed all the paraphernalia having to do with the Brewster furniture business. "Dated 1937. This design line would have been an entirely new direction for us."

I only needed a glance at the drawings to recognize their tantalizing modernity, sleekly angular, low-slung pieces in which form and function had been transformed into art.

"Our first European co-venture, this was to have been, with Enzio in charge of the Italian end of production." Mr. Julian turned the sheets. Elegantly streamlined chairs and tables, cabinets and credenzas, grids filled with intricate upholstery patterns rendered in colored pencil passed before my eyes. "He created all these templates. Inspirational! Look at this sofa-and-rotating-endtable combination: who but an artist could have dreamt *this* up? And most amazing of all was that Father bought into the concept, oh he did, hook, line, and sinker. That was the second summer Enzio visited us here."

Before I could ask the fate of the undertaking, or follow up on the hint about Enzio and Julia, Mr. Julian pushed one of the photo albums between us. My eye caught the date 1928 inked in the white margin of one of the small sepia photos that filled the page. "All our yammering about travel the other day gave me the itch to have a look at these albums. Took G.G. hours to locate 'em." He pointed. "That's me in front of the Duomo, my first trip to Italy. I'd arrived in Florence the night before, dazed and dazzled." And, there, indeed he was—an even younger version of the handsomely waspish young man of the Sorrento oil that hung in the drawing room, not yet as aloof as the man of the portrait, though he held his head—hair slicked with pomade—with a haughty tilt that hinted at the man to come.

"Whole family made the voyage, here's a shot of Julia and me on Ponte Vecchio. It had rained that afternoon, and the air smelled so fresh, I remember the scent as if it were yesterday. That's my sister Adelaide, in the courtyard at the Bargello. I suspect she was having an *affaire de coeur* with that serious-looking gentleman, Father's secretary. Father would have locked Adelaide up in a convent then and there if he'd suspected; you can see the hardness in his eyes"—he was pointing to a photograph of his eagle-nosed father—"not a nice man. Not a nice man at all." He paused. "Of all my friends, the only one he didn't mind was Enzio. Odd. He saw the artist in him, like the rest of us."

"How did you meet Mr. Sorrento?"

Mr. Julian turned to a second album, embossed *Italy 1931* in gold letters on its jade green leather cover. "At an art opening in Florence, through some New York friends. It was my first solo trip to Europe. Enzio couldn't believe I hadn't seen the Signorelli frescos at Orvietto, so he drove a group of us down by car, to gape at the Torments of Hell for ourselves. Here we are, outside the cathedral."

I squinted for a closer look at the image that Mr. Julian's manicured fingernail was tapping. I easily recognized my benefactor, dressed in a striped summer linen suit, fedora in hand so that the sunlight glinted off his slicked-back blonde hair. Beside him stood a man of perhaps thirty, shorter, boxy, and dark-haired, flashing a smile under a trim moustache as he carelessly dangled a cigarette from the edge of his curved lips, one eyebrow cocked higher than the other. Even in black and white, the olive hues of his closely shaved face were apparent. So this was the mysterious Enzio.

"That evening we had mountain boar roasted with sage—such fragrance!—and of course Orvietto bianco..."

As Mr. Julian turned the pages of the album, a series of close-ups of Enzio as he clowned for the camera—blowing smoke rings at the photographer, lasciviously licking a cone of gelato, laughing with mouth wide open at what he seemed to think the world's funniest joke—whetted my curiosity to learn more about the man who, apparently, had won the hearts of both Julian and his sister Julia. Shots of the painter in his studio, another of Mr. Julian looking out Enzio's windows over Florence's terracotta rooftops, just as in the portrait that hung in the drawing room. Pictures memorializing the tourist attractions of Florence, Venice, Rome, sometimes the two of them joined by faces I recognized from the group in Orvietto. And then pictures of a trip to Urbino, with its fairy-tale castle turrets and cathedral dome soaring above the city walls, and the villa in the countryside just outside Raphael's birthplace where Enzio's parents and sisters lived. They were a boisterous clan, from the looks of it, dining al fresco at long tables laden with food and wine bottles. A young Mr. Julian smiled, bashfully, in their midst.

Mercurial as ever, Mr. Julian snapped the album shut. "I don't know why I bothered."

I put my hand on the portfolio of furniture designs before he could tie its ribbons closed. "These are beautiful. I'm glad you showed me."

Mr. Julian turned his quavering blue gaze on me. "Well, that's something, I suppose."

"Do you have any of these pieces, I mean, the real thing?"

He pried the portfolio from my hands, not without gentleness, as he shook his head and pushed himself to his feet. I rose, as well.

"No more questions, my boy, not now."

He shuffled to the bookcase, slipping the binder among the family business catalogues. "Have a look any time you wish," he said. "*Memento mori*, that's all they are to me. Quite useless, really. Let me show you something else."

He returned to the griffin-legged table and unlocked a drawer beneath its top. Amidst stacks of letters tied in colored ribbons, he found what he was looking for: a wooden box whose lid was breathtaking: an intricate inlay whose many grains and hues together formed a curious design. At first it appeared to be a maze. But when I tilted the case so that it refracted the light, I seemed to discern, as if from an elevated perspective, the rendering of a formal garden.

"It's Quattrocentro," Mr. Julian said, by way of explanation. "But the design on the lid was added by Enzio—there, you can see his initials carved into the wood."

He opened the lid and removed a creased sheet of watercolor paper, folded into a small packet. Carefully, he prized the stiff paper open; two keys spilled out, one large and one small, both very old, and attached by a ring. On the inner face of the paper, six inches wide and nearly three feet in length, an arabesque design was painted in brilliant tints. It looked like the plan for a decorative frieze and consisted of a series of rectangular stone columns from which sprouted the torsos of mischievous-looking satyrs, arms extended overhead to hold aloft floral garlands that drooped in symmetrical swags connecting one figure to the next. As startling as the herm-like erections that marked each column midway were the female breasts attached to the chests of each of these otherwise masculine figures "A little *jeu d'esprit* that Enzio may have copied from some fresco in Pompeii," Mr. Julian said. His voice sounded far away as he dangled the two keys from fingers that trembled slightly. "Very mysterious. Enzio sent these to me shortly before he died, wrapped in this watercolor and enclosed in this box. Why, I haven't an earthly clue."

"What do you think the keys are to?"

"Who knows? A safety deposit box? A hiding place? Enzio's studio? The homestead outside Mazzaferro? A location long since bombed out of existence? It's a mystery to me."

He refolded the watercolor around the keys, replaced the packet in the box and handed it to me. "Why don't you keep this? It's a silly whimsy, but humor this old man. I'll like knowing it's with you."

*

One more memorable event occurred that afternoon. Mr. Julian had asked G.G. to show me out, as he was heading straight for the elevator—rehabilitated or not, using the stairs exceeded his abilities. In the gloomy entry hall, G. G. paused awkwardly. Again, I noticed the dark circles under his eyes, the sunken hollows in his cheeks.

"Excuse me, Mr. Newt, I need to ask a favor. I was hoping that you wouldn't mind having a word with Samson."

This was a surprise, as I never expected the proud man to ask *me* for anything. "He's all right, I hope?"

"*He* thinks he is. I think his head's stuck up his butt"—G.G.'s slight profanity startled me anew—"or maybe just too far up in the clouds." He clicked his tongue. "That fool of a boy's got a serious mind to drop out of school, with just one year to go. He has this notion it's now or never to pursue this boxing craziness of his." G.G. shook his head glumly as he opened the front door. A shaft of sunlight fell on my high tops. "Wasting all his God-given talents—and for what? Some fool dream of glory and a smashed face."

G.G. stepped out with me onto the front terrace. "You being so smart, and getting educated like a man of the world, I thought maybe you could talk sense to him. He doesn't pay any attention to this old-ster, ohhh no."

Inwardly, I quailed. Samson and I hadn't seen each other since he'd barged in on our ménage at the pool. But before I fabricate an excuse, G. G. took my silence for a yes and said he'd let me know once he'd spoken to his son to arrange a meeting time and place.

G.G. added, "He's always looked up to you."

Perhaps once. As I exited the front gate, I wished I were already back at Phipps, where the only Newt Seward that people knew was the one that I wanted them to know, not the boy haunted by ancient and not so ancient secrets.

19

CONTINUED TALES OUT OF
SCHOOL

The last week of my trip home passed peaceably enough. I slept in, looked up old school friends, played tennis with Jubal, ran errands with Mother. A few relatives paid visits to gawk at the family oddity who'd deserted the South for "Kennedy Country." In the evenings, propped up on the top bunk in Jubal's room, the heavy scent of the June night and the sound of crickets drifting through the open window, I read Victorian novels till I fell asleep.

No doubt to Scotty's chagrin, I visited Mr. Julian a few more times before I returned North. I first reappeared on Tuesday, when Mr. Julian invited me to a luncheon to which, happily, neither Bruno nor Scotty were included. Afterwards, we took a stroll to walk off B.B.'s fine cooking, Mr. Julian briefly resting his arm on mine as we stepped off the rear terrace onto the lawn. He pointed to the break in the shrubbery that led to old formal gardens and we slowly but surely made our way through the decorative arch cut into the hedge. The garden looked much the same as ever, straggling boxwoods outlining the parterres, and everywhere rank weeds, Queen Anne's lace, and pokeweed competing with a few unkempt rose bushes—everywhere except the quadrant where G.G. tended his kitchen garden. There a black hose curled across the path like a python intent on waylaying us, ending in a rusty sprinkler set in the middle of G.G.'s well-weeded spot of dark loam and pale shoots. As we sidestepped the hose, salamanders warming on the pebbles scurried to join other unseen critters rustling in the underbrush. When we reached the grape arbor at the garden's rear, I uprighted the two corroded chairs that looked least likely to collapse under our weight, and we sat down under the translucent green leaves and miniature grape clusters, looking over the ruined garden in silence.

Too much silence, however, disagreed with Mr. Julian, and he returned to a topic we'd touched on earlier. "Mary Jo is *wild* about seeing you in Cambridge. Says it will be like having a second brother at hand." He crooked a frosty eyebrow. "Maybe a better brother than Marxist Markus of late. Of course, they've always been too dependent on each other. Being twins, and then their parents' deaths, one understands, but still... dear Julia and I were close, but never *that* close! And now Marky thinking he can scrap his education and become a Movie Star overnight!"

I corrected him, mildly—Marky wanted to make films, not *star* in them—but Mr. Julian swatted my words aside like pesky flies.

"Oh pooh, I *know* you won't hear ill of your pal. He is charming, that I grant him. Well, perhaps you can be a good influence on the reprobate."

Then Mr. Julian returned to the topic at hand.

"We'll have to fit you up with a proper wardrobe, so you can squire Mary Jo about and keep her admirers at bay when they get too annoying. Oh, she'll have her hands full, she will, those Harvard men'll know a good thing when they see it. Suitors aplenty. And it's *your* task, my boy, to make sure she chooses the right one—I'm counting on you!"

I assured him that I looked forward to seeing Mary Jo and that I would be more than happy to escort her whenever she needed a companion—but I rather disliked the idea, seemingly fixed in Mr. Julian's head, that my role was to be her watchdog and his spy.

"You *would* enjoy squiring her about, wouldn't you? Yes, you would! Imagine your classmates' faces, were they to see Mary Jo hanging on your arm, oh you'd enjoy *that*. I shouldn't be surprised if you end up falling half in love with her yourself. Now that would make Marky jealous!" Those blue eyes twinkled with a light I didn't quite like—all too reminiscent of Marky when he set about needling me just to watch me squirm. "Just don't let her break your heart. Because the vixen will, if you don't take care!"

I had a premonition that my heart would need very little encouragement, in years to come, to break when faced with the possibility of romance, and break again and again. But perhaps, so I scolded myself in that wry second voice always carrying on in my head, I'd been reading too many Victorian novels of late.

*

When I got home that afternoon, Jubal presented me with a blue envelope, barely containing his curiosity as he followed me into the kitchen. It was from none other than the recent target of Mr. Julian's dire predictions—Marky himself—forwarded to me from Andover by Miranda. A pity she weren't here to deliver it in person, so that she might astonish Jubal with one of her tumbling runs. Retreating upstairs for privacy, I raised the envelope to my nostrils to see if it carried the odor of foreign climes, relishing the suspense as I peeled back its flap.

For once Marky hadn't just scribbled a note on the backside of a postcard but penned a three-page letter filled with excitement at the news he wanted to share: he'd met a director who planned to shoot an avant-garde documentary about the Jefferson Airplane in Manhattan next year, and he'd promised Marky a spot on the production team— no salary but what a way to learn the trade! The added bonus was that after the shoot Marky would travel up to New England to visit his sister and me. In prose, at least, Marky seemed to have lost none of his ironic wit, proceeding to amuse me by lampooning the more flamboyant contacts in the film world he'd been making. Exempted from his humor, however, was an aspiring director-writer he'd recently befriended, Bernardo B., an Italian living in Paris; the two of them had (actually!) spent a drunken evening discussing visual aesthetics in the company of (gasp!) Godard himself. When the Maestro left a pair of his signature sunglasses on the bistro table, Bernardo had pocketed the frames as a good-luck talisman. Included in the letter was a Polaroid of Marky posing in said glasses, beret aslant his long dark hair and scarf dramatically looped around his neck. He cheerfully predicted that he'd be enjoying a successful career long before I'd decided on a college major. Take that, institutionalized education! The loquacious letter overflowed with so much of the old charisma that had filled our days last summer that I felt as if Marky were by my side.

Wednesday brought another old acquaintance into my orbit. Mr. Allbright dropped by to see how I was getting on and, before leaving, pulled me aside to deliver a message from George Geronimo—Samson would meet me at four o'clock Thursday. The next day I found myself waiting for Samson at the designated rendezvous spot: the crest of the hill above Mr. Julian's estate, beyond which Browntown tumbled downhill, an unkempt border zone that in the evening doubled as lovers' lane and likeliest place to score drugs in town. I tacitly understood G.G.'s decision that it wouldn't do for Samson to meet me on the Brewster estate, where any of its curious inhabitants might happen upon us. So here I waited, killing the time by kicking loose used condoms embedded in the hardened clay. I was attempting to dislodge one such fossil of spent passion with the toe of my Keds when Samson loped into view.

I froze. For a split second I felt as exposed as I had been the day at the pool when he'd last laid eyes on me—all of me. Then he smiled, sheepishly, and I saw nothing in his eyes but his own embarrassment at his old man for having seen fit to confide his paternal worries to an outside party such as myself. The slight hesitancy in his athletic gait as he approached was all about him, and not about me.

"So, Scholar, how's it feel to be a man of such fine prospects?"

I wasn't quite sure if his irony were directed towards my good fortunes or the view of Browntown below the embankment where we stood. He wore his usual overalls, more patched than ever.

"Meeting like this is weird," I admitted as we shook hands. "I didn't have the heart to tell your pa that it's not my place to tell you what to do."

"He's hard to refuse. Don't I know!"

We agreed to put his worries aside for the time being and moved to the graffiti-covered bench that overlooked the view, settling back on the countless initials and arrow-pierced hearts scratched into the bench's painted surface, their sentiments vying for space with crude illustrations of a decidedly more sexual bent. Samson rolled us cigarettes as in days of old. Haltingly at first, then picking up speed in response to his questions, I found myself narrating the high and low points of my past half-year, and he responded in kind to my inquiries.

So we talked, and blew smoke rings into the air, until we got around to the awkward reason that G.G. had brought us together.

"Don't you see, this place is strangling me. School's your way out, these fists are *mine.*" Samson sparred at the air. "If I go profession-al this fall, at least I'll get to Roanoke. Then I'll have a shot at Rich-mond; and if I do okay in Richmond, it's D.C., and, damn, I'm a free man. I could have a career before you're out of college!" His words uncomfortably reminded me of Marky's similar boast in his recent letter. "That's all I want, a future that's my own, can you blame me?"

How could I say anything other than that I understood, since his feelings were so close to my own? But I also argued—with passion, because I believed in what I was saying—that a high school diploma was his most secure means of escaping Rocky Hill. What I didn't say but was also thinking was that the color of his skin handicapped him in ways that made his present choice all the more critical. If those were thoughts too tender to voice outloud, they didn't stop me from pressing forward on other fronts. What if he were injured in the sport early on? Without a diploma, how far could he expect to go if he had to leave boxing behind? What of the threat of Uncle Sam if he dropped out of school? His sponsors, he countered, had connections that would take care of his draft status. Only a year, one more year, I advised—and then do whatever you want. Wherever.

So our words flowed back and forth as the summer sun lazily made its way towards the western horizon, bathing the tin roofs of the dilapidated houses below in illusory radiance. I couldn't begin to fathom whether I'd said anything to change Samson's resolve, but he hadn't acted like there was any reason to avoid me. That was enough for me.

*

At the end of my stay, Dad arranged to drive me back to Roanoke to catch my train. On our way out of town we made a last-minute stop at the Brewster estate so I could deliver a gift that Mother—"it's the least *we* can offer, after all *he's* done for you!"—had purchased for me to present the old man: a bottle of the Bailey's Cream he relished as a nightcap. Since I only planned to stay a few minutes, Dad kept the car idling outside the gates as I paid my call.

Walking down the graveled drive, I couldn't shake off Dad's casual mention, just seconds ago on the drive over, that the same Hank Atwater who'd stormed out of the dealership last year had just returned to town, supposedly contrite and asking for his job back. Dad was inclined to forgive and forget, which struck me as unwise but all too typical of my father. He woefully remarked that a year earlier Jean-lyn would have read him the riot act for considering Hank's request, charging him with being mush-minded as well as softhearted. But now she was so preoccupied with her career plans that she merely arched an eyebrow, remarking that he was free to treat his own employees as foolishly as he pleased.

Thoughts of how rapidly my parents' lives were moving in different directions distracted me as I sat on the Duncan Phyfe and paid my respects to Mr. Julian. Inflecting the role of stentorian sage with his usual theatricality, my former employer urged me to disappoint neither himself nor my family once the school year resumed, all the while cradling my gift like a precious newborn. Scotty looked on from a distant chair where he'd been ordered to sit, watch, and learn.

"Remember we're counting on you!" Mr. Julian declaimed, as if addressing an audience of twenty rather than two. And then he lowered his voice, winking knowingly. "Never forget how much we're all invested in your success!"

Just as earnestly, he made me swear to keep an eye out for Mary Jo's well being once she arrived in Cambridge.

"And you can accompany the dear girl down here next Christmas, now that would gild my holiday!" he brightly added.

I left him in the gloom of the drawing room, sitting by the Enzio Sorrento portrait, after I shook his hand farewell. George Geronimo silently appeared from nowhere when I reached the entry, moving forward to open the carved door for me.

"I thought you might like to know, seems like Samson might be coming around. *Might*. Thanks for talking to my boy."

I was glad to hear it, I said, and shook G.G.'s hand heartily. He wished me a fruitful summer and a productive school year to come and added, as I stepped outside, not to be a stranger to folks back home. I grinned. "Not possible."

Little did I suspect that this would be the last I would see of Samson's old man. George Geronimo had a fatal heart attack before the summer was over and was buried in the all-black cemetery west of the city limits. I heard the sad news from Samson, who wrote to say that he was sticking around for his senior year. His mother wouldn't hear of his taking off, not under these hard conditions, and Samson felt he owed it to the memory of his pa to help out around the Brewster place until Mr. Julian found a new aide de camp. That, I knew, would be a next-to-impossible task: how to replace the man who had been his faithful companion for nearly two decades, who knew his moods and whimsies inside out, who forbore his outbreaks and silences, and who knew better than to beat him too many times in games of gin rummy and double solitaire? Little as I expected never to see G.G. again, even less did I suspect that the next time I rang the Brewster doorbell, it would be answered by Hank Atwater, his Elvis smirk and slick pompadour in unsettling contrast to the oversized formal livery he wore.

But that is getting quite ahead of myself, and first I must attend to the series of events that unfolded before I again walked down that graveled drive, before I again passed between its row of elms from which the last leaves had fallen, before I again watched the old house rise out of the gloom of a late December afternoon while Mary Jo, the fur collar of her smart jacket turned up against the chill that had set roses blooming in her cheeks, walked by my side.

20

TRICK OR TREAT

When she approached Harvard Yard that October, I had only to catch the scent of her expensive perfume, the hint of Gauloises clinging to her corded turtleneck sweater, and the pastille-flavored breath that she exhaled, to conjure out of airy nothings the fragrance of the Parisian autumn she had left behind. She had not yet spotted me, although I was waiting mere feet away, slouched against the brick pillars of the entrance to the Yard opposite the Square. For the last half-hour I'd pretended to be one of the undergraduates passing in and out of the gate as the temperature dropped by the minute. And then she arrived, inhaling New England fall and exhaling French autumn.

Or, so it seemed to me, since I could only imagine the heady odors of the fabled city I had yet to experience for myself. Undeterred by such petty realities, however, and fed by the overactive imagination of a bookish sixteen-year-old, I had no problem summoning from her proximity the alluring attar of exotic foreignness. For here in front of my eyes, detached from the motes of fallen leaves floating in slanted shafts of late afternoon sunlight, transcending the roar and stink of traffic, Mary Jo stood an arm's length away, her back to me as she expectantly scanned the crush of students passing in and out of the Yard—undergraduates armed with stacks of books and chattering with all the intensity middle America associated with their elevated lot. Watching Mary Jo standing so close, part of yet so distinct from these passersby, I wasn't ready to break the spell by calling out her name. But all of a sudden she spun on her heel and faced me, as if she'd known all along that I was spying on her, and that's when I caught the scent of her mint-flavored breath as she drolly enunciated, in the rich tones that she and Marky shared, "*Allô, mon cher frère, allô!*" She made it seem as if our running into each other in Harvard Yard were the most normal occurrence in the whole wide world. But to me the moment marked an epoch.

"I can't believe you're here—that I'm here—and you look totally, wow, amazing," I blathered inanely as we embraced and pecked each other's cheeks French style.

"Only fourteen months, and look at you! What a gentleman you've become, Newt!" Mary Joe appraised me from parted hair to tasseled loafers. "A stranger would think you'd been at Phipps for years!" She removed a fine doeskin glove and stroked my cheek. "It becomes you."

I wanted to say that I'd dressed up for her, but bit my lip.

"There's only one change I regret," she continued, as she crooked her arm in mine and guided me towards her favorite café. "What's happened to that accent I used to adore? What an effort you must have put into making it disappear!"

I solemnly vowed I had done no such thing, but she would have none of it as she gently continued to tease me in a way that made me feel ever more special, transformed beyond my wildest dreams.

The rich odor of Turkish coffee greeted us we swung open the door to the basement café, abuzz with students and no townies in sight. Phipps had taught me to spot the difference. Mary Jo unwound the scarf that draped her neck and pulled off her gloves as we found seats on a pillow-strewn divan by a low, round, copper table. "There's no question about it," she said with mock-flirtation. "I'm quite relieved to see what an acceptable Escort you'll make when you take me to the South House Winter Formal, so grown up you look now. Uncle intends that you to keep an eye on me, you know."

"A *formal*? Never!"

I recalled that Mr. Julian had said something about suiting me up in my own tuxedo, but nothing had ever come of it. I'd dismissed the idea as one of his whimsies of bygone sartorial splendor, harkening back to years spent in Manhattan among a circle more accustomed to supper clubs and opening galas than today's campus dress codes.

Sipping the muddy coffee that was the specialty of the house, Mary Jo belittled my trepidations. "There's no way out. Uncle's got it into his head that the December formal is *the* event of the semester we must attend together. He's even made me promise to send him a studio photograph of the two of us all tarted up."

"So he can slip copies into the Christmas cards he sends his Brewster relations to make them squirm?" I took another sip of coffee, and, perversely, its viscosity conjured up memories of Dillard Crick and the summer afternoon we'd spent skinny-dipping there. For the residue clinging to the bottom of the glass cup in my hand was as fine as the silt that Mary Jo had molded to her skin. I remembered how it had slowly dribbled down the slopes of her breasts, parting to reveal the pale skin, the perfect nipples, that once, in a dream, I had touched. To my discomfiture, I felt myself getting aroused. And I'd vowed not to think such thoughts today, our first reunion, of all days.

"You're blushing, silly boy." Fortunately Mary Jo mistook its source. "I know it's a chore, but, seriously, think of the fun we can have. There's a reception and dinner at the Fogg, then the Hilton for the dance. What a pleasure it will be to have you by my side! I know you think *I'm* the snob, but wait till you meet the girls I live with!" And she continued, in that siren's voice, second nature to her, that I found as impossible to resist as Marky's laconic wit. "My triumph will be showing up with you. My roommates will be agog at the changeling prince I've conjured out of thin air—a man-boy with the face of an angel and the body of a god! They'll be fighting for a chance to meet you: just you wait, Newt Seward."

But in my private thoughts I was already spinning another scenario: a candlelit fantasy that involved swirling across a marbled ballroom floor with Mary Jo in my arms. This fantasy, however, dissolved the instant I recalled I'd never learned a dance step beyond the twist, mastered in the privacy of my bedroom after watching Chubby Checker on the Ed Sullivan Show. Miranda, by contrast, frequently bemoaned the number of gym classes that Adams Academy devoted to dance instruction—classes that she strongly believed should be dedicated to proper athletics. Miranda, it dawned on me, would be thrilled to instruct me in these finer, if frightening, social arts.

Mary Jo and I moved on to other topics that kept us chattering *à toute vitesse*, as she was fond of saying, for the next two hours. She traded stories of Radcliffe for my tales of the life I'd begun crafting at Phipps—from the stage set I was helping build for an production of "Anything Goes" to my new courses, from the colorful inhabitants making up the topsy-turvy world of the Fortinbras household to last summer's job at the Andover Spa, where my primary customers were sheepish men who came in after midnight to buy the cellophane-wrapped skin magazines we kept under the counter—issues whose glossy displays made the *Playboy* I'd appropriated from Judge Leroy years ago seem quite lame.

And, of course, we talked about Marky.

I asked if it were strange to be living so far apart for the first time since their parents' deaths. "Strange, yes." Mary Jo put her hand over mine and squeezed it. "And that's why I'm so glad you're here. Unlike Marky, a brother I can count on." Her touch set the veins in my wrist pulsing—a perturbation she remained quite unaware of as she attached her delicate fingers to my rougher ones. Contradictory emotions warred within me: her touch, like her presence, spontaneously rekindled last summer's sexual heat, yet the firmly fraternal terms in which she calmly cast our friendship left me feeling like a spayed lapdog, despite the turgid swelling between my legs.

"It's hard to explain," she continued. "It's odd enough being twins, knowing the world contains another version of yourself, someone whose thoughts and emotions and skin you've known as intimately as your own. But now he's changing...."

Mary Jo went on to talk about those changes. By now she had met most of Marky's new friends—a clique of dreamers, hipsters, anarchists, and occasional visionaries bitten by the desire to revolutionize cinema, would-be auteurs one and all.

"I've got to give them credit, I can't imagine ever caring about anything quite so passionately." Nor could she fault Marky for merely being a dreamer; he was building connections as likely to open doors as any number of university lectures.

"So of course I miss seeing him nearly every day. But I was already starting to miss *my* Marky Joe all this last year. I just can't *comprehend* this new political fervor—it's all-consuming. He's not letting me *inside* anymore. He still knows the inner me in a way no one else will—not even you, Newt. Yet he's choosing to shut me out."

Later, Mary Jo walked me to the subway entrance, and, brushing lips to both cheeks but no more, we parted to the roar of cars careening around the Square. I turned to watch her walk away—watched, as long as I could, the gleam of her dark hair shining in the glow of streetlights that had come to life while we were drinking coffee—watched, as she disappeared into the mass of parkas, London Fogs, and pea jackets moving past the Coop in the direction of Radcliffe.

So began a fall and winter in which Mary Jo and I became friends all over again—each of us finding in the other a zone of comfort, an oasis of familiarity. Knowing that she was in Cambridge, a phone call away, added an unexpected glamour to my life and, I dare say, to my reputation at Phipps. While I still found myself working around the clock, I no longer felt as if I were falling impossibly behind. I was making my way; gaining new friends and acquaintances; meeting the challenge of Greek while continuing to excel in Latin; earning the approbation of my teachers. In the midst of this swirl of activity, the promise of spending time with Mary Jo, of catching glimpses of the enticing world that lay behind the gates of Harvard Yard, inspired me to succeed all the more.

*

Halloween came and went before I got to see Mary Jo again—the most memorable Halloween I've ever experienced, and costuming was the least of it. Miranda had taken me aside, shortly after my visit to Cambridge, to reveal a deeply troubling development in the Fortinbras household. We were sitting in the den, watching as much of the Olympics on ABC as our schedules would allow. It was the year of the Mexico City games, and while my particular interest was tracking Debbie Meyer's freestyle strokes to a record three golds, Miranda exulted in Vera Caslavoska's gymnastic victories, imagining her own future tumbles to glory. Last week's raised fists during the awards ceremony by the U.S. 200-meter sprinters had been an ongoing subject of debate at the dinner table. Why was this expression of black solidarity so reviled by press and public alike, Miranda asked, while the same commentators lauded Caslavoska's equally bold protest of the U.S.S.R.'s invasion of Czechoslovakia—she had turned her head away during the Soviet national anthem—as an act of heroism?

Seated across from Mick, I registered a series of subtle emotions flickering across her face during these boisterous discussions. I wondered, too, what Samson would have to say about the black power movement; I thought about Browntown clinging to the western slopes of Rocky Hill as if about to slip off the face of the earth; and, for the first time in a long time, I recalled my terrifying encounter with the Leroy's maid-turned-convict at Furnace Creek.

All these impressions flitted through my mind as I looked at Mick, trying to fathom her thoughts as she passed the roasted potatoes while the pros and cons of black militancy were bandied about— Mick, who never pointed attention to her mixed racial heritage, who instead fiercely charged through life as if her skin color couldn't possibly be on anyone else's minds. Years later, I realized this was her modus operandi, absolving all of us from confronting the anomaly of her position.

But black power had reared its fist in a style that couldn't be ignored that autumn in Mexico City. Miranda and I had finished watching the long distance relays and pole vaulting finals, just the two of us slouched on the sofa, when she stood up to turn down the volume on the eleven o'clock news and swore me to absolute secrecy. It appeared that my surly roommate, Dewey-Do-It, was again proving the wisdom of those academies from which he'd been expelled: over the past month he'd exposed himself in front of Miranda on two occasions. Little as I thought of the spoiled ex-pyromaniac, I had no idea he would stoop this low. He'd never liked Miranda—too tomboyish for his taste, too immune to the testosterone-charged blandishments by which he attempted to appeal to the opposite sex—and now it appeared he had found a sick way to exact revenge. Even in a house as teeming with activity as the Fortinbras fortress, there were abundant nooks and crannies where you could find yourself alone—and it only took seconds, Miranda observed laconically, to flop the hardware out for a brief airing, then dash away before your shocked victim had time to react.

Now, I knew from sharing a room with the lout that he had more than enough to flaunt, as he liked to swagger naked from the bathroom into our shared quarters, belching, farting, and picking at his balls. His penis looked as mean and ugly as his sullen personality—size, in his case, had nothing to do with appeal. I was utterly appalled by Miranda's revelation and made her promise to tell me the instant he gave her any more trouble or threatened her in any way.

"Threaten *me*? I could flip him over my shoulder before he had time to shriek."

Miranda executed a karate move that made me flinch. Her prowess not withstanding, I urged her to tell Wim about Dewey's behavior. The day my mother had been assaulted flashed before my eyes, rousing once again all my feelings of guilt at having failed to be home to protect her.

"And give Do-It the chance to say I'm making it all up because I'm a sex-crazed virgin? No way. Besides, he's not going to *do* anything—it's the exhibitionism he gets off on, I've read all about it."

"I still think we should do something," I grumbled.

"I didn't say I'm not thinking of things."

Miranda's voice reverberated with mystery. I made her promise to keep me in the loop.

Which, in a roundabout way, she did.

Halloween was upon us, and since the date fell on a school night, festivities had been forwarded to Saturday evening. My charge was to squire Kirby and Daisy Fortinbras around the neighborhood, so that Mick could stay home with the youngest infant and distribute the candycorn balls we'd spent the morning rolling in caramel. Mick had assured me the children would have it no other way, which I seriously doubted, but I was happy to accompany Kirby (dressed as Einstein) and Daisy (dressed as a daisy) on their rounds. With Kirby's aid, I'd already carved three suitably grotesque pumpkins to decorate the Fortinbras's door stoop and we'd covered the front yard boxwoods with cobweb-like material that Kirby had spun in his laboratory out of God knows what toxic chemicals.

So the three of us set off, into the not unpleasantly chill night, while Mick manned the front door and Snodgrass stayed upstairs—spooks and shrieks were too much for his nervous bladder (earlier in the week Dewey had unkindly suggested that Charlie outfit himself as a urinal). As for himself, Do-It had leagued with a quintet of football team buddies (Do-It himself was too lazy to play for the squad) draped in bedsheet togas proclaiming themselves the Walking Roman Orgy. Their sole goal was to undo as many bra straps as possible at the Adams-Phipps social, and they swore to consume enough contraband liquor to live up to their moniker. Miranda and her girlfriends had opted to skip the school event for a downtown screening of "Night of the Living Dead."

The evening passed with no greater incident than Daisy falling asleep in my arms before we had made it halfway round the neighborhood and Kirby getting a belly ache from prematurely overindulging in his loot of sweets. The house was quiet by the time I crawled into bed. Dewey had not yet returned, and Snodgrass was already tossing and turning under his blankets.

The next thing I knew, Miranda was at my side, shaking me awake and making shhhing sounds.

"What is it?" I rasped, still half asleep, then bolting upright as visions of a flashing Dewey flashed through my brain. I looked at his bed, and saw that he was still missing in action. The nearest alarm clock gleamed 1:30. Even Dewey had to obey the Fortinbras's weekend curfew hour of 12:30, so he was in trouble.

"Follow us downstairs," Miranda whispered, tilting her head towards the door.

That's when I realized that Snodgrass wasn't in his bed, either. He was standing by the doorway in his stained pajamas, and even in the moonlight I could make out the excited gleam on his face. I reached for my robe and trailed after Miranda and Snodgrass. Stepping over Rover, the black lab who'd stretched out at the bottom of the staircase and had no intention of interrupting his bird-chasing dreams for our convenience, we tiptoed past Mick and Wim's closed door and down the front stairs.

"What are we *doing*?" I whispered.

Snodgrass held up his backpack.

"Tag-time," he said conspiratorially. I was stumped.

"Hush!" Miranda hissed as we reached the entry hall. She gingerly slid back the half-opened paneled doors that led into the living room, every squeak and groan magnified by the silence. The living room's heavy draperies had been drawn earlier in the evening, and when Miranda closed the doors behind us, we found ourselves suspended in pitch dark. A faint odor, slightly sweet, slightly sour, caught my nose, and then a sound—a rattling snore—rocked me in my socks.

That's when Miranda flicked on the flashlight she'd been carrying in her pocket, and I saw, stretched out flat on his back on the couch, my third roommate, arms and legs akimbo and body emanating the stench of stale whiskey and staler beer. Half strangled by the rumpled sheet that had served as his toga, he looked more Mummy than Centurion at present.

Hail Caesar, indeed.

"He's been out an hour," Miranda whispered. "Nothing's waking him now."

Snodgrass handed me his backpack and Miranda gave me her flashlight, motioning me to hold the light steady as the two of them stole to the edge of the couch. I looked on with disbelief as they untangled Dewey from his costume.

"Moment of truth," Miranda whispered, motioning me forward as she slipped on a pair of yellow dishwashing gloves. We three stood looking down at our disrobed victim, whose ugly wanger rose and fell before our eyes in semi-tumescent somnolence. Its owner's open mouth wheezed sour fumes into the close air. "He won't be flashing *this* once we're done."

Snodgrass swallowed a gleeful giggle. "It was *my* idea!"

Since when had Miranda also made a confidant of Snodgrass? I was more dumbfounded than ever.

I wasn't dreaming, however; the muffled rattle coming from Snodgrass's backpack when he took it from me was real enough. Opening the flap, he extracted three cans of spraypaint. He and Miranda, having settled on their knees, signaled for me to direct the beam of flashlight on Dewey's family jewels.

"Blue here," she instructed, cool as a cucumber, pointing. "As in..."

"Blue balls," Snodgrass confirmed with a nod.

"We *can't*!"

"Of course we can." Miranda set about her task as clinically as if she were in her Botany 101 lab, delicately if disdainfully lifting Dewey's shaft with the tips of two gloved fingers while Snodgrass pointed the cobalt blue canister and pushed the nozzle. The operation only took seconds, but to my panicking sensibility the hiss sounded as loud as a firing squad. The slumbering giant, however, slumbered on. Nonetheless wet tingle of the paint was stimulus enough to rouse the object of our artistic endeavors to nearly full glory, such that Snodgrass, with a look of disgust, had to prop it upright while Miranda sprayed the length gangrene green and finally applied to the glans a florescent orange that glowed as pumpkin-bright in the dark as the jack o'lanterns outside.

"Mission Accomplished!" Miranda murmured with aplomb worthy of Barbara Bain.

"Not quite yet," Snodgrass announced.

Whereupon our surprisingly intrepid compatriot produced a razor from his pack, with which he proceeded to shave off the line of hair running from Dewey's navel to his pubis.

Producing a black laundry marker, he wrote, on the now smooth expanse of Dewey's white belly

DO-IT-NOT

in convincingly prohibitive block letters.

"The Eleventh Commandment," he said, sotto voce. "Indelible ink."

More than ready to abscond from the scene of our crime, I helped Miranda arrange Dewey's toga-sheet back over him and killed the flashlight. Deep snores shook the couch as we exited the room and slid the paneled doors shut.

Charlie chortled. "My bladder's about to burst, I'm so excited!"

Heaven only knows what prank Dewey thought his drinking buddies had played on him when, the next morning, he stumbled to the bathroom to take a piss and looked down. All I can say for sure is that he looked sorely unhappy, in addition to sorely hung-over, when he appeared at Sunday lunch and made a mess of his ham steak, his face turning sallow as Mick plopped the fleshy pink meat on his plate. No doubt even indelible ink and spray paint wear off with assiduous scrubbing, but it was months before Do-It swaggered out of our attic bathroom without a towel firmly secured around his waist, and I suspected he wasn't going to be making any sexual conquests in the next several weeks, at least not with the lights on. Even more happily, Miranda reported that his days of flashing in the Fortinbras household proved to have been a flash in the pan.

21

TUXEDO NIGHTS

Having served as accomplice in Miranda and Charlie's scheme to keep Dewey's pants zipped, I was a bit put out to find Miranda less than enthusiastic when I proposed she save me from humiliating myself at Mary Jo's formal by giving me private lessons in ballroom dancing. True, my role in the Halloween escapade had been less hands-on *artiste* than that of terrified spectator failing to hold the flashlight steady, but I'd expected a little more *quid pro quo* from the one person in the Fortinbras household who was my best friend, confidant and, in my academic ambitions, faithful enthusiast.

"What next?" Miranda asked, eyes rolling and pulling at her frizzy red hair, as if she had reason to be exasperated with me. "Really, Newt, what's to become of you!"

Generous-hearted person that she was, however, Miranda felt guilty for her outburst and apologized ten minutes later. Soon enough, exercising the overzealous determination with which she charged into all discussions or projects—a trait inherited from her mother—she had me practicing ballroom steps so frequently that I was nearly driven to distraction. The rhythm of fox trots, waltzes and polkas so infiltrated my consciousness that they punctuated every action of my daily life: Latin verbs, atomic particles, the backstroke—all took on the tempo of those annoying steps. Because I demanded privacy, the basement laundry room adjoining Kirby's chemistry lab, whose strange odors kept the house's occupants away from these nether regions, became our de facto studio. I lugged Miranda's heavy phonograph to the cellar, and she outlined dance steps in chalk on the frigid concrete floor—frigid, I well knew, because she made me practice in stocking feet to save her toes from my clumsy steps. Truth be told, the stubbed toes were more often my own, since Miranda constantly had to stymie her natural tendency to lead, even though she stood at all of five to my nearly six feet. Thankfully, our only audience was Daisy, watching mesmerized from her perch on the basement stairs and fully caught up in the sing-song counts that Miranda kept chanting: "And-a-ONE-two-three, ONE-two-three," which my partner would sometimes recast as "MAR-y-jo, WATCH-Newt-go, LOVES-her-so, CAN'T-say-no." Daisy was convinced that Mary Jo was a princess coming from a foreign kingdom to whisk me away, and I had to promise the teary-eyed child at every lesson that I wasn't about to abandon her.

As a result of these basement instructions I was well on my way to becoming a competent if wooden dance partner by the time Mary Jo paid her first visit to Andover. Having heard so much about my glamorous friend, Mick had issued an open invitation to "come up and stay over" any time she wished, and "any time" finally materialized over the long Thanksgiving weekend. Mary Jo arrived by train on Tuesday night, and all of us who could fit into Mick's battered station wagon rallied to meet her at the depot. Mick greeted her with open arms, never happier than when she was enfolding yet one more body into her overflowing home; Kirby looked at her as if she were an interplanetary creature that his rocket ship designs had brought to earth; and Daisy danced circles around her, lisping "ONE-two-three, ONE-two-three, WALTZ-with-me, I'M Daiii-see!" Miranda hung a step behind the rest of our entourage, brimming with curiosity and skepticism as she waited her turn to be introduced to the guest of the hour.

Our boisterous welcoming party was nothing compared to the ritual induction into the Fortinbras world of plenty and mayhem that Mary Jo underwent on Thanksgiving Day itself, when the household numbers swelled to twenty-eight. Mary Jo handled herself with consummate grace and came off a grand success. But before she was subjected to the masses on our national feast day, I gave her the grand tour of campus and my favorite haunts about town. The weather was glorious: cold without being unbearable, brilliantly blue skies. Mary Jo wore a dazzling new coat—knee-length suede with an extravagant, upturned fur collar of a glistening ebony hue that cradled her flawless cheeks as if its fur and her flesh were on the most amorous of terms. As we ambled arm in arm, glowing with laughter and high spirits, I was conscious of people turning to look at us—or, rather, at her. And as I walked her across the yards of Phipps, I was secretly glad at the number of classmates who had not yet departed, so that they could see me in such striking company. With each admiring glance, my sense of my own stature rose exponentially.

Mary Jo turned to me as we passed one group of ogling boys. "Proud as a Peacock, are you?"

I colored while she compounded my embarrassment by kissing me full and wetly on the lips.

"There. That should give the poor lads something to squirm about!"

She rubbed a trace of lipstick from my mouth.

And then there was Thanksgiving itself. The sliding panels separating the living room on the left and the dining room on the right from the entry hall had been pushed back, so that the series of trestles and card-tables that had been added to either side of the dining room table—repositioned in the entry—extended in both directions, making the longest feasting board I'd ever seen, excluding the summer potlucks held on the lawn of First Methodist. How Mick's cluttered kitchen managed to turn out two perfect turkeys simultaneously, I can't imagine, but the browned birds anchored each end of the table while a molded concoction of rice, nuts, and mushrooms for the vegetarians commanded table center, emanating odors of sage and savoy. In addition to the Fortinbras family, the Thanksgiving diners seated higgledy-piggledy around the makeshift table included a few faculty from up on the hill, a sprinkling of relatives, a dash of students not going home for the holiday, neighbors, two stray waifs from Mick's latest social project, the town mayor and his wife, and three of Andy's posse. Since Snodgrass had gone home for the break, we didn't have to worry about one of his spontaneous charleyhorses upending the table, but Dewey was in attendance. Mary Jo's presence had the most unusual effect on him. I'd never seen him take note of an attractive girl without leering in a most unbecoming manner; but on this occasion he looked like a Sinner hit by the True Word at a revivalist tent meeting—dare I say dewey-eyed for the first time in his life.

The regal calm and poise Mary Jo maintained amid the swirl of personalities, competing voices, and general clatter was remarkable;

she was at her best, exuding an intoxicating combination of warmth and distance, of interest and mystery, that made everyone desire a turn talking to her. I swelled with pride. One of the rules at Fortinbras holiday bashes was that guests shift places every half an hour, giving everyone the chance to talk to as many tablemates as possible. Hence, even though Mary Jo and I had begun the feast side-by-side, by the time the brandied plum pudding surrounded by dancing blue flames materialized from the kitchen to general applause, I was seated at the end of the table extending into the living room, while Mary Jo, at the opposite end, solemnly listened to Wim's octogenarian uncle. Daisy cuddled in her lap while Dewey, two seats away, gazed on stupidly.

Mary Jo having thus been introduced to my Andover world, it was only fair, two weeks later, that I undergo the same ritual. Oh, what a fuss Mick and Miranda made over my fitting for a tux at Mr. Ted's, the local haberdashery! The ever-frugal Mick couldn't quite get over the fact that Mr. Julian had sent a check to cover the purchase of the formal wear. "Lord knows when you'll stop growing, Newt," she clucked her tongue, "and it's not going to be tomorrow!" And such fretting over all the choices, from cut of jacket to style of bow tie!

Mick and Miranda were adamant that I err on the conservative side—"It's Radcliffe, not John and Yoko's wedding," Miranda scolded me as she vetoed the electric-blue cumberbund I held up for approval—and Mick set her foot down when it came to purchasing a new overcoat: Wim's camel-hair would do quite fine, thank you. Then there was the issue of the corsage, which Miranda, in whispered phone conversations with Mary Jo, settled to the satisfaction of both.

So, on December 9, the day after I turned seventeen, I approached South Hall wearing my very own tuxedo and a borrowed overcoat, armed with a corsage of creamy miniature orchids ever so lightly streaked with magenta, fragrant freesia, and pristine snowbells encircling a dark pink rosebud that Miranda promised would look ever so stunning against Mary Jo's dress. As a sign of how seriously the Fortinbrases took the event, Wim and Mick had given me permission to drive the station wagon to Cambridge all by myself.

The moment I found parking near Radcliffe, snow began to fall as if on cue, delicate whorls animated by the streetlamps, and by the time I entered campus, a fine white sheen dusted the Quad. A growing sense of trepidation filled me as I merged into the stream of groomed, self-assured young men converging on South House and entering its elegant foyer, where our overcoats were appropriated by smiling black matrons in frilly white aprons. The sensation of being trapped in an echo-chamber of brash, confident voices quite overwhelmed me, and when I caught my reflection in the gilt-framed mirror hanging in the entry, the tuxedo I'd proudly modeled before my host family an hour ago now looked the pathetic disguise of a plebian upstart. I entered the Commons Room feeling more like a convict facing execution than a young swain marveling at his good fortune.

Crossing that threshold was like stepping into a perfume shop in which all the flasks had been unstoppered, and my senses swam in the dizzying array of feminine finery that greeted me. The sensory overload was almost too much to bear, and I panicked at not seeing Mary Jo in this colorful blur of vivacity.

But then I spotted her, and my world righted itself.

It was hard *not* to spot Mary Jo. She stood out among the milling throng of young women like a Botticelli hanging on a wall of Verrochios. Most of her peers wore evening clothes incorporating the popular trends of the year: rainbow-hued paisley prints, flowing patchwork ensembles, gipsy skirts and gauzy sleeves, beads and glitter rendered expensively if noisily formal. But Mary Jo had gone classic. She moved across the room towards me in a close-fitting, burgundy-colored, sleeveless satin gown that followed the clean, athletic curves of her body and shimmered in gradations of deepest red. Her dark hair was swept up from her neck, long white gloves encased her arms, and a single strand of diamonds sparkled on her neck—a piece of jewelry that her father had once given her mother, perhaps to compensate for the discovery of yet another of his mistresses.

"So you approve?" she asked archly, as she took my hands in her own and carefully pecked my cheek so as not to leave a red imprint.

"I do," I solemnly swore. *I do I do I do.*

"I know I'm no substitute for the Southern belles you grew up adoring. But I'll do my best not to shame you." She straightened my bow tie as I pinned the corsage on her dress, my fingers electric against her smooth skin as they slid under her shoulder strap to complete the operation. The bouquet complemented her dress perfectly, as Miranda had promised.

Taking me by the arm and guiding me forward, Mary Jo prepared me for the first obligatory ritual of the evening. That consisted in being formally introduced to a steely-eyed House Mother who made sure I knew that the men in her family had chosen Exeter over Phipps, then to a Senior Rep who checked my name off a list, and finally to Mary Jo's three suite mates (one vapid, one bored, one brainy) and their escorts, all Harvard Men. Disengaging ourselves from that tongue-numbing conversation, we enjoyed a brief reprieve at the non-alcoholic punch bowl until it was time to queue for our photograph—Mr. Julian would get his portrait after all. Then we gathered our wraps and joined the line of couples waiting for the cars hired to transport us, in groups of four, to the museum for the next, more alcoholic, and altogether more enjoyable stage of revelries.

It so happened that the wife of the director of the board of trustees of the Fogg Museum was a House alumna and, as it was their daughter's senior year, they had secured the museum's majestic lobby and front gallery for the formal reception and dinner. Within these awesome premises we were joined by a stream of select faculty, moneyed alumni, and Boston luminaries. The event was carried off with a storybook magic that only hugely endowed Ivy League institutions can get away with in this day and age: yuletide toasts under the gleam of Old World masterworks; banisters festooned with creeping fir and red velvet bows; rounds of champagne cocktails in which pink sugar cubes fizzled in effervescent bliss; tasteful harp music in the background; reverential silence as a few well-chosen professors read seasonally-appropriate passages from august works of literature; a clarion call on trumpets summoning us to sit down to a five-course dinner served by white-gloved, impeccably-groomed Harvard freshmen whose silent presence left me feeling both curious and envious, as well a little smug, since after all they were serving *me*.

After dinner, waiting for the arrival of the limousines that would whisk us to the Hyatt Regency ballroom, Mary Jo excused herself to "powder her nose," at which point I found myself joined by a cheerily rotund Frenchman with white hairs sprouting from his ears. When we'd arrived at the Fogg two hours earlier, I had noticed him throwing glances our way across the crowded foyer—knowing glances that at the time made me feel as if I'd been caught out for a fraud in this distinguished throng. Some minutes later, as Mary Jo and I had stood admiring a Sargent in the adjoining gallery, we discovered the same gentleman rubbing up at our elbows, using the occasion to point out similarities between the gown in the portrait and the one Mary Jo was wearing. Proper introductions were made; he was an art dealer associated, in some vaguely entrepreneurial way, with the museum; he was only in town a few days before returning to Paris; yes, of course, he had heard of Mary Jo's excellent preparatory *école*; indeed, the moment he laid eyes on her, he assumed she was French, as she was the only *jeune fille* exhibiting true taste in this sea of overblown American roses.

"So we meet again, Mr. Seward!" the eccentric character now greeted me anew, his eyebrows—scarcely less white than the thickets sprouting from his ears—jerking up and down like Venetian blinds out of control. "Very beautiful, *n'est-ce pas*? The *fête* has surpassed my expectations!"

He gestured broadly around the room, and I couldn't help but notice his stubby, coarse fingers—indeed, they swept by so close to my nose I had to step back. And, noting those fingers, I couldn't help but take note, as well, of the odd contrast between those plebeian digits and his fingernails—each of which, perfectly manicured, reflected a sheen of clear polish. "*Oui, oui!*" he chuckled as he caught my gaze and winked conspiratorially. "We French care about such details!"

Whereupon the most bizarre event of the whole evening transpired, as he opened his dinner jacket and extracted an elegant fingernail file from an inner pocket, twirling the instrument before me like a magician's wand. It flashed brilliantly in the light, pure silver, studded at the top with a ruby-red stone as he filed his ring finger. "I never travel unprepared—nor, pardon me for saying so, should *you!*" He laughed from deep in his belly, as if he'd either said the funniest, or the most meaningful, thing in the world, re-pocketed the file, winked again, and took his leave, wishing me the best of luck on life's journey.

"Perhaps our paths will cross again!"

Moments afterwards Mary Jo rejoined me, lipstick freshened and eyes twinkling. "Are you ready to lead, Mr. Astaire?"

And dance we did, once we arrived at the Hyatt. Silently blessing Miranda for her thankless hours of instruction, I guided Mary Jo as competently as my nerves allowed across the buffed ballroom floor. All the champagne I'd consumed no doubt helped bolster my mobility. Through it all, I was warmly conscious of Mary Jo resting in my arms, her body brushing against my own, as she playfully teased me with a light-hearted archness for which there was no recourse but to respond in kind.

"Do you think she's pretty? Tell the truth!" Mary Jo whispered in my ear as a honey blonde that we agreed bore an uncanny resemblance to the recently departed Sharon Tate swept by us on the dance floor. It was a game she'd been playing all evening.

"Ravishing."

Mary Jo persisted, teasingly. "Prettier than me?"

"Impossible." I paused, deliberately. "That's not saying much, mind you. I never had a thing for deceased blondes."

And so we bantered back and forth, Mary Jo soliciting my judgment of the various couples whirling by as she acerbically evaluated the mating rituals occurring on and off the dance floor. Although I laughed in return, her quips left me all that much more aware of the simple fact that no such rituals were, to her mind, occurring between us.

"And *her*?" Mary Jo directed my attention to a sophomore who had a "reputation" and was glancing our way beneath mascaraed lashes. "I do believe she's flirting with you!"

"Then, in addition to possessing a reputation, she obviously possesses good taste."

"Would you sleep with her?"

"Perhaps I have."

"Cheeky fellow! Uncle Julian will be quite alarmed to learn that you've been bedding my housemates, when you are supposed to be protecting my honor!"

Thus we passed the hours—performing a sophistication beyond

our years—till the music ended sometime after midnight and the limos, now capped with three inches of snow, lined up to take us back to the Radcliffe campus. Those of us who were out-of-town "gentlemen guests" were convoyed to Harvard Yard, where we had been allocated vacated beds in a freshman dormitory. Clearly, neither hall reps nor House Mother deemed after-hours *pas de deux* in South House an acceptable finish to such a lofty social event. Lying in the narrow bed in the room to which I'd been assigned, an unfamiliar quilt drawn up to my chin, I listened to the staccato hiss of the radiator—more cha-cha-cha than fox trot—and I watched the snow fall on the Yard, etching invisible tree limbs in luminous white, and I was unable to fall asleep for all the excitement pulsing through my limbs. And I futilely wondered whether Mary Jo, in her room, was also lying awake, unable to relinquish the glamour of this long evening and whether, as I was thinking of her, she was thinking of me.

22

"I'M (NOT) ALL RIGHT"

I didn't see Mary Jo again until Christmas recess. As he'd earlier hinted, Mr. Julian summoned his niece to share the holiday with him, delivering his invitation in an imperious tone that couldn't be ignored,
so she declined the holiday invitations of more proximate relatives in
Connecticut and more distant friends in Paris to accompany me on
the long trek to Virginia. It was the same route that I had taken six
months ago, except that Mary Jo and I caught an overnight express
that arrived in Washington in the morning and Roanoke in early afternoon. From the Roanoke station we transferred to the Greyhound
depot to take the bus to Rocky Hill; and since it passed within a block
of the Brewster estate, we disembarked at Honeysuckle Heights and
walked the few steps to the gates of Mr. Julian's home.

Thus it was that Mary Jo and I found ourselves ambling down
that graveled drive between the now-leafless rows of elms, as the dark
stones, faded bricks, and storied timbers of the house rose before us
that late wintry afternoon. I remember the moment vividly. Mary Jo
was wearing her suede coat with the black fur collar. I was carrying her
two bags and my own, and she had threaded her gloved hand through
my arm. I entertained the fancy that, to any onlooker peering out of
the blank windows of the old mansion, we appeared happy newlyweds returning home—though in reality we more closely resembled
siblings whose affection for each other was filial and no more.

My imaginings were rudely interrupted when the massive front
door swung open and I found myself staring at Hank Atwater, wearing George Geronimo's livery and smiling at me with the hint of a
smirk on his thin lips. Mary Jo had no reason to be aware of my as-
tonishment. She'd heard Mr. Julian had hired a replacement to fill
the void left by G. G.'s death so, announcing herself as Mr. Julian's
niece, she carelessly slipped off her jacket, handing it to Hank as if
his presence were of no more significance to her than a coat rack, and

asked him to carry her suitcases upstairs. He nodded obsequiously, and before I recovered from my surprise enough to acknowledge our acquaintance, he'd turned away, still smirking.

Mr. Julian waited in the drawing room. He'd heard us in the foyer, and his piercing blue eyes eagerly looked over the reading glasses perched on his nose with something close to delight as we entered the chamber. He was sitting in the deco-inspired French leather club chair by the fireplace, where a blaze was voraciously devouring the kindling, and I noticed that the book in his lap was a traveler's guide to Europe. The mantel was festooned with boughs, as were the valences over the French doors leading to the back terrace, and the scent of cedar mingled with his Chanel cologne. There was no tree, at least yet, but the old man certainly seemed to be making an effort to mark the season, not only in décor but in his unusually jovial demeanor.

"So you've delivered my charge to me, safe and sound!" he chirruped as he rose to receive Mary Jo's kisses and return my handshake. "My lovely grown-up niece! I trust Newt hasn't been neglecting you?"

Mary Jo assured him that I'd been a knight-in-shining-armor all semester long.

"That's as it should be. Newt doesn't mind, either—eh, Newt?" He winked at me. "A little port, my dears? A wee early in the afternoon, but we *are* approaching the holidays, aren't we, and *this*"—motioning us to the sofa—"is quite the special occasion indeed!"

He chuckled and walked to the Sheraton sideboard, where a decanter and small crystal glasses awaited. There the photograph Mary Jo had sent her uncle of the two of us in our formal splendor was displayed in a lavish silver frame. Mr. Julian seemed as pleased as punch to be able to serve us, for once, rather than be served himself.

"Sit next to each other, so I can look at you both: such a handsome pair, even more splendid in person!" The feline Mimi materialized out of nowhere and, leaping onto the sofa, rubbed against my side as if she actually remembered me.

Mr. Julian wanted to hear about our journey, and we made the polite answers the occasion called for; then he wanted to hear about our terms, about which there was too much to tell, even though the prospect of finals still loomed for both of us after New Year.

"Well, you will just have to hold study-hall in the library!" he said brightly.

I reminded Mr. Julian that I needed to call my parents to pick me up. But the old codger would have none of such talk, not yet, and made me sit tight while he poured us another thimbleful of the sweet port and redirected the conversation to a topic close to all of our hearts—Marky's wellbeing. He seemed determined to tease forth our worst fears, quizzing us about his nephew's state of mind, his suspect acquaintances, his latest vices. The more Mary Jo and I improved ourselves, the old man bemoaned, the more the reprobate's demerits loomed large. We must prepare for the worst.

Fortunately, neither Mary Jo nor I said anything too disparaging about Marky. For at last Mr. Julian could no longer contain himself and broke out laughing till tears ran from his watery eyes. We looked on, bewildered. "Surprise, surprise!" he called out. On cue none other than Marky emerged from the library entrance, just out of sight on the other side of the Heppelwhite highboy, a shit-eating grin on his face, a gigantic red bow wrapped around his waist, and a Santa Claus hat on his head.

"I decided to give you two your Christmas present early," Mr. Julian triumphantly announced, shaking with mirth at the fine joke that he'd pulled on us.

So it turned out that the old man's perverted sense of humor had not disappeared but had merely been lying in wait, under the veil of jovial sociability that had greeted our arrival. He clapped his hands and rocked in laughter, no doubt thinking he was as clever as the illusionist who's just reassembled the lady he's sawn in half, blithely unaware that his version of Genie was equal parts Grinch.

Mary Jo and I gaped at Marky's magical appearance, each at a loss for words though for different reasons and with different emotions. I had long feared this moment of reencounter, ever since that afternoon at the pool when he'd stood behind me, urging me on. Marky enveloped his sister in an embrace that lifted her off the ground, then squeezed me in a brotherly bear hug. He seemed as delighted at the prank as his guardian, too much so to notice my perturbation. I half-listened in a daze as Mr. Julian explained how he'd plotted for

Marky to arrive a day before us. Mary Jo was ecstatic, of course, to see her brother, and, shooing Mimi off the sofa, seated him between us, fully intent on monopolizing his attention. But before he gave himself over to his sister, he turned my way, and fixed my eyes with his cat-like gaze. In those green depths I saw neither denial nor challenge, and I breathed a sigh of relief. Seconds later Marky had repositioned his Santa hat on Mary Jo, who made it look almost fashionable. As she deluged her brother with questions, Mr. Julian smiled approvingly from his chair. I took advantage of the interlude to scrutinize Marky.

He had entered the room and thrown himself on the couch with the same easy savoir faire that had so impressed and intimidated me the first day we met; and yet something subtle in his demeanor had changed. For one he simply *looked* different, more mature than I remembered; he had become lean, one might even say gaunt, although not in an unattractive way. His hair was longer than it had ever been, and instead of the elegantly casual clothing he had once sported, he was carelessly attired in rumpled black jeans and a ratty black sweater pulled over a faded tee shirt, which, abetted by the dark circles under his eyes and two-day stubble on his jaw, lent him a world-weary, cosmopolitan, indeed Gallic mystique: doubtless the intended effect.

Amid all the affection he showered on Mary Jo, and the sparkling eyes he turned to me and his uncle as the siblings's conversation expanded to include us, I also sensed something different in the energy he emanated—it was more electric, more edgy, more prone to shifts of mood than I remembered. All these slight changes added up to a totality that was more than mere pose; they signaled a change in how he saw the world—perhaps in how he saw us. Even in those first minutes of being reunited, I understood, dimly, Mary Jo's feeling of having been left behind as Marky moved into orbits of his own choosing.

But the magnetism was still there, and it held me, as it did his sister, in its spell. And on this day, at least, none of the teasing insinuations or taunting jests that had sometimes fretted me were in evidence; just the charm, pure and simple, and with it, Marky's contagious sense of fun. Another hour passed before I remembered to call my family. When I did, it was clear that they'd been waiting with anticipation, and, shame to say, I didn't feel as badly as I ought to have.

And that became the pattern for the rest of my vacation: whenever I was with my siblings and parents, I was calculating how much longer I must wait before finding an excuse to slip back to the Brewster mansion. Mr. Julian was no help. As the presiding genius of his domain, he egged the twins and me on in our renewed intimacy, dismissing us to go "play" after he'd had a taste of our company, giving Bruno a long holiday that eliminated his presence in the house (Scotty, per George Geronimo's predictions, had been fired last August, and Hank Atwater was smart enough to keep his distance). When the four of us dined together by candlelight, the old man supported our daydreams of a future in which we three would roam the globe together, finally settling down to live in the same foreign capital. In my heart I knew these were pipe dreams, as different futures beckoned each of us: Marky's commitment to cinema; the stipulations that my benefactor had set on my own education; the unspoken expectation that Mary Jo was destined to make a spectacular match that would bring credit to the family. But for now, under the long spell cast by our being reunited for this finite duration, we were able to suspend those realities and indulge in fantasies of an undivided future.

As I moved between my home and the Brewster mansion in shuttlecock fashion, Christmas came and went, and so did New Year's Day. Marky's nine-day holiday ended, and before I knew it Mary Jo's departure also loomed—Radcliffe's finals began before Phipps' winter break ended. Our last evening, the two of us went to see Zeffirelli's "Romeo and Juliet," which—released the previous summer—had finally reached Rocky Hill, and although we'd both seen it twice, we looked forward to experiencing its magic one more time. If I entered the theater sad that our time together was drawing to a close, I also nursed a warm glow in my belly, the result of the sheer relief I felt at knowing that the three of us had rekindled the best parts of our friendship without awakening its more ambiguous eros.

Of course the spell of the film's lush score, its dewy-eyed leads, and, above all, the presence of Mary Jo seated inches away was just too much for a romantic dreamer as myself. Exiting the theatre, I effused about true love, tragically thwarted desire, eternal beauty— hoping against hope that my lyric musings would spark in Mary Jo

a kindred feeling that would (what else?) flame into iambic declarations of undying love. Or maybe kindle into just enough heat to
warrant a drive to the Overlook, where we would park at a discrete
distance from the four or five cars already there, and neck in the front
seat while the stars glimmered their approval.

Mary Jo interrupted my encomium to Shakespearean love with a
soft laugh. "You are so cute, Newt. Really."

"Are you making fun of me?"

"I mean it." She chastely touched my cheek. "Let's go home."

I pulled Dad's car to a stop at the end of the Brewster driveway,
near the old carriage house. It was the clearest of winter nights, thousands of stars twinkling icily above our heads, and we lingered as we
crossed the hushed silence of the back yard. The lights of the empty
drawing room fell in shafts across the flagstone patio and spilled onto
the gray lawn, ending near our feet. A soft glow lit Mr. Julian's bedroom windows—he must be reading in bed. As we approached the
drawing room, we saw Hank enter and begin tidying up. By mutual
consent, we slowed our steps.

"It's hard to believe he attacked your father." Mary Jo's breath
condensed into evanescent goblins in the dark. "I don't like him, any
more than you, but he's been as quiet as a church mouse since I arrived."

"He's just biding his time." I'd quizzed my father once I'd discovered Hank working for Mr. Julian. Dad had indeed rehired him last
summer, but Hank had handed in his resignation six weeks ago without a hint as to his prospects. Why he'd returned to Dad's employ,
then left it so soon, and for what, had remained a mystery to my father
until I'd told him about Hank's new mode of employment.

Mary Jo suppressed a chuckle. "Look on the bright side. He
doesn't seem to be pocketing the silver. And now's his opportunity."

We walked further away from the house. The sky was awash with
milky pinpoints of shivering light, and for a few minutes we stood
looking upwards, playing a game that our trio had invented—discovering fictitious constellations, then improvising myths to accompany
the fantastical names we gave them.

"Are you cold?" Mary Jo asked, once we turned our eyes back to our more earthly surrounds. "I don't feel like going inside quite yet. Let's stroll a bit longer. If it's all right with you."

Compared to those distant stars, so cold and so aloof, her words seemed tantalizingly warm and close. My seventeen-year-old self hardly dared hope that those simple words held the promise of something more, yet the air around us seemed to vibrate with unannounced expectations. Our arms linked I allowed Mary Jo to draw me more deeply into the darkness of the far lawn, and we wandered into the ruined garden, which on any other night would have seemed unbearably haunted at such an hour. As we rambled, our steps led us without my quite being aware of it—so caught was I in a state of suspended reality, trying to calm the pounding of my heart—through the archway cut into the hedge, now much overgrown and brushing against us, and into the secluded recess of the swimming pool.

Despite the black shadows cast by the surrounding hedge, the pool and dressing rooms stood out as distinctly as if outlined in white ink. The temperature had hovered below freezing for the past several days, and as a consequence the surface of the pool, which had not been properly drained without George Geronimo to tend to it, had frozen into a sheet of ice strewn with the detritus of winter and neglect. We walked to its edge, looking down—the water was two feet below its normal level and, frozen, gave off an alien glow—and Mary Jo took my gloved hand and pressed it. I sensed she wanted to speak.

As I waited, my eyes scanned the surface of the dark ice. I could make out clumps of leaves, branches, a battered sheet of newspaper, a glint of silver I realized was a gum wrapper that had frozen into the ice. Then my eyes caught something else, something that looked out of place, and I pointed.

"What is it?" Mary Jo breathed.

We knelt, still holding hands, peering at the splayed shape. It took a few seconds for the form to materialize into the bloated corpse of a kitten, a scrawny malnourished thing with twigs for limbs that had met its death in the watery expanse—chased over the pool's edge by another animal, unable to scramble out?—and whose little body, floating to the surface, had been embalmed in the ice.

"That's heart-breaking," I said.

I wanted to look for a rake to pry it from the icy grip that held it fast, but Mary Jo stopped me.

"No, Newt, not now," she whispered, turning to me, her face inches from my own. She took both my hands in her own, her face turned down and dark hair hiding her eyes.

"This place," she said, slowly turning to look up at me. I couldn't read her eyes. "That day, two summers ago. What happened—it was Marky's idea. He made me promise to go along with it. You see, I think it was you he wanted."

I felt dazed, out of my depth. I started to protest, but no words rose to my lips. Instead a wave of nausea slammed me.

"I thought you should know," Mary Jo repeated. Her voice sounded as distant, and she seemed as impossibly removed from me, as the cold stars glittering overhead.

"I'm all right," I said, answering a question that hadn't been asked.

"But don't you want to talk—"

"I said I'm all right." In glum silence I turned, and then she turned, and we walked through the frozen landscape back towards the house.

23

SITTING OUT AND GETTING IN

Eleven months later the minds of most eighteen-year-old American males were preoccupied with graver concerns than mine. Richard Nixon had been sworn into office at the beginning of the year; the draft lottery had been reinstated December 1; and me?—obsessed with composing the most dazzling college admission essay the world had ever seen. My days at Phipps seemed to be rushing, suddenly and relentlessly, to an end—a reality that would have been depressing were not that terminus touted as the entrance into an even more exciting realm. Ensuring a smooth transition across that threshold, indeed, was the goal upon which the Academy's reputation was staked.

Ever since our return to Andover after Christmas vacation, it was hard for any of us uppers, as eleventh-graders were called, to escape the shadow of our impending collegiate prospects; the very structure of Phipps encouraged such a mindset, mandating our participation in a series of advisement sessions with counselors whose purpose in life was to guide us successfully through the hurdle of next fall's college application process, which they did by handicapping our odds and advising us accordingly.

"Timmy's down for Princeton, Daveen for Harvard, Simon for Brown," so these Gods ordained, which meant that Timmy's chances at Harvard or Brown had decreased by half.

An adviser's hearty "By all means, apply to Yale, excellent choice! But really, Jonas, take a *serious* look at Dartmouth or Williams!" was shorthand for another message altogether: we've already determined our top five competitors for Yale, and you are not on that list.

I don't mention Yale lightly. Ever since Yale's announcement that it was going coed, the New Haven campus had become the Ivy of Choice for Phippsian lads salivating at the notion of leaving all-male education behind once and for all. But Elihu Yale's institution wasn't the prize to which I aspired. From the first day I visited Mary Jo in

Cambridge, I began stoking other fantasies—what better culmination to the story of my progress than entering Harvard, the nation's most storied institution of higher education? And what better way to guarantee my intimacy with Mary Jo than attending Radcliffe's "sibling" college?

Though the seeds of this desire had been planted as early as the fall afternoon I waited for Mary Jo by the corner entrance to Harvard Yard facing the Coop, and though it continued to grow with subsequent visits, I didn't realize the Faustian lengths I was willing to go to join this exclusive club until the spring of my junior year. The occasion was the takeover of Harvard's University Hall by Students for a Democratic Society, in response to the Corporation's refusal to alter its policy of allowing ROTC on-campus recruitment. To those of us in the Fortinbras household crowding around the television to watch the news on the evening of April 9, 1969, the images of that day's events were as spellbinding as any World Series playoff: the locked chain placed on the door of the administration building; the gleeful occupiers flashing peace signs and power fists from the windows while waving SDS flags; and most of all, the fate of the dean who, refusing to vacate his office, found himself hoisted aloft in his desk chair and indecorously expelled by a dozen students. We were abuzz—the student protests that had seemed so distant when Marky had written from the front lines of Paris last year had breached our shores.

But it was at breakfast the next day that matters turned really interesting. It was still dark outside, and we three boarders and Miranda were blearily crunching our way through bowls of Wheat Chex. We were the perennial early risers, as we had to set out for morning chapel a good hour before Wim dropped Kirby off at his elementary school. So we were surprised when Andy bounded down the stairs and into the kitchen with fire flashing in his eyes—after working late shifts at the Spa he usually slept in. "Listen up!" he announced, flipping on the radio buttressing the row of cereal boxes on top of the refrigerator.

"What are you *doing*?" Miranda moaned as he fiddled with the dial. "Too much static in my brain already!"

"Too bad, kiddo." Andy turned to face us. "The four of you need to wake up and tune in. I've been following this story since late last night." That's when we learned that President Pusey had summoned the State Police to remove the occupiers of University Hall en masse. Even at this ungodly hour the early news was filled with outraged spokespersons for campus and Cambridge communities who— whatever their feelings about the student takeover—condemned the President's middle-of-the-night decision to involve state police in a university matter.

Andy drew up a chair and leaned forward into the huddle we made around the milk-spotted Formica tabletop. He looked at each of us conspiratorially. "*Fuck* Phipps and Adams." Nodding upwards at the creaking floorboards overhead, a sign Mick and Wim had arisen, he continued. "No need to involve the Parental Unit. You're coming with me to Cambridge to see what's going down. No ifs, ands, or buts—if there was ever a day to go rogue, *this* is it. I've got the station wagon today, and I'll meet you at the corner of Rosewood. Get your book-bags and coats and set off like normal. Now move!"

What's amazing is how quickly we acceded to Andy's plan, swept along by his urgency—and, just perhaps, by the thrill of so blatantly doing something that we knew was, if not exactly criminal, an infraction for which we would later be held accountable. The sheer audacity of breaking my perfect attendance record was enough, in and of itself, to propel me out the door and into the Fortinbras station wagon when Andy pulled into Rosewood. Dewey, of course, needed no excuse to cut class; Snodgrass was too gripped by the moment to consider consequences; and Miranda saw Andy's proposition in moral terms: he was one of the draft-age men who might be forced to serve in the war the Harvard students were protesting.

An hour later, Andy wedged the car into a parking space that one of his friends had staked out for us with dented trashcans in front of his triple-decker off Central Square. I used a payphone to call Mary Jo, who agreed to meet us in front of Widener Library. The crowds walking along Mass Ave swelled as our posse passed the Orson Welles Theatre, and soon we found ourselves swept up in waves of slogan-chanting people of sundry ages and motley lifestyles bearing down on campus. At Andy's suggestion, we veered from the crowd to enter the Yard through the back entrance on Prescott in case the police blocked off the Mass Ave gates—and by the time we neared Widener, the quad had grown thick with excited students and spectators spilling across the lawn. A group of young men dressed in army fatigues, faces painted like death masks, passed by, waving an American flag whose center had been burnt out as with raised fists they chanted "Outta Nam!" Another group bearing the banner "Professors and Students Unite!" was calling for the resignation of President Pusey, whose effigy, seated in a desk chair, had been lofted overhead. The black student coalition was dispersing Panther pamphlets. A trio of beaded hippie minstrels sang protest songs and dispensed free joints.

Anxious-looking campus security officers patrolled the crowd, and I noticed a roving crew of newscasters from Channel 5 at the same time that I spotted Mary Jo waiting at the bottom of the library steps, cheeks flushed. A trickle of students, books in hand and heads downcast, scurried to morning class. The excitement in the air was palpable, as, with Mary Jo in tow, we plunged into the roving multitude.

At the top of the library steps, a frizzy-haired young man with a red bandana tied around his brow and a megaphone pressed to his lips began exhorting the onlookers gathered nearby. Another crowd gathered in front of Memorial Church where, rumor had it, students were debating the ethics of boycotting class. Tension ran highest, however, in front of University Hall. Supporters of the SDS cadre that had been dragged from the building in the early morning hours were venting their rage in growing numbers. Some bore flags with the black letters STRIKE! emblazoned across a raised crimson fist, others carried placards supporting the rights of campus workers and protesting the Corporation's support of ROTC. Despite the peace symbols decorating many of the posters, the undercurrent of fury uniting the mass of demonstrators was anything but peaceful. Here, more than anywhere else, campus security and uniformed officers, probably National Guard, warily stood at alert, keeping a path clear for those administrators gutsy enough to enter the reclaimed building. Protestors openly heckled officers whose darting eyes belied their stock-still postures, tensed to spring to action at the first sign of violence.

Which inevitably erupted. Close to entrance of University Hall, someone shoved a security officer, and as his comrades in arms moved en masse to remove the protester, other spectators started pushing the officers from behind, backed by a swelling chorus of angry voices chanting for the removal of the pigs PIGS *PIGS*!

Within seconds the lawn was a hornets' nest of chaotic frenzy as people pressed in from all directions, buffeting our little group. "Up here!" called Andy, motioning us to retreat behind the Chinese stele and step onto the concrete seating that ran the length of the side of Widener. From this perch we looked down at the mass erupting in violence.

In no time Channel 5's cameramen had arrived to catch the melee. A general fisticuffs had broken loose amid enraged shouts and terrified screams. A Pepsi Cola bottle surreally met one officer's baton midair, spraying slivers of glass and liquid in all directions, and a uniformed guard wrestled a screaming youth to the ground. A woman turned my way, blood running down the side of her face, and for a timeless second her stunned eyes stared right into mine. Another officer hit the ground. The excitement grew too contagious for Andy to resist, who after exhorting the rest of us to "stay put!" jumped down from our observation post and joined the mass of bodies surging back and forth in front of the Hall. All the while, an intrepid news anchor threaded the mass, shoving his microphone into people's faces to record their spontaneous reactions as the cameraman at his side captured their stunned expressions. Then the cameraman lifted his camera and, panning across the crowd, turned his lens in our direction and zoomed in.

This was too much for me.

"We need to leave," I shouted to my companions. "It's not safe."

"Don't be such a fucking wimp," Dewey sneered.

"We should be all right here." Miranda put her arm through mine to reassure me.

Snodgrass, goggle-eyed, was too mesmerized by the action unfolding before us to respond in any way other than pinching his privates through his khakis to avoid spontaneous overflow, but Mary Jo turned my way.

"College life too much for you?" she asked, an ironic arch to her brow.

"You want to end up on the news?" I pointed to the camera crew. "I still have to get *into* college and I don't need a black mark on my record. Especially if I want to get in *here!*"

There—I'd said it. In those few seconds, the paranoid idea that I might be risking my chances of admission should I be identified as a participant in the violence escalating before our eyes overwhelmed me. Not until this instant did I realize how very much I wanted to go to Harvard: the idea of a chance mishap intervening to ruin my hopes propelled me into an unreasoned state of panic.

A look of incredulity fluttered across Mary Jo's beautiful face.

"What *would* Marky say?" Her voice was cool, and I flushed. Seconds later, she whispered something in Dewey's ear. For once living up to his moniker, Do-It stepped off the concrete benching and, placing his hands around Mary Jo's waist, lifted her down to his level. Smooth—you would have thought he was Rudolf Nureyev partnering with Margot Fontaine. The two of them, waving saucily, vanished in the press of angry bodies.

Miranda, who had anxiously watched our outburst, spoke up. "Maybe you're right, Newt. The others know where to catch up with us later. Come'n, Charlie"—she tugged authoritatively at Snodgrass, who followed wherever led—"time to ditch this scene."

Thus ended my first foray into student activism. The second Mary Jo had cast her icy look of judgment my way, summoning forth her brother's political convictions in the process, I felt utterly caught out, having revealed an ambition that, till then, I had not quite admitted to myself. Intuiting my conflicting emotions, Miranda tried to distract me. Snodgrass remained oblivious, gaping at the piebald pageantry swirling around us as we regained the calmer crowds by Houghton.

Later in the day, we gathered at Bartley's Burgers—our predetermined meeting place should we get separated. When Mary Jo and Dewey joined us, breathless and thick as thieves, I was relieved to see she no longer wore the withering look of scorn my cowardice had earlier occasioned. The two of them were much too engrossed in trumpeting their heroics—they'd rescued one protester by tripping the officer about to handcuff him—to notice my emotions. My heart sank as I looked at the stupid grin decorating Dewey's face since I knew there was no one but myself to blame for his surge in cockiness, and for my fall from grace as Mary Jo's chevalier in waiting.

24

THE CURTAIN RISES

Almost exactly one year later, I waited with tens of thousands of other seniors across the nation as admission and rejection letters were posted to our mailboxes on April 1, 1970. The first news was good: UVA, my fall-back school, was a go, and so was Wesleyan, my preferred of the smaller colleges. Rejected at Yale, to which I'd only half-heartedly applied; in at Dartmouth; rejected at Williams; and then the news I'd been waiting for: Harvard had accepted me. It was a dream come true, the perfect climax to my final year at Phipps. As fortune would have it, all three of us Fortinbras boarders opted for universities in the Boston area: Dewey would be attending Tufts, a few blocks above Davis Square on the Cambridge side of the Charles, where he would only have to work moderately hard; and Snodgrass was confident his eccentricities would find a welcome home with the other science nerds at M.I.T., right down Mass Ave from me. The weekend after we made our decisions Mick and Wim hosted a special dinner for the three of us, replete with any number of toasts and heartfelt offers to return to Andover as our home-away-from-home any time we felt the need for some TLC or home cooking—a possibility that our future proximity actually made feasible. At the Fortinbrases' invitation, Mary Jo had taken the train up to join in the celebration. Since each of us had been asked to invite a favorite teacher (an opportunity only Dewey declined), I had invited my classics mentor, Dr. Vance, as his endorsement of my developing aptitude in Greek as well as Latin had played a crucial role in my admission; and Pastor Pete, everyone's favorite, had come at Charlie's invitation.

News of my triumph had reached Rocky Hill, too, of course. Mr. Allbright sent word that my anonymous benefactor was especially pleased that my diligence had paid off so royally. In addition to the already stipulated financial arrangements that had been laid out for my education, I would now be receiving a generous spending allowance as long as I remained in good standing. Meanwhile, Mr. Julian—as if I must keep up the fiction that he hadn't already rewarded me beyond all expectations—made me the gift of a post-graduation weekend trip to Manhattan in Mary Jo's company: express train tickets to Grand Central, rooms at the Algonquin, and orchestra seats to see "Applause" at the Palace Theatre. My parents too were duly impressed at my achievement; even for them, the name "Harvard" was magical—although the fact that I wanted to pursue a degree in Classics was a puzzle no amount of explanation elucidated.

I didn't get to gloat too long over my success; more immediate matters lay at hand. I'm not talking about simply finishing classes, but about my role as the director of the spring production of the Phipps and Adams Drama Clubs—an honor perhaps inspiring Mr. Julian to make my graduation present include a Broadway outing with Mary Jo. My involvement with the club, which had begun as a lark, had become a passion, along with swimming and deciphering Classical texts. I'd gotten involved in the Phipps-Adams club the fall of my junior year when I helped build and paint art-deco drops for Cole Porter's "Anything Goes." While the lure of the spotlight never struck me, I quite reveled in returning to the Fortinbras home from the prop shop at midnight smeared head to toe in layers of acrylic paint, sawdust, and epoxy that took half an hour of scalding water to dissolve. And in the process of learning to build sets I discovered a talent for set design itself—despite a childhood spent sketching elaborate floor plans and furnishings for mansions I'd never inhabit, I'd never thought of myself as possessing an artistic bent before.

The following spring I was charged with creating the set for the annual Shakespeare production, "The Tempest" (it was an iron-clad tradition that while the clubs could choose any vehicle—most often a musical—in the fall semester, the spring production must be Shakespeare and coordinated with the Senior English instructors). In dreaming up a surreal version of Prospero's island, replete with rising levels and sinking holes, a landscape in which all green foliage had been replaced with coral, and a sky that was either malevolently violet or mellow yellow—all very Sergeant Pepper—I must have revealed some latent affinity for island fantasies. For the following autumn I took on the set design for "South Pacific." Bali Hai never beckoned so luminously as it did under my touch, as a simulation of the isle made of neon lights descended over the gasping audience during Bloody Mary's solo. Rumor has it the custodial staff grumbled for the next decade about the sand that my team had hauled from Swanscott Beach to cover the aisles of the auditorium, down which audience members were forced to tread in multicolored flip flops handed out in the lobby.

The spring semester Shakespeare production always occurred during graduation weekend, so that parents could take in the show along with myriad other activities designed to convince them that their pocketbooks had been drained for a good cause, but planning began in the fall. The pre-selected tragedy was "Hamlet," and I campaigned to assume the role of director—being set designer no longer sated my aspirations. Once I received the nod, I launched a crusade to mount an "interpretation" that rendered the Bard's themes newly relevant for our age: namely, Stoppard's retelling of "Hamlet" from the perspective of the hapless peons Rosencrantz and Guildenstern. Production rights, however, far exceeded our club's budget, a bump in the road that only inspired my more audacious scheme: to convince the Board to allow a student to write a creative adaptation of Shakespeare. I hardly need add that the very concept was heresy to Phippsian tradition. Or that the student-author I had in mind was myself.

My revisionist efforts began with a simple reversal: to explore what might have been the consequences for Hamlet's Oedipally tortured psyche had his mother Gertrude—in my revision, the beloved queen of the Danes—been the victim of poisoning by her husband, the regent prince who murders her so that he can marry her manipulative, carnally possessed sister Claudia, the object of his own incestuous desire. In this retelling, the ghost of Gertrude appears not to Hamlet but to her god-daughter Ophelia, asking for her intercession in helping poor Hamlet sort out his confusion, and Ophelia becomes the mad-appearing "secret agent" who attempts to bring about rightful action in a world that sees her as nothing more than an object of royal barter ("oh that this too too sullied flesh" gained new significance coming from Ophelia's lips). In the course of events, Ophelia fakes her suicide to incite Hamlet to action and ownership of Danish destiny, only to see how inconsequential all her efforts prove to be: in the process she becomes the play's voice of existential angst ("to be or not to be" she laments) and the ultimate victim of the male-motivated violence that erupts in the blood-strewn finale.

As might be imagined, Miranda was quite delighted at my proto-feminist revision. She also proved to be one my most insightful critics.

"Why do you have to follow Shakespeare's ending down to the last corpse?" she asked. "Any story has multiple possible outcomes; there's always the big *what if*—what if we'd taken a different turn in the road? Does Ophelia have to die just because Hamlet does?"

That inspired me anew—not simply to rewrite the ending but to present *two* endings: first, the one in which Ophelia dies; then one in which she survives the carnage. Instead of this being a restoration of order, of wrongs set right, however, she faces a new "to be or not to be" moment: whether to embrace her destiny as heir to the kingdom or set out on her own, unknown, path. In effect, the choices of what to believe happened are left up to the audience.

I finished my first draft over Christmas break and, as the fates would have it, the timing was perfect. With one eye on the student protests roiling campuses nationwide and the other on the growing disdain of elitist education among America's youth that was leading to a drop in private school enrollments, Phipps was searching for ways, within limits, to trumpet its openness to new ideas and creative education, to advertise, in other words, its Hipness—and my concept of (as the playbill judiciously worded it) "honoring Shakespeare" by giving his most famous tragedy "an innovative twist that speaks to our times" fit the bill, since the school saw how well it might serve their own agenda. There were caveats: I had to agree to rewrites with Phipps' creative writing tutor and consult with the senior English instructor to make sure the "spirit" of Shakespeare lived on in my revision. Some of my more radical ideas were vetoed, but I carried the larger point—staging my own play.

I threw myself into the task with a passion, determined to leave a mark on Phipps with this parting stroke. Once the student newspaper championed our effort as radically anti-establishment, Phipps boys and Adams girls joined our effort in record numbers, eager to be part of what was shaping up to be the season's event. Never had so many hands volunteered to paint flats, erect ramparts, post publicity, sell tickets, and swell the cast as occurred that April and May. I basked in my role as minor campus celebrity, and I took my multiple roles— writer, director, and (because I wouldn't give up my first love) set designer—ever so seriously in those final months of our senior year.

By the end of May, we were ready: the week before graduation had seen our rehearsals move from galling to galvanized, and our two-night run on graduation weekend met with boisterous approval from our fellow students—who in cheering us on felt they were cheering on the spirit of the times—and with many a perplexed look among the politely applauding parents in the audience. I daresay my script was awful, but I was supported by an often talented and always enthusiastic cast; what my writing lacked was allayed by my unexpected competence as a director; and the construction team's realization of my abstract set design gave Elsinore's beetling cliffs, rank gardens, and arras-covered walls a broodingly psychodramatic ambience far eclipsing my attempts at iambic pentameter.

Thus the spring semester of my senior year passed in a theatrical blur; first the suspense of awaiting the results of my college applications, and then, before I had barely had time to exult in that good news, the onset of nightly rehearsals that, juxtaposed with the work involved in finishing classes, led to the defining pinnacle of my Phipps experience: graduation weekend. Our production played on Friday and Saturday nights, bookending the Saturday afternoon graduation ceremony. Inundated by a range of emotions, I stood backstage that final evening before taking my seat in the darkened auditorium and, putting my face to a small rent in the worn crimson curtain, peeked out as the auditorium filled with spectators. Diploma in hand: I had come this far, and now I was ready to make my final offering to an epoch that I was convinced had transformed me in a mere two years. While stagehands fussed with the smoke machine that would wrap Elsinore's ramparts in ghostly mist, and while Horatio and the Ghost of Hamlet's mother paced backstage, deep breathing in preparation for their entrances, I inhaled the dusty scent of the velvet drapery as I surveyed the audience.

There, on the fifth row, with the best views in the house, sat my parents, proud of if not fully comprehending the magnitude of the threshold I had just crossed. Dad appeared tragicomically uncomfortable in a Sunday suit that buckled around his shoulders and a tie that choked his Adam's apple. Mother, despite the loss of her Grace Kelly French twist, managed to look coolly glamorous in a professional-woman manner, her turquoise, beige, and white twill suit complemented by faux pearl earrings and a circular gold pin on her lapel signifying her recent election to the post of President of the Franklin County Better Business Women's Association. My siblings had come up to New England with my parents and sat flanking them: Katie still sporting a Joni Mitchell hairstyle but otherwise reformed of her most outrageously flower-child tendencies, and Jubal, taller than ever, taking in everything and everybody with intelligent eyes.

Given the narrow aperture through which I was looking, it took some craning to get the proper perspective, but soon I found my two roommates, along with Miranda, seated in the front row of the balcony: Miranda and Charlie had returned to see the show a second time for the sheer joy of cheering me on; and Dewey, who had grown imposing sideburns over the past semester, had elected to join them, perhaps because he knew that the two seats they were saving were for Mary Jo and her date. I scanned the audience as it continued to fill, picking out friends here, teachers there, and teammates sprinkled throughout; and I felt myself yielding to a wave of nostalgia before the present had even become the past as I pondered everything, good and bad, that had befallen me at Phipps. I wished that Mr. Julian could be here, too, to witness what, through his curmudgeonly beneficence, I had achieved. But he was off reaping his own well-deserved reward, having departed three weeks earlier on the QE II with Bruno as his aide de camp, bound for Europe on the long-fantasized vacation that his recuperation had now made possible.

Wim and Mick Fortinbras, looking out of breath as if (as always) they had rushed to campus at the last minute, had now taken the seats I'd reserved for them by my parents. They kept bobbing their heads and smiling good wishes my way—had their many years at Phipps bestowed them with preternatural knowledge that the director of the spring production would be stationed behind this exact fold of stage curtain, nervously surveying the audience? Settling into the seats around them were Andy and his new girlfriend, as well as Kirby, looking seriously critical, and Daisy, bouncing up and down in her seat in misguided anticipation, no doubt, of a dance extravaganza in which I would lead Mary Jo in a lively polka across the stage floor. The Fortinbras household had fairly been bursting with activity over graduation week. Not only were Wim and Mick putting up visitors who had come to town for graduation, but Wim's first-born, Larry by name, happened to be paying one of his rare visits from France. Looking every bit a successful CEO, down to the balding spot on the crown of his head, he'd flown into Boston a week earlier on business and arrived the day before in Andover to spend a few days of leisure with his father and stepmother. I spotted him lingering at the rear of the auditorium, checking his watch: he was waiting for a companion arriving separately by train from Boston.

That put me in mind of Mary Jo: I hoped that she hadn't missed *her* train. Lifting my eyes to the front row balcony, I saw that I need not have worried: for there she was, Mary Jo Sumner, whose personal radiance made up for the fact that her date was annoyingly handsome in a collegiate, silver-tongued sort of way. I wasn't the only envious party; Dewey was aggressively thrusting his chin in his competition's direction.

The lights in the theater started to dim; it was almost time for the show to begin, and I confess my eyes watered as I turned to make my way down the side hall to the lobby, where I would enter the auditorium and take my place on the back row. I reached the lobby as the warning buzzer sounded, sending a final influx of elegantly clad gentlemen and ladies scurrying from the restrooms. I waited by the padded door as an usher held it open for these stragglers: other ushers stood ready to help them find their aisles in the darkening auditorium. The buzzer sounded one last time, and for a millisecond I found myself measuring the approach of a splendidly dressed, regal-looking black woman of middle-age wearing Jackie Onassis sunglasses, a woman whose beautifully coiffed hair, draped by a gold-threaded scarf casually knotted under her chin, and diamond-studded jewelry spelt wealth and leisure. As she removed the glasses and put them in her Gucci leather bag, I felt with surety she must be a celebrity I couldn't quite place—an opera singer, perhaps, or a recording artist, or a novelist—for minor celebrities did make it to our campus on occasion. Her ebony eyes, set off by lavender eye-shade and long mascaraed lashes, caught my inadvertent stare as she brushed past me, and her carefully penciled eyebrows lifted ever so slightly as she smiled the courteous but distant smile that one stranger bestows upon another in polite circumstances. Looking into the auditorium, I noted with curiosity that Larry Fortinbras had immediately approached and given her his arm, as she murmured something in French to him that reverberated in a rich contralto voice whose echoes, if not meaning, reached my ears. Before I could observe more, they had moved down the aisle to take their places in the darkness.

The lights now completely extinguished and the audience lapsing into expectant silence, I slipped into the cavernous room and lowered myself into my aisle seat on the last row. I was ready; I was filled with anticipation for what would come, as come it must.

And then the curtain rose: it was night, and drear, and an unlikely ghost stalked the stony ramparts of Elsinore, while icy waves crashed onto the dangerous rocks below.

PART THREE

25

PATHÉTIQUE FOR MARY JO

That triumphant exit from Phipps, one and all confidently assumed, was mere precursor to the similar triumph that would await me four years down the road. But four years later the truth turned out to be quite different indeed.

"A matter of some urgency": that is how I put it when, in the spring of 1973 I asked Mr. Allbright, as my benefactor's representative, to meet me in New York City. I knew that so monumental a discussion as the one I needed to initiate was best held on neutral terrain, and I knew that I must plan carefully what I needed to say. To Mr. Allbright's credit, he immediately sensed the gravity of my summons and responded with a detailed plan: he would arrive in Manhattan on Thursday of my spring break, the first free day his schedule allowed, and meet me at Schrafft's on Fifth, where his secretary had made us a seven o'clock dinner reservation. Surveying the staidly upscale dining room upon my entrance, I was grateful I'd worn my blazer and coaxed my long hair behind my ears—the days of shearing my locks to win Mr. Julian's approval had long since passed. Seated in a discreetly lit booth, our orders taken by tactful waiters in a room that slowly filled with business associates who sipped martinis, ordered well-done steaks, and spoke in hushed baritones that the thick table linens seemed designed to absorb, I was reminded of the future that I did not want to have.

Even though I arrived fifteen minutes early, Mr. Allbright was already ensconced in our banquette, enjoying a Manhattan as he invited me to order my highball of choice. "After all, you've been of legal age nearly five months!" His version of a droll wink added little expression, droll or otherwise, to his impartial face. "Though I suspect," he continued, in a spirit of raillery meant to ease us into the conversation that had brought us here, "you've had no trouble finding establishments happy to serve underage Harvard men. Including that dining club of yours—the membership fees should cover your bar tabs for a century!" He picked the cherry from his glass, sucking it from its stem with a smack of satisfaction. Our waiter approached. "Manhattan, or are you a martini drinker?"

To be contrary, I ordered a kir. Which Mr. Allbright brightly pronounced a "very Continental choice!" Of course, once I began to broach the subject on my mind, I wished I'd ordered a drink with more kick. First, I wanted Mr. Allbright to know that I was considering abandoning my concentration in Classics—a focus that I'd previously justified as a respectable stepping stone to a career in the diplomatic corps, or, if I decided to enter the ranks of academe, the necessary prerequisite for a Ph.D. My aptitude in Latin and Greek had continued to soar at Harvard, helping me to shine in a modest way among the constellation of intellects that surrounded me—my Latin tutor told the head of Classics that I had the makings of a first-rate Ciceronian. But of late my passion for what I was doing had waned—precipitously waned—and left me feeling as ossified as the languages in which I'd so happily immersed my energies only months before.

In a word, I felt dispirited and cut adrift. I hadn't realized just how dispirited or adrift until last month, when Mary Jo announced her engagement to Frederick Bentley Offenbach, perhaps the most wooden—and one of the more wealthy—of the Harvard suitors who'd paid her homage since her arrival at Radcliffe. That indignity was the last straw, and suddenly I saw myself as a bit of flotsam eddying down the stream of life with neither direction nor goal. While Mary Jo was readying to marry into Manhattan money, I'd betrothed myself to the realm of the irrelevant, facing a solitary future sifting through inscriptions of a long-dead past.

Naturally, I didn't confide the personal cause of my dissatisfaction to Mr. Allbright. His immediate response had been relief—his legalistic mind probably suspected much worse misdeeds preying on the conscience of a young man with too much money in his pockets and too many miles separating him from home. "Well now, Newt, no use crying over split milk," he declared. "There are other concentrations, some frankly more suited to a man of your intelligence. Mind you, I simply speak as a neutral observer. But spending the rest of your life establishing a fragment of Pindar!" He flicked a speck of offending lint from his jacket sleeve. "No doubt the life of a professor is an honorable pursuit. But we both know your Harvard education can open doors, *important* doors. You might consider a degree that will prepare you for law school—so many directions a bright lawyer can take these days—think District of Columbia or Wall Street! Yes, you'll fall back a semester or two changing concentrations at this late stage, but I'm sure I can make the case to your benefactor. Perhaps Political Science interests you?"

This being the longest speech I'd heard Mr. Allbright deliver since the December evening he came to Willow Woods to announce my good fortune, I hated to deflate it with the bombshell that I now dropped—namely, that I doubted Harvard was the institution where I should be pursuing *any* interests. Confronted with this heresy, Mr. Allbright's countenance—always so kindly impassive—registered something akin to a grimace, as if he had bitten into a particularly obstinate piece of gristle that, detaching itself from his steak Diane, had wedged its way between his molars.

"Won't do. Won't do at all, young man. You can trust that I am speaking for your benefactor when I say it won't do at all. Harvard's the number."

Over the awkward dinner that followed, we inched towards a compromise. A certain person's heart, Mr. Allbright firmly stressed, was set on my receiving a Crimson degree, and surely I didn't want to jeopardize said person's patronage. But neither, I countered, did I want to jeopardize my own happiness. Finally, Mr. Allbright convinced me, and I convinced myself, that it was in my best interest to take a leave of absence in the fall, during which time I would contemplate my direction and, according to the good lawyer's script, sow a few wild oats, realize the folly of my desires, and, thoroughly chastened, return to Harvard in the new year to finish the story of my rise as splendidly as it had begun.

What Mr. Allbright didn't count on was that I would extend that one semester's reprieve into a second, packing my bags in January of 1974 and, without asking approval this time round, taking Marky up on his offer to join him in his new residence in Rome. True to form,

Marky championed my heretical cause and, now that he had come of age and into control of his inheritance, he was all too willing to help abet my flight. I, Newton Horatio Seward, officially become a college dropout.

Thus began a new chapter in my life. Of course, in leaving the Cambridge of my dreams I wasn't simply abandoning the spell that Harvard Yard had cast over me years ago. I was attempting to abandon the fantasy that had coexisted with that dream: the hope, however deluded, however crazy, that Mary Jo would someday come to love me as much as I believed I loved her.

For Mary Jo was the theme that gave meaning to all the experiences I had undergone since enrolling in Harvard three years ago; the thought of her proximity, even when she was too busy to make time for me, was the inspiration for the inward melody that gave my days their rhythm, their harmony, their soul. So pervasively did the idea of Mary Jo inhabit my thoughts that the music bombarding the airwaves seemed composed to express my deepest yearnings. When I heard B. J. Thomas's "Hooked on a Feeling," I thought of Mary Jo; when Gordon Lightfoot sang "If You Could Read My Mind," I thought of Mary Jo; when Chicago played "Color My World," I thought of Mary Jo. *As time goes on,* my inner recording artist crooned in the studio of my romance-besotted mind, *I realize just what you*—yes, *you,* Mary Jo Brewster!—*mean to me.* Absurd fantasies for an admirer nearly two years younger than the object of his desire, but that did not make them any the less real. Absurd fantasies, as well, for a youth who had been clearly told by Mary Jo, one winter's night by the frozen pool, that the one erotic moment we'd shared had been a sham: "he made me promise to go along with it," she had said of the orgiastic frenzy that Samson's inopportune arrival had derailed. But the reality of her words didn't lessen the sexual charge her presence kindled in me, one that became even more of a fixation the older I grew and the longer I managed to repress her complicity—and her brother's intentions—in egging on my desires.

Absurd fantasies, as well, given my foreknowledge of the future that awaited Mary Jo. Throughout our overlapping years in Cambridge, she faithfully kept me abreast of her suitors, sometimes even brought me along on outings with her beaux; in short, did nothing to contradict the impression that she intended, sooner or later, to embark on a well-made marriage. So I should have been more prepared when, in the March of my junior year, she calmly announced that she and the offensive Offenbach would be tying the knot. But I *wasn't* prepared, and the foundation on which I had staked my claim to be at Harvard gave way like a mudslide in Appalachian spring.

Where to begin the story of the rise and foundering of the romantic illusions that scored those seasons of my youth? From the day I arrived on campus, Mary Jo was as solicitous as any caring older sister might have been, giving me the space I needed to make my own friends but also making sure that I never felt too lonely—the secret curse of all freshmen, whether they admit to it or not. We shared any number of heady experiences that first year, both in her world and in my own. There was, that fall, the exhilarating rush of the casino party her Radcliffe house sponsored at the Lodge in the Pines. The theme was the Roaring Twenties, and accordingly we dressed in flapper-era garb and gambled at tables set up for blackjack, using Monopoly money to place our bets at the rate of one dollar to each Monopoly "hundred"—proceeds earmarked for the Jamaica Plains Children's Center. Officially, the outing was a double-date—Mary Jo had cajoled me into escorting her "little sister," a shy girl, as newly arrived to Cambridge as myself, whose father had had the fortune of inventing the century's premiere garbage dumpster, while Mary Jo was escorted by a senior from the varsity football team who needed no pedigree beyond his pigskin prowess. He proved most interested in hanging out by the gin bathtub—part of the décor in keeping with the Twenties motif—where he got suitably plowed, while one sloe gin fizz was enough to render my date so woozy that the house chaperone sent her back to campus early. Meanwhile, Mary Jo and I tried our hand at the tables, raking in paper money by the tens of thousands in a run of luck that made us the charity event's biggest "donors."

And there was the equally memorable winter evening when Mary Jo joined a group of my friends in the Commons Room of my freshman house. Bearded Ricardo, who hailed from Brazil and—bizarrely to us—dressed his salad greens with lemon juice, played folk songs on his guitar as we sat by a fire smoldering in the carved stone fireplace. The mellow mood became magical when David Berger, who roomed across the entry from me, broke into a spontaneous Dance of Liberation. The occasion of David's "dance" was memorable for more than fancy footwork. Mary Jo had arrived in the company of a classmate, Sondra Szeikel, whom she'd known in Paris and reencountered at Radcliffe. Sondra's parents, the girl told us with a French accent that positively purred, were Austrian aristocrats who, von-Trapp-like, had escaped the Nazi occupation over the Alps on foot, family jewels sewn into the hems of their greatcoats. Where else in the world, I marveled, could a person like Sondra share such a story while seated next to my sandy-haired roommate, whose German nuclear physicist father had been abducted by American intelligence in 1943 and relocated to the States? Yet here we were, joined together by a dance of liberation executed by proudly Jewish David Sprott Berger.

On the occasions when Mary Jo spent time with my friends, she was as winsome, and as winning, as she had been with my Andover cohorts and my family back in Rocky Hill. When I spent time with her crowd, she shielded me from the worst of their pretensions, making me laugh with her self-ironic awareness of the pettiness attending the elite circles in which she seemed naturally to move. And we spent an inordinate amount of time in the company of one or the other of her suitors.

Despite Mr. Julian's solemn injunction for me "keep an eye" on Mary Jo's beaux, I hadn't suspected I'd be observing so many at so close a range—or that my role might be so craftily bent to serve her purposes. To this day I marvel that she convinced her dates to put up with me. At the same time I marvel at my blindness in dreaming I was the favored one, rather than a pawn whose presence was an effective way of inciting the jealousy of her admirers and keeping them panting, panting, panting at bay. I couldn't help but feel badly for Billy Buckley, on the Saturday in April when he came to fetch Mary Jo for a spin in his new Opel GT two-seater, only to find my freshman self waiting beside her.

"Newt *must* come, he's never been to Mt. Auburn!" she insisted. We piled in the tiny car, Mary Jo and I wedged in one bucket seat, Billy exiled to the driver's side of the gear shift.

Spring had come upon Boston in a rush, and the legendary cemetery was filled with young lovers seduced by the scents of the season. Under pale-green leaves unfurling in the shape of telltale hearts and frothy fruit-tree blossoms filtering the sunlight as it dappled the marble sepulchers, Mary Jo led us forward with her infectious laughter. No fool, that girl: she showered Billy-Buck with just enough attention that he couldn't help but forgive her my irksome presence—spontaneously taking his hand, pulling him into the azalea bushes behind a lichen-encrusted stone angel about to depart skyward just long enough to let him nuzzle her parted lips. And I didn't mind, because I intended to triumph over all these fools, as surely as I believed that her banter—engaging me in tales of our past adventures, recounting her brother Marky's exploits and Mr. Julian's idiosyncrasies—was designed to remind Billy-Buck of a shared history that excluded him. There were others, too, suitors she seriously auditioned for the role of future mate and left less sexually frustrated than Billy. For she was nothing if not forthcoming when it came to sharing the gruesome details of carnal siege, retreat, conquest, and victory. As jealous and turned on as her stories left me, suffusing me in an ecstasy of unhappiness, I was palliated to see that sooner or later she always grew tired of the mild attractions of flesh or mind these conquests offered, discarding them as easily as she lured them on. For all her worldly experience, consuming passion was an emotion she held at bay—and I convinced myself that the sheer force of my desire, and *only* my desire, would someday remove those barriers.

Thus I fed my hopes. So too did the subtle enticements of Mr. Julian, who, once he'd returned from his triumphant European tour, wrote weekly letters demanding updates on Mary Jo's suitors. Their names and personalities, their backgrounds and pedigrees, their appearances and ambitions—his craving for detail was voracious, and from the information I dutifully supplied he wove webs of speculation in spidery handwriting on monogrammed stationery, or during long-distance calls crackling with static when he was too impatient to await my written response, or over cups of Earl Grey tea in his embalmed drawing room when I returned home on school vacations. Into those webs I also fell. For he encouraged me, alternately teasing,

cajoling, and sympathizing in ways that fed my hope that he too envisioned a future in which I would play a role in his ward's life other
than that of chaperone or informant.

At first, he lured me on with slight innuendoes. "Why Newt, I
hope you don't mind—" he'd wheedle when I was reluctant to enu-
merate the attentions of Mary Jo's latest fellow—"don't tell me you're
jealous!" Or, "mind, you'll be growing sweet on her yourself, if you
don't beware!" But as the semesters passed, and my enamored state
became too obvious to hide, innuendo gave way to archness.

"Don't fret so much, Newt," he'd say, patting my hand as I refilled
his cup of tea. "The girl's too smart to settle for *that* oaf! Who knows,
my boy, perhaps she'll tire of them *all*—and realize that all she wants
is *here*!" Another pat on the hand. Or, leaning so close on the Duncan
Phyfe sofa that his stale breath brushed my cheek: "If you adore her
beyond all reason, never give up faith."

At the same time, he played me both ways. His unfeigned exul-
tation over the social prospects opened up by Mary Jo's dating life
filled me with a sense of foreboding, underlining the gap between my
origins and the glittering set towards which she so easily gravitated.
The news that Mary Jo had been invited by a Rockefeller Jr. to spend
the weekend at his Oyster Bay family home so excited Mr. Julian that,
as I talked to him from the pay phone in my entry stairwell, I feared
he might hyperventilate with joy. I was now a sophomore, and the
fact that the suite I shared in Eliot House, looking out on the Charles
River and the crew team's boathouse, opened onto the same stairwell
as young Rockefeller's more spacious rooms, only added to my sense
of exclusion.

How I ended up living beneath the aquamarine dome of Eliot
House was a mystery that caused my friends to marvel. With my intellectual pursuits and theatrical propensities, everyone assumed I
was Adams material. It was no mystery to me. I'd listed Eliot, that
bastion of privilege, athletes, and spoiled brats, as my top choice because I knew that most of the Harvard men Mary Jo deigned suit-
or-worthy resided there. If I inhabited the same space, if I wedged
my way into their cliques, then I bettered my own chances when, as
went my reasoning, my sun rose and Mary Jo found herself struck

by its beams. Despite the grating sense of social inferiority that I felt whenever I was brought face-to-face with the disparities between my upbringing and the charmed lifestyles of the young men with whom I daily sat down to dinner, I tried my best to carry myself off as an Eliot man—even if the only attributes that qualified me for its ranks were my prowess on the swim team and my willingness to sky steel in the weight room with other Eliot jocks.

Needless to say, in the process of trying to fit in, I became something of a prick, and in the process of striving to maintain a style of life commensurate with my environs, I contracted expensive habits, spending far more of the installments that Mr. Allbright deposited into my bank account than was prudent. Yet no matter how many times I treated other Eliot men to a round at the Archer Club, or laughed at their tales of wenching, or ghost-wrote their essays, I never really passed: they tolerated me, with good enough humor, as their resident oddity, the Classics nerd who raised the house's grade-point, turned a good backstroke, and knew the most attractive girl at Radcliffe.

Pining away for Mary Jo didn't mean that I remained celibate. That problem took care of itself the spring of my freshman year. David Berger's parents had a summer place in Chatman, jutting out of the elbow of Cape Cod's long arm, to which we descended for a weekend in April. Mary Jo declined, but Sondra had come, eager to pursue David over sand dunes, as did my roommate Tom, musical Ricardo, and two of Tom's high school friends attending Brown, Milt Morrissey and Missy van der Donk by name. Bundled in cable-knit sweaters, trousers rolled to our knees as we trolled the mushy gray beach, we spent our first day plucking wet sand dollars and whorled shells from the surf as we guzzled brandy wrapped in a paper sack. While Sondra clung to David at the head of our convoy and Tom fanned the breeze with Milt, I found myself keeping step with Missy. Ricardo, strumming his guitar, brought up the rear, serenading the gulls with Brazilian ballads that wafted out of earshot on salty gusts of wind. There was nothing mysterious about this young woman from Yonkers. Missy was everything that Mary Jo wasn't, from effervescent personality to sunny appearance: true to her Dutch heritage, she looked like a

Rembrandt lass born into the twentieth century—flushed pink and flaxen blonde, freckled cheeks and unabashed curves.

That night we built a clambake on the beach, and when we decided to wade in the ebbing surf at midnight, we discovered that the sand turned phosphorescent green wherever we stepped. With such magic twinkling at our toes, it was perhaps inevitable that the electric charge of the microscopic creatures underfoot coursed through our limbs and caused me to reach for Missy's fingers at the very instant she extended her hand toward mine. The rest of the weekend followed equally inevitable stages, culminating in an affair that robbed us both of our virginity and waxed bright for several giddy weekends before it gently waned, like those phosphorescent organisms haunting the Chatham surf.

So, strangely enough, you might say my sexual initiation was actually all about Mary Jo: to make the plunge I needed to find her mirror opposite—which Missy van der Donk, with her cheery openness, so generously provided. Other girls followed—my libido was primed to repeat the raptures of a newly discovered virility. But none formed into lasting relationships; part of me always stopped short. I wanted to believe it was the part of me tethered to the hope that I was the one man destined to thaw Mary Jo's heart. And I wanted to believe that the other unspoken desires that sometimes surfaced in my thoughts were ephemereal.

As I've said before, I was fully aware that Mary Jo led her suitors on, seductively provoking and simultaneously withholding. I still believe I was the one person she didn't deliberately deceive; she was always perfectly, even mercilessly, honest about how she felt towards me, and warned me more than once not to act silly. What she wanted when we spent time together, just the two of us, was a respite from the world of expectations and an intimate friend who could also be a surrogate brother, a kindred spirit. I provided both—along with a fidelity that she felt free to exploit when it suited her ends.

How far those ends were removed from my own, I had to wait till the spring of my junior year and the announcement of her engagement to Fred Offenbach to discover.

26

HOOKED ON A FEELING

If Mary Jo wronged me during those college years, it was in her ability to deflect what must have been her suspicion of my feelings for her. Perhaps she thought it was enough to confide every sordid detail of her sex life to me with a frankness any rational person would have found an antidote to attraction. But her siren call had become too much a part of my inner life to be silenced; and the truth is, I both sounded the call, and responded to its beckoning.

Only once did she withhold details of her dating life and that was during my sophomore year when she reconnected with my old Phipps roommate Dewey at an inter-collegiate event. Two years had passed since they'd merrily joined the ranks of protesters in front of University Hall, and Dewey, whose attraction to Mary Jo I had always found downright criminal, asked her out on the spot—the effrontery of a sophomore from Tufts courting a Radcliffe senior was apparently beyond his cognition. That Mary Jo proceeded to accept his invitation despite my revelation of his behavior to Miranda three years before sent me through the roof. For the only time I can remember, I screamed at her so angrily any onlooker would have surmised I hated rather than loved her. No wonder she chose to share no details of her dates with Dewey—that is, until one drunken evening some months later when I stupidly challenged her on her dubious ethics. Miranda had just been in touch with Mary Jo. My spitfire, would-be gymnast confidant was the only girl I knew wholly exempt from Mary Jo's irony, and Mary Jo—who always maintained the warmest regard for my foster family in Andover—was pondering a high school graduation gift worthy of her friend as we were having drinks at Passim's.

I finally exploded. "You *say* you care so much for Miranda. Didn't stop you from going out with that *pervert* Dewey last semester."

"For God's sake, Newt. Do I really have to explain my every action to you?"

"You're only saying that because you know damn well there's no sane explanation. What were you *thinking*?"

Weariness crept into Mary Jo's voice. "You should know me well enough by now to know he never meant anything to me. That's why I played around with the foolish boy, till he became too boring to bother."

"*Played around* with him?" I slouched in my chair.

Mary Jo's eyes grew mischievous. "You *do* know what I mean? Playing as a euphemism for S-E-X? I was curious to see if your spray paint decorations had left his legendary attributes impaired." Of course I'd told her of the Halloween revenge we'd exacted on Dewey, hoping to make him all the more cringe-worthy. After a suitable pause, she delivered her coup de grace. "They hadn't."

To keep myself from striking her triumphant face, I stormed out of the bar.

Perhaps, on some subliminal level, the knowledge that she had done it with Do-It bolstered my determination to end the thrall that had frozen me in desiring limbo far too long. I began to plot a scene of seduction that would let me know where I stood once and for all. The fact that she would be graduating in months only strengthened my sense of urgency, my feeling that I must act now or never—although in point of fact Mary Jo would only be moving across the river, come fall, to begin work as an assistant editor at Little and Brown. Four years of unrequited feelings was quite enough, even for a romantic masochist like myself. So I jumped at the opportunity when she proposed that we take our books to Boston Commons, just the two of us, no boyfriend in tow, and I began to lay my snares.

It was the first Sunday in May, a green delight, and I felt the world lay all before us.

We made quite the pair as we wended our way across the grassy expanse of the Commons. Even among my conservative Eliot cohorts—future Wall Street tycoons, Republican politicians, CEOs— long hair was now fashionable, straight, frizzy, or otherwise, and I gathered mine into a ponytail from which loose strands continually escaped, dangling over my reestablished sideburns. I wore bellbottom jeans, frayed hems scraping my Wallabies, along with a stonewashed denim shirt with hand-stitched Zodiac embroidery. As the finishing touch to my sartorial whimsy, I'd donned the love beads that Mary Jo had strung me our summer in Rocky Hill. In contrast, Mary Jo looked like she'd stepped out of an alternate reality. She wore an expensive tweed skirt, and her fine black cashmere top was offset by an onyx pendant dangling on a silver chain that broke, tantalizingly, over the firm line of her breasts. She had the gift that money and taste together bestowed, the gift of looking both classic and current, of her time yet of no time at all. I would have been envious were I not so enamored of the élan she projected without even seeming to try.

We began our outdoor study hall with the best of intentions. Reclining on a blanket spread over newly mown grass, I read my *Life of Luther* and she her volume of James's letters while long-tailed kites danced in the breeze overhead. But before long I couldn't resist the distractions surrounding us on that gloriously spring day and pulled Mary Jo to her feet. Together we wandered through the Commons, taking in the hucksters performing card tricks and a mime impersonating Henry Kissinger, walking down the hill to the pond in the Garden where swan boats filled with children and lovers plied the water.

As the afternoon waned, I proposed that we stroll down the shaded boulevards of Back Bay, where we watched the lights blinking on in elegant brownstones that seemed right out of Henry James (Mary Jo, concentrating in English and French literature, was writing her senior thesis on adulterous triangles in *The Golden Bowl* and *Les liaisons dangereuses*). Which august façade was sheltering the perfect rental for Mary Jo? It had to be on the drawing room level, boast a ceiling with plaster moldings, retain its original wainscoting, and include a second bedroom for Marky should he ever join her in America. Or for me, I added, if I crashed for the weekend. As darkness fell, we fell into conversation with a stoned usher outside the Copley Square Cinema where "Easy Rider" was playing; he snuck us in via the exit door. Shifting from Henry James to Dennis Hopper, from drawing rooms to biker brigades, seemed perfectly natural, part of our proud versatility, as did the transition from a vegetarian dinner at Avocado Dreams in Central Square to my dorm a short walk away, where I proposed we listen to jazz favorites I'd already stacked on the turntable.

Equally calculated were the scented candles I had strewn around the room, the two bottles of champagne chilling in my mini-refrigerator, and the more-or-less clean sheets on my bed. After I dimmed the lights, lit the candles, and uncorked the first bottle, we flopped on my single mattress and sank into the oversized cushions propped against the wall, finding, as we always did, unending topics to discuss as Sarah Vaughn's velvety voice soothed our ears and the dusky scent of patchouli filled our nostrils. Time melted away, as slippery as pocket watches in a Dali landscape, and, somewhere into our second bottle of bubbly, I took the liberty of resting my head against Mary Jo's shoulder, shaved cheek meeting thin cashmere.

"I wish you weren't graduating so soon."

"You silly boy." Mary Jo tugged my ponytail. "I'll only be across the Charles."

"You'll be in France all summer."

"Don't be maudlin, you've got your own travel plans." True, I was going home for two weeks in June, and on my return I planned to visit the Fortinbrases before settling back into Cambridge to work for my Latin professor.

"Still." I snuggled into the curve of her neck where cashmere yielded to scented skin.

"I'll envy the time you spend with the Fortinbrases."

She may have meant it, but I was much more engaged in brushing the tip of my nose against her earring, an onyx pendant that matched her necklace, making the most of a moment of physical contact that was beginning to turn me on big time.

Miles Davis replaced Sarah Vaughn, and I pulled Mary Jo to her feet. "Let's dance."

"The idea petrified you three years ago."

"It's taken me this long to come to my senses."

I folded her in my arms and we swayed in place, hardly moving. My hands played up and down Mary Jo's back in rhythm to Davis' sonorous melody, fingers lightly stroking the soft cashmere in anticipation of the softer skin beneath.

"Miranda taught you well."

The rhyme that Daisy had created to accompany my waltz lessons, "MAR-y-jo, WATCH-Newt-go, LOVES-her-so, CAN'T-say-no," came out of nowhere and momentarily eclipsed Davis's beat. *YES I will, MAKE you mine, DON'T say no, MAR-y-jo.*

"I remember your dress. You looked ravishing."

"I remember the girls casting covetous glances your way."

"And your House Mother turning her nose up at my mention of Phipps!"

"How about that odd Frenchman singling us out at the Fogg?"

"And your corsage—I knew Miranda was consulting you, of course."

We slow-danced in silence for several minutes, memories gliding over us like quicksilver and burnishing us in imagined moonlight.

Mary Jo lifted her head from my beating chest. The tipsy slur in her voice endeared her to me all the more. "You should pay more attention to Miranda."

"Why?" I hugged Mary Jo tighter.

"If you'd just open your eyes, you'd see the crush she has on you—I can't imagine a more perfect girlfriend for you, Newt."

I stiffened. Being told who was perfect for me by the very woman whose warmth was beginning to give me a hard-on was rather much to bear.

"You can't? You really can't?" My steps slowed to a standstill, and I forced Mary Jo to look me in the eye. "You have to know. You *have* to. I'm so *into* you."

Desperation and desire gave me the courage to lean forward and kiss Mary Jo as deeply, as passionately, as I had ever hoped or dreamt. For what seemed like years my lips held her lips, while my hands slipped under the back of her top and found the clasp of her bra. I was conscious of my erection straining past the top snap of my low-riding jeans.

Mary Jo pulled back, her sapphire eyes flickering inches from my own. "Newt, what's gotten into you?"

"I think I'm in love with you."

Mary Jo looked down towards my low-hung belt and smiled. "I don't think what's happening down there, dear boy, has anything to do with love."

I forced her body back against my own. "I want you *because* I love you." I tilted my face forward till my nose nestled in her dark hair, smelling of lilies at Easter. "I need you," I whispered, trembling but resolute. "I need *this*. I need..." My words trailed off, as the thought completed itself silently: I need to know.

"Are you sure, Newt?" Mary Jo's voice was low, no longer light-hearted but deliberate, serious. "*This* is what you want? This is *really* what you want from me?"

I answered by pulling her to my bed. Again, I found her lips, and she didn't resist as we sank into the softness, my hands again finding the clasp of her bra and next the fullness of her breasts as I pulled the cashmere over her head and brought my lips to her nipples, chill bumps sparking up and down the length of my body as I exulted in the arrival of a moment fantasized for a lifetime. I reached to unbuckle my belt, but her hands intervened, undoing my fly, button by slow button. I let out a moan as she lowered my jeans. This, too, I desperately needed, Mary Jo's hands on me with no shadow of her brother reaching from behind.

When I finally came, I nearly levitated as my sperm unspooled from deep in my loins and, rushing forth with it, my spirit, giving itself over without limits to the living pulse, the marvel, that was Mary Jo.

Afterwards, as we lay regaining our breath, I dizzily pushed myself upright so that I could look down on Mary Jo's body. It glimmered in the wavering candlelight like the prized golden apple of myth.

So beglamored, I couldn't restrain myself from whispering, "I'll love you forever." But before Mary Jo could reply, stars exploded in front of my eyes, and I blacked out for the first time in my life. When I came to, roused by a pressing need to urinate made worse by the turgidity of my erection pressing into Mary Jo's thigh, I saw that it was three in the morning.

Mary Jo lay spooned in my embrace, facing the door, so to exit the bed I had to hoist myself over her body and onto the floor in a single motion, a feat made all the more perilous by the groaning springs of the soft mattress and my spinning head. I guess I wasn't as soundless as I'd hoped, for when I returned from the john I saw that Mary Jo's eyes were open.

"Sorry I woke you, Sleeping Beauty," I whispered, kneeling by the side of the mattress where her cat-eyes watched me in the flickering light of the one candle that had not burnt out. I leant forward and kissed her, my heart in my lips and on my tongue as I caressed the dark hair that fell across her forehead and shadowed her cheek. "In my whole life I've never felt so happy as now." Taking a deep breath, I rushed on, no censoring my words tonight, not at this pinnacle of bliss. "When we came tonight, I felt like the universe was cracking wide open."

Silence hung in the air, much too long, before she responded.

"Oh, dear Newt, don't you understand?" She guided my hand under the sheets, down her body and between her legs, till my touch met a warmth that was no stay against the chilling words she uttered. "I don't *feel* anything. *This* means nothing to me."

She pushed my hand away and sat up, pulling the sheet to her breasts. "I repeat: I feel nothing. You wanted me, so we *fucked*. Now we're done with it, once and for all."

"Done?" A quaver entered my voice.

"Listen to me, Newt. I gave you what you asked for, I wanted you to have that much, this one time. But sex leaves me cold. So now I hope you understand why you and I will never do this again." She grasped me by the shoulders, holding them firmly as an uncontrollable fit of trembling overcame me. "You want passion, you want romance, and I can't give that to you or to any man. I'd rather you accept the kind of love I *can* give you, little brother."

At first her words were too much for me to comprehend and so I denied them. We've just *made love*, I kept telling myself. But as reality sank in, and as I finally looked into her shining eyes—eyes so calm, even kind, and yet so deadly serious—I read my fate and my heart shattered. As the light went out in my soul, bitterness made me reckless.

"The kind of love you can give me? You don't even give me half the love you give Marky. You probably *fuck* him, too."

The words sprang from my lips faster than my brain processed the thought—a thought always lingering somewhere close to consciousness. Worse than the silence that met my accusation was Mary Jo's serene lack of surprise. Even in this instant, shrouded in my rumpled bed sheet, she was a vision of beauty as she stretched her neck so that the candlelight exposed the underside of her chin while leaving her face in voluptuous shadow.

"And?" she finally spoke. After so long a silence, I wasn't sure whether that single word was an answer, a provocation, or a transition. Then she turned to me and let her own cruel dart fly into my heartsick misery. "At least be man enough to ask, if that's what you want to know."

"So you do."

"Marky can make me *feel*, like no one else."

Breathing slowly, I became aware of the bedspread that had slid to the floor during our frenzied coupling. I became aware of the lingering odor of patchouli choking the air, and I became aware of the whispered beat of the stereo needle skipping, skipping, skipping, at the end of an LP that had long since ceased playing.

Mary Jo reached forward to touch me on the cheek, where I still knelt by the bed.

"You'll find this hard to believe, but tonight doesn't matter. Lie back down beside me." Numbly, I obeyed, and it was now she who wrapped my body with her own. "Sleep. Everything will be all right tomorrow."

Tomorrow came, as Mary Jo promised it would, and even as an inner part of me protested that nothing would ever be right again, I saw in the coming weeks that *she* was miraculously able to carry on with our friendship as if nothing earth-shattering had happened.

Her example gave me the strength, at least on the surface, to meet her overtures in kind. But in my most private thoughts, even as I found myself looking back across the river of spent passion whose banks marked a clear *then* from *now*, I willed myself to believe that no Rubicon had yet been crossed, that my devotion might yet heal her unfeeling heart—such was the power of the desire that had woven itself into my illusions for so long. I would not bow to the inevitable until Mary Jo announced her engagement the following March.

When that blow fell, I discovered how truly adrift I really was.

27

GUY TALK

If Mary Jo was a constant thread, always on my mind, an ever-present source of happiness and heartache in the warp and weave of my college existence, thoughts of Marky marked its pattern in more subtle ways. When I traveled home for Christmas vacation my freshman year, I got an earful from Mr. Julian. The old man and Bruno had returned from their six-month European trip in October, and although I was aware Mr. Julian had seen Marky in Paris, I knew few details until my former employer fulminated at length on the wintry afternoon I stopped by the Brewster mansion with my Christmas present. Our gifts displayed an eerie symmetry: I'd gotten him an African mask from the Peabody Museum's gift shop, while he presented me a lacquered carnival mask he'd purchased in Venice. I might find it useful in my next rewriting of "Hamlet," he noted with raised brow.

Naturally, I was eager to hear all about Mr. Julian's trip, and since Bruno had been ordered to keep his Instamatic at the ready, there were dozens of images commemorating what looked to be a triumphant return to the scenes of Mr. Julian's young adulthood and middle age: Italy, France, Switzerland, England. The photographs of Paris were the trigger for his rant about Marky. Mr. Julian had stayed at the Crillon—only the best on this return voyage—and was appalled when Marky showed up for high tea in the mirrored salon wearing ripped jeans and dark glasses, hair unkempt, reeking of cigarettes and looking, the old man swore, as if he'd just emerged from an opium den. How the nephew whose wellbeing had been foremost in his mind these many years could evince such disrespect was beyond comprehension—he'd personally had to assure the concierge that Marky hadn't come to stage a protest in the lobby!

After the maitre d' lent Marky a blazer to hide his offending tee-shirt, the boy had had the nerve to ridicule the room's patrons, calling them—"and I quote," Mr. Julian declaimed, "'the dying vestiges of a bourgeoisie whose collective neck, like that of their noble predecessors two hundred years ago, is again on the chopping block, only they haven't looked up yet.' Not that our budding Marxist," Mr. Julian added with a snort, "wasn't above gaping like a starstruck fan when he recognized the actress sitting three tables away!"

Dinner at the Brasserie Flo two nights later hadn't improved matters. Marky and Mr. Julian got into an argument over the U.S. withdrawal from Cambodia before the seared foie gras arrived, then over Prime Minister Heath's Conservative victory in Great Britain, which practically ruined the goose breast sliced over stewed prunes. The liberal sentiments Mr. Julian had entertained among his Manhattan set having long since faded, his mind had narrowed to the vaguest of generalities when it came to politics. Not so Marky. Even when totally wasted, he could propound a perfectly logical argument in seconds, particularly if the subject were social injustice or political corruption. The fact that the nephew's verbal triumphs were witnessed by their dinner partners—Bruno, Marky's roommate Jules, and Jules' friend Sylvie—only increased Mr. Julian's irritability, ill-disposing him to harbor warm feelings for Marky's *amis*.

"That Jules character gives new meaning to vanity!"

I barely had time to repress a smile at the thought of Mr. Julian holding forth on vanity, given his habit of coloring his hair at his age, before he turned an offended eye to my locks. "It's truly dispiriting how young people are running to seed these days—and you *fancy* you look fetching! Mary Jo is the last of your generation to understand the meaning of style!"

Ever curious, I contrived to get Mr. Julian to tell me more about Jules. No, he wasn't an aspiring film auteur (my guess) but a "mere" clerk at Le Bon Marche, having recently been promoted from the men's cologne counter to the Yves St. Laurent boutique under the building's vaunted stained-glass ceiling. Even though Mr. Julian derided young Jules' vanity and disparaged his trade, such put-downs couldn't repress the old man's grudging respect for Jules's knowledge of French fashion—a national trait Mr. Julian associated with Evolved Civilization—and it took all my self-control not to laugh when he let slip that he'd accepted Jules's offer to use his employee discount to buy the old man several dress shirts. Nothing, however, could redeem poor Sylvie, an aspiring folksinger. "Such a dreary creature. Reminded me of those humorless women who flooded the Village back in the day" (by which I presumed he meant *his* day) "with voices rough as sandpaper!"

Luckily, not all Mr. Julian's interactions with his nephew were disasters—Marky arranged a twilight trip down the Seine on a bateau mouche that was irresistible, and a shopping spree for antiques in Montmartre yielded a suitcase of souvenirs—though Mr. Julian couldn't resist telling me that any *sensible* guardian would write such a wayward, impertinent nephew out of his Will. I didn't add the obvious rejoinder—Marky would come into his own sizable inheritance within the year and have no need of Mr. Julian's largesse.

Looking at Mr. Julian's photographs gave me an inspiration. What if I took a number of vintage images from his pre-war European scrapbooks and paired them with Polaroids shot in identical locations? I suspected he'd be charmed by the "before and after" effect. So, two days later, while Bruno was administering Mr. Julian's physical therapy, I crept into the library to pilfer photographs from the original albums, slipping them from the black corner holders that affixed them to the yellowing pages. I selected twenty images for which I located counterparts among the recent Polaroids and arranged them side-by-side in a handsome leather album.

Despite the gap of nearly five decades separating the pairings, the settings had barely changed. And Mr. Julian, however wrinkled and wizened with time, was still, ineluctably, Mr. Julian. I found myself preferring images of the older man, whose goofy grins and sheer elation as he took in the tourists milling about the Bridge of Sighs, or as he stood with a halo of pigeons circling his thinning pate at Trafalgar, seemed more humanly approachable than the studied aloofness of his younger self. However, there was no glossing over the one jarring discord between the two sets: the replacement of Enzio Sorrento with Bruno Epps. Bruno's boast of Italian blood may have allied the two companions on some dim ancestral plane, but the association stopped there: Enzio's alert-eyed raffishness was worlds removed from Bruno's square-jawed Italian-American brashness.

The gift was well received when I presented it on New Year's Eve. Outside, the afternoon sky darkened with snow-filled clouds readying to unload their icy arsenal. We sat side by side on the Duncan Phyfe, amid dust motes floating in the golden light of the Foo Dog lamp, as Mr. Julian turned the pages, savoring each image like precious candy from Fauchon. And as he extemporized on all the likenesses and changes between the paired photographs, he grew uncharacteristically confidential.

During the Italian leg of his travels, he now told me, he'd attempted to track down any remaining Sorrentos, just to lay to rest the ghost of his old friend Enzio, who'd died in a mysterious car wreck back in 1943. Tragic to be surrounded by war's horrors, only to fall victim to a blow-out that caused his car to careen off a narrow pass in the Apennines—although why he had been speeding through snow-covered mountains on an icy road in March in the dead of the night, when he was supposed to be attending a reception at an art gallery in Milan, none of Mr. Julian's Italian contacts could explain.

"And the cruelest irony," Mr. Julian said, slapping the arm of the sofa so forcefully that Mimi bolted to the other side of the room with an alacrity she rarely mustered these days, "the cruelest irony of all, is that Enzio's father outlived his son by a decade—that flint-hearted, ruthless man! He gave *my* father a run for the money when it came to making the lives of his progeny perfectly miserable."

Mr. Julian, in Bruno's company, had made a pilgrimage to Florence to see if he could locate the studio where Enzio had painted his portrait those many decades ago. Prior to his departure, he had asked me to return the keys in the Quattrocento box he'd passed along to me. "I had a fancy that I might find his studio intact, waiting all these years for me to unlock it to the light of day—foolish dream! The entire block had been razed and replaced with gruesome postwar flats—not a redeeming aesthetic feature among them all! Enzio would have shuddered."

More successfully, the two men traced the matriarch of the Sorrento clan to a nursing home outside Urbino. The discovery proved a dead end, however, since the senile Senora, well into her nineties, didn't recognize Mr. Julian, much less respond to the name of her long-departed son. The two were about to abandon their quest when a parish priest in Mazzaferro, a village near the old Sorrento villa, recalled that Enzio's youngest sister, Angelica, had joined a Carmelite convent in Rome after the war. Adhering to the order's vow to shun the outside world, Sister Angelica declined to see Mr. Julian. But she did send him a brief note, in which she offered her prayers to those who honored the memory of "my dear, poor, doomed brother"—*mio fratello, caro, povero, condannato*, Mr. Julian intoned from memory—"forced early from this world by an unforgiving and unrepentant father, may his lucre-encrusted soul burn in Hell for eternity."

"*Condannato?* Why doomed?"

What she meant was a puzzle to Mr. Julian as well. As far as he knew, Enzio's death had been a freak accident, a rotten throw of the dice.

When dusk fell, Hank interrupted our conversation to kindle a fire in the hearth, sidling in and out of the room with an unctuous smile that fit him as ill as the livery he wore.

Mr. Julian sipped a thimble-glass of Bailey's as he gazed at the blaze leaping from one log to the next, the firelight dancing in his watery blue eyes and conjuring forth visions I couldn't fathom.

"Julia died two years before Enzio," he recommenced once Hank left the room. "Their Great Romance, *that's* what turned out to be doomed. He was heartbroken when it ended, and I couldn't help but be heartbroken for him."

I asked what happened. "Fathers, that's what happened. My father broke the engagement off after Sorrento reneged on his end of their business partnership. The man walked off with the tens of thousands we'd invested in the Italian branch of the furniture venture, didn't even have the decency to fabricate an excuse. My father was livid at having been taken in—and since he didn't want to blame himself, he blamed Enzio in absentia for having proposed the collaboration, and me for having introduced Enzio into the bosom of our family. He declared no daughter of his would ever enter a union with such a family of vipers." Likewise, Sorrento Senior forbade his son to return to the States or communicate with Julia. "Under the threat of—I don't know... disinheritance, excommunication, incarceration.

He was that kind of a man."

"So Enzio wasn't part of the fraud?"

"Preposterous! He was an artist, not a businessman. He believed in his marvelous designs, and he believed kismet had led him to merge his talents with Father's business acumen, just as he believed kismet had led him, through me, to Julia. What damned romantics we were! Of course, tensions in Europe were heating up, there's no way the enterprise would have survived once Mussolini tied his ambitions to Hitler's. But that didn't make Father any the more forgiving."

"Julia must have been devastated."

"She wept for months, starved herself, begged our father to relent, blamed him for what she was sure would be the death of Enzio when Italy entered the war. Lord knows the torments Enzio underwent." Mr. Julian stared moodily into the fire. "But before you could say jackrabbit, Julia started seeing this attorney from Manhattan. When Enzio and Julia fell in love, I admit I *was* jealous—after all, Enzio was first *my* friend—but in the end he brought Julia and me closer. Not so Nelson: I was entirely cut out of the equation. She moved to Manhattan—*my* city—to be closer to Nelson once they got engaged. The saddest irony of all is that she and I saw less of each other residing in the same place than we did when we lived four states apart. To this day I rue the fact that I hadn't seen her for over a month when she died."

"It was an accident?" I remembered Samson telling me as much at Dillard Crick.

"She and Nelson. They were sailing off Long Island when they got caught in a late summer squall. I was the first relative to reach the morgue once their bodies washed to shore, that was four days later. Hers was so bloated I barely recognized a feature." He paused. "Damned stupid of them to go sailing that day, what with the weather warnings. But Nelson thought he *ruled* the world."

I reached down to stroke Mimi, who'd rubbed her way through a forest of chair legs—fluted, scrolled, cabrioled, clawfooted—on her way back to our side of the room.

"I can't impress upon you how dreadful her corpse looked. When I returned to Rocky Hill to take care of Mother, the first thing I did was move Enzio's portrait of Julia to my room. Looking at it was the only way I could erase that frightful image of her body laid out in cold storage. Julia in '41, Enzio in '43. He died without even knowing she had preceded him to the grave. What do I have left? Her portrait and his signature."

What wrecked lives, I thought, youth's egotism assuring me that such muted tragedy and lingering morbidity would never be mine. I remembered that Mr. Julian's return home to nurse his mother was to have been temporary. Did the devastating news of Enzio's demise contribute to his failure to return to his comfortable life in New York? What other invisible factors had gone into the making of the crusty bachelor who for the next two decades rarely ventured from the decaying family mansion where his eccentric behaviors festered unchecked? I looked at the leather album that lay open in my lap— black-and-whites paired with color Polaroids—and I was glad that in this last year Mr. Julian had finally broken the spell that had bound him to the family home, locked in old habits and older resentments.

And I was glad, too, to have heard reports, however exaggerated, of Marky, the "delinquent" nephew upon whom Mr. Julian enjoyed bestowing affectionately unkind aspersions. Soon enough I saw Marky in person, not just filtered through Mr. Julian's or Mary Jo's accounts or his quirky postcards. I'd aced my May exams—marking the official end of my freshman year—when he flew into Boston to visit Mary Jo and me. His persona as artist-rebel was on full display, yes, but he was also the Marky whose quick tongue and quicker response to all that he found preposterous in life made the time spent with him a lark, even when I found myself the unwilling butt of his irony, which was not infrequently.

Too quickly our reunion was sundered: Mary Jo and Marky took the train to Connecticut to visit their Sumner relations while I made good on an invitation from a future Eliot House suite mate, Bill Havilland, to spend the month at his family compound on Nantucket along with three of his other Harvard friends. Since Marky's plan had been to fly back to France after visiting his relatives, it was a shock when, in the midst of my Nantucket sojourn, he called from Hyannis to announce his arrival on the afternoon ferry for a spontaneous two-week stay. In the ten days since we'd parted, I'd fallen in love with the island, wandering the town's cobble-stoned streets, cycling to the beaches, playing tennis at the boating club when we weren't taking cruises on the family yacht.

And then Marky, as wry and mordantly sardonic as ever, inserted himself into our circle. It was assumed that as my friend he was welcome to stay in the Havilland compound, a sprawling structure whose shingled front commandeered the bluff overlooking the marina. But within hours Marky wore out his welcome, at least as far as my Eliot cohort was concerned. I'm sure it was intentional, the way his pronounced yawns and raised eyebrow made it clear that their activities bored him, the way he was forever devising schemes to detach me from the group. Marky had the unique power of making my housemates squirm on two fronts—on the one hand, using his European savoir faire to trump their own pretensions to class, on the other, injecting his discomfiting Marxist rhetoric into nearly all our conversations. Havilland and company didn't stand a chance in the face of this double-whammy, and although I had no desire to find myself a pariah in Eliot before I even took up residence, I secretly enjoyed watching Marky get under their skins without their quite knowing how it had happened. But I also knew when enough was enough and, to protect my own future standing, I decreed it was high time to help him locate his own lodgings.

We found digs perfectly matched to Marky's bohemian tastes on Upper Liberty Street, in a fraying Victorian whose rickety sun-porch, tacked on the back of the house in a later era, had been converted into a minuscule bedroom for rent. The room leaked buckets when it rained, as Marky was to discover, and it lacked privacy—its row of uncurtained windows peered over the backyard gardens of three adjacent houses—but its makeshift charm appealed to Marky's imagination. The first and second floor bedrooms were filled with state-college students who'd ferried over for the season to work in the island's eateries and get stoned; free spirits that they were, they didn't mind the peeling floral wallpaper, rusted sconces that perpetually blew fuses, or buckling plaster ceilings. And every bit as atmospheric as the house was its landlady, Mrs. Myke Sizemore, a twice-married divorcée who had converted the dank basement of the old house into her living quarters and worked as hostess at the Golden Finch.

Even to my inexperienced eyes, Myke Sizemore exuded the aura of a woman of the world: from her closely cropped, graying blonde hair to the Virginia Slims dangling from her lips, from the violet circles under her eyes to the psychedelic caftans she wore till it was time to dress for work. She drifted through the house like a chthonic presence, unfazed by the wafts of weed seeping from under bedroom doors, or the wails of "Layla" repeating on the stereo, or work uniforms left to dry on the ledges of the second-floor windows. For the residents of Liberty Street, she was an imperturbable earth mother who turned a blind eye to their sex partners, drug habits, and late hours, and who barely yawned if the rent were a few days late.

Not that the latter was Marky's problem; he paid in advance for his stay as soon as he laid eyes on the back-porch-turned-boudoir. From that day, I schizophrenically split my time between my Izod-shirted friends and Marky as the two of us explored the island: body-surfing at Madaket, inveigling girls to join us for strawberry daiquiris at The Brotherhood of Thieves, hiking through sand dunes covered with scrub-pine and wild roses at 3 a.m to watch the Aurora Borealis pulsate in the northern sky.

Soon enough, I learned, Marky was splitting his time, too—between me and, of all people, Myke. One late evening Marky returned to his room at Liberty Street and was undressing for bed when he noted a small red light glowing in the back yard just beyond his windows. Curious, he exited the rear door of the house and found its source: Myke sitting in a lawn chair in her bathrobe, smoking one of her Slims and taking swigs from a pint of vodka while rubbing bare feet that ached from standing all night in the platform heels that were part of her hostess attire. Marky's ghostlike apparition in his silk boxers didn't startle her, since it turned out she'd been watching *him* through his windows, and she invited him to draw up a chair. At some point in their desultory conversation, Myke recalled some heavy cartons in the cellar that needed moving. That hint was enough, and Marky followed Myke down rickety stairs into her underground lair, whose earthy odors mingled with her Virginia Slims. Bending to step through tie-dyed sheets that had been hung from the low ceiling to divide the cellar into sections, Myke reached behind to take Marky's boxers by the waistband, stubbed her cigarette out in a scallop shell with a worldly sigh, and tugged my friend to her rumpled bed.

"How very Mrs. Robinson," I commented as Marky gleefully recounted his amorous adventure the following day.

"It was *perfect*." Marky swiveled his crotch in pantomine. "She was a damn pro. Shot my bolt three times, God knows how many times she O'ed—"

My plea for less detail only made him more explicit. "To be frank, Newtie-boy," he concluded after doing his best to gross me out, "an older woman like Myke could teach *you* a thing or two. What have you got to show for the summer—deep-tonguing Miss Prissy-Pants at the yacht club last week? No comparison, *mon frère!*"

The affair continued for the rest of Marky's stay on the island, to the mutual satisfaction of both. Once he departed for Paris, careless and carefree as ever, I had just enough vacation time left to play contrite with my hosts at the Havilland compound, doing my best to fit in a world where the days were measured in endless tennis matches, boating cruises, and a haze of alcohol. But part of me was still with Marky in spirit. For part of me idolized him, wanted to *be* him, be as audacious as him, all over again.

*

Almost exactly twelve months later, at the end of my sophomore year and just two months after that fateful spring day with Mary Jo that began on Boston Commons and ended in my dorm room, I returned to Rocky Hill to visit my family, as well as bring Mr. Julian news of his niece's graduation—he'd wanted to attend but a month before suffered a ruptured disc that put travel out of the question. As no glamorous invitation to Nantucket awaited me upon my return north this summer, I was in a funk when I arrived in Rocky Hill. Mary Jo's graduation reminded me how much I was still smarting from the rejection that formed the anticlimax of our one and only sexual encounter. Even my father picked up on my mood, and announced, to my embarrassment, that if I ever had "gal-problems" I could always count on the advice his experience had granted him—something I gravely doubted. In his nearly fifty years on this planet he remained more innocent in the ways of the world than my kid brother.

"You can't let 'em know you're pining after 'em, son," he said, tapping his forehead with one finger and broadly winking. "Jeanlyn didn't pay me a lick o' attention till she thought that vixen Sally Mae Sullivan was throwin' her cap at me..."

Whereupon Dad settled into a wistful reminiscence of his and Mother's courtship—the Grease Monkey wooing the Bootleg Princess with after-church drives that culminated in their being elected King and Queen of the Senior Prom. Kneeling on the dais by her throne, he'd taken a ring from his tux jacket pocket and popped the question to the applause of the entire senior class. As he came to an end of this narrative of his glory days, Dad sighed. Mother's ascent into the echelon of Rocky Hill's business entrepreneurs—by all measures a success if the number of decorating jobs coming her way were a sign—was leaving him behind. She, though, was happier than ever, reveling in her new role as president of the Chamber of Commerce and keen to show me the bold color palettes she was assembling for her latest client. I had to hand it to Mother, the walls of my old bedroom, stripped of the French Impressionist posters I'd taped there years ago, had become a feast of color: day-glow bright paint samples dabbed everywhere, overlapped by fabric swatches favoring geometric designs pinned into the plasterboard: the overall effect attested to a visual logic nearly as arresting as the Monets and Renoirs they'd replaced. And I had to hand it to Mom, her decision to replace the living room set of Ethan Allen furniture with Danish contemporary was long overdue.

So as Mother zipped forward into the new decade, Dad, softhearted and unassertive as ever, slipped backwards in time, more befuddled as each passing year's newness left him ever more astonished. Going about his daily routines—particularly at the dealership, since home itself seemed too much a part of the dizzying world of change and surprises—he could still make a go of it. But outside that zone of comfort, his raw-boned awkwardness stood out more than ever.

I felt bad for him, a victim of passing time—congratulating myself, in the meantime, on moving with such confidence into the future. I can only say that I was blithely unaware that my own past was readying to jump me from behind.

28

MEDAL OF VALOR

On my third day home, I borrowed the family station wagon to drive over to Mr. Julian's for a very special and unexpected reunion. Two autumns ago, as the ancient elms littered the pathways that bisected Harvard Yard with a shroud of golden leaves through which my eager freshman feet had shuffled, Samson's post-high-school pugilistic career in Roanoke had ground to a less than golden halt. Uncle Sam had caught up with him. A college deferment wasn't an option for Samson, as it was for me. Although his boxing sponsors had assured him that they would "take care of matters," whatever deals they had made with the draft board to keep his name off the books lasted little more than a year, for in October of 1970 Samson received his notice to report for a physical.

So, while I was acclimating to life as a new college student—applauding David's dance of liberation, listening to Professor Thernstrom's lectures on the fallacies of the Domino Theory, trying to raise my grade in Miss Thrall's Expos class—Samson hunkered down at Fort Jackson for basic training. A year later, while I was doing my best to measure up to the standards of an Eliot House man by running up tabs that had left me no recourse but to ask Mr. Allbright to provide me advances on my monthly stipend, Samson was touching down in the Mekong Delta. These updates I garnered from Mr. Julian, who, with a paternal attention not uncommon among white Southern aristocrats, maintained contact with the Washington family out of respect for G.G.'s many years of service. On Mr. Julian's part, I sensed feelings that ran deeper than gentrified shows of concern. Last year I discovered the memorial that he'd installed in the quadrant of the ruined garden where his companion had tended his kitchen garden—a slab of polished black granite into which were carved G.G.'s name, dates of birth and death, and, compliments of A. E. Housman, three lines of verse:

GOODNIGHT; ENSURED RELEASE,
IMPERISHABLE PEACE,
HAVE THESE FOR YOURS.

Before he shipped out, Samson sent me a postcard with a cartoon image of an angler being slapped in the head by the fish he'd just reeled in. On the reverse he'd quipped that he doubted he'd be doing any troutfishing in Nam but recommended that I read Richard Brautigan anyway. Only this spring I'd learned from Mr. Julian that Samson's tour of duty had been cut short by injuries incurred in combat. After two months in physical therapy, he'd been transported home with an honorable discharge; and this fine June day he was coming to the Brewster estate in the company of his mother to pay his respects. Mr. Julian was sure I would want to be present to salute his homecoming as well.

Thus I found myself, once again, keeping company with Mr. Julian in his drawing room as we waited for the door chimes to sound. And as I sat watching shafts of sunlight filter through the faded sheers overhanging the French doors, holding a glass of lemonade beaded with sweat that Sassafras had delivered from the depths of the kitchen, inhaling the scent of Mr. Julian's Chanel cologne, time seemed to melt away, and for all I knew I could have been fifteen, nerving myself for my first interview with my future employer. Around me were signs abundant that time had indeed pressed forward, but even those changes seemed to have begun to move eerily backwards. Mr. Julian looked less the hale man who, flush from Bruno's miraculous "cure," had set off for Europe two years ago as wide-eyed as a first-time traveler. His pale skin seemed more translucent than ever, and, thin as he already was, he had lost weight—his white linen trousers and button-down blue-striped shirt from Le Bon Marche slid over his bony frame as if unable to gain traction.

As the hum of his tinny voice filled the space between us, I noticed another change that now seemed no change at all. One of Hank's first and, to my mind, only salutary services upon taking G.G.'s place had been to repair the grandfather clock, so that for the first time in years it ticked off the minutes in harmony with the Greenwich mean. But the fix had apparently run its course—the second hand now jerked without moving at twenty to the hour, five minutes behind its former frozen time. As I set my drink on a jade coaster on the side-table, I noted the film of dust on its surface. The detail augmented a sensation of entropy that sent a chill shudder through me as I sat, sweating, while Mr. Julian held forth from the straight-backed chair in which, due to his slipped disc, he sat as stiffly as a Sunday school teacher as we waited for the door chimes to break the stillness of that tomb-like room.

When Samson entered, his mother at his side, and stepped down into the drawing room, I didn't know who to look at first. Samson had become a man, a full-fledged grown-up, since I'd last seen him two years ago; there was no question of calling him "Pockets" now. Standing even more ramrod straight than Mr. Julian sat in his chair, olive green uniform pulled smartly over chiseled body, boxer's shoulders squared and broader than ever, dark face unreadable and jaw clenched, his fleshed-out presence exuded an adult solemnity that made me feel like an adolescent all over again. The woman by his side was a revelation. I don't know what I expected, but not this speck of a gray-haired woman in her Sunday best. She barely reached Samson's shoulder, and her skin, lighter than either Samson or Geronimo's, was peppered with age spots. There was no signature of the boxer to whom she had given birth in her frame—bird-thin legs and sloping shoulders, concave chest beneath which protruded a round belly that made her appear pregnant in old age, and eyes that preferred to trace the faded patterns in the carpet at her feet rather than meet our own. Samson introduced her, and Mr. Julian graciously motioned Mrs. Lillian, as he addressed her, to take a seat on the musty sofa by her son, to whose left arm she nervously clung.

That's when I noticed Samson's right hand. It drooped lifelessly from his wrist, two fingers missing. The back of the hand was swollen, and through the dark skin I could see the grotesque shadow of gray cartilage pushed to the surface, striated with pink scars lighter than the skin of his palms. So this was his war wound. He led with his right in the ring.

Mr. Julian noticed the mangled hand at the same time. He breathlessly asked Samson to recount the story of his injury.

"This medal for bravery"—Samson tapped one of the insignias attached to his uniform—"is nothing but a cover-up for stupid tom-foolery." He spoke in a deadpan voice as he sat upright on the edge of the sofa, feet solidly on the ground. Shiny black boots, I noticed, not the sneakers of yore, nor one dab of red clay to diminish their luster.

"My squad leader selected me for a Special Mission all right," Samson said when pressed by Mr. Julian to tell his story. "It was my job to deliver a crate *critical to the war effort* to a general hunkered down in a valley crawling with Viet Cong northwest of our base. You'd have thought I was carrying top-secret files, the way I was in-structed never to let the damn crate out of my sight while a special convoy helicoptered us in. We had to fly low, because our mission was off record, and enemy fire nearly downed us twice."

"Top-secret files!" Mr. Julian clapped his hands in anticipation of more to come.

"No, sir, that crate was filled with something far more precious: twelve bottles of French champagne pilfered from the cellars of the Hotel de Ville in Saigon—we're talking bottles from the 1940s. Turns out the general had good taste. But he was mad as a hatter. When he jimmied the crate open and lifted out the first dusty bottle, he let out a hoot anybody within twenty miles must have heard. We'd flown in two chests of dry ice, as well, and come midnight, he decided the bub-bly was chilled enough to serve—to his team of advisers, not to me, I was just waiting for daylight when the pilot could fly me back to my base—and he was pouring the stuff into real wine glasses he'd gotten God knows where when a round of gunfire ripped loose. We hit the ground in no time flat but not before a round hit the washtub where the bottles were chilling, and damned if they didn't explode like dy-namite. Pieces of glass wedged here, and here"—Samson touched his hand—"and obviously here"—he gestured where fingers used to be.

Pale as he already was, Mr. Julian blanched.

"I was lucky, another shard flew straight into the pilot's eye, sliced it through like a pitted olive. Anyway, I was lying there, holding onto what was left of my hand and trying not to make a target of myself while we exchanged fire. It was over fast; they disappeared quick as they'd come. That fucking four-star general—excuse my French—was kind enough to give me a few sips from the one bottle that hadn't exploded to stay the pain till the medics arrived to bring me in."

Mrs. Washington looked down at her round lap while Samson used his left hand to hoist his right by the wrist. The remaining fingers flopped around like putty. "Glass severed some nerves, it's still hard to feel anything though they promise a bit of sensation might return one of these days. So that's how I earned my badge of honor."

We were all silent. I knew this meant an end to his boxing career. Samson sat stock still, his body radiating fury. Mrs. Lillian, who had heard her son's monologue as many times over as relatives had come calling since his return, came to our rescue. Patting Samson on the shoulder, she spoke for the first time. "Your father would've been proud of you. Lord bless my dear Thelonius if he didn't get his leg all tore up in the Pacific doin' the same as you. Serving our country. Don't fret yourself so."

Thelonius? I'd always understood G.G.'s full name to be George Geronimo. And his limp to be the consequence of polio contracted as a child. I remembered, distinctly, my conversations with Mr. Julian and Samson regarding their contradictory explanations of G.G.'s middle name. Evidently the man, so transparent on the surface, had nurtured more than one mystery about himself and taken them all to the grave.

Mr. Julian picked up the conversational thread, turning to the question of Samson's future plans—"There's always the G.I. Bill, so maybe Samson will see you at Harvard, Newt!"—and sharing local gossip till Sassafras appeared with a plate of toast points spread with homemade pimento cheese. Mrs. Lillian used the occasion as an excuse to disappear into the kitchen to fetch a glass of water—"Ice hurts my gums," she apologized as she exited with Sassafras. The three of us chatted on, Mr. Julian coaxing anecdotes of bunker life from Samson and nudging me to fill the pauses with tales of my sophomore year. Trivial as they seemed in face of Samson's ordeals, I stumbled through my repertoire to please Mr. Julian. A faint hum of chuckles emanated from the kitchen, where Mrs. Lillian seemed to have come into her own without us menfolk looking on.

Mr. Julian ended the social hour by telling Samson that he would be in touch—there were surely some tasks around the place where he might, God forgive the ungracious pun, lend a helping hand. And he invited me to return on Thursday, for a swim and lunch for old times' sake. Mrs. Lillian reappeared from the kitchen, carrying a covered dish that Sassafras had put up for her and looking relieved that her time in the cavernous mansion was at an end. I fancied I saw a glimmer of relief in Samson's tired eyes, as well, as they exited the front door where the climbing rose and wisteria still fought to topple the other to the ground.

No more bouts for our local war hero. If only I could say something to make him feel whole again. The best I could do was to remember to extend my left hand to grip his good one as we parted.

*

When I returned on Thursday, it turned out that Mr. Julian was feeling "a mite puny."

Again, the thought that his health wasn't what it had been a year ago crossed my mind. Lunch by the pool being out of the question, I was instructed to take my swim anyway, and if he felt better by the time I was done, then perhaps we might enjoy B.B.'s shrimp salad with iceberg wedges remoulade in the kitchen.

The pool area wasn't being maintained to its old standards and the pool house smelled damply of mildew, concrete, and decaying wood, but the water felt bracing as I dove in and swam my 100 laps. I'd just finished rinsing off in the dim changing room—the ancient overhead shower still managed to plash a respectable stream of warm water—when I heard footsteps. Instinctively I jumped, almost slipping on the wet floor as I stepped out of the narrow shower stall to reach for my towel. A figure stood silhouetted in the entrance. I couldn't make out his face, but I knew Samson's outline, there was no mistaking it. And I could see that he was dressed in civilian clothes—the uniform of his previous visit had been donned at Mr. Julian's behest.

"You surprised me," I said, holding my towel in front of me.

"Thought I might find you here," he answered in a tone that made me vaguely uneasy. He didn't enter, just stood silently watching. I suddenly felt conspicuously naked and turned away, still dripping, to step into my boxers. But before I could lift a foot, he'd crossed the room in a flash, he was standing right behind me, and my boxers dropped to the wet floor as he pushed me roughly against the dark green tiles, pinning me against the cold wall with the solid weight of his body, his good arm holding me down, breathing hard. Panic gripped me as I felt my damp cheek slide across the tiles, oddly aware of the smell of mold in the grouting and the stench of liquor—rye or bourbon?—on Samson's heaving breath.

From my left eye I saw the two of us reflected in the speckled mirror over the pale green pedestal sink. I couldn't move: his bulky muscle more than made up for the inch or two I had on him in height. Insanely, all I could think as I watched our frozen image was that his clothes were going to get wet if he kept bearing down on me so fiercely. Then he leaned back, just a fraction, but enough to start pummeling my flesh with his good fist: rhythmic, bruising punches anchoring me in place as he brought his lips to my left ear and whispered, still breathing hard, "I'm no idiot. I saw you. I saw the three of you."

Again, he pushed his considerable heft against my back, much as Marky had done those years ago. I could feel the anger that pulsated through his hard flesh into mine, and shame immobilized me.

"You fool," he hissed into my ear. "Don't you get it? He was fucking me, *me*, that whole summer."

I clenched my eyelids shut as his words ricocheted through my skull and amplified his whisper to an unbearable roar. I had had no clue that Marky had even registered Samson's existence.

"Yeah," Samson continued, his voice breaking. "He was fucking the butler's boy, when what he really wanted was you."

There it was again—the words I had heard spoken by Mary Jo and that I had repressed, on a starry winter's night by this self-same pool: *he wanted you.* Samson stopped drumming his fist into my back, held tight to me in a fierce clinch, and spat out four words: "And so did I." I felt the wetness from his eyes trickle down my neck as he pressed hard against me with the pain of all the betrayals he must have felt, and I felt him twist his body as he lifted his bad arm and brought his wounded hand to rest against the side of my face. I watched, through wet eyelashes, as the puckered nubs where two fingers had ceased to exist brushed my cheek. As his wounded flesh touched mine I choked down a sob that arose from the depth of emotions that I was just discovering.

"I'm sorry," I said. "I'm—"

Samson's body shuddered violently, as if he hadn't heard me, and he jerked away, suddenly another person as he violently, repeatedly, struck his forehead with his good hand like a wild man.

"What the fuck am I doing? Damn you damn you, Newt Seward, I hope to God I never see you again."

He gulped down a heaving sob and dashed out of the room before I could stop him.

*

The magnitude of Samson's revelations slammed me like Hurricane Edith trawling the Louisiana bayous, bringing to its surface a mass of hitherto hidden inhabitants of the deep.

How could I have not known? This time I couldn't, I wouldn't, allow myself to ignore what I had just learned, what I had *felt* in my muscle and bone when Samson shoved me against that clammy wall of tiled lotus stalks and blooms. From our first meeting, watching the summer hailstorm cross this very pool, I had been attracted to Samson—even though such feelings had been too dangerous to allow to surface in my thinking mind. And, it appeared, so he'd felt the same for me. But now any chance of realizing those feelings were utterly wrecked. Till this moment, I had never fully known myself.

And Marky? The fact that he'd been fucking Samson was a total shock, even more so than what this revelation implied about Marky's desires. Behind his quips and insinuations, the way he liked to mess with my head as if *I* were the one harboring secrets, I had surely suspected, even if I refused to acknowledge my suspicions. But fucking *Samson*? My head reeled.

For the first time I envisioned seeing our ménage à trois at the pool through Samson's eyes—that is, the eyes of Marky's sexual conquest, the eyes of my fishing buddy, now an angry stranger who had just acknowledged his own desire for me. My head grew dizzy at the enormity of the missed connections latent in that frozen instant.

But, most of all, Samson's choked confession—*so did I*—even as he pummeled my back changed my world, and I knew I would never be the same. I wasn't ready to explore these realizations yet: not now; not at Harvard where everyone knew me as someone else. I was too scared; but I was also exhilarated. Someday soon, I could no longer afford to turn away from the possibilities that the bruising impact of Samson's fists on my flesh had scored into desire. In place of fistmarks of frustration bruising my skin, I wished that his arms had embraced me.

Instead, he had disappeared, shouting he never wanted to see me again. Ever. That made it painfully clear that the first man in my life would never be Samson.

And I mourned.

29

SHERLOCK IN THE STACKS

The first time I entered Widener Library's hallowed halls, I thought of Mr. Julian's library and how my current academic life had its origins in that lofty, windowless room overflowing with books piled in perilous columns. Its stately carved bookcases and frescoed ceiling had nothing in common with the antiseptic gloom of Widener's industrial stacks, whose tomb-like tiers descended stories underground, or its cold metal shelving. But the ineffable smell of all those books, pages crumbling into invisible particles that, once inhaled, became part of me, was the same: the odor of inks, bindings, glue, mysterious alchemies of print and paper, these blended together like a rare perfume.

Widener formed a crucial part of my double life at Harvard. Whenever the roster of social engagements and moneyed one-up-manship that was everyday existence for those of us living in Eliot—from cathedral dining hall with its seating hierarchies to dorm suites with their vertical hierarchies, from interior quad where upperclassmen tossed footballs and Frisbees to Master's residence where all were invited to weekly high teas but only an appointed few were asked to dinner when the Head Master entertained the occasional Captain of Industry, Congressman, or Nobel Laureate—whenever any of these pressures grew too oppressive, I grabbed my backpack and escaped to Widener. There I shook off my fear of being an impostor by doing what I did best.

Eight months before my fateful encounter with Samson, during the fall of my sophomore year, on a halcyon October afternoon when Eliot Quad had filled with its resident men and their Radcliffe dates performing distracting rites of courtship on blankets spread across the manicured lawn, I had taken my books to the library to get a leg up on my seminar paper for an elective on international modernisms. Each student had been assigned a country and time period, and Italy's interwar years had fallen my way. Starting with Italian Futurism, I began by investigating an art movement I'd never heard of before—the *aeropittura* movement of the early thirties. That directed me to the careers of Fortunato Depero and Enrico Prampolini, artists whose interests in stage design and the decorative arts piqued my curiosity. Depero was particularly intriguing since he had spent two years in Manhattan when Mr. Julian lived there. Not only had Depero worked on avant-garde theater productions, as had Mr. Julian, he'd created interior designs for wealthy clients in Mr. Julian's circle. These were also the same years Enzio Sorrento came to America to visit Mr. Julian. In tracking Depero's movements, I imagined myself tracking Julian and Enzio's steps as well.

Back in my dorm room, the folder of Enzio's furniture designs stood on the shelf over my desk, propped upright by the Quattrocento box that Mr. Julian had passed on to me for caretaking—he'd returned the set of keys I'd sent him prior to his European tour, which once again nested in the folded watercolor encased in the box. Last Christmas I'd asked Mr. Julian if I might borrow the design portfolio as well. When I found myself too tired to continue my schoolwork, it soothed me to untie the satin ribbons of the mottled binder and behold its sheets of tracery. Often they sent me back to my own projects energized and inspired.

So that gorgeous autumn afternoon of 1971 found me, perversely, in the shadowy depths of Widener, reeling through microfiches of *Il Giornale* and *La Stampa* in quest of newspaper coverage of a 1934 exhibition in Naples, *La Casa d'arte, o l'arte del futurismo,* for which Fortunato Depero had famously gathered a roster of Italy's top industrialists as backers. My gift for languages and the smattering of Italian I'd learned with Mr. Julian made it easy enough to skim the headlines. Depero's exhibition had caused a sensation because of its bold manifesto: the time had come to bring art to a mass audience through a merger of the creative arts and industry. In time I located what I was hoping to find: a lengthy article detailing the exhibition's opening ceremonies. It was accompanied by a grainy photograph of the contributing artists standing shoulder to shoulder with a group of industrialists, flutes raised in a toast: an unholy alliance of Finance and

Aesthetics if ever there were one. Imagine my shock when I skimmed the caption in search of Depero's name and one even more familiar to me leaped from the fine print: *Enzio Sorrento*.

A ghost breathed down my neck.

It was easy to pick out Enzio's rakish face, despite the poor quality of the image: he stood to the left rear, champagne glass barely raised and face far more grim than the one I remembered from the playful photographs in Mr. Julian's albums. Skimming the listed names, I discovered a *second* Sorrento—Eduardo—among the group. Ticking off names against figures revealed this Sorrento to be a confident-looking man, solid as a piece of Pavonazzo marble, shaking Depero's hand as the two smiled at the camera from the center of the photograph. Instantly I realized this financier must be Enzio's father, the man who had destroyed Enzio and Julia's happiness and sundered Enzio and Mr. Julian's friendship in the process.

Filled with a detective's sixth sense as he hovers on the brink of recovering the missing murder weapon, I opened my dictionary and pieced together the contents of the article. After heaping praise on Depero for conceiving this unique collaboration between art and enterprise, the reporter turned his attention to the senior Sorrento, hailing him as the power broker who had charmed his more hesitant associates into supporting the venture. He'd also used his considerable connections to insure it had the highest stamps of approval, including a congratulatory message from Il Duce himself. Even more intriguing was the article's identification of Sorrento as a most respected art collector and a dealer in Old Masters. His son Enzio earned mention both for his modern furniture designs and his equally striking oil portraits. It seemed amazing, and wonderful, that my research had unearthed a link between a Fascist-endorsed Italian art exhibition and my Virginian benefactor's deceased friend. But how, exactly, did Enzio fit into this picture?

In due time I finished my paper on Depero's contributions to modern theater design, but not so my delvings into the hazy past of the Sorrento clan: I was determined to see what other facts I might unearth. The next discovery occurred when I came across a biographical notice of Enzio in a 1938 directory of contemporary Italian artists. It reported that two years before the 1934 Naples exhibition, Enzio had mounted a solo show in Paris hailed as his big break and increasing the demand for his portraits. He remained one of the country's more promising young artists and had recently moved his studio from Firenze to Roma. The writer's one criticism was that Sorrento didn't more aggressively use his talent to reflect the glory of the new Italian empire. That entry sent me in quest of information on Enzio's Paris show of 1932, and I located a witty interview in *Paris Match* accompanied by a photograph of the debonair artist in his Florence studio, standing by a window whose vista was uncannily familiar to me from his portrait of Mr. Julian. Enzio's responses were simultaneously self-deprecating and charming in ways that recalled his whimsical poses in Mr. Julian's photographs. "An artist? No, no, I simply take pleasure in peering out windows—and into faces—far too much." Then there was the posthumous evaluation of the artist that I located in a Sotheby's catalogue from 1958. Sorrento's career had been curtailed by the War, the catalogue reported, and his reputation had suffered following criminal charges brought against his father for "unorthodox dealings" in the art world, but Enzio's respected if small oeuvre was demanding renewed attention from discriminating collectors.

It was late December by the time I finished compiling this portfolio of information, so I didn't have to wait long to surprise Mr. Julian with the fruits of my sleuthing. And Mr. Julian's face did light up, when, the Tuesday before Christmas, I braved the aftermath of the winter storm that had covered Rocky Hill with four inches of life-defying sleet to pay him a call. Indeed, I lost my balance crossing the front terrace, grabbing at the front door just as Hank opened it, hardly bothering to disguise his amusement at my clumsiness. The fir wreath on the door, dishearteningly, turned out to be the sole attempt at decorating the house for the season. Following Hank, I stepped down into the drawing room, which felt drearier than I remembered, despite the fire smoldering on the hearth. Near the fitful flame Mr. Julian was seated in his old wheelchair, whose reappearance startled me. Mimi curled on the throw covering his lap, and my benefactor's head bobbed in light slumber until my greeting returned him to the land of the living.

"Come to see the old man, have you? What Crimson tales have you brought to spice up our sleepy Yuletide holiday? No, no, *don't* make a to-do about the chair." He stopped me short. "Fit as a fiddle; I simply took a nasty spill in the kitchen the other day. Hank or Bruno trekked in snow from the terrace and I slipped in the puddle it left and wrenched my hip." Mr. Julian craned his neck in order to stare accusingly at Hank. "Damn careless, neither cad admits to the deed, all I know is that it wasn't B.B., it was her day off."

Hank squirmed under his master's glare until, finally, Mr. Julian dismissed him and beckoned me to sit on a low stool, where the ruddy firelight warmed my cheeks. He looked down at me as I sat with my long legs stretched on the carpet. Mimi jumped from his lap and resettled in mine as if it were time I returned to my duties. A pensive look crossed Mr. Julian's face.

"Harvard is doing well by you, Newt; you are becoming a handsome *adult*. And you turned twenty this month—it's all beginning, my son!" Then, like the Southern gentleman he had been raised to be, he made polite inquiries about my family. "I must say your Mother's name seems to crop up in the *Chronicle* every time I open it!"

I confirmed that Mother's standing in the business community was indeed on the rise; beyond her interior decorating and real estate businesses, she'd used her authority on the Chamber of Commerce to push through City Council a proposal for Rocky Hill's first shopping mall, she'd lured in the investors, and its Christmas sales were setting records. Rumor had it that Jeanlyn Seward had the stuff to become Rocky Hill's first Lady Mayor if she were so inclined. It tickled the old man to imagine her rampaging over a whole new realm of minions—she who had first practiced her leadership skills by keeping us Sewards in line.

"And sister Katie has grown quite respectable, sir, does the books for Mother, and just got engaged to the new pharmacist at Davis Drugs."

"Quite the contrast to our Rat of yesteryear," Mr. Julian commented.

Personally, I found it of a piece that Katie had ended up with yet another beau intimately involved with drugs—albeit of the legal variety this time round.

"And your brother?"

"Jubal keeps surprising me. He's got more of a head on his shoulders than I did at his age." I smiled. "I find myself growing to admire him."

Further reports from the Seward world were interrupted by Sassafras's entrance. She hobbled forward on arthritic ankles as wobbly as Mimi's paws, bearing a tarnished silver tray that, in G.G.'s day, would have never looked in such need of a vigorous polish. "You're a sight for sore eyes, Mister Newt," she greeted me as she served up hot spiced tea, gingerbread men fresh from the oven, and slices of tinned fruitcake. The commingled scents added a sorely needed note of holiday cheer to the stuffy room, and Mr. Julian and I saluted each other's health in the spirit of the season.

"But it's not *my* family I came here to talk about."

This I announced with a theatrical pause worthy of Mr. Julian himself.

To heighten the suspense, I picked the candied cherries out of the whiskey-soaked fruitcake, savoring them one by one until Mr. Julian demanded that I explain myself. Whereupon I presented my research on the Sorrentos, handing the old man the items I'd photocopied so that we could peruse them together. Mr. Julian pulled his bifocals from the pocket of his burgundy cardigan and listened avidly as I summarized their contents.

Yes, he of course remembered the Paris show that had made Enzio's name—in fact he had attended the opening at the gallery on the Rue Guissarde, near Place Saint Sulpice. But he didn't recall having seen the interview ("How *could* he have neglected to send me a copy?"), so translating its contents with me gave him special pleasure. Of the 1934 art and commerce show in Naples, Mr. Julian shook his head darkly. Julia was in Italy with Enzio for the event, as they had been making the rounds of Enzio's relatives to announce their engagement. It was the exhibition's emphasis on commerce as much as art that had helped persuade Mr. Brewster to consider seriously the international collaboration between his furniture company and Mr. Sorrento's manufacturing resources that Enzio brought to the table on his visit to Virginia the following year.

"I do remember how disturbed Julia was—not by the show itself, not even the concept of art for profit, but because dear Enzio felt so utterly humiliated by the way his father had *bullied* his associates into supporting the event—and then had made sure reviewers singled out his son's contribution for hyperbolic praise. Of course, Mussolini's endorsement embarrassed Enzio and Julia terribly. For years Enzio had lamented his father's politics and business ethics—if a quick profit were involved, no one knew better how to grease the system! What irked Enzio most was that the dirtier his father played, the more he came out looking as pure as the Virgin Mary and as golden as the Vatican treasury." Mr. Julian frowned. "Knowing all that, perhaps I should have asked more questions when the collaboration between our families was on the table. But it *seemed* above board. And Enzio's designs *were* heavenly!"

I took up the *Casa de l'arte* article, reading aloud its description of Signore Sorrento as a "most respected" art collector—*molto rispetta-to*—and a dealer in masters old and new.

Mr. Julian frowned. "There *were* some excellent paintings in the Urbino home, I remember a medieval altarpiece and a few Renaissance paintings—and, yes, one lovely oil, unattributed but clearly Florentine and hardly bigger than this sheet of paper. Ragazzi shaking cherries—or was it olives?—out of a tree. Quite charmed me. Thank goodness I majored in art history, since art was the only thing Il Signore and I had in common." Mr. Julian emitted a delicate snort. "Not that we formed any endearing bond. My work in the theater made me just one more dilettante in his eyes, no better than his son, whose artistic ambitions he lost no opportunity to mock in private—even though in public he demanded his son's genius be recognized. The fact I was the offspring of an American millionaire was no doubt my one redeeming quality. So he 'dealt' in art, they say?" Mr. Julian snorted again. "The question of aesthetic empathy aside, I would hardly have expected him to have the patience or honesty to become a so-called *respected* player in the field."

I smiled in my turn. "Clever as he was, Mr. Sorrento didn't always come out smelling like a rose. In fact, just after the war ended"—I paused in order to heighten the revelation of my ultimate discovery—"he was put on trial... for fencing stolen art."

So saying, I handed a second set of xeroxed newspaper articles to the wondering Mr. Julian.

In 1947, Signore Sorrento had been charged with taking advantage of the chaos that ensued upon the Allies' drive into southern Italy and Mussolini's retreat north to smuggle several "disappeared" Italian Renaissance and baroque artworks to clients in France, Germany, and Austria. The prosecution, in building its case, also charged him with using his highly placed governmental connections to supply various of Mussolini's associates, at home and abroad, with art treasures the regime had been confiscating from Jewish families since the Thirties. The trial had been spectacular, building on a popular backlash against the country's recent fascist past and public outrage at the pilfering of the nation's artistic heritage for the personal gain of Axis connoisseurs, but it had not resulted in a conviction: too many documents destroyed in bombings, too many critical witnesses conveniently disappeared just before the trial's start.

"Don't you know the wicked man had a hand in that!"

"The story gets even better. In trying to establish a history of shady art dealership practices, the prosecution brought to light a former incident, a hushed-up affair from the late Twenties. You see, Eduardo Sorrento had been accused by a client of deliberately selling him a Pollaiuolo Mantega that turned out to be a cunningly executed fake. Now guess what artist's name, his career just beginning, gets tangled up in the potential scandal?"

"No!"

"Yes, poor Enzio himself."

I explained that I'd found an article in *Pettegolezzo*, the Roman tabloid of the day, gleefully reporting the rumor that Sorrento had pressed his talented son into producing the Mantega, along with a series of other forgeries. There was no evidence to substantiate the charge ("Of course not!" Mr. Julian exclaimed indignantly), the only connection being that Sorrento's son happened to be an artist. Ultimately, a pre-trial settlement spared Sorrento Senior any charges, his integrity fervently vouched for by Bernard Berenson, with whom Sorrento had a mutually beneficial professional relationship. Nonetheless when the 1947 trial became daily news, these old charges resurfaced to join the newer ones, and public opinion against the accused was buttressed by tales of the cutthroat business practices that had made Sorrento both feared and wildly successful for nearly a half-century. I was beginning to understand how so unscrupulous a parent might have terrorized someone of Enzio's artistic temperament, the weight of the father's ego bearing oppressively down on the son until Enzio's untimely death in 1943. "Was Enzio running away, that night he died?"

"Or carrying out another of his father's unsufferable commissions? In either case, the 'unfortunate son of an unforgiving and unrepentant father.' Doomed."

"*Mio fratello, caro, povero, condannato*," I recited, for I too remembered the somber words that Enzio's sister, Angelica, had written Mr. Julian from her Carmelite cell. "Well, sir, you'll be happy to know that the unrepentant father finally got what was coming to him. Even though he was acquitted, his empire collapsed and his health suffered for the rest of his life."

"I never knew any of this." Mr. Julian lifted his unholy blue eyes to meet my gaze, marvel in his voice. "Fencing stolen art—with Brownshirts and Nazis, no less!"

"For once he didn't choose the winning side."

Mr. Julian lapsed into silence as Sassafras reentered the room to fetch our plates. She took the liberty of rearranging the throw on Mr. Julian's lap—which he of course protested—then looked at me, massaging her sore back as she straightened up. "I hope you ain't been tellin Mr. Brewster any dreary tales. He's been moody enough all this autumn without you adding fuel to the fire! What this house could use is some Christmas cheer." She shuffled over to the liquor cabinet and produced a bottle of port, filling two crystal stem glasses with the ruby liquid.

"A touch to lighten the mood. Doc B.B.'s orders!"

Mr. Julian returned to our conversation once Sassafras left the room.

"All your research makes me wonder if Enzio suspected what his father was up to those last years. If only I had Julia's correspondence with Enzio!" He sipped his port. "There was one strange letter she *did* share with me, it arrived just before the furniture collaboration went up in smoke. Enzio was writing to assure her that he would do whatever it took to keep his hands clean, no matter how much his father pressured him, until he rejoined Julia on this side of the Atlantic. At the time, we assumed he was referring to the usual demands his father placed on all his progeny. In retrospect we wondered if Enzio had been trying to warn us that the furniture collaboration was going south."

All of a sudden Mr. Julian clapped his hands together. "Funny how it comes back in bits and pieces—there *was* the oddest reference in that letter. I remember now, because neither Julia nor I knew what to make of it, something to the effect that all Julia and I needed to consider was Caravaggio's 'Job before Eliphaz' to understand how strongly resolved Enzio was *never* to deliver the work of innocents into the hands of the unworthy. But Caravaggio never painted such a scene—I checked it out. Delivering 'the work of innocents into the hands of the unworthy': was that his way of telling us his father was fencing stolen art?"

"How he must have hated his father."

"Not only that. For Enzio, art was an inheritance to be shared by all, a visual record of how far we'd come as a human race. Not something to be bartered for money." Mr. Julian exhaled meditatively. "I want you to fetch me something."

From his pocket the old man produced his familiar jangle of household keys, dangling from a silver clasp that he'd purchased at Tiffany when he was only slightly older than me and newly arrived in New York City. His shaky hand fingered one small, brass, single bolt skeleton key.

"This unlocks the drawer to the reading table in the library," he said. "Fetch me the packet of letters tied with the blue ribbon."

I stepped across the fraying carpets, entering the chillier gloom of the book-lined chamber. At the walnut table where I'd labored so assiduously four summers ago, I bent to unlock its drawer—the same from which Mr. Julian had taken the Quattrocento box. It was lined with stacks of yellowed letters tied with different colors of fragile satin ribbon, among which nestled the small packet bound in blue.

"These are the few letters from Enzio I saved," he explained when I delivered the stack into his hands. "I can't forgive myself for burning the letter he wrote me after the breakup with Julia—I was too upset to consider his apologies, too angry to entertain his plea that our friendship meant more than any barriers our fathers could place between us. I relented later, wrote him several times when it became clear Italy was going to war, hoping my letters would get through. They came back, unopened, and I only heard from him once more, three years later. Here it is. Read it out loud."

He sat back and closed his eyes as I unfolded the pale sheet of stationery he handed me. I slowly deciphered the cursive script that had faded to a pale lilac, penned in surprisingly good English.

3 VIII 1942

My dear Julian—

Forgive me the brevity of this communication after so long a silence, but I must hurry if this package has a chance of reaching you safely. I never received a reply to the letter I wrote you after your father ended my engagement to Julia and my father used his influence to have my passport revoked. I fear that silence means you never want to hear from me again. But I must write, once more, to try to make—what? amends? There can hardly be any. Reparation for Julia's heartbreak? There can be none—I pray she someday finds happiness with a good man who gives her the joy we were denied. All our dreams so hellishly broken, first by our fathers, now by this war.

But in the name of our friendship that once was, I beg you, mio migli-or fabbro, to accept these tokens. If the world survives and I do not—the latter I fear increasingly likely—it is my dream, however fanciful, however remote, that the enclosed may in the future lead to some small recompense for the misery that I have brought upon your family. I dare not commit more to paper, nor would I entrust these talismans to anyone else in this world. But someday follow their lead, and please know that what lies on the other side is rightfully mine, and upon my death, rightfully yours and your sister's. I think of you and Julia constantly, trying to imagine how you are spending your days, your hours, your minutes. It solaces me, it whispers of the pleasures we once shared. Don't try to imagine my life now—there is no pleasure left in the circle of hell I inhabit. I have an ominous feeling that all will end badly very soon—I will rest better knowing that I have passed this on to you.

Your loving friend, Enz—

The bottom of the page was water-damaged, blotting out half of Enzio's signature and, below it, what appeared to have been an address, of which only the words *Studio d'Ar—* and *—oma* and the number *31*—or was it *87*?—remained decipherable.

Some intuition—perhaps it was trying to decipher those numerals—made me glance back at the date at the top of the page.

"Julia died in the late summer of 1941, didn't she?"

"August third."

I exhaled, filled with wonder at the coincidence. Without knowledge of Julia's death, Enzo had written exactly a year later. Mr. Julian nodded in silent agreement.

"And what did he enclose with this letter?"

Mr. Julian's unearthly eyes glimmered in the firelight. "Something *you* have in your possession, my boy. That lovely inlaid box I passed on to you, along with that scrap of watercolor wrapped around the keys I returned to you when I got back from Europe."

"You fancied they might be keys to his Florence studio—but he'd relocated to Rome by the late 1930s, hadn't he?

"Yes, but I was never there and don't remember the address—somewhere in the Ghetto, I remember him describing the Turtle fountain and jesting the ruins of the Teatro Marcello were practically in his backyard." Mr. Julian took the letter from my hands, gazed at it with watery eyes. "For a long time I puzzled over these words, trying to fathom what Enzio was telling me. But I finally gave up. He was dead, Julia was dead, where was the use?"

On an impulse I leant across the space that separated us and placed my hand on Mr. Julian's. A piece of burning wood dropped through the grate, sending out a shiver of sparks that bounced against the hearth screen. We heard the front door open, sturdy footsteps abused the entry hall's tiles. Bruno entered the drawing room, saluting us as he unzipped a parka dusted with snow and tossed it on a Queen Anne chair. Now he uses the front door like he's master of the house, I grumbled to myself. And throws his coat where he pleases.

"It's snowing again," he announced, rubbing his strong hands together as he strode forward. "Harder than ever. Is my charge behaving?"

My palm was just recovering from his handshake when I noticed Mr. Julian twisting to his left side to screen the table by the side of his wheelchair.

Bruno immediately took note.

"What are you hiding? Damn it!" An ugly flush colored the skin behind Bruno's five-o'clock shadow, and his brows lowered in displeasure as he spied Mr. Julian's glass of port. "I've told you a thousand times, no unauthorized stimulants! You must follow my rules to a T if you expect me to restore you to health! What else has that woman been slipping you? Sweets?—I see it on your face. I warned you—"

Indeed, telltale pink circles had popped out on Mr. Julian's pale cheeks. It took me a moment to realize Bruno wasn't being facetious: his ire was palpable.

"You eat and you drink what I give you, from my hands, with my medicines, when I tell you. Or I'll walk straight out of here. You want that?"

"Forgive me," the old man quavered. His show of servility seemed as improbable as Bruno's anger. I had to bite my tongue to keep from barking at Bruno that it was a holiday, let the old man enjoy his pleasures. But this was their domestic dispute, not mine, so I remained silent until Bruno had stomped out of the room, taking Mr. Julian's glass with him. I feared Sassafras was in for it.

"That seemed uncalled for," I observed.

Mr. Julian's hands danced in his lap, his face quivering. "Oh, he's right, I *know* he's right. You saw the miracle he worked on me three years ago. His connections are supplying him with special vitamins and medicines, I'm on a strict diet that will heal me, oh I do believe so! But I've upset him, and he does *not* like to be disobeyed. I best summon him back and make our peace. Put these letters back, and on your way out, my dear boy, press the button to send Hank in. He'll know where Bruno's sulking. Oh a-Lordy, a-Lordy, a fine mess I've made of it!"

I left Mr. Julian all aflutter. On my way out, I noticed that Bruno's parka, so carelessly tossed on the side chair, had slipped to the parquet floor, where a puddle of melted snow had now collected, and, shaking my head in wonder at the levels of dysfunction pervading Mr. Julian's domestic troika, I quietly let myself out the front door.

*

If, with my recent twentieth birthday in mind, Mr. Julian had found fit to salute my entrance into a new epoch—"it's all beginning, my son!"—so too I celebrated another rite of passage on New Year's Eve. At the beginning of December, on the counsel of Mr. Allbright, I had declared my A1 draft status, betting on the odds that the draft would never reach 323, my lottery number—unless, God forbid, the country launched World War III in the next month. As the clock ticked towards midnight and 1972, I breathed a sigh of relief, knowing once and for all I wouldn't be forced to leave school and, like the less lucky Samsons of my generation, face a foreign war in a foreign clime. Jubal had taken me to a New Year's Eve gathering at the house of one of his school friends, whose parents were either open-minded or foolish enough to permit the mostly underaged guests to party to their heart's content. When midnight arrived, the teenagers surrounding me broke into a carefree rendition of Steely Dan's "Reeling in the Years." No "Auld Lang Syne" for this generation.

Spending the evening with Jubal was eye-opening. Over the holidays, he'd plied me with questions about colleges as he made me privy to his ambitions and dreams—next year, as a senior, he hoped to apply to a range of schools that fell within the family's budget—and I realized what an intelligent, thoughtful young man he had become. Now, witnessing the ease and good humor with which he interacted with a roomful of friends who clearly adored him, I took note and pondered.

So midnight came and went. Jubal was still happily dancing with his friends, showing no signs of stopping when I signaled that I was going to walk home now and leave him the family car. He flashed a peace sign and kept swaying in rhythm to the music as I stepped into the icy night. My path took me down Main Street, where the flashing neon sign over the Tavern on Main, a hole-in-the-wall bar, was the only object showing any sign of life in the deserted downtown. Years ago Marky, Mary Jo, and I had tried to get served in the narrow, dark-paneled establishment, but even the twins' sophistication and our doctored IDs failed to convince the doorman we were of legal age. Tonight I was seized by a whim to pop my head inside for a few minutes before calling it an evening.

I unfurled the woolen scarf from my neck, breathing in the warm air as I settled on a wobbly bar stool, ordered a beer, and looked around me. A battered plastic Santa by the cash register and a string of Christmas lights looped over the shelves of liquor behind the long bar announced the season. Usually the Tavern was home to serious drinkers who prefered to imbibe in disgruntled silence, but tonight the dozen or so celebrants lining the bar were, by Rocky Hill standards, a veritable crucible of conviviality. In a meditative frame of mind, I leaned forward on my elbows, pondering my wish list for 1972. So much achieved in sixteen months since I'd begun college; so many unrealized dreams on the horizon.

Having drained the last suds in my glass, I set off to locate the men's room. A small antechamber at the end of the bar led to the restrooms on the right, and, on the left, through a doorway framed with worn red velvet curtains hanging from a metal rod, to a small room lined with a half-dozen wooden booths where food was served during the day. Finding the men's room occupied, I leant against the door frame, fingering the velvet—and with a rush I recalled standing backstage at Phipps Auditorium on the final night of "Hamlet," so full of expectations as I peered through the rent in the stage curtain. I was still smiling at the recollection when my thoughts were broken by the voices of the only people sitting in the dining room.

The hum of those voices was familiar: one a commanding baritone, the other a needling whine. I peeked around the curtain and saw that the room's two occupants were Bruno and Hank. They sat across from each other in a cramped booth, engrossed in a conversation whose serious mood was worlds removed from the jocularity reigning in the main bar. It unsettled me to see them so intimately engaged—I had always imagined that they disliked each other, wary competitors sparring for Mr. Julian's favor. Quietly I drew back from the doorframe, listening as hard as I could. Their muffled conversation took on the tone of a debate and Hank's voice rose in peevish frustration.

Before I could make out Hank's words, the occupant of the men's room exited and another customer crowded into the antechamber, obliging me to duck into the gents' for my turn. By the time I'd relieved myself and washed my hands with a very dirty bar of soap, Bruno and Hank had left the premises.

I did the same. The collar of my jacket turned up and my scarf wound round my neck to ward off the numbing chill, I walked home. It was one thing to sleuth in the stacks, quite another to spy upon men I didn't really like at all, men that I wished, with all my heart, might one day fall from Mr. Julian's good graces into deserved oblivion.

30

"I DO"

My romantic fantasies about Mary Jo, so rudely curtailed the one night we slept together; my reencounter with Marky on Nantucket; the discoveries I shared with Mr. Julian of the Sorrento family history; the self-knowledge set into motion by my encounter with Samson in the poolhouse; and, not least, my growing disillusionment with the elite world of Harvard and my even more profound sense of being set adrift once Mary Jo announced her engagement to Offenbach— all these factors formed links in the chain, be it iron or gold, thorns or flower, that began the dreamlike day Mr. Julian hired me to arrange his library and that culminated in my resolve to take a leave of absence from college at the beginning of my senior year.

The fateful dinner at Schrafft's where I announced that decision to Mr. Allbright occurred in April of 1973, near the end of my junior term. Eight months later I found myself again standing in a tavern on a New Year's Day—only this holiday the establishment in question was not Rocky Hill's rough-and-ready Tavern on Main but the fabled Tavern on the Green in New York City's Central Park. It was the first day of 1974.

The occasion? None other than Mary Jo Sumner's wedding to Fredrick Bentley Offenbach. The "I do's" had been pronounced, the festivities in the Tavern's west wing had begun, and with thoughts of the long evening stretching before me—six-course dinner and dancing yet to come—I quaffed three flutes of icy champagne in a row to numb the ache in my heart as I gazed out of the Tavern's frost-covered windows onto a white landscape that mocked the vernal vistas promised by the restaurant's name. The orchestra had just struck up "Lara's Theme," and the twelve-inch bafflement of snow, along with the lethal icicles dangling from every limb and lamppost in the Park, brought to mind the ice-encrusted dacha where Julie Christie and Omar Shariff had made passionate, furtive love in "Doctor Zhivago." Why Mary Jo had chosen to tie the knot in the dead of winter in the frozen North-east escaped me—in *my* fantasies I'd always imagined our nuptials taking place in early summer on the manicured lawn of one of her Newport relations. Instead, floating among the two hundred guests in a confection that looked as if it might melt at a touch, Mary Jo was alabaster perfection, the Snow Queen of a glittering world that reflected the gelid one outside.

"January? What was she *thinking*?"

So I said to Marky and Miranda we watched Mary Jo glide from one cluster of guests to the next, arm hooked in Fred Offenbach's, do-ing bride's duty with the grace, and graciousness, that came to her like second nature. Miranda, having acquitted herself as Mary Jo's maid of honor with a patience that belied her feminist qualms about partici-pating in such rituals, was enjoying a moment of respite. The events of the past two days had given Miranda her first chance to meet Mary Jo's fabled twin, who tonight was looking fabulously dapper in his Armani tux. Like it or not, he had been included among Offenbach's best men. The "Offensive Offenbach" we called the groom behind his back, and not because he had played offensive tackle for the Yale Bulldogs in his glory days.

"Can't you *see*, Newtie? She had to move the ceremony up. All that lace is hiding a baby bump." Mary Jo's twenty-two-inch waist clearly belied the accusation.

Miranda poked Marky. "*You're* being the Offensive one now!"

Miranda was more offended, however, by the arrival of a brides-maid who insisted she join the group of girls awaiting the toss of the bridal bouquet—which Miranda, as she was led away, assured us she would do her best to avoid catching. I was left alone with Marky: the friend who, I now knew, had fucked Samson and, presumably, had wanted to seduce me.

The big news on Marky's front, following his move to Rome the previous year, was that he was living in the carnal embrace of a young Italian man named Nicola. Marky's official coming out shouldn't have been that great a shock, given all I had learned. Still, his revelation had taken me off-guard—perhaps I was afraid his openness would demand the same of me, before I was ready to lay myself bare to the world. Marky's disclosure followed a season of letters, mostly to Mary Jo, first mentioning a new chum, a young Italian in Paris that his filmmaker friend Bernardo had introduced him to. Next, we learned that said Nicola was returning to Rome. So was Bernardo, who'd been hired onto a Visconti shoot, and Bernando promised Marky a crew position if he wanted it. Before we knew it Marky announced he was relocating to the Eternal City, where he'd be sharing digs with Nicola.

That spring, the same month that the *Times* announced Fred Offenbach and Mary Jo's engagement, Mary Jo flat-out asked Marky *what* was going on during one of their expensive international phone calls. Yep, Marky declared, as cavalier as ever, he and Nicola were shacking up and he was gay. Mary Jo accepted her brother's "conversion" with a mix of relief and peevishness; relief because she'd always found his attitude towards women deplorable, peevishness because she was growing weary of the myriad shifts in his personae that she felt had already created too much distance between them.

Arriving in New York for Mary Jo's wedding, I was very curious to meet Nicola, whom I assumed Marky would be bringing if only to rile his relatives. There was no Nicola to meet, however. Marky explained the romance was quickly unraveling.

"But there will be others," Marky grinned. "My reprobate reputation is at stake!"

Mr. Julian's absence from the festivities was a more pronounced dearth; even with the stalwart Bruno's help, he'd grown too feeble over the past year to dare such an expedition. What should have been, by all rights, a reunion of benefactor and his three charges was thus pared to Mary Jo, Marky, and me. And now there were just us two, standing on the periphery of the swirl of activity of which Mary Jo was radiant center.

As if she'd been reading my mind, Mary Jo disengaged herself from a regal elderly lady who had been offering felicitations far too long and floated our way, gloved arms outstretched to close the gap between us.

"Aren't you both dashing!" She air-kissed our cheeks as she took our hands. "Thanks for being such stoics—how you must loathe this frippery! Once I've done the obligatory turn on the dance floor with my new husband, we'll dance—the three of us."

"What will the Offensive Offenbach say about that?"

Mary Jo refused her brother's bait. "Wait for me."

And off she glided to the next ringlet of guests.

"Since when have we witnessed Mary Jo *waiting* for anyone? And you, Newt, are *you* still waiting?" Marky squeezed my shoulder. "Dear God, what *is* ahead for you?"

Good question that—if only I knew. Ever since I'd announced to Mr. Allbright my desire to take a semester's leave, thoughts of the future had preyed on my mind—and they only grew more pressing as my semester of freedom ticked away. The bombshell I had lobbed Mr. Allbright's way last spring, however, was nothing compared to the proclamation he'd traveled north to deliver to me in person mere weeks ago, over the Thanksgiving holiday.

"In a word," Mr. Allbright had announced, "your expectations have come to an end."

In the instant that it took for those words to travel from his lips to my brain, life as I'd lived and breathed it for the past five years had been blown to smithereens—and, as Marky knew, I was still reeling from the shock. As I took in Mr. Allbright's announcement, my life passed before my eyes, I swooned and nearly passed out.

"There, there, Newt, buck up! It's no fault of yours, let me assure you."

For reasons the lawyer was not at liberty to disclose, my benefactor could no longer fund my education or supplement my immediate future. The money, simply put, had evaporated as completely as a rainbow after a summer thunderstorm, undoing the promise of a pot of gold at its terminus. "You must believe me when I say that this has nothing to do with your recent decision, rash though it was; no one saw this catastrophe coming."

On the bright side, Mr. Allbright added, tuition for the coming spring semester had been set aside in advance. And there was a nominal sum—a very nominal sum—left in my account that should see me through a few more months if I practiced thrift.

"That amount would have been considerably larger. But what you chose to do with it was your decision, and no use crying over spilt milk!"

So Mr. Allbright referred to my decision, made late last spring, to gift 10,000 dollars from my account to my brother Jubal for his college education. He deserved more than our parents' modest savings could afford. It was one of the few decent things I've done, and later, when I was in a frame of mind to think reasonably, I was relieved I'd seen to the transfer of funds while they were still to be had.

"Destiny's dealt you a blow." Mr. Allbright's poker face stayed in place as he concluded his thankless missive. "Embrace it like a challenge, it will make a better man out of you!"

I might have agreed with Mr. Allbright had I been in a calmer frame of mind, but I was so confounded by my new circumstances that I felt only the panic of a shipwreck victim tossed from a capsizing lifeboat into freezing ocean water. The foundations on which I'd formed my identity since leaving Virginia vanished in a split second. And once the enormity of this change sank in, my reflex was to feel wretchedly guilty. Deep inside I was convinced that I'd somehow let my benefactor down, terribly let him down, or this calamity wouldn't have descended on me like a deadweight pulling me underwater.

Slowly, over the next weeks, I adjusted to my fate. Cast off as I felt, I wasn't left homeless. When I'd moved out of Eliot House in June, I began sharing an apartment near Davis Square and took a job at the Brattle Street Bookstore. I'd continued the rental this fall since, of course, I couldn't live in Eliot while unenrolled. Not that I would have wanted to. Along with the malaise that had descended on me earlier in the year as I began to question my commitment to Classics—a malady that clung to me like a second skin by the time Mary Jo announced her engagement late spring—I'd grown profoundly unhappy living in Eliot, blaming its residents for character flaws that were, in no small part, projections of my own inner disgust. I'd grown weary of the expensive tastes and spendthrift habits my housemates encouraged, of the beliefs I pretended to champion in order to fit in, of the affectations that had infiltrated my better self. Striving to be someone other than I was began to exhaust me, and even the pleasure I had taken in Greek and Latin came to seem as elitist and worthless as the milieu in which I lived.

There was no better example of the depths to which my better self had sunk than when, the fall of junior year, Dad wrote out of the blue to announce he had weighed the matter long and hard and, despite his stubborn belief that travel was a betrayal of hearth and home (I remembered Mother's unsuccessful attempts to convince him to take the family on edifying vacations), he'd come to realize that it behooved him, as one who had always been partial to my welfare (and so he had, ever my stalwart defender in the face of Mother's bursts of ire), to renew our father-and-son bond with a trip to Cambridge.

The threatened visit, I confess with great shame, sent shivers down my spine. What would my compatriots think if they met him? I spent hours devising plans that would put as much distance between Father and Harvard Square as possible. Meanwhile, I wrote home bemoaning a class schedule that allowed scant time for the quality of visit that we both desired. Dad proved not quite so tin-eared as I imagined him and wrote back that perhaps this wasn't the right time, allowing that the last thing he wanted was to do was make an impression that would leave us less than what we both at heart were: ever the best of friends.

I felt horrible. I'd not only been seen through, but I began to see through myself. I didn't make my usual June visit home, my excuse being my full-time job. Truth be told, I didn't want to face my family's queries about my decision to take a leave of absence. I was even more reluctant to face what would surely be Mr. Julian's invective at this alarming detour in the course of my upwardly mobile aspirations. Then, at the end of August, Uncle Rafe died. Of all my aunts and uncles, he had taken the greatest shine to me; the silver dollars commemorating my birthday arrived till I turned eighteen. I begged a leave from the bookstore and bought a plane ticket to Washington— at this point I still assumed I had plenty of cash to spend on such frills—and made my way to Waynesboro to join my parents for the interment. From there I traveled, with some ambivalence, to Rocky Hill for the final night of the long Labor Day weekend.

I shouldn't have been surprised that Mr. Julian got wind of my arrival in Rocky Hill despite the fact I hadn't contacted him. We Sewards were finishing an early supper when he rang. His raspy stage whisper of a voice struck me as odder than usual; he hissed that I must come over *immediately*, he'd be on the lookout for me. *Now*, he emphasized, hanging up before I could ask questions. There was little else to do than obey his command.

Curiously, the gate to the estate didn't swing open when I pulled up in Dad's car, so I parked on the side of the road and manually let myself in. The house at the far end of the drive looked like a mausoleum in the grim twilight, all its windows unlit. More curiously, although I jabbed the front buzzer repeatedly, no one answered. I walked to the rear of the house to try the French doors to the darkened drawing room. The black panes of glass reflected the desultory lightning bugs flickering across the lawn behind me as I rattled one locked door after the other. Then I heard, faintly, a familiar voice from above.

"Pssst, up here, boy!"

Mr. Julian leaned out his bedroom window, comically ghoulish in his white nightshirt. "No need to raise the dead—I told you I'd be on the lookout, didn't I? Here, catch these, and fix us some hot cocoa on the way upstairs."

The keys he tossed wildly missed the mark, landing in a bed of geraniums where, luckily, the glint of metal revealed their location. Unlocking the door, I felt my way through the drawing room to the kitchen, where I switched on the light and lit the hob. As I waited for the milk to simmer, I entered the butler's pantry to fetch the Sèvres teacups I knew Mr. Julian preferred. These I found soon enough, but I noticed that several of the silver pieces that used to gleam on the shelves were absent. Soon enough, carrying our cocoa on a tray, I backed out of the elevator into Mr. Julian's lamp-lit bedroom, where I found him fidgeting by the side of his unmade bed, ebony cane in hand as he shuffled back and forth with antic energy. Blonde-white hair floated above his cranium like a fractured halo. Barely had I set the tray down on the tea table and drawn up two chairs than he grasped my wrist with preternatural strength.

"I'm glad you're here, boy! I've *so* wanted to see you!"

I'd arrived so sure of the tongue-lashing that lay in store for me for dropping out of school that I was thrown off-balance by the strange eagerness lighting Mr. Julian's face.

"So precious to have this moment just to ourselves," he whispered as we sat down. His fingers trembled too much to lift his cup by its delicate handle; he needed both hands to raise it to his lips. "It's Hank's day off, and Bruno's taken one of his Tarts to the movies. What a godsend when Mr. Allbright sent word you were coming to town. But how *cowardly* of you not to let me know... shhh!" He peered into the shadowy depths of the room and raised a finger to his lips. "These walls have ears!"

I began to suspect, uneasily, the man had grown deranged since I'd last seen him. He was a scarecrow of his former self, long nightshirt a makeshift tent for scrawny limbs and brittle bones. His garment, I also noticed, was soiled, and the sheets on the unmade bed behind him looked like they hadn't been changed recently—a lapse in housekeeping G.G. would never have permitted.

"Is something the matter?" Mr. Julian's conspiratorial whispers had grown contagious and I had unconsciously lowered my voice as well. "You can tell *me*."

"If I could only put my finger on it—if I only knew where to begin! Maybe it's all up here" (he lifted both hands to his head, pressing his temples) "but I feel so *strange*! I take my medicine religiously" (a sweep of his hand indicated the phalanx of pill bottles lining his bed stand) "but something's wrong... I sleep all day and hardly leave this room. Then, at night, I wake up—and see... things!" He pointed to the portrait of Julia. "Last night, she stepped out of the frame—she was standing at my side, chiding me for a silly prank I'd played on her in childhood!"

"Sir, you were dreaming," I said, gently as I could. I tried to bring the topic back to the state of his health. "How is your appetite? Are you eating properly?"

"That's *another* thing. B.B.'s on vacation—visiting relatives in Florida, but the good it does me it might as well be for a year! She knows what dainties set best with me. Inmates at County get better than the gruel Bruno and Hank have been preparing me—Bruno says it's pumped with vitamins, but bah! it tastes like bone meal!"

When I asked how much longer B.B. would be gone, Mr. Julian admitted ignorance: she'd absconded in something of a huff without

specifying the date of her return, having had a major to-do with Bruno who'd insinuated that she'd been pilfering knick-knacks from the
premises. I mentioned that indeed some of the silver in the pantry
seemed missing or misplaced. "But never, in a hundred years, would
I believe Sassafras capable of making off with anything. She's as loyal
to you as George Geronimo was."

"Oh, for the days of G.G.!" Mr. Julian sighed distractedly. "As for
the silver, you haven't heard? There's been a regular series of burgla-
ries on this side of town. As a safeguard Bruno's stored most of the
portable valuables in the basement vault. And just in the nick of time!
My heart palpitated when he told me he'd come across a prowler on
the premises two weeks ago—he and Hank gave him a good chase,
but the rascal escaped. What's to become of us if we aren't safe in
our own beds? Now they make sure to lock all the doors if I'm here
alone—to keep me from harm's way!"

If silver or any other items had indeed gone missing, I was more
inclined to suspect Hank or Bruno of fencing them on the sly and
feeding Mr. Julian misleading stories. I resolved to convey my qualms
to Mr. Allbright and ask him to alert Sassafras, on her return, to keep
an eye out for anything unusual. Frankly, I was more worried about
Mr. Julian's poor health, psychological and physical, than a few missing items. As Mr. Julian had smugly confided to me all those years
ago, the most valuable objects in the house were the heavy pieces
of furniture—Sheraton sideboard, Hepplewhite highboy, Lannuier
Federalist bookcase—that the family assumed were Brewster reproductions but that in fact were originals and worth a fortune. Even if
Bruno and Hank were in on the secret, which I strongly doubted,
they weren't going to be able to pirate those heavy treasures from the
house on tiptoe.

I asked if Mr. Julian had seen a doctor lately.

"Oh dear me, yes. Bruno's specialist comes in regularly from
Richmond, he says I'm *on the brink* of recovery if I heed Bruno's instructions. Sometimes, I can feel the Regime working, I feel positively euphoric! But then, again, sometimes... have I told you what *happened* to Mimi?"

"No, sir."

"Tragic, Newt, tragic! Hank found her on Honeysuckle Heights Boulevard, a *bullet* through her skull!" Once again Mr. Julian leaned towards me, grasping my arm with unearthly strength. "It was a warning," he fiercely whispered. "There are Demons prowling this earth, strange forces!"

I was growing quite alarmed. The paranoid thoughts infiltrating my benefactor's musings revealed a mind no longer functioning logically.

"My Brewster relatives are behind it. The harpies have always tormented me, and now they've leagued with the spirits to drive me mad and get at my money! But wait till they read my will—" He let out a crazy laugh, but soon his thoughts drifted elsewhere. "Have you heard about Samson Washington? He finished his first year at Spellman, and he's transferring to Georgetown this fall. With advanced standing! Who knew? It will be the making of him!"

Once he'd used the same words about me.

"But *you*! Are you mad, dropping out of school? We had *faith* in you, silly boy, and what have you gone and done?"

My heart was in my throat. I attempted to explain my leave of absence, but I saw that Mr. Julian had again grown distracted, making it useless to continue.

"What can I do to help you?" I asked. "Help you now?"

He sighed. "I'm so weary. If you would be gentlemanly enough to help me to bed, this tired body would take it most kindly."

So I held his arm and slowly walked him to the canopied bed, and I did my best to smooth the soiled, wrinkled sheets as I brought them up to his chin, and I gently stroked his forehead as he closed his eyes and sighed the sigh of a man who hoped that no new spirits chose to visit him this night.

Just when I thought he'd drifted off, his eyes blinked open and fixed me with that relentless watery gaze that I knew so well. "Still, I wasn't wrong to hire you, was I? You restored the library to its glory days. I shan't forget that." For a millisecond he seemed somewhere else.

He again closed his eyes and laced his fingers over the coverlet, still as a marble effigy in a cathedral's crypt. I put my hand on his, and I felt the pulse beating under his veined skin. When his breaths became shallow snores, I dimmed the bedside lamp, returned to the ground floor, and let myself out. Again I resolved to talk to Mr. Allbright as soon as possible, suggesting he bring in specialists he trusted to assess the poor man's failing health. Looking up at Mr. Julian's bedroom windows before crossing the back lawn to the driveway, I pondered his final words. Had it been a good thing, hiring me? What had it done but propel me into a labyrinth of dreams and desires whose ends I could no longer clearly make out? I pondered, too, the disappointments that had stranded my benefactor in a maze of delusion and decay that seemed to spell a sad conclusion.

*

It was three months later that I learned Mr. Julian, unpredictable to the end, had curtailed my expectations without a word of explanation. When Mr. Allbright delivered the bad news in late November, I found myself tugged between contradictory emotions as I pictured my one-time benefactor wasting away in his sickbed: flashes of keen anger and betrayal, keener regret for having fallen out of his good graces, but, keenest of all, pity for the state to which he had been reduced, once again the bedridden prisoner in his decaying home, in his failing body, in his yet frailer mind. Perhaps the financial reasons for ending my means of support were genuine, perhaps not, but I suspected the signs of dementia I'd witnessed in August factored into the abrupt decision to cut me loose. As soon as I returned to Boston, I did reach out to Allbright, who promised to check into Mr. Julian's care as well as alert Sassafras to keep an eye out for mischief on the part of his employees. But the lawyer confessed, with regret, that the more the patient ailed and the crankier he grew, the less heed he paid to the advice Mr. Allbright attempted to proffer, and he refused, outright, medical intervention.

Thanksgiving came and, with it, Mr. Allbright's bombshell—which, in a state of shock, I shared with Mary Jo in person and Marky by post. They had always been amused by but proud of their guardian's unacknowledged support of my education, and they were as baffled as me by his decision to cut my resources off. When Mary Jo attempted to broach the subject in a telephone conversation, the old man grew flustered and changed the topic to the evils that his Brewster relations were visiting on him as they plotted new ways to drain his coffers. His decline was an unhappy state of affairs, an anticlimactic end to the vistas that his acquaintance had opened when I first walked through the gates of the Brewster estate and found George Geronimo waiting in the shady lane to escort me across the mansion's threshold.

So when Marky asked me what I intended to do with my life—as the waiters at the Tavern on the Green passed by with their gleaming trays, and as we watched Mary Jo float from guest to guest—he wasn't speaking idly; he knew I had critical decisions to make, sooner than later. The wedding dinner followed, the cake was cut, a soloist sang Roberta Flack's "The First Time Ever I Saw Your Face" as Mary Jo and Fred took to the dance floor and danced cheek to cheek, and I discovered that although my heart felt as heavy as lead, it was still beating. "Wait for me," she had promised us. And as the floor flooded with others, young and old, couples and groups, eager for stimulus after so much gorging on such rich food, we three had our dance together—not slow, mind you, but fast, loose limbed, laughing at the ludicrousness of this strange thing called life. And when Marky and I walked off the dance floor some fifteen sweaty minutes later, leaving Mary Jo in the arms of her father-in-law, Marky uttered the only words that, in that whole long day, penetrated my numb heart and made complete sense to me.

"Fuck going back to school, Newt. Come to Italy with me. Do!"

So three weeks later, instead of moving back into Eliot House to begin my belated senior year, that is exactly what I did.

PART FOUR

31

ROMAN DESIGNS

For some tourists, Rome in January may disappoint—no golden glow from the declining sun to set cobble-stoned piazzas theatrically aflame or add radiance to the peeling facades of Renaissance palazzos. Temperatures hover just above freezing, pedestrians with designer scarves draped around pinched faces do not linger, the lines at popular gelaterias have disappeared, and bone-chilling showers fall from gray skies every few days. But for me, experiencing Europe for the first time in my life, Rome was the most beautiful place I'd ever seen. Navona glistening in the aftermath of a downpour, the Colosseum emerging from a chill fog, Palatine Hill all to oneself—Rome in winter has its own beauty, which it shared with me daily as I sallied forth from Marky's apartment, anticipating the layers of history through which even the most casual walk was sure to take me. And the promise of the sweet life of summer days to come lived on in the warm interiors of the city's trattorias, caffès, and bars: in steaming bowls of *cacio e pepe* and the pungent aroma of Abruzzo wine; in the rich cadences of voices competing in ever louder cacophony; in the exquisite expertise with which young lovers transformed any available public space—door frame, stone bench, church steps—into a private bower of bliss, making out with a dexterity that Americans, if they aimed for such heights at all, saved for the bedroom. Monuments dirtied with grime and soot, history crumbling under foot, exhaust fumes burning one's eyes—as immense and tiring as Rome was, I loved the city from the day of my arrival.

Marky lived in the Jewish Ghetto, a medieval warren of streets that were hardly arms-length wide. Upon hearing of Marky's impending move, Mr. Julian, censorious and capricious in one breath, had first declared his nephew's plan yet another symptom of his steady decline, then as quickly insisted that Marky look for a place to live in the Ghetto. The old man regaled his nephew with reminisces of its hidden wonders (mostly gleaned from praises that Enzio in his letters had heaped on the Jewish enclave buried in the heart of Christendom's Eternal City when he moved his atelier to Rome). He wrote with as much relish as if he'd actually ventured further into its labyrinths than the Fontana delle Tartarughe, where the marble fingers of lissome boys delicately lifted turtles to the pool of water overhead.

At any rate, Mr. Julian's hint stuck in Marky's mind, for he and Nicola had found an apartment in the quarter located off a street whose name seemed longer than its length: the Via della Tribuna di Tor de' Specchi. On its western side, the rust-colored, seventeenth-century building abutted the rounded nave of the church attached to the Monastero delle Oblate di Sta. Francesca Romana. To the east, a marble stone's throw away, the remains of the Teatro di Marcello, its upper echelons fantastically converted into residences, presided over a graveyard of fallen columns and stacked capitals where legions of feral cats sunned by day and prowled by night. In those days, the Ghetto wasn't the magnet for artisans, owners of boutiques, and upscale restauranteurs it has since become; it was a down-on-its-heels neighborhood where one strolled with open eyes—by day to avoid the animal droppings dotting the cobblestones; by night to avoid suspect figures materializing from its shadows. But as Enzio had discovered decades before, it was a remarkably cheap place to live, and the second-floor apartment that Marky and Nicola shared was a bohemian dream—irregularly shaped chambers made to fit the angled dimensions of the building, a squat Roman column half-buried in the exposed wall of the front room, wood-beamed ceilings higher than the rooms were wide and bearing hints of painted tracery, tall windows with folding shutters from which, if you craned your neck, you could see the bend where the street stretched uphill towards Piazza Margana. Oversized, baroquely ornate furniture, from carved chests and leggy Risorgamento tables to lumpy sofa and unsprung easy chairs, crowded the space, and Marky and Nicola had made the walls a carnival of art: dark oils still to be had for a dime in the flea-markets of Trastevere, a decomposing strip of medieval tapestry, Italian movie posters. A kitchen the size of a closet jutted out of a corner of the front room, on top of which a cramped loft space was entirely occupied by a thin mattress whose begrimed ticking dared sleepers to seek comfort on its surface.

Here I made my nest while Nicola and Marky spent the first two weeks of my stay thrashing out the end of their *grande storia d'amore* behind the closed door of the bedroom at the other end of the oblong flat, a "discussion" that resulted in Nicola decamping with a malediction on Marky specifically and on Americans in general. After his departure, Marky and I began to carve out our parameters as roommates: I acclimated myself to Marky's tendency to stumble into the apartment at all hours of the night reeking of wine and tobacco, and he habituated himself to my propensity (so he claimed) to break into snores that rumbled all the way down the long crooked hallway at the first hint of dawn.

"More predictable than a goddam rooster," he complained over morning espresso, dark circles under cat-green eyes that, even when he was sleep-deprived and hung over, twinkled seductively.

Speaking of seduction, you might well wonder how our living arrangement accommodated the unspent residue of eros that had, without speaking its name, suffused the earlier years of our friendship. The subject had given me pause as I decided whether to make good on Marky's offer to move to Rome. Had we reached a zone of friendship where I could put his prior innuendos behind me, or would I still have to contend with his sexual vibes in spite of his relationship with Nicola? More importantly, what did *I* want?

With Nicola out of the equation, these questions overflowed the brim of our companionable equanimity like carelessly uncorked prosecco. A week after Nicola's huffy departure, Marky had insisted that I indulge his desire for one evening of self-pity by getting plowed with him—not on prosecco, however, but vodka. I could hardly refuse the newly minted bachelor one night berating the fickleness of love. So we propped the Stoli liter between us as we sat on the sofa, downing slugs as Marky happily vented and grew more lugubrious by the minute. By the time the bottle was half empty, I was loose enough to ask the questions that had preyed on my mind all year—questions I needed to ask before I laid myself bare to what was sure to be his inquisition of me.

"So you *say* you didn't really know you were gay till Nicola swept you off your feet. Then what in the fuck do you call what you and Samson were doing back in Rocky Hill?"

"You know about *that*?" The sensual tilt of Marky's lips grew a tad—but only a tad—sheepish as he slouched further down the sofa, his chest nearly prone with the seat cushion. In the process his ratty sweater slid up beyond his navel, revealing a trail of dark hair that he twirled with a forefinger—new growth that I hadn't seen before.

"He told me. Years later. And he didn't sound all that happy about it."

"Didn't seem to mind at the time." Marky made a show of batting his long eyelashes—an effect, frankly, that his sister used to much greater success when she wished to distract her interrogators. "*Besides*, Newtie-boy, if you hadn't been playing so hard to get, I wouldn't have had to resort to him."

"What are you saying? That you were only trying to get in my pants all that time? That day at the pool—honestly it *fucked* with my head. What did you and Mary Jo think you were *doing* with me?"

Marky took a swig directly from the bottle.

"Dude, we didn't mean to fuck you up. I told Mary Jo I thought you might be a fag, that maybe we'd find out your secrets if we—well, if we put you in a position to see how you reacted. You were such a mystery, Newt, I wanted to know what made your balls tingle."

"So you wouldn't have to deal with what *you* really wanted?"

"We were young and stupid, all three of us—and, besides, I was horny as hell." Marky shrugged his shoulders. "Mary Jo wasn't so keen on the idea, if you must know. I put her up to it, long before that day."

"A pissing contest to see who *got* me? Wow, that really makes me feel good about myself."

"Newt, don't you get it? You were a fucking *prize*. You were golden." Marky belched. "And you didn't even know it."

That merited more vodka.

"How about all those female conquests you were always rubbing in my face—Myke on Nantucket—was any of it real?"

"Down to every orgasm. Sure, maybe I embellished, but I've done it all. Now I *know* what really turns me on and it's cock. Plain and simple. Or should I say big and hard?" Marky gave me a look of drunken defiance. "At least I know what I want."

I met Marky's gaze. "Don't presume anything."

"Yeah, like what? You've found another Mary Jo to fall hopelessly in love with?"

"No. I had sex with a guy while you and Nicola were yelling at each other. It was my first time. And, oh, again last week."

"What the fuck? Newt Seward, damn you, tell me more!"

At which point I told Marky about the adventures that I'd had over the past three weeks. I'd made the plunge with a man cruising me over winter vegetables in the Campo di Fiori. It had been easier than I ever imagined, allowing myself to return his gaze. Then there'd been the ragazzo I'd followed into an empty church. He'd motioned me to step with him behind the curtain of a confessional absent a priest officiating on the other side.

"You've got to be kidding—in a church? in Rome? That's hotter than the Mile-High Club. I always told Mary Jo you were the sly one, not the shy one."

As the night wore on, and as we drunkenly exchanged notes, dirty detail by dirty detail, I felt a load lifting from my chest. Even if this was my time to explore sex with guys, I avowed I could still imagine settling down with the right woman. Bisexuality, Marky countered, was "a coward's out": sure, he could still fuck women as easily as men, but what he really wanted was the hard flesh, the greedy lust, of other men's bodies pressing against his own: once you experienced desire like that—urgent, hot, masculine—there was no turning back.

"Speaking of hot lust, what about us, Newtie?" Marky shifted his position so he could throw his legs over my lap while inclining his head on the arm of the sofa. "Haven't we deferred the inevitable long enough?" He rubbed his stocking foot against my crotch. "Don't deny it, you've always wanted me."

I removed his foot. "You're not *everyone's* First Choice. Or even Second."

"Come'n, you know you can't resist me." Marky lowered his voice to its most sultry register, and with an energy that belied the state of his inebriated limbs, he undid his belt, raised his hips to slide his jeans past his knees, and, seizing my most proximate hand, clamped it over the flesh stirring to action within his silk boxers. "You fuckin' *want* it."

Actually, I didn't.

As charismatic as I still found Marky after all these years, his personality as magnetic and his wit as alluring as ever, there had always been for me, from the beginning of our friendship, the Marky whose cocksure confidence in his seductive powers, whose insistent need to bend me to his will, smothered desire for him as surely as a fire brigader's hastily tossed bucket of bracken water reduces gorgeous but dangerous flames to muddy ashes. And that was the Marky who at this moment lay with legs sprawled akimbo over my lap—the Marky could not hear me say no simply because he assumed I couldn't resist him.

So there I sat, nearly as drunk as he, watching his cock rise from the open seam in his boxer shorts as unashamedly as a well-pampered groundhog emerging to contemplate a cloudy February sky, and I still wasn't moved. Titillated, yes, for in response to the hardening flesh against which my fingers had involuntarily been pressed I could feel my synapses begin to fire. But this scenario was not one I desired. That knowledge was a revelation.

"Trust me, Marky—this is not what I want from you."

He tried to insist, struggling to a sitting position and throwing his arms around me as he aimed a wet kiss at my mouth. His lips, however, missed the mark and skidded across my cheek, wetly lodging in the vicinity of my ear. In the process, he lost balance, pawing at the air while his dropped trousers straightjacketed his thrashing legs.

"Aw, come'n." Marky looked at me under his long lashes from where he'd landed on his side of the sofa. "Be a pal and at least let's help each other get off."

"How about getting off my case? Face it, the only reason you're acting like a horny letch is history: you didn't succeed before, so you think you're still owed a try." I laughed, feeling a renewed surge of conviction in spite of my spinning head. "Look, now you've *tried*, and I'm saying no. You're my best friend, and that's even a pretty awesome cock you've got going there, but I *don't* want you. Let me help get you to bed."

Marky flopped back in resignation, extending his legs as I bent to shimmy his scrunched jeans over his knees and up to his waist. His lower lip protruded in a dramatic pout—the way he must have looked when, as a truculent child, he didn't get his way.

"Up you go!"

Marky swayed on the brink of passing out as I helped him to his feet but he rallied, at least enough to clutch me with both arms and lean the dead weight of his body full into mine. Positioned thus, we sidled down the long, angled hallway in a macabre simulation of sexual congress.

Finally we reached his bed. "You're mean." He burped. "Newtie's mean to Marky." And then without a losing a beat he collapsed, face forward, onto the mattress, which groaned as loudly as the reader of a badly written romance novel might have expected such a bed to groan, and instantly he was dead to the world.

Luckily, Marky seemed to recover from my rejection—or what he remembered of it—with aplomb, and as the weeks passed the routine of our shared life shifted into a fraternal intimacy that overpassed sexual desire. Now that he embraced his gayness, perhaps he felt less need to play the role of tempter that he had so insinuatingly deployed during the timeless, shameless summer that had initially brought the twins and me together. His sexual exploits over the next few months were legion—against which my experiments with either sex paled—but by early summer the impossible happened: he had the extraordinarily good fortune of meeting Fabrizio, a young Dante professor at Sapienza who was the best thing that ever happened to him. Marky, of all unlikely candidates in the world, had hit the jackpot—so much so that he began to contemplate, albeit not altogether convincingly, the virtues of monogamy.

The hyperactivity of Marky's extracurricular amours was matched by the relentless pace of his working hours, where as aide de camp attached to various film projects he was absorbing skills like a sponge. The Visconti shoot had wrapped, he was working on a Zeffirelli project, and the affable Bernardo—to whom I'd been introduced as soon as I arrived in Rome—was completing a script that consumed his and Marky's free time. Marky's participation was a given, Bernardo teased me, since his treatment was based on tales that Marky had told him of our youthful threesome; he'd simply transposed our Virginian idyll to the Paris of the student protests Marky knew so well. I grinned and said I'd wait to see the movie before judging—judging, that is, either his filmmaking talent or our own lives.

*

As I grew to feel more and more at home in Italy that first winter and spring, news of the other homes that I'd left behind crossed the Atlantic on a regular basis:

Jubal, April 15: *"I'm going to William and Mary! My FIRST choice and I'm jazzed. Thanks bro, you're the best! Everyone here fine. PS— Mom and Dad won't let on, but they are worried about what you're doing with your life. You ever coming back?"*

Mother, January 31: *"You must be settled in by now. It's some relief that we've met your roommate, who seemed such a polite boy when we met him years ago at Bonner Lake. I hope he's a good influence. Do remember to visit the fabric outlets listed below and send me as many swatches as you can. Don't forget to drop Mr. Brewster a note. Unconscionable as it was for him to cut you off, it is still in your best interest to STAY IN TOUCH. Sassafras's sources say his heath continues to decline. Those greedy relations are beseiging his house."*

Mr. Allbright, January 15: *"A most grave decision you've made, Newton, jumping the pond like this. I can't say I approve, but you already know that. My disappointment is not the point. I am writing to wish you well in your endeavors while urging you not to let Mr. Brewster's nephew lead you astray. Harvard has agreed to defer your readmission yet one more semester—but ONLY one more. Take heed. They will hold the tuition that's already been deposited—and will remit with a penalty if you don't enroll next fall. Till then, you'll have to make do with what remains in your account. As for other matters of concern to us both: from all the intelligence I can gather, Mr. Brewster seems in a poor way. I say seems because the man no longer welcomes my company, a consequence I suspect of the questions I've raised about the quality of care he's getting under Mr. Epps, who seems to have thoroughly brainwashed our friend. I was turned away at the door the last time I tried to visit. Epps has fired Sassafras—claims she was slacking on her job, undermining their authority, other nonsense. She's mad as a hornet, of course, at the unceremonious way she's been let go. Swears all those pills Epps's doctor is feeding Mr. Brewster are messing with his mind. As a kindness I've taken her on one day a week, and recommended her to your Mother, who says she needs someone to cook for your father and Jubal now that she's working fulltime."*

Father, February (undated): *"Dont fret about us Oldsters—we're fine and dandy, Lonesome as We'll be once Jubal leaves for W&M. Good thing your Mother hired Sassafras. She cooks a heap better than me, thats darn sure! Dont forget Us, you hear? Never to soon to visit, and and never to often. Ever best of buds, Dad."*

David Berger, January 19: *"This is heavy, dude! Though it kinda rocks you're shafting Harvard TWO semesters in a row!"*

Mr. Allbright, March 9: *"Your Wachovia credit card is overdrawn from charges that date back to last spring. Interest mounting. Please advise. Gravely disappointed!"*

Mary Jo, January 21: *"It will come as no surprise to the two of you that honeymoons—like husbands' libidos—are highly overrated. Of course I had no great expectations, so I'm less than devastated. I trust Fred will learn how to Obey Me now that we've settled in the apartment here on Fifth. He shows some signs of rebellion but soon I'll render him docile as a lamb. The Bermudas were warm and lovely, of course, so perhaps I'll grow nostalgic about our honeymoon in frigid winters to come."*

Miranda, May 1: *"You'll never guess who I just met. A group of us went to DC for the weekend—we were clubbing in Dupont Circle, and guess what EXTRAORDINARILY HUNKY sophomore transfer to Georgetown I happened to encounter? Here's a* CLUE: *ex-military, honorable discharge, born in Rocky Hill, and rumored to have gone fishing with you.* YES, *I've met Sam Washington! Did you know he's thinking about attending law school at GT, just like me, after he finishes his BA? So we had* LOTS *to talk about. Need I also say, the guy is built like one of those Michelangelos you're seeing on a daily basis. But something tells me that the fairer sex are not among those who flutter his heart, so I shan't embarrass myself by batting my eyes at him. We spoke affectionately of you, Newt, we hope you are happy doing what you feel you have to do. We had such fun, we're getting together in two weeks' time."*

Mr. Julian, January 15: *"Silly boy, what are you doing? Leaving Harvard to run away with that troublemaker nephew of mine?!? I thought you had a brain. You mustn't let the downturn in your fortunes send you off the deep end. Screw that sensible head of yours back onto your broad shoulders and don't waste your life!"*

Mr. Julian, April 24: *"... more dizzy spells today. Oddest thing happened last week, I woke up in the middle of the night to find myself in the drawing room—no idea how I got there. And then I fainted in heap, right in front of my portrait! I want you to have the Sorrento, of course, if anything ever happens to me. I trust you haven't mislaid Enzio's drawings and keys in your precipitous move. Don't be a stranger to Rocky Hill. Newton Seward in* ROME *with my* NEPHEW—*what a quirk of fate! If I weren't so vexed at you, I'd say what larks!"*

*

I couldn't afford to be the idler that everyone from Mother to Mr. Julian seemed to think me. Life might be a "lark," as Mr. Julian put it, but it didn't come free of charge. As it happened, I found gainful employment—one might even say I found my calling—more easily than I ever dreamt. I was walking down Via del Monserrato on a Tuesday evening in February when the sleekly crafted furniture on display in a shop window, shining under spots like precious icons in the gathering dusk, stopped me in my tracks. The shop's name, *Vita moderna*,

Disegni moderni, proudly proclaimed its distinction from the neighboring vendors of antiques and furniture restorationists, old hands
for whom the term "modern" barely included the eighteenth century.
On a whim I entered the establishment and was instantly greeted by
the proprietor, who introduced himself as Carlo Bigelli and warmly
accepted the compliments I delivered in my stilted Italian. Sensing
my genuine interest, he became more voluble by the minute in his
equally stilted English, his rich baritone filling the space as he held
forth on his design concepts and construction techniques. Soon he
was unfurling rolls of trace paper filled with drawings of his true love,
sleek modular units that—opening, folding, sliding in various directions—served multiple functions.

An hour passed before we knew it. Running a hand marked by
a journeyman's nicks and scars through wavy salt-and-pepper hair,
Carlo declared *"Basta!* no more customers this evening," and proposed we have an espresso a few doors away. He promptly flipped the
APERTO sign hanging on the front door to *CHIUSO,* as if intent on
proving the adage that Italian store-owners only obey their own in-
ternal clock: for while the stenciled numerals on the front door *orario*
clearly announced closing time as *alle 20:00,* church bells all across
the neighborhood were declaring the hour six p.m.

Standing shoulder to shoulder in the tiny bar, we tossed back
our espressos as if they were shots of whiskey while Carlo told me
how he'd come into the design enterprise. For decades his father had
operated a furniture restoration business out of the same building,
whose metal front in the old days rolled up like a garage door to let
the sawdust and chemical fumes escape. His father had inherited the
business from his father before him, which meant that when Carlo re-
modeled the premises and made it a showcase for his contemporary
designs, the entire Bigelli clan pronounced it an insult to tradition
and family—although nearly all, Carlo slyly added, "made nice" once
the business began showing a profit. In time, he asked me what I was
doing in the Eternal City. I admitted I had yet to find out.

"*Interessante,*" he said, eyeing at me quizzically. "You must be
running from something. Family troubles? Girl problems? Boy problems? No worry, we talk about it on our way. Zippa your jacket, it's
freezing outside."

On our way where, I sensibly asked, although I already implicitly trusted the man.

Carlo, as he insisted I call him although he was twice my age, said that he was taking me to his workshop across the river, where his team created the designs on display in the Monserrato shop and assembled the larger modular units that the store couldn't accommodate. After all, he explained as we briskly paced Via Guilia towards Ponte Sisto, if I *were* to accept his offer to be front man in the Monserrato shop, I needed to understand the operation from the bottom up. Your Italian, it passes, he continued in his own just-passable English—and, at any rate, he added, the majority of his customers tended to be Brits, Americans, the occasional Frank. Hiring me to watch over the gallery would allow him to spend more time in the workshop itself.

"But you hardly know me!"

We paused midway across the pedestrian bridge. The panorama was incomparable—the illuminated dome of St. Pete's emitting a glow as otherworldly as the half moon rising on the horizon, the windows of the buildings on both sides of the Tiber twinkling in the dark, millions of stars glittering in the clear winter sky overhead.

"Oh, I know *abbastanza.*" Carlo's voice reverberated in the dark, like an oracle. "The artist senses the presence of another artist."

Those words seemed the greatest compliment ever paid me, and I proclaimed my wish to work for him with the same fervor I'd accepted Mr. Julian's offer of employment in my youth. Winding our way east of Viale de Trastevere and south of Genovesi, Carlo guided us through a working-class neighborhood to a nondescript building whose barreled roof arched over an immense room filled with table saws and router tables, drills and planers, shaft shapers and mallets. The cornucopia of chisels, grips, adzes, jigs, awls, and other tools spilling everywhere made me flash upon the original chaos in which I had found Mr. Julian's library. But this disorder appeared to have a hidden logic, one that Carlo knew by heart as he gave me a tour. What I most vividly remember of that first foray into the world of fine-woodworking was not the physical space, not the half-assembled pieces of wood and laminate, not the bolts of upholstery waiting to be cut to size, not the exotic varieties of lumber sorted into overhead bins—what I remember most vividly was the intoxicating smell of the wood particulate itself, a thousand shaved scents floating in the air, subtle perfumes shifting from one part of the room to another.

"I'll want you to spend a few hours observing here every week—to explain the product to *padroni* you must understand the process."

So I found myself working at "Vita moderna" full-time, opening and closing the shop, greeting the customers who wandered in, keeping the books, scheduling deliveries, running errands, and, on the fly, learning first-hand from Carlo about furniture design and hand-crafting. It was hard to believe that, only a year ago, I was a college student—and equally extraordinary to realize that I had left the pursuit of Classics to live in this vast remnant of the classical world. Instead of waking in a dormitory, I now woke in a fusty apartment as old as Harvard, and instead of a view of the Charles from my window, I now looked out over terracotta rooftops beyond which the Tiber cumbrously flowed on its way to the sea. Instead of cafeteria-style breakfast in Eliot's dining hall, I now grabbed a cornetto on my way through Piazza Farnese. Marky and I often met in the evening for dinner; my world of acquaintances expanded to include Carlo's co-workers as well as Marky's friends; and the shopkeepers up and down Monserrato began to return my *buon giorno*. As the hours of daylight grew longer and as window dressers fitted mannequins with spring fashions, I began to think of Rome as a place I might call home.

32

THE HERM'S MESSAGE

"We've *got* to do something with all your books," Marky announced in April. "And find a place to store this junk you've been collecting!"

I may have arrived in Rome with little to call my own except for the two suitcases I'd stored under Marky's bed, but over the past four months I'd been collecting second-hand volumes en masse, currently stacked around the perimeter of the living room, along with flea market bargains I'd picked up all over the city. The apartment's only built-in shelves, recessed into one wall of the hallway that ended in Marky's bedroom, were already overflowing with his own formidable collection of LPs and film books.

Spring-cleaning fever was on us. In an apartment lacking closets and crammed full of the bulky furniture that had come with the premises, we agreed that we must find a better way to arrange our possessions so that we weren't always stumbling over them. One of Marky's tricks had recently taken a nasty spill when, in the darkened living room, he'd tripped on an oversized eighteenth-century folio of chair leg designs that I'd left propped against the base of the sofa. As he fell, he scraped his chin on the peaked cowl of a cracked wooden statue of St. Francis I'd rescued from a trash bin behind the monastery next to our building. If he had to get stitches, he screamed on his way out, I'd be hearing from his lawyer. Poor lad had ambitions of becoming an Armani model. I refrained from saying a dashing scar might enhance his look—just as the dribble of blood he'd left on St. Francis's cowl had added a welcome dash of color to the lifeless icon.

Faced with this overflow, Marky decided it was time to install extra shelving, and the only room with wall space to spare was his bedroom, which, not untypical of Roman apartments irregularly carved out of the former rooms of much grander buildings, was nearly as large as the living room. Since the objects destined for these shelves were mine, I was put in charge of installing the half-dozen particle boards we hauled home from a hardware store ten blocks away, terri-fying more than a few pedestrians in the process. So, on a bright Sat-urday afternoon, a fine layer of plaster dust settled on me as I drilled holes for the supporting brads. Marky kept me company by setting about another overdue task.

"Let the sunshine in!"

So Marky sang as he raised the pair of pruning shears he'd bor-rowed from a friend lucky enough to have a small garden patio. Mar-ky's bedroom, immense as it was, boasted a single window, and years ago a bougainvillea vine had entirely covered the casement, replacing the view with a viscous green glow that made me feel, whenever I stepped into the chamber, as if I'd sunk to the bottom of a fish-tank long overdue a cleaning.

Bougainvillea, however beautiful from afar, boasts more vicious thorns than the deadly briars surrounding Sleeping Beauty's castle turret. Many curses and a dozen scratches later, Marky succeeded in clearing an unobstructed view. I joined him at the now-open window to take in the vista. Below us stretched a cloistered garden attached to the monastery and church whose apse abutted our apartment build-ing; the rears of buildings of varying ages, heights, shapes, and states of dilapidation hemmed in the other three sides of the empty garden, towering above the portico that wrapped the boundaries of the rec-tangular space below.

The design of the garden was at once typical and unique. Not un-like the formal garden in back of Mr. Julian's house, it was divided into four quadrants, each consisting of an octagonal flowerbed plant-ed with severely pruned rose bushes that had seen better days—that was the typical aspect. What was unusual, to my eye, was the fact that the raked gravel paths typically connecting such quadrants were here replaced by two streams of water running in shallow basalt channels set at right angles to and bisecting each other. Unless the Sister in question were to lift her robes to leap over the basalt barrier, there was no way to move from one quadrant to the next. The visual effect from above was that of a large, dark cross. While the symbolism of this shape befitted its sacred setting, a disconcertingly pagan note was provided by a rectangular stone column topped with statuary located at the point of the crucifix below and to our immediate right. A jet of water gushing from its midpoint fed the two channels of water.

"I think that's a herm," I commented. The statuary rose at what apparently formed the head of the cross shape—the two quadrants on either side were proportionately smaller than the two forming its base. I found Marky's binoculars and peered more closely.

Sure enough, the column-turned-fountain was topped with the muscular chest, truncated arms, leering face, and tufted horns of a satyr. A steady arc of water spouted from the hole midway up the front of the column where a stone phallus had once projected like an antique coat-rack ready to accommodate any number of togas. Had its organ been removed to protect the immaculate imaginations of the cloistered sisters whose garden this was?

Marky took his turn at the binoculars and chuckled. "Damn, his pecs are so big they might as well be tits!"

I was only half-listening, because an idea was buzzing in my head, struggling to take coherent shape. I felt like I was seeing a vision that I had once glimpsed in a dream.

Finally, it was the herm itself that triggered the train of associations that fell, bit by bit, into place. First I remembered the watercolor wrapping that enfolded the set of keys that Enzio had sent Mr. Julian, in which a row of priapic herms held flowery swags aloft with gleeful sneers. Then, as Marky's words echoed in my brain, I recalled that Enzio's otherwise hypermasculine herms sported female breasts. I recalled, too, the Quattrocentro box in which the watercolor had arrived, wrapped around the two keys. And now I remembered the design of the inlaid top that was Enzio's creation.

In a flash, I was down on my hands and knees, reaching for one of the suitcases I'd stored under the bedframe. Marky stared like I'd gone crazy. Unsnapping the clasps, I dug through my winter clothes till I found the box Mr. Julian had placed in my care years before.

Passing it to Marky, I explained its origins and, by the light of the window, showed him how the geometric design on the lid, intricately composed of slivers of wood of different patinas, seemed to change when viewed from different angles. Tilting the box, I found the image that was stored in my memory—and, yes, at this angle the design on the box lid mirrored the layout of the garden below. Every important detail was there: the cross, the octagonal rose beds, the cloistered walkway—and, directly facing the viewer, at the far end of the cross, the herm. I recalled the newspaper interview in which Enzio had joked about being a voyeur whose artistic inspiration came from looking out windows.

In this case, no joke at all.

Where, I asked Marky, might Enzio have stood to replicate the design's perspective?

Marky scanned the far side of the interior courtyard. "See that building, the gray one facing the herm across the way? One of those upper windows I bet."

Here, in my hands, was a veritable map to Enzio's studio. The thought blew me away. I opened the box to show Marky the watercolor design wrapped around the two keys, explaining the contents of Enzio's enigmatic letter to Mr. Julian that had accompanied this gift.

Unfolding the watercolor to its full length, Marky whistled at Enzio's whimsical representation of the double-sexed herms. "So that"—he pointed to the statue in the garden—"was his inspiration for this"—he tapped the watercolor.

"Which means these might be keys to his studio—over there."

I peered more closely at the building Marky had singled out with his binoculars. Rising above the covered walk at the foot of the cross-shaped waterway, it was one story shorter than the ochre building to its left, and narrower than the pinkish structure to its right. The windows on each floor were shuttered, all traces of paint having long since peeled from the casings. In contrast, laundry hung out of an open window to the house to the left; and those of the building to its right opened onto balconies crowded with plants, mops, toys.

Marky turned to me, emerald eyes twinkling. "Well, Sherlock?"

*

In this case Marky proved the superior sleuth, I a mere Watson. We bounded down the stairs and proceeded north on Tribuna until we reached, on our right, Piazza di Campitelli, the street that the monastery and adjacent buildings faced. If our hunch was correct, the rear of one of these had once housed Enzio's studio. No two façades were alike: some had arched entrances capped by elaborate open-air ironwork, and others doors outlined in marble blocks; some flaunted distinct fenestrations for every floor, and others simple window grills; some were medievally solemn, ruddy brick showing behind the crumbling plaster, others garishly rococo. We counted off the buildings till we found ourselves facing our goal: number 81, a boarded-up structure narrower than its companions, looking as if the larger structures leaning on it from either side had, over the centuries, squeezed the life out of it. Set back six feet from its neighbors, it seemed to recede, before our eyes, into the shadows. The windows on the ground and first floors had been filled with brick; those on the top two floors were shuttered. One of the shutters on the third floor window to our right, however, was missing, and the glassless window frame had been stapled with heavy plastic.

We rattled the metal-studded wooden door; it was bolted from inside.

Across the street two tables signaled the presence of a small caffè, so there we headed to contemplate our next move. Once it became clear that our bored, youthful server was unlikely to provide any useful information about the building across the way, Marky asked him to send out his nonno, nodding over his lottery sheet at the back of shop. The old man was delighted to have an audience and shooed his grandson into the kitchen to fetch us a plate of *dolci* as he regaled us with the history of the street. Yes, he had lived here seventy-nine years, he had been born in a room upstairs, and oh, the changes! He remembered when the monastery overflowed with noviates from all over Italy, but those days were long gone. And the building Marky was pointing to? It had gone into foreclosure some three decades ago, been tied up in litigation ever since; no, he didn't know who owned it now, no doubt some bank? The family that once rented out its apartments had vanished during the war. I asked him, in my slowly improving Italian, whether he recalled an artist who may have had a studio there in the late 1930s and early 40s but such details, no, he couldn't remember. Artists had always lived in the Ghetto, but they came and went while the locals like him barely hung on. This caffè had been opened by his father before he was born and used to be always abuzz with activity, but now, a customer an hour if fortune smiles on us!

As he continued to reminisce, we took in the unhurried life of the street, doors opening and closing as housewives departed on late afternoon tasks, children gathered to play soccer, husbands in business suits heaved their way home. Old, staidly middle-aged, or very young: that seemed the demographic of this quiet street until a pretty girl our age, dark hair bunched on her head and dressed in the uniform of a waitress, exited the ochre-hued house across the way. She was clearly in a rush but, when Marky winked at her, she nevertheless lifted an eyebrow and returned a pert smile.

When she turned the corner, she did so with a backwards glance.

I turned to Marky. "You're incorrigible. She hasn't a clue you aren't interested."

"Who says I'm not?" Marky looked at me askance. "What kind of sleuth *are* you? Didn't you see her leaning out of her window, up there, before she came downstairs?" He pointed to the third story above ground level. "And see that adjoining side window, next to Enzio's building? *Presto!*" Indeed, the side window to which Marky called my attention was in arm's reach of the unshuttered casement we'd noted earlier. Well, a very long arm's reach. More like a body's length. I was skeptical.

Marky grinned.

Being more practically minded, I spent the next two mornings threading the labyrinthine bureaucracy of the Registry of Deeds in quest of any records about the owner of the property at Piazza de Campiletti, 81. After waiting in interminable lines and being met with more indifferent shrugs than a hapless tourist asking for directions to the Trevi Fountain, I was no closer to an answer than when I entered the maze.

Sunday morning Marky casually announced, as he brushed the last flakes of sfogliatella from his lips, that I might want to stay in this evening. *He* was going out, but really I should stay home—he might have need for me later.

"You're being a little too mysterious for my taste."

"Trust me. And if I were you, I'd keep Enzio's keys handy. Or hand them over!"

"Not an option!"

Yes, Marky had met the waitress, Alessia Martina by name, from around the block. Trailing her to the trattoria where she worked, he appeared at closing to walk her home, and on Friday he'd taken her out for an espresso and bought her a rose. Sunday was her day off, and Marky had promised to make the evening one she would never forget if she consented to spend it with him.

"You can't *possibly* think—"

Mark held up his hand. "Show a little team spirit! Just stick around tonight in case I need you. And have a flashlight handy. I'd hardly look like a convincing lover if I showed up with one bulging in my pocket."

"Maybe she'll just think you're excited to see her."

Marky grinned at my Mae West imitation.

Reading Stendhal to stay awake that night proved a mistake. It was one a.m. when Marky, breathless, burst through the door and found me snoring on the sofa.

"I rose to the occasion—quite admirably I might add—and the moment is now ours!" Marky took a bow as I rubbed my eyes. "Got the keys and flashlight?"

"You're joking."

"For *you*, Newtie, I've been an absolute charmer, an unflagging stud, a height-defying daredevil—all in an evening's work!"

As Marky dashed and I stumbled down the worn marble stairs and out into the late evening air, he filled me in. A very romantic dinner with Alessia Martina, too much wine (most siphoned into her glass), a romantic stroll by the Tiber, and, once in her bedroom, acrobatics designed to ensure she fell asleep afterwards like a baby. At which point Marky made for the side-window in the front room. Thank God for the clay drainpipe that ran between the two buildings, without it he'd have never been able to pull himself from one window ledge to the other, punch out the plastic covering, unhinge and push open the window frame, and, as cool as Cary Grant's cat burglar in "To Catch a Thief," hoist himself into a room reeking of petrified pigeon shit. Locating the door, he'd felt his way down the stairs in the pitch black to the front entry, whose bolts slid back with surprisingly little resistance.

He'd left the door propped a fraction open for our reentry.

The street was deserted when we entered it, and we melted into the shadows cast by the recessed facade of no. 81 as we breached the threshold. My flashlight revealed stairs speckled with rodent droppings that led upwards into the dark. So long shut up, the foyer smelled of age and decay and—remarkable after all this time—traces of garlic.

We agreed to try the keys on the rear apartments, one by one, and two landings up we hit pay dirt. The larger key slid easily into the lock and we heard the click of tumblers falling into place once, twice, three times. With a groan intimidating enough to frighten away any lingering spirits, the door swung open.

The beam of my flashlight took in a large, almost bare chamber. Facing us on the far wall were three tall shuttered windows. I motioned Marky to the central one and, working together, we folded the interior wooden panels into their wall pockets, then tugged open the begrimed glass casements. Unhasping the exterior shutters was a greater challenge—weather had corroded the clasps and hinges. But when we finally pushed them outwards, we knew that we were standing where Enzio had stood, those many decades ago, when he conceived the design for the lid for the Quattrocentro box.

Below, glossy-black in the moonlight, the long crucifix shaped by the cloister's waterway stretched across the rectangular space, and directly opposite, at the apex of the cross, the silhouette of the herm glimmered in the moonlight.

Turning to the interior of the room, I rotated my light. A crippled easel leaned in a corner. A long worktable stood against one wall, abutting a deep porcelain sink. On the table were heaped dozens of tubes of dried oils. A moth-eaten woolen jacket hung on a peg. From a pile of rubbish I unfolded paint-splattered newspaper pages dated 1943.

"The year Enzio died," I murmured.

There was only one other door, located on the interior wall to the right of the windows. I rattled its porcelain handle, but decades of damp had swollen the frame shut.

Marky joined me in the effort. It took both of us throwing our shoulders against the door before it gave way, and it sprang open so suddenly we landed at the same time on a gritty floor that hadn't been cleaned since before our births.

The flashlight had fallen from my hand, rolling to a stop against the baseboard. In its diffused light I was aware of dusky red hues hovering above us and porcelain glimmering at eye level: we'd landed in a surprisingly spacious bathroom. I reached for the lamp and was plying it around the space as we rose to our feet when I caught my breath.

Marky saw what I saw. "Holy shit."

The upper half of the bathroom was painted a Pompeian red, and the lower a yellow ochre. But what riveted our attention was the space between: an elaborate, hand-painted frieze separating the two hues and running the room's circumference. As I aimed the beam at its surface, a band of priapic satyrs leered at us in still-vibrant colors. Their heads sprouted from rectangular herms, their muscular arms held garlanded wreathes aloft, their masculine chests sagged with female breasts. The sixteenth-century shepherd who accidentally breached the Aurea Domus for the first time since Nero's reign could not have been more surprised than us.

"Exact design as the watercolor."

"So this *is* where we are supposed to look." Marky paused. "But for what?"

The answer to the riddle dawned on me, clear as day. "Of course! Remember the castrated herm in the garden?"

"So?"

"Lacking his key, as it were? Is one of these herms lacking *his* key?"

Two keys had been enclosed in Enzio's box, and we'd only used the larger one. I dangled the smaller key up for Marky to see. He instantly grasped my meaning, and we set about investigating the genitalia of the painted figures, one by one, under the golden orb cast by the flashlight.

"How pervy! Seems obvious where Enzio's interests lay." Marky's fingers grazed yet another erection. It didn't escape our attention that each phallus was differently detailed, whereas the breasts remained identical.

"There was Julia, remember."

"Doesn't mean he and Uncle weren't getting it on."

"We can hope."

We continued our investigation, methodically brushing our fingertips over the lacquered images in search of any discrepancy: past the pedestal sink, past the towel rack missing its dowel, past a blackened toilet bowl and flush chamber suspended high on the wall.

And, then, at last, directly above the spigots of the claw-footed tub, my fingertips touched metal. Where the herm's phallic glory should have been painted there was a lozenge-shaped indentation, a keyhole hidden in plain sight.

In my excitement, I dropped the attached keys into the tub, perilously close to the open drain. Marky retrieved them for me.

"Steady there, buddy. I'll hold the light..."

With a sense of imminent revelation, I fit the smaller key into the disguised opening. Before it had turned a quarter of an inch, it stopped, stuck.

Marky placed his hand over mine and we pushed together, till I feared the thin metal might snap. But then we felt the release of a latch giving way, and a square section of wall swung out towards us, exposing a small compartment.

Within the otherwise empty space rested an envelope.

"Holy shit," Mark said for the second time.

I reached for the thin enclosure. It bore a single inscription written in the same violet script I'd seen in Mr. Julian's library two winters ago: "For J.A.B." *Follow their lead,* Enzio's letter had said, *and please know that what lies on the other side is rightfully mine, and on my death, is rightfully yours.*

Had we reached the other side?

I prized open the flap of the envelope and extracted a folded sheet of paper. Marky held the beam on the page as we leaned in to read its single sentence, written in English in Enzio's impeccable script: "Call this number, identify yourself by name, and the prize will be yours." The next line was composed of a series of numerals—and nothing more.

We departed the apartment building as furtively as we'd entered, leaving the front door invisibly ajar so we could return. Neither of us slept well, so eager were we for Monday morning to arrive when we might reasonably attempt to ring the number Enzio had left behind. The numerical sequence looked unfamiliar, so we were wary of getting our hopes up. Nonetheless, when after a dozen rings an operator interrupted to say we'd dialed a nonexistent number, we were sorely disappointed. To come so close to deciphering the meaning of Enzio's final communication with Mr. Julian, only to be deprived of that magical moment when an unknown voice on the other end would respond with a hearty *Pronto!* was wrenching.

We weren't giving up yet. The next day I let Carlo know I'd be locking the shop for a long lunch break so that I could visit the central telephone office, hoping the sequence of numbers would make sense to someone with a memory for old phone codes. Waiting in line for information wasn't quite the disaster as my foray into the Registry of Deeds. After a mere hour of misdirections, I learned that the number designated a Paris exchange from the early 1940s, one that had long ceased operation. Marky's multiple calls to Paris provided no further illumination. We'd reached a dead end. By way of commiseration, Marky reminded me that at least I could now explain to Mr. Julian the mystery of Enzio's box and its contents. Whatever catharsis he might gain from our narrative must be our recompense.

We returned to the studio the next night—this time with two flashlights and a camera—to take snapshots to send Mr. Julian and make sure we had missed no other clues.

We hadn't, I was finally forced to admit.

The herm in the garden had yielded its secret, directing us to the message that had been awaiting Mr. Julian all these decades. But Enzio's attempt to communicate beyond the grave had stalled amid ambiguities whose meanings were now lost in the voids of a personal history that, having tantalizingly flared to life these past few days, now faded, part of an infinite regress reverberating with unfulfilled dreams. As we left the building, we pulled the door shut behind us till the lock clicked shut, consigning Enzio's studio to the same silence that had shrouded its secret for three decades.

33

SUMMONS TO PARIS

We were getting on, Marky and I, living out our separate versions of *la dolce vita* in the same city and under the same roof. Another spring came and went, it was 1975, and I was as poor, and as happy, and as carefree, as I had been in a long time. I hadn't ventured out of the country since I'd arrived, as much from necessity as desire. Once it became clear I wasn't returning to Harvard, the institution had remitted the tuition (after withholding a punitive amount as promised) to Mr. Allbright. Sad to say, the entire sum went to pay off my outstanding debts. I regretted the folly of those overindulgent evenings at my dining club, the strippers I'd hired to entertain the swim team when we placed third in state competition, and the expensive clothing purchased on Newbury Street that, in my rush to leave Boston, I ended up donating to Goodwill. Now, counting every lira I pocketed, I was able to cover my share of living expenses, with just enough left over to browse the city's flea markets and used bookstores and eat all the cheap pasta I desired. A little went a long way in Rome—these were the days when travel guides advertising "Europe on 10 Dollars a Day" flirted with possibility.

Work and play complemented each other in an easy rhythm for both Marky and me. Carlo increased my responsibilities at the Monserrato shop, and I tried my hand sketching a few concepts. Carlo patiently showed me what worked and what didn't, and I was exhilarated when I completed the design for a console that earned a *bravo!* instead of the usual *basta!*—a design that drew its inspiration from the half-dome arch supports of Roman basilica architecture. Even more encouraging was Carlo's suggestion that I use the workshop after-hours to carry the design to completion. While his wife dropped by to feed us pastries and his daughters frolicked in the sawdust of the Trastevere workshop, I found myself cutting, grooving, aligning, and assembling the pieces as Carlo offered commentary. Marky's career

was taking even more auspicious turns. Bernardo had secured backing for his film project, which he'd cleverly pitched as "Jules and Jim"
meets "Last Tango in Paris," and Marky was slated to serve as first
assistant director when shooting began.

Not all was work, as I've said—it was impossible to live as a
Roman without experiencing the myriad pleasures making up every
Roman's daily existence. As my circle of friends grew, so too did my
sense of adventure and daring; and I risked putting myself forward in
ways that the boy who had come of age in Andover and the teenager
who thought he had achieved the acme of sophistication as an Eliot
man would have never dreamed. Marky introduced me to the hedon-
istic world of dance clubs springing up across the city—his film connections got us on the VIP list to Jacky-O's. I learned on my own to
cruise the paths of the gardens of Capitoline Hill in the twilight, lingering by the Tarpeian Rock for encounters that were crude, immediate, and sometimes dicey; I ventured into saunas that, pale echoes
of the Domitian and Caracalla baths of ancient Rome, made good on
the promise of mindless rounds of pleasure; I joined the throngs of
other young men and women using the Spanish Steps as the backdrop
for their mating rituals, awaiting the returned glance—sometimes
a man's, sometimes a woman's—that might lead to conversation,
drinks, after-hours intimacy. On flush evenings I spent hours with
friends people-watching from one of the tables lining the Via Venuto.
For the first time in my life, I let myself experience everything: as for
so many of my generation, "anything goes" had become my password.

Marky, of course, spurred me on in my sybaritic adventures—
although, ironically, his own sex life was becoming less and less epi-
curean the more time he spent with Fabrizio. Their relationship, however, had to weather any number of crises, most of Marky's making
when, aghast that he might be settling into Bourgeois Complacency,
he periodically attempted to sabotage the romance with one-night
stands. Blessed with a wisdom that belied his years, Fabrizio refused
to take the bait, waiting for the moment when his philandering lover
returned home, proverbial tail between his legs. It amused me to witness the revolutionary who had taken to the streets in Paris coming to
terms with his need for the less radical but perhaps more challenging

pleasures of domesticity. So we worked, and we played, and I created a life that was sweet in a world far removed from my origins.

Periodically Marky threatened to fly me back to visit Rocky Hill on his own dime before I forgot my roots altogether. Some quirk in my personality rooted in the Protestant upbringing I'd otherwise forsworn, as well as regret at my more recent extravagances, made me cringe at the idea of accepting his charity, however much I missed my family. But of late new circumstances were forcing me to rethink my resistance—Mr. Allbright had written that Mr. Julian had been hospitalized with bronchitis and that matters did not look good at all. Marky had visited him over Thanksgiving and, on his return, warned me that I might want to do the same sooner than later. Mary Jo confirmed as much after making a trip to Rocky Hill in January. Her habit was to ring our apartment late evenings, in hopes of finding either Marky or myself—or if she were lucky, both of us—at home. "Late evening" our time was mid-afternoon Eastern Standard Time while Fred was conveniently at work. There was no love lost between the Offensive Offenbach and the Roman Roomies. Nor, apparently, between Offenbach and Mr. Julian. Despite the latter's alarming decline, Fred had refused to accompany Mary Jo on her visit, declaring she could have the aged degenerate to herself. Poor Mr. Julian! For years he had woven elaborate fantasies about the brilliant marriage Mary Jo would make, only to dislike her choice as much as her choice disliked him.

A disturbing incident had occurred during Mary Jo's visit. She had gone to bed—the old house drearier and more rundown than ever, she told us—only to be awakened in the middle of the night by shrieks coming from the floor above. In spite of his weakened state, Mr. Julian had managed to sleepwalk out of his bedroom and up the stairs with a lit candle in hand, at which point he'd stumbled and set his robe afire. His screams roused Hank Atwater (whose room, like G.G.'s before him, was on the third floor). Rushing into the hallway to find his master in flames, Hank wrestled him to the ground, holding his thrashing body tight until the conflagration petered out. By then the ruckus had awakened not only Mary Jo but also Bruno, who now occupied one of the grander bedrooms in the east wing. The three of them rushed the hysterical man to the emergency room at Franklin

General. The burns he'd suffered were far less damaging than the scars the incident scored on his psyche, feeding his feelings of paranoia and adding to his feebleness of mind.

So thoughts of travel were stirring in my brain when at the beginning of June I received an urgent summons to pack my bags—but an entirely different destination was being asked of me. The call came from Mary Jo while I was preparing dinner. Marky was away shooting a commercial on the Amalfi Coast.

"You're where?" I crooked the receiver between my neck and shoulder as I added pasta to boiling water. "Paris?... Calm down, I can barely make out a word."

"I just flew in, I would have come to Rome but that'd be the first place Fred would look for me—he'll assume I've taken shelter with my brother."

Mary Jo's voice, which rarely projected anything but maddening serenity, sounded unsettlingly agitated.

"I don't understand—is everything all right?"

"No, everything is *not* all right and that's why I need to talk to you and Marky now." I explained Marky's absence. "All the better, I might not be able to bear his *I told you so*. I need to talk in person. Will you come up tomorrow?"

"I can't just take off from work."

"Newt, I need to talk to someone I trust *now*. It's a matter of days—who knows, hours—before Fred tracks me down and there'll be hell to pay. I'm depending on you."

If the part of me that had never stood a chance with Mary Jo was pleased, in a grim sort of way, that she might be ruing her choice of mate, the part of me that had adored Mary Jo for so long couldn't resist the siren call of her summons. I asked Carlo if he might spare me while I dealt with a "family emergency"—take a week, he genially offered—and I borrowed against my salary in order to purchase a round-trip train ticket, since, in her urgency to see me, Mary Jo hadn't considered the fact that I no longer commanded the kind of income that was second nature to her.

Twenty hours later Mary Jo greeted me in the lobby of an elegantly appointed but appropriately discreet hotel in the fifth arrondissement. Embracing me with nervous fervor, she directed the bellboy to take my bag to my room. For a woman normally the color of bronze by summer's beginning, she looked uncharacteristically pale.

"Let's find a place to sit and talk," she said, locking her arm in mine. "Who better to serve as my confessor than my second brother?"

We stepped out in a lovely June afternoon I'd barely had time to notice in the rush of my arrival. Having studied French since I was fourteen, I felt that Paris was already part of my bloodstream, and I had to keep reminding myself that I was actually *here*, here in the city of light and lovers. Paris in early summer has a beauty that rivals Rome—a balmier feel to the air, cloud-stippled skies a softer blue than Rome's cobalt dome, the palette more pastel than ochre, the flora more playful than austere—and all of these differences were bathed in rays of sunshine that seemed to sparkle and dance, as opposed to the steady burnished glow that makes even the cobblestones of Rome radiate sensual surfeit in the month of June. I was famished after my hastily orchestrated journey, so we found a quiet bistro where we could sit at outside, facing a verdant park islanded between three boulevards where manicured flowerbeds had been elevated to high art. I ordered steak frites while Mary Jo asked for a martini.

"Afternoon martinis are de rigueur at our place. I find it helpful to have finished my first before Fred gets home. He catches up soon enough." Mary Jo paused. "After his third drink, he gets ugly."

I listened.

"I know how Fred *appears* to you and Marky: a little stuffy and a lot boring, a tin-ear when it comes to our cultural tastes, a team-player in the office and a pushover at home."

"Something like that. Perfect match. I congratulate you."

"Newt." Mary Jo's look warned me that flippancy, in her present state, was not to be tolerated. "I thought I knew exactly what I was in for too. I had made my peace with it."

She put down her cocktail and spread her beautifully manicured hands for me to see—they shook uncontrollably, making all the more noticeable the size of her engagement ring, whose flashing diamonds and central sapphire—the shade of her eyes—bespoke wealth beyond my imagining, even in the days before my expectations were curtailed. "Look! Trembling like a schoolgirl facing her Mother Superior for a minor infraction. Whenever did you know *me* to be cowed by *anyone*?"

I took her hands in mine and brought them to the table.

"You need to tell me exactly what's going on."

"I said Fred *looks* like a pushover. On that point I was definitely mistaken. Before we married, every command I uttered, as they say in novels, was his wish to perform." Bitterness entered her voice. "But once we returned from the Bermudas, he made it painfully clear that *his* desires were mine to... to submit to."

"He's a Wall Street shark. Did you think he got to his position being a wimp?"

"Newt, you aren't *hearing* me." Mary Jo looked me in the eyes. "He doesn't just order me around. He beats me."

I paled. No way was I prepared for this.

"And when it comes to... sex—" Mary Jo stopped and looked away. "He's deliberately violent—he *likes* making me hurt, and he *likes* forcing me to beg him to stop when I can't take it anymore."

Weakly, I protested she must have known of his sexual kinks before tying the knot.

"He was aggressive, he took control, I confess I liked that since it meant I didn't have to pretend to feel anything. But it's different now; his biggest turn-on is to humiliate me, to force me to admit I'm unresponsive—that I can't feel anything but the pain. Real, physical pain."

Mary Joe tugged at the neckline of her blouse, so I could see the ugly blue and yellow bruises that stretched from shoulder to breast, and she told me of other, worse, injuries she had suffered.

"The wretched irony is that my failure to get aroused is what brings him off." She laughed bitterly. "When he beats me, my mind freezes, I lose all will to resist—and that frightens me most."

I was so shocked I didn't know what to say.

"I know how proper he appears." Mary Jo attempted to control the waver in her voice. "But when it's just the two of us, he's a beast." She paused. "Do you think, Newt, that deep down... I deserve it?"

"My God, Mary Jo, no!" The words erupted from my lips with unexpected vehemence. I steadied myself. "What are your plans? How can we help?"

"I need space to figure that out," she said. "That's why I left New York. Soon enough he'll find me and try to force me back. Then I don't know what will happen."

"You have to file for divorce, or at least a separation."

Mary Jo took a deep breath. "There's more, Newt. In March, I found out I was pregnant. I couldn't stand the thought of all those Offenbachs smiling at the news, or what he might *do* to the child someday. So I had an abortion. Fred found out, and now he's remorseless. He says he's going to 'knock me up' for good. Those are *his* words. I'm sure the pun is intentional."

I wanted to knock Offenbach down. The hatred that filled me had no bottom. "Mary Jo, Mary Jo, listen to me—you *don't* deserve this." I paused to think. "For starters, you need to hire a lawyer who isn't on your husband's Rolodex. I'll get in touch with Mr. Allbright. For Mr. Julian's sake alone, he'll want to do right by you. Trust me."

"And when Fred finds me? He'll hire professionals, you know." I do not think I had ever seen Mary Jo cry before, but tears now trickled down her cheeks.

"He can't, he has too much to lose," I said, assuming for her sake a confidence I didn't feel. Rising from my chair, I went to Mary Jo's side and, kneeling, folded her in my arms. She felt as fragile as a Dresden figurine dangling from a toddler's careless fingertips.

*

Mr. Allbright, as I predicted, was a lifesaver. His imperturbable calm came to the fore as he researched New York's divorce statutes and advised Mary Jo that her case would be much stronger were she to return to the States to make an affidavit, help him gather testimony, and establish a case—her sudden flight to Europe could be twisted by Fred to make her seem the guilty party. Within days, he filed for a restraining order and arranged for Mary Jo to stay with the Fortinbrases upon her return to the States; even if Offenbach successfully fought the order, it would stay in effect for thirty days. The rub came,

Mr. Allbright warned, with New York State's lack of no-fault divorce, which meant that both spouses had to agree to end the marriage; and the possibility of Offenbach refusing to let Mary Jo walk free was a distressing reality, especially if it appealed to his sadistic impulses. A separation of indefinite duration was the most plausible immediate solution, and Mr. Allbright was of the opinion that in time the Offenbach clan could be made to apply pressure on Frederick, lest allegations of abuse besmirched the family name more than they found profitable. Mary Jo still had her inheritance, like Marky, which was ample enough to live on; and if she were willing to separate without making financial claims on Fred—if she were willing to swear she would not bring charges of his physical violence to public attention—there was a chance that the cad might be persuaded by his betters to allow a divorce to proceed. It was sure to be tricky, but Mr. Allbright set the wheels in motion.

In face of these recent crises, thoughts of visiting Mr. Julian had been driven from my head. So when Mr. Allbright called on July 12, with a note of urgency in his voice equal to that in Mary Jo's when she'd rung me a month earlier, the first idea that flashed through my mind was that Offenbach had violated the restraining order and abducted Mary Jo. My second thought was that Mr. Julian was dying and I might not make it home in time to see him.

What Mr. Allbright had called to communicate, however, was far different: I was being summoned, once again, to Paris, on a mission that had to do neither with Mary Jo nor with Mr. Julian but, so the lawyer announced, everything to do with me.

34

BASTILLE DAY

So once more I found myself bound for Paris, taking the overnight train in order to reach Mr. Allbright by the hour he'd designated for our meeting.

"I am flying in tomorrow night. Meet me the day after at the Hotel Quai de Voltaire. Be there by noon." Mr. Allbright's tone brooked no dissent. "This is a matter of utmost importance. A certain person is ready to exchange words with you."

I was baffled. If that "certain person" were my benefactor, we both knew he was recovering in a hospital in Rocky Hill.

"Neither here nor there, Newt. You'll learn what you need to learn when we meet. We shan't take a NO for an answer."

Marky offered to come along, as curious and concerned as me about this mysterious summons. But my gut instinct said I needed to go alone. When I asked Carlo for more time off, he drolly responded that perhaps he should open a Paris branch for me to run. He then pressed into my palm a curious object, withered and brown. Plant, animal, mineral—I had no idea.

"Don't even ask. It's a family good luck charm. Old crone from Sicily gave it to my nonna when she was a little girl and it's worked wonders ever since."

Rubbing the unidentified object in my pocket with one palm while I rubbed the sleep out of my eyes with the other, I approached the Hotel Quai de Voltaire. "Tired" does not do justice to how I felt. All night I kept falling asleep to the thrumming sound of the train only to dream of Mr. Julian going up in flames; jerking awake, then again falling into fitful slumber in which Mr. Julian appeared as wraith floating above the old swimming pool; waking with a gasp only to lapse into a dream in which Bruno and Hank, joined by Samson and George Geronimo, jeered at me, why I didn't know until I saw that I was stark naked and had fallen down the pit in the well-house, turning somersaults in slow-motion for what seemed an eternity as they heckled and called me names, and as I passed the stones making up the damp walls of the shaft, each precisely identical, I confounded their identities with my own. Inexplicably, Sassafras replaced the jeering chorus, lowering into the well an oaken bucket until it fished out a minuscule infant, who was myself, shivering in fetal position. When Sassafras hoisted me aloft, the light scalded my newborn skin.

Paris seemed brighter and fiercer than it had a month ago, sunlight turning the Seine into a glaring mirror and suffusing the limestone blocks of the Louvre, directly across from the hotel, with white heat. I paused by a plaque at the hotel's entrance advertising Oscar Wilde's distinguished patronage at the end of the last century, ran my fingers through disheveled hair, and realized that it was Bastille Day.

Mr. Allbright picked up his fedora as soon as I entered the lobby.

"Thank you for coming, Newt, but we're already running behind. We'll hail a taxi."

I felt like I was still dreaming as I stumbled back into the glare. A cab pulled up, Allbright gave the driver an address, and off we zoomed to an unknown destination. I had the uneasy sense, as I watched the lawyer glance out the rear window, that he was checking to make sure we weren't being followed, although in the blaring traffic I couldn't fathom how one would know.

From the corner of my eye I glimpsed the awning of the Café de Flore as our driver zigzagged south, skirting the edge of the Luxembourg gardens before connecting with Rue Raspail and entering a network of interlacing streets on the south side of Montparnasse cemetery. The one time I tried to speak, Mr. Allbright raised a hand. "It's not for me to tell. Soon enough, you'll have your explanation. Afterwards, we'll talk." He touched his scented handkerchief to his lips. Onwards we journeyed in silence, until the taxi stopped in front of a black door on the obscure Rue Georges Sache.

"Here we are!" Mr. Allbright announced. "Press number four, you'll be buzzed in. Take the elevator to the third *étage*, fourth floor if you're thinking American style—that is, if the lift's working today, I've found it temperamental of late."

I looked at Mr. Allbright wonderingly.

"I'm to go in there alone?"

"I'm following instructions." He tucked some francs into the breast pocket of my shirt. "Taxi money to return to the hotel. Tonight, I promise you a very good dinner, and you may ask all the questions you wish."

"But, sir," I said, faltering as I opened the taxi door. "What am I supposed to *do*? I don't understand."

"Be a good lad, now, and ring the buzzer. Someone is waiting."

I listened to the taxi drive away with a sinking feeling. Once I buzzed my way in, the heavy front door slowly swung shut behind me, leaving me alone in a dim foyer where a narrow stairway wound upwards, its oval bends enclosing a filigree iron cage that housed the two-person elevator Mr. Allbright had spoken of. Nothing happened, however, when I jabbed its operating button, no whir of machinery sounded to indicate that it had been brought back to life. So I took to the stairs, my right hand gripping the polished railing and my left trailing the flocked designs in the burgundy wallpaper as I ascended in the close darkness. On the third landing, I paused and felt for the light switch. A single sconce flickered to life, and I saw that one apartment, its double doors inset in the wall, faced me. I lifted the heavy knocker and brought it down once, twice, three times, my heart beating in anticipation of what I did not know. Beads of sweat formed on my forehead and dampness pooled under my arms.

I touched Carlo's charm for good luck.

Someone swung the right panel of the wooden door open, and as if in a dream I saw, outlined against the dimly lit room behind her, the regal shape of a woman who, in a deep contralto, asked, "Is it you, Newt?" Before I could mumble a reply, she gestured me inside and bolted the door. The small entry where I stood opened onto a crowded sitting room right out of the Belle Epoque. The weight of heavy brocaded curtains looped at the sides of tall windows dimmed the light, and as I turned to look at my host, I saw that she was a mature woman, a woman with queenly bearing and penetrating eyes, a dark-skinned woman of unmistakably African origin, and my mind flashed to my graduation from Phipps, to the lobby of the theater as the curtain was about to rise on the final performance of "Hamlet," to the instant when I locked eyes, ever so briefly, with the late-arriving audience member who turned out to be Larry Fortinbras' guest, and, feeling that I must be hallucinating, I saw that the one and same woman was now curiously looking me up and down, with an air of being pleased by the sweating, unnerved sight she beheld.

"You really don't recognize me?" she finally asked, and smiled wryly. "I expected more of Newton Seward, the Deacon's boy."

She extended her hands, taking my damp palms in her expectant clasp, and as I stupidly looked down at her beautifully shaped, mahogany hands—and at her exquisitely manicured fingernails, gleaming fuchsia red and tipped with perfect white crescent moons—time melted away and the truth came crashing down on me, as violently as if the ornately plastered ceiling above had just given way and pinioned me, helplessly wrestling the choking debris, on the floor. I might have preferred the guillotine.

"Zithra?" I uttered, pulling back my hands in shock. "Zithra Jackson Brown?"

"Actually, dear boy, Mrs. Thomas Ravenel Beauchamp now. A widow as of two years ago. Shall we sit?"

She motioned to two gilt chairs standing by the brocaded curtains, and I followed, dumbly. The morning gown of silver and lilac hues loosely belted around her waist trailed behind her like moonbeams or memory, tugging me in its wake. The majesty with which she glided forward bore not one trace of the panting fugitive I had last glimpsed lurching through twilight gloom pricked by fitful fireflies down by Furnace Creek.

We sat. She looked at me; I looked at her. In her face I saw a sophisticated Parisian lady, and in her face I also saw my convict.

"I owe you a debt of gratitude, Newton Seward. I was one desperate woman that day we ran into each other, and Lord knows you were one frightened slip of a youngster. But you acted noble, you did. You were just a whimpering little white boy I never thought I could trust, and I was an escaped criminal. But you brought me everything I asked for and more, not telling a soul, and for sure I wouldn't be sitting here all high and mighty today if you hadn't cracked open the door for me. I hightailed it through that door, son, like there was no tomorrow, but I never forgot about you or what you did for me."

The lips that had once seemed so threatening curled in a bemused smile. The gold front tooth seared in my memory had been replaced with a porcelain one. "Haven't you guessed, Newt? It was me. I made you what you are"—her voice reverberated with a strange pride that made my heart recoil in panic—"and I'm glad of it! You made the world possible for me, and I wanted the same for you." She sighed, looking every bit an opera diva who has successfully completed her final aria, just before she realizes the villain has silently appeared by her side and is about to drive his dagger into her bosom. "I was crushed that I wasn't able to see your fortunes through to the end. But look at you—you've become a man, as handsome and educated as they come. You've done me proud, Newton Seward!"

While she uttered these words, locking me in her hungry gaze, I began to tremble, reliving adolescent terrors I thought I'd locked away.

"It was *you*, all these years?"

"It was *me*, single-handed. With a little help from Mr. Beauchamp, I admit—that man was ever so generous when it came to my whims, he was plumb *crazy* about me. But the idea of sending you off to school, making you independent, that was all my idea! A brilliant one, if only my husband hadn't passed away on me without a word of warning!"

She let loose a ringing laugh. "Never count on the money, dear!" Then she softened and reached over to take my hand, which I yielded numbly. I was in a state of shock: my world had turned upside down, and I no longer knew who I was. *Mr. Julian Mr. Julian Mr. Julian* I kept thinking.

"I am sorry the money dried up, honey," Zithra continued. "I'm sure it's been awful after all the good years feeding off the fattened calf. I should know, seeing we're in the same boat. But why in heaven's name did you drop out of school? I wanted the very best for you and Harvard was the top of the heap!"

My mind was elsewhere. "So it *was* you, at the Phipps graduation? With Larry Fortinbras?"

Zithra laughed again, now with childish delight as she clapped her hands. "Oh, don't you know Larry warned me it was a risk, but I just *had* to see my protégé on his special day! My husband got me a fake passport—bless his soul, he knew how to go about *those* kinds of things—and for a whole week I traveled in New England as Ms. Loretta Fishbone and not one soul was the wiser! Tommy and I had a good chuckle about it once I made it back safe and sound. That man always admired my sense of adventure!"

"Tommy?"

"My husband of course. Tommy Ravenel Beauchamp. Although" (and now she snorted in a rather unladylike manner) "*some* say I don't have the right to call him *husband.* You see" (her penciled brows levitated) "he never divorced his second wife proper-like. Although *I* certainly didn't know *that* when we took our vows in that sweet little chapel in Geneva... what a road I've traveled! Whoever supposed, in their wildest dreams, that Zithra Jackson Brown's prison break would lead her *here*"—Zithra made a grand gesture that seemed to include herself, the room, all of Paris—"isn't that the truth?"

I nodded mutely. It saved me the effort of having to respond while I continued to absorb one simple, colossal fact: the illusions under whose spell I'd labored for so long were false. I felt utterly lost.

"Just look at the wall behind you, the whole story's there."

Beyond the old furniture, chintz upholstery, curios, and gewgaws that competed for space in the darkened room, I made out the oddest display of framed pictures arranged in three rows—some photographs shot in high resolution, some illustrations cut from magazines, some in color, some in black and white, one pastel. But the one thing that they had in common was their subject matter: disembodied hands in different positions and poses, sometimes waving in the air, sometimes demurely crossed, sometimes resting on a cheek or bare shoulder or stockinged thigh, the fingers always prominently lit and their tips always gleaming with immaculately applied polish.

"I was Tommy's top model for his hand products," Zithra announced with pride. "To his dying day he said I had the most beautiful hands and nails he'd ever laid eyes on. Sweet man, that's what first attracted him to me. Once I slipped out of the States—*that's* a story for another day!—I came straight to Paris, folk back home always raved about how the Frogs *fancied* our kind. It was fall, I was sitting at an outdoors cafe near Luxembourg, wondering what I was going to do with my new life, when this gentleman at the next table gasped out loud as he noticed my fingers lifting that dainty cup to my lips. I'd just gotten a perm, and I was wearing my first real-to-goodness French dress, so I admit I was looking *fine*—but it was these hands he noticed. Oh my! My Tommy did have a *thing* for hands, specially on a black lady, and so we fell to talking, and soon enough he tells me he's created a line of beauty products for Women of African Origins, Élégance Ébène, Ebony Elegance. Made him a fortune in the Sixties. Tommy was launching a new line of nail polishes with the tagline

BLACK IS BEAUTIFUL,
BUT SO IS THE COLOR
OF YOUR **NAILS**!'

and yours truly became his Number One model for the label. Something about the sheen of my skin, he always said, set off any nail color to its best advantage."

She waved at the images on the wall. "These hands have been in more fashion magazines than you can count. Tommy decorated his office with these pictures for everyone to see. Poor dear was besotted, I've never seen a man so gone on his woman. A year later he divorced Wife Two—or so I was led to believe—and we said our vows in Geneva. That's around the time I asked him for a special favor. Namely, to advise me on how to reward *you* for your help, as my career was bringing in money the likes of which I'd never imagined. I told him the whole story of that day by the creek, and he got so caught up in my brainchild he decided to go whole hog and open his coffers so I could do something Big. He's the one who put me in touch with Larry Fortinbras, who told me about Phipps, and when all the pieces were in place I made Mr. Allbright, a man I already had every reason to trust, our agent."

Feverish as my brain felt, the dots began to connect. I remembered the phone conversation I'd overheard the evening we dined at the Leroys, as Tom Allbright solemnly delivered to the distraught

Judge the details of Zithra's terms for returning his sordid black book page by page.

"Yes, life was glamorous for your ole Zithra from the moment Tommy made me his Star Attraction. Bought me beautiful clothes and taught me how to act elegant and talk polite—not that I always care to—and I took to it like a duck to water. He liked to show me off at all the best places—the restaurants, the opera, the fashion shows, St. Moritz in the winter, Santorini in the summer, and didn't I enjoy it all! Paris loved me, and I loved Paris right back. I thought it would last forever, till he dropped dead two years ago." Zithra took a moment to find a lacy handkerchief and dab eyes whose tastefully mascaraed lashes complemented her nail polish.

"Clogged arteries. Poor thing liked his foie gras. Well, he lived to see 78, I hope I'm still kickin' when that number rolls around. If the fool had only left me an income!"

Ah, I thought. Zithra dabbed more freely at her cheeks.

"I'm in dire straits, Newt, I'll be heading to the poorhouse before I live to see another year!" Discreetly looking around the room in which we sat, I couldn't help but think that its ornate furnishings might provide Zithra with enough income to keep the wolves from the door. She must have read my mind. "Ha! I'll be lucky to keep the clothes on my back, much less those pictures on the wall, once Tommy's creditors have done with me!" She leaned forward confidentially. "Son, you might think there's no ruder shock than finding out your marriage vows were a sham, that the love of your life was still legally tied to *that* woman. Wounded my pride, oh yes it did. But the real shock came when I learned there was no provision for me in his will—and he'd promised he'd change it so many times, silly duck! Now *that* hurt more than my feelings, it hit me in the pocketbook. His coffin was hardly in the ground before the creditors swarmed out of the woodwork like Carolina termites on a feeding frenzy. Turned out Tommy owed everyone right and left, he liked to speculate on the wildest business ventures as much as he liked his goose liver. They've been eating the foundation out from under me ever since, Newt, they're claiming a right to every item I possess! The executors emptied the bank accounts to pay off the debts—honey, those accounts was where your money was coming from, I never thought of opening my own after I met Tommy. Now a whole new set of bigmouths are claiming Tommy owed them big time and I better make good on his debts *or else*. It's a nightmare. Newt, your Zithra is down and out!"

Zithra also found herself nearly out of breath, and for an instant I detected, under her contralto vibrato, the wheezing sounds I'd heard on top of the stony mound at Furnace Creek. It was also beginning to dawn on me that, like the greatest of actresses, she was able to shift her vocal register at will: from elegant lady-of-the-world to woe-be-gotten sufferer to child of the South. She steadied herself, patted her still ample chest, and began again. "After a few months of wrangling with the executors I agreed to sell our beautiful place near the Opera and found this cheap little apartment, taking just a *few* things Tommy and me purchased together, sentimental whatnots. My financial advisers and Mr. Allbright tell me I have enough valuables to keep myself going for years if I sell 'em off bit by bit. But a month ago a brand new set of hooligans started in on me, saying I've held onto portable property that's rightfully Tommy's and hence rightfully theirs—the jewels, the art, the furs, the antiques, down to these old worn-out Persian rugs under your feet. They're circling me like vultures. I'm ruined!"

The tears flew thick and fast. I was in a state of shock, reeling from the realization that the bedrock on which my dreams had rested for six years had been financed by a petty convict and her shady paramour. Yet I couldn't help but feel for the woman who sat noisily sobbing before me. Whatever the truth of the tale she'd just spun, her intentions toward *me* were clear: to give me a leg up, to allow me to escape, as she'd done before me, the confines of Franklin County. But I didn't know what she wanted from me *now*. With a sinking feeling, I feared it was something Big.

A few minutes later the shower of tears had ceased, and Zithra took a compact from the pocket of her dressing gown, sat up, and patted her cheeks dry. Her face was a dark marvel rendered even more marvelous by fine beauty products, from ambient lip gloss to purplish eye shadow to the iridescent umber powder with which she now dusted her cheekbones. Tommy Beauchamp's favorite model—whom I reckoned to be in her mid-fifties—was still the best advertisement for Ebony Elegance that ever breathed.

"Mrs. Beauchamp, I'm sorry for your troubles, and I truly thank you for trying to help—indeed for helping me, all these years. It was uncalled for, such generosity—" A cry shook loose in my heart and burst from my lips. "But *why* didn't you let me know that you were my benefactor before? Why only send for me now?"

"Don't be calling me Mrs. Beauchamp—I hope I'll always be Zithra to you! Besides," she added with a dramatic grimace, "if what They tell me's true, I guess Mrs. Beauchamp ain't my legal name after all."

As she stopped to ponder this further hitch in her rocky career, I feared she might burst into tears again. Instead she drew herself up grandly.

"Why didn't I tell you? Oh, I may not know much but I *knew* your family wasn't about to accept money, no matter the sum, from the next-door maid who'd sprung herself from prison, cut up another woman, and put Rocky Hill in a tizzy. Plus Mr. Allbright was adamant I not risk the exposure—why, the federal marshals would have jumped for joy if they'd found out Zithra Jackson Brown was still alive and living the high life in France. And I was *done* with jail. So, between protecting you and protecting myself, I made my peace with being an invisible guardian angel, and, to be honest, honey, I came to enjoy looking on your life from the outside, relieved that you'd never have to know your money was coming from a common criminal. But I had the strongest itch to lay my eyes on you at least once—that's why I cajoled Larry Fortinbras into escorting me to Massachusetts, so I might spy you in your finest moment. Saw you I did, though I was almost late for your play! And, dang it, if you'd just stuck out your last year of college, don't you know I'd have snuck back one more time to see you waving that Harvard diploma in your hand, knowing *I'd* helped put it there—it would have been like I was getting that degree too! Well, *that's* not to be, is it? My fault for allowing the good Mr. Allbright to convince me to let you take that semester off, it gave you a wicked taste for freedom! Then the crash came, what with Tommy's death and Them scooping up all the savings; and without money there was no carrot to tempt you back on track."

Zithra sighed, heavily, before she continued.

"It made me feel sick to my stomach, it did, wondering how you felt when Mr. Allbright broke the news. I was sure you were thinking dark thoughts about the person who'd given such sums, then taken 'em away without the decency to explain why. One day, I dreamt, I'd have the chance to tell you face-to-face what really happened, hoping you might forgive this sad self. When I heard tell you'd moved to my side of the world, well, I fantasized more than ever about us meeting. Now that God Knows Who is threatening to rip the shirt off my back, I decided the time was now or never." She squeezed my hand. "I knew it would lift my spirits to see the gentleman I made of you. And I wanted you to meet me while I still *look* like a queen, even if I don't live like one no more!"

As Zithra unfolded her tale, I had found myself increasingly dreading, with an irrational return of the paranoia that the initial crossing of our paths had planted deep in my psyche, that any moment she was about to make impossible demands of me. I recoiled, precisely because my conscience told me that there *was* a claim, there *was* a duty, involved in this unsolicited tie that chance had knotted.

Fortunately, Zithra misread the look of dread showing on my brow. "Here I am dumping my woes on you and forgetting your own! What's eating at you, dearie? I can see it on your face. Is it the money?" I blushed, since I'd actually been thinking how little I wanted to entangle myself in the financial problems of this revenant, however transformed she might now appear. As my cheeks reddened, Zithra's eyebrows raised. "I know! Newton Seward, you're in love!" Her face beamed with delight. "Is she beautiful?"

"That's not it," I stuttered—the *she* in question was another ghost of the past I had yet completely to lay to rest. "Well, yes... but it's over." I paused. "She *is* beautiful."

It turned out Zithra had a sentimental affinity for love stories, whether they ended happily or sadly. As she drew me out, I found myself unfolding bits and pieces of my long history with Mary Jo, a history that also entailed explaining who Marky and Mr. Julian were—although, for fear of hurting Zithra's feelings, I refrained from revealing my belief all these years that the old man was my benefactor. Another hour passed, and another, as we relived that Fourth of July at Furnace Creek and talked about how Zithra had first espied the Judge's black book and begun to hatch the plot that only came to fruition after her arrest and escape, the stratagems by which she had eluded the authorities hot on her trail and contacted Mr. Allbright as she made her way out of Virginia, and her adventures assuming false identities in order to leave the States. The more we talked, the more accustomed I grew to her presence. By afternoon's end she had become an elderly lady with perfect comportment who nodded in empathy as she listened to me, more beneficent fairy godmother than the glowering convict whose countenance, for years, had permeated my thoughts like a stain that wouldn't fade away.

"Come back, tomorrow," she said, when I finally rose from the chair in which I had sat for hours, first numbed to the core and then spellbound. "Let me see you one more time. Tomorrow morning at nine?" She put her hands on my shoulders and looked up at me with those eyes I remembered so well—"So tall! so handsome!"—and I bent my head so that she could kiss my cheeks. Perhaps she left the faintest trace of lipstick, I do not know, but as I turned to exit, and as she smiled at me, waving those famous hands, I saw that the gloss on her lips remained as perfect, undisturbed, as ever.

35

DAYS OF RECKONING

As draining as Zithra's revelations had been, the immediately following days proved even more emotionally wrenching. One morning I
had been sitting in my actual benefactor's drawing room, paying my
second call and beginning to lay out a scheme for placing her beyond
the reach of those she called her persecutors; two mornings later I
was sitting in the drawing room of Mr. Julian's house on the other side
of the Atlantic, my mind void of all earthly plans as I contemplated,
with sadness and pain, the imminent demise of the man who had fed
my belief that I owed my good fortune to him.

I sat on the worn Duncan Phyfe sofa with Mary Jo; Marky
sprawled in his usual easy chair. An unexpected addition was Miranda Fortinbras, who occupied a nearby loveseat with Mr. Allbright
and glanced at our downcast faces with sympathy. Having returned
to Andover for her summer break, Miranda had generously offered
to accompany Mary Jo, still sheltering with the Fortinbrases, on the
long trek to Virginia. For years Miranda teased me with the threat of
visiting my place of origin to see how many of my Southern tales were
pure fabrication. This pilgrimage was far from the pleasure trip she'd
envisioned.

Worn out by our hasty travels, we had fallen silent. Mary Jo and
Miranda had arrived yesterday afternoon; Marky, the dark circles under his eyes darker than usual, had flown in from Fiumicino late last
night; Mr. Allbright and I had landed in Washington D.C. direct from
Paris in the wee hours of the morning and driven a rental car to Rocky
Hill. Hank Atwater hovered restlessly in the background, shifting
from foyer to the kitchen area without so much as offering us a glass
of water, so Mary Jo took it upon herself to brew coffee. I hadn't seen
Bruno Epps, who was upstairs keeping vigil with the on-duty nurse.

Two weeks before, his bronchitis having finally abated, Mr. Julian had been released from the hospital. But over the past few days

his health had taken a severe turn; both the doctors retained by Bruno and the physician from Franklin General agreed that the end was nearing and that the best course of action was to allow Mr. Julian to pass his remaining time, barring a fresh medical emergency, in his home under round-the-clock supervision. Over the past twenty-four hours the final downwards spiral had begun. Mary Jo had been able to spend time with Mr. Julian when he was awake yesterday; this morning Marky and I were awaiting word that we might go upstairs and pay our respects.

Every now and then I surfaced from my dazed state to look at the dreary room—dreary as my thoughts. The house was finally succumbing to entropy and ruin. The sheers hanging by the French doors had so yellowed that they were dissolving into shreds. I sat on a rent in the Duncan Phyfe upholstery where the cushion's stuffing inched its way forward like a cancerous fungus. A stain of mysterious origin had obliterated much of the design in the carpet under my feet. Even more dispiriting was the fact that Bruno had set up his gym— weights, dumb bells, pressing bench—on the back patio in direct view of the French windows. I noticed that the Ming era Foo Dog ceramic lamp that always held pride of place on the side table by Mr. Julian's reading chair had been replaced by a cheap brass contraption no doubt purchased at the downtown Woolworth. And I noticed that my favorite piece of statuary, a late-Roman bronze likeness of Adonis, wasn't standing on its pedestal. Perhaps it was under lockup, with the other valuables that Mr. Julian had once claimed thieves were plotting to steal. Perhaps. It was as likely that Bruno or Hank, anticipating Mr. Julian's death and the loss of their positions, had hocked it for a tidy sum. Well, I thought grimly, they'll have their comeuppance when I make it known that the most valuable antiques in the house had been standing under their noses whole time, the massive Sheratons and Heppelwhites from which the old man's legatees stood most to gain.

I didn't feel like wasting my emotions on such petty crooks, not at a moment like this. Other, sadder thoughts pervaded me as I tried to imagine how I would feel standing before Mr. Julian with my altered understanding of the source of my prospects and ambitions. What twisted part of his fancy had so enjoyed toying with the hopes of a vulnerable sixteen-year old boy? It was cruel. The inward pain to which such thoughts gave rise was almost too great to bear.

Only three nights ago, back in Paris, I had asked Mr. Allbright the same plaintive question—*Why did Mr. Julian lead me on?*—once we finally sat down to dinner after my return from Zithra's apartment. I had left my true benefactor's apartment mentally and physically exhausted; seated across from Mr. Allbright at the Brasserie Balzar, a bustling bistro downhill from the Sorbonne, I discovered I was ravenous. The fine Chateau Montrose St. Estèphe that Mr. Allbright had selected helped numb the complicated emotions the afternoon's discoveries had unleashed in my thoughts. Previous occasions had taught me that Mr. Allbright was no stranger to fine wines and dining. Now I learned that he was no stranger to Paris and other European capitals. The fact that he had traveled as widely as Mr. Julian in his day revealed unsuspected depths behind his placid demeanor. Next I'd learn he had a beautiful mistress awaiting his arrival in every city.

"Shoot away, Newt," he said as we settled into our food. "After the ordeal you've been through, you've earned the right to ask anything. All's fair game tonight."

I took up the gambit by asking the most pressing question on my mind: why had Mr. Julian let me believe he was the maker of my fortunes?

"Too much time on one's hands, and too solitary a life, shut away from the world in a big house like that, can do strange things to a person's mind," Mr. Allbright replied. He straightened his place setting. "Mr. Brewster was already something of a local legend when I arrived in Rocky Hill. I sensed something had broken in him when he moved home for good."

"Do you know what happened?"

"Oh, there were rumors that he'd been involved in a scandal that made him fearful of returning to New York. From a legal point of view, I take gossip of that sort with a grain of salt. Contrary to popular opinion, in my line of work I've found that the effect, the aftermath, is the important thing to examine. Pay heed, Newt: origins are much overrated. Causes remain a muddle to the end, shrouded in the mysteries of the human heart. In the case of Julian, there were so many possible origins for the disposition that came to be—the tensions between him and his father, the deaths of two siblings, decline of the family fortunes, a broken heart, who is to say?"

A good dinner unlocked a degree of loquacity in Mr. Allbright that belied his reputation as a man who kept his opinions to himself and his words to a minimum.

"So much for origins. From the moment Mr. Brewster became my client, I saw the effects: a fragile man hiding his hurts under a mask of whimsy and imperiousness that, over time, ate into his soul and transformed him into the invalid you met—the old man who delighted in dominating others, who could be petty and mean. That's not to say I believe he was being deliberately cruel in leading you on. No, I think he'd lost touch with some essential aspect of reality, after spending so many years in the bubble he'd built around himself. Once you, Newt, entered that bubble, you became part of his fantastical construction of things, and it so appealed to his fancy that you would think him your secret benefactor that the fiction became real to him."

Bestowing me with a look of tacit commiseration, Mr. Allbright extended his wine glass to clink it against mine. "Yes, it *was* wrong to encourage your illusions, and yes, it gave him an unhealthy sense of power, but he didn't mean to *hurt* you. However perverse his actions struck me then and strike you now, they were warped signs of affection. Sad thing is that he wanted your approval, wanted you—a smart young lad who showed every sign of moving up in the world with *or* without anyone's help—to think of him as a man capable of goodness, of generosity." As for his own role in these proceedings, Mr. Allbright had felt bound to honor Zithra's anonymity until she wished her identity to be revealed. Nor had he revealed it to anyone else, although Mr. Julian threw more than one hissy fit at Mr. Allbright's refusal to let him in on the mystery. Mr. Allbright had also let his client know what he thought of encouraging me to believe he was the architect of my expectations.

"But I felt I couldn't steer you otherwise without distracting you from the goal, the *effect*, that Zithra had in mind—producing an educated, sophisticated, genteel young man who could hold his own with the best, a young man for whom the world was possible. I saw the risks in her plan, but I trusted—not incorrectly I hope—that your powers of self-reflection would put you back on track whenever the temptations of having so much capital at your disposal became too great."

"I'm not sure I am a better person."

"I *know* you are. Cheer up! And, for the record, your mysterious benefactor's generosity was actually an inspiration to Julian. There's no reason you would know, but he's been bankrolling Samson Washington's college education; his allegiance to George Geronimo for standing by him all those years was deep and strong. And he's always done well by Mary Jo and Marky, and although they don't need it, they'll be the major beneficiaries of his estate. You didn't hear it from me—far from me to raise hopes after all you've gone through—but you'll find yourself remembered as well. Bitterness has twisted his heart, but he does care for others. And *we* can take heart in that!"

We talked, as well, about Zithra, my secret patron and shadow. Mr. Allbright had represented her when she'd been charged in the insurance fraud scheme that landed her in the county penitentiary. He'd taken the case *pro bono*—he made it a point to represent, without fanfare, a few impoverished Afro-American clients every year; he considered it a moral obligation. His aversion to the injustices his forbears had heaped on the race ran deep, revealing yet another side to the man most denizens of Rocky Hill took for granted.

"Not that that gal was anything but guilty as heck. She was a crafty one— always had an agenda going." He chuckled. "Saw that instantly. But I also saw some fire there, some grit, that intrigued me enough to take her case on, even though she didn't stand a chance of escaping conviction. But she was sharp as a tack and a born survivor. Still, I was shocked when she called me days after her prison break with her audacious scheme: how like her, to have gotten her hands on the Judge's black book just when she needed the leverage. She had it all figured out."

Flush with a second bottle of wine and a flood of reminisces, Mr. Allbright conceded that he was a perfect advocate to execute Zithra's plan: he'd seen enough back-of-the-courtroom action over the years to suspect Leroy's hands were dirty as they came, and he had no qualms about being the agent of the Judge's comeuppance, as long as his actions appeared above-board—and Zithra, he said, knew just how much *not* to tell in order for Mr. Allbright to carry out her commission without getting involved in whatever illegalities she was committing to leave the country. He chuckled, once again clinking our glasses as he added what was becoming obvious to me. "I may look like a boring man, but I've got my passions, and serving justice is one of them!"

Zithra had come a long, long way from her beginnings to the woman who ended up in Paris as Tommy Beauchamp's last love. Mr. Allbright explained that she had told him how she first became aware of herself when she was a very small girl apprehended for thieving tomatoes from a garden. All she knew was that her name was Zithra Jackson Brown, and that someone had abandoned her along a sandy country road, and that she had been hungry for a very long time. Mr. Allbright supposed her parents had been Depression era vagrants, and either she'd been left to fend on her own, or had wandered away from a campsite, somewhere in what he deduced was eastern North Carolina. After the owners of the garden had caught Zithra belching up the tomatoes that she'd ravenously devoured, unripe and rotten alike, the authorities placed her in the county orphanage, where she learnt that survival meant outwitting the other wards in an eat-or-be-eaten universe. She was always a strong girl, big for her age, strapping arms and legs—which, Mr. Allbright mused, was probably why she was taken into foster care by a sharecropper's family. "Till she was ten or thereabouts, her memories were mostly of working the tobacco fields dawn to dusk, not understanding why she wasn't allowed to go to school like the four white children who had their own room to sleep in while she was obliged to make up a pallet in the pantry."

Suspecting she was missing out on something called life, she ran away one summer's evening, blindly heading north, where a kindly retired minister of the United Colored Methodist Church took her in. Turned out he wasn't so kindly, or so retiring, once she reached puberty; for the next two years he crawled into her bed at his whim and had his way with her. But by day he taught her how to cook and clean house, and she attended school for the first time in her life, so the experience, however traumatic, added to her arsenal of survival tools. The sexual abuse ended when a schoolteacher finally got wise to the minister's carryings-on, and Zithra found herself in another orphanage—somewhere west of Richmond, she vaguely remembered. There she remained till she was fifteen and ran away again, this time with another girl from the institution. They grubbed out a living, stealing what they could, doing odd jobs, camping in the woods. Sometimes her friend turned tricks for money, but Zithra declared she never once sold her body—she gave it where she chose.

Eventually her friend fell under the influence of a pimp, and Zithra split before he had a chance to sink his fangs in her. Around that time she met Johnny, a grifter who swept her off her feet, and the two of them lived in various locales across western Virginia, skipping town before too many people caught onto their game: more survival skills under her belt. Zithra's late twenties found her settling down with a new boyfriend who held a respectable job as a car mechanic, and eventually the two of them relocated to Rocky Hill. There, Zithra lived the straight life—tried out her hand as a beautician but finally got tired of straightening hair day in and day out, then hired herself out as a maid to a series of middle-class households, including the Leroys. She began to weary of such a tame life. Meanwhile her boyfriend started drinking too much and she threw him out after one too many fights. So Zithra was ready and primed, in all the wrong ways, for Sherlene Williams' proposal that they partner together on an insurance-fraud scheme that involved stealing the identities of old widows and collecting their annuities.

Zithra's judgment may have lapsed in allowing herself to be taken in by Sherlene, but her brainpower was running full throttle once she'd left Sherlene bleeding in a ditch, happened upon me at Furnace Creek, contacted Tom Allbright, and—to this day he didn't know exactly how—acquired the passport that landed her safely in Paris.

And then, as she'd already told me, life began again the September afternoon Thomas Ravenel Beauchamp spied her hands caressing that delicate demitasse cup.

"Ah, Tommy," Mr. Allbright chuckled. "I met him several times, and a character he was! A savvy entrepreneur and something of a playboy, yet a sentimental goof at heart who thought he'd gone to Paradise when Zithra became the new love of his life. Lord knows what his parents would have made of his high jinks! His mother was one of the Ravenels from Louisiana. Mr. Beauchamp, Tommy's father, was a Frenchman she met on her grand tour, and she never looked back. The two of them beat the Lost Generation by a decade in discovering the modern art scene in Paris. You see, Tommy's father ran a smart galley not far from here, just north of the Luxembourg. He was one of the first to show Cézanne and Matisse, so soon enough he was rubbing shoulders with the American newcomers. Tommy started out in his father's business, but he itched to play higher stake games than waiting for the next expat to plunk down a wad of cash for a jumble of paint, so he started investing here and there, poking his finger in this and that enterprise, some on the up and up and some, I leave it to your imagination, flying under the radar."

Mr. Allbright signaled for the waiter to bring us brandies. Between the emotional roller-coaster I'd been on all afternoon, the evening's rich food, and the inexhaustible flow of wine, I found myself floating on an astral plane where the words made sense, but the complete picture was broken into as many pieces as in the cubist paintings sold by Beauchamp Sr.

"Like Zithra, Tommy had a bit of the con-artist in him. In that way they *were* the perfect match. The last war wiped out most of his fortune, but by selling some art he inherited from his father, he managed to start over again, and right around the time you were born he began his cosmetics empire." And when he came up with the idea of a special line for women of African heritage in the Sixties, he hit pay dirt.

"It was a smart business move, but it also sprang straight from Tommy's heart—he'd always had a thing for black gals—maybe it was a reaction to his mother's Dixie roots. His first wife hailed from the Caribbean and created a sensation in the Follies back in the 1920s. Right after the war he married again, another black woman, this one a singer. Héloise turned out to be high maintenance, especially after her career tanked, but, shrewd harpy that she is to this day, she made it impossible for him to shake her completely. Long after they separated, he bought her the Place Vendome apartment where she still lives in style, and he footed most of her charge accounts to keep her off his back—that's the dirty little secret he forgot to tell Zithra. Like I said, he was a sentimentalist. I imagine he kept telling himself he'd get around to divorcing Héloise and marrying Zithra proper, and I imagine he meant to provide generously for Zithra. He's not the first financial wizard I've known to neglect putting his house in order before being called to the Pearly Gates."

"Tommy really left her nothing?"

"That's the truth of it. I've done a little digging, with the help of our mutual acquaintance, Larry Fortinbras. All Tommy's assets—everything was in his name—went to pay off the loans he'd taken out to finance business schemes that went bust or investments that didn't earn back their cost. So the lenders are basically taken care of, far as we know. He left Héloise a life insurance policy and some valuables, so she's not hurting. But Zithra got nothing but the possessions she claims were her own or were gifts—everything you saw crammed into that little apartment."

"What do you make of this gang of thugs she claims is harassing her now?"

"You're touching on the real problem. I suspect they're fronts for a power-broker in one of Tommy's shadier business ventures, some silent partner left holding a tab who's royally pissed off—in a word, someone who couldn't make an official claim on the estate since his dealings with Tommy were off the books. He's hired these goons to frighten the wits out of our friend since he suspects she's sitting on a load of valuable loot."

"Is she?"

"Between the jewelry Tommy lavished on her and her collection of antiques, there's a small fortune sitting in that apartment."

I asked whether Zithra were in danger. Mr. Allbright bit into of one of the chocolate truffles that the waiter had left with the bill. "We aren't in Sicily, but Paris has its home-grown Mafia. It's not a pretty picture, and Tommy should have known better. *Danger* isn't too strong a word."

"Then we've got to get her out of this situation. I owe her that."

"I've been pondering it." Mr. Allbright set his American Express card on the bill without looking at the sum. "The hard task is convincing Zithra she has to relocate to a place where no one knows her till this blows over. With as much property as we can get out of the apartment without tipping anyone off."

"So you suspect she's being watched?"

"Count on it." Mr. Allbright nodded knowingly. "I've hired a private investigator to check it out. I've put him in touch with Larry Fortinbras as well. We'll puzzle a way out of this."

We stood to go.

"I want to help."

"That's very decent of you, Newt. Zithra may not have been your ideal benefactor, but she did mean well. Between you, Larry, and me we'll see to it that she lands somewhere safe. It's good you're here to help us." He gave me a wink. "Consider this our own little walk on the wild side!"

*

How surreal to think that conversation took place only three nights before I found myself back in Virginia. As planned, I paid Zithra a visit the following morning, but when I returned to the hotel Mr. Allbright met me with a grave face. Mary Jo had just reached him with the news that the end was in sight for Mr. Julian; she'd also alerted Marky, who was departing as soon as he could book a flight. The next morning Mr. Allbright and I took off from Orly and now we all sat in Mr. Julian's living room, thinking our separate thoughts.

The faint whir of the elevator coming from the direction of the kitchen snapped us to attention. Footsteps followed, and Bruno Epps walked into the room, dressed in his usual outfit—hospital-style scrubs—and he looked as formidable as ever. Obviously he'd been putting the gym on the patio to good use, as his chest threatened to split his shirt in two. His nightlong vigil at Mr. Julian's bedside had left him with a rough beard.

"Doctor Faraday increased the dosage on the palliatives last night," Bruno announced, as if he were holding a Presidential press conference. "Mr. Brewster's mind has been wandering badly, and his moments of hallucination were unnerving him. With the extra seda-tives, he calmed down and slept most of the night, and now he's alert and thinking clear enough. He's asking after you. He'd like Mr. All-bright to step upstairs first, if he would."

He turned, and Mr. Allbright followed him. When the lawyer re-appeared, twenty minutes later, he took me aside. "He asked about us being in Paris together, and I filled him in—I figure it can't hurt at this point. So he knows that you've been introduced to your proper benefactor, though I didn't tell him the specifics. He's ready to see you now."

As I entered the familiar bed chamber, shimmering with its worn red and golden hues, I saw that a hospital bed had been set up on the opposite side of the room from the canopied bed, directly under Ju-lia's portrait. If Mr. Julian cared to turn his head, he could look out the windows onto his ruined domain. Instead, he turned his head to look at me, as I waited my signal to approach.

"Is it you?" he asked.

"It is I, Newt," I answered.

The nurse who had been sitting by his bedside quietly depart-ed, leaving me her chair. Bruno paced at a distance, and Hank leaned against the wall, chewing his nails. I was annoyed to see them both lingering with no intention of giving us privacy. I forced myself to will them out of mind as I took Mr. Julian's thin hand in my own.

His sunken face looked ghastly, a wreck of what had it had once been. His pale blue eyes seemed even paler as they struggled to fix me in their gaze. His feathery hair had not been colored for weeks, so he was now haloed by half an inch of white roots that clashed with the blonde tips.

"You've come home."

"I've come to be with you."

"Rome is home now, eh? And the *two* of you living there!"

"Almost like old times," I tried to jest.

"I think not."

"You're right. Marky and I *have* changed. We're getting on with our lives."

"Mr. Allbright tells me you've recently made a discovery."

"I've met my benefactor. You did know, didn't you, that I thought it was you?"

"Forgive me, Newt." His hand tightened on mine, his blue eyes grew watery. "I should have been a better man. Don't despise me."

"I want forgiveness and direction too much to be bitter with you."

I kissed him on the forehead. His clammy skin tasted of metal.

"Will you keep an eye on Mary Jo? I worry, she seems so sad."

I smiled. "You asked me to keep an eye on her when she arrived at Radcliffe, years ago. I always have, and I always will. You *know* how much I once loved her. I'd still give my life for her."

He was silent for a minute, then asked: "Does it hurt?"

"I can bear it."

"And Marky? He's going to make his mark, after all, isn't he? Marky's mark! I would have never guessed he'd be the first of you three to realize his dreams!"

"I wish I had his passion."

"Maybe you do. You just have to unlock it." Mr. Julian chuckled faintly, as if something had just occurred to him, and he pointed a frail finger at a stack of photographs on the nightstand. "The key's already in your hands. Just find the lock, like you and Marky did when you found Enzio's studio."

The photos were the ones Marky and I had sent him documenting the dim interior of the studio: the bare room itself, the broken easel, the view from the window, the date on one of the discarded newspapers, the design on the bathroom wall, the hidden compartment.

"You and Marky came so close, so close, to unraveling it all!" Mr. Julian reached under his pillow and extracted the envelope we'd sent him as well: *For J.A.B.* He mustered a smile. "To have this is nearly enough."

I squeezed his hand, and he fell into a drowse. I sat, in silence, looking from his face to the portrait of Julia above his bed, and I compassionated us all.

When he returned to consciousness, with a gasp of breath that rattled his chest with a frightening noise, he looked at me wildly, and then he seemed to breathe a sigh of relief.

"Bruno, send up the twins. Newt, you stay here, by my side. It's your place."

Mary Jo and Marky entered the room and affectionately kissed their guardian. The sight of Marky, his long dark hair flowing around his face, was enough to inspire in the old man something of his familiar, sardonic, mad cackle.

"The sight of you, the sight of you!" he wheezed as he tugged at Marky's hair, choking on his own sense of the hilarious.

Mary Jo lifted a water glass to his lips and the choking subsided. Then he motioned for me to rise and stand beside my friends. We linked arms.

"All three of you—what a sight!" he chuckled merrily. The cornflower blue of his eyes seemed to wane, as if he were seeing through us. "Then and now, now and then, happy threesome, where did all the time go? Are you there?"

His eyes closed, and he was gone.

34

THE OTHER SIDE

After the funeral, we barely had time to catch our breath before plunging back into our tumultuous lives. Returning with Miranda to New England, Mary Jo continued to parry a barrage of erratic messages from her estranged husband: nasty threats alternating with pleas that he'd never lay another hand on her if she just returned. Meanwhile his lawyers' behind-the-scenes bulletins suggested that Offenbach might submit to a no-fault divorce after a face-saving separation of some duration. Marky flew to Rome, already several days late for a shoot. Urgent business that had amassed in Mr. Allbright's absence forced him to remain in Virginia for a few more days, rather than accompany me back to Paris. So I returned alone, armed with the lawyer's instructions for setting into motion the first stage of our plan to extricate Zithra from her situation. I thanked the stars that Carlo was the most accommodating boss in the world. He seemed less concerned about having to schedule around my absence than about my being able to return to Rome in time to complete my latest whimsy of a design—a desk combining brushed copper and Deco-inspired wood veneer— so that it might be displayed in his fall line.

Mr. Allbright's undercover Parisian contacts, working in tandem with Larry Fortinbras, helped determine my course of action once I unpacked my bag in the sweltering top floor room of a fleabag hotel—lodgings that befitted my reduced circumstances—on a particularly raucous street in the Latin Quarter. Prior to a planned meeting with Zithra, I joined Larry for petit déjeuner at a nearby cafe. On my left Notre Dame's twin towers rose above the linden trees bordering the river, on my right waves of eager tourists blinked like moles as they poured out of the St. Michel metro exit. I hadn't seen Wim's eldest offspring since he'd brought Zithra to my Phipps graduation; what had been a mere bald spot now encompassed most of his shaved cranium, and, sitting in a Pierre Cardin suit, tie properly Windsor-knotted, speaking to the waiter in flawless French as he glanced at the menu through bifocals balanced on the bridge of his nose, he looked and sounded every bit the august financier that he had become, seamlessly blending into the city that was now his home. Like Mr. Allbright, he possessed one of those deadpan faces that gave away little, though every now and then I thought I spied some of his father's sageness about his eyes. After exchanging a few pleasantries—having just seen Miranda, I was more caught up on the Fortinbrases than he—we settled into the task at hand.

"Tom and I agree that the first order of business is to put Zithra beyond reach of her harassers, which means getting her out of Paris. But as you've no doubt already discerned" (Larry let flash a rare smile) "she's an imperious lady with her own mind. Which makes all the more difficult persuading her it's imperative to leave behind the high life she and Tommy Beauchamp shared. Stubborn as a mule, but what a class act! A stranger would never guess her past."

I asked how he and Zithra had met.

"Through Tommy—he'd brought me on board as a financial consultant for the new cosmetics line, and he couldn't stop crowing about the latest love of his life. We were on quite friendly terms, he'd taken a fancy to me and liked to think he'd taken me under his wing— though, quite frankly, a week or two of looking at his books made it perfectly clear he was the one who might need some serious taking care of. Be that as it may, he took me to dinner one evening at La Tour d'Argent where Zithra joined us. She walked in that restaurant like she owned the place. Over dessert, she started in on This Boy she wanted to shower with enough advantages to make something of himself. The way she talked about you, Newton Seward—like you were some kind of wonder! It confirmed my suspicion there was more to the woman than met the eye. Honestly, how many glamorous models that double as the Boss's mistress do you find fantasizing about becoming a fairy godmother? We talked over possible scenarios, I mentioned Phipps, my father's boarders—and the rest is history."

My history. All the more reason to help Zithra now.

I asked Larry what he made of the most recent threats, noting that Zithra genuinely seemed terrified.

"She's been running scared since Tommy's death. It wasn't just finding out that he hadn't divorced Héloise, or learning that he'd never got around to revising his will. Tommy, you need to understand, was the foundation on which she had built an entire new self, and losing that equilibrium has shaken her severely. Her reaction's been to bunker down in that apartment, hardly leaving for fear she'll return to find it stripped bare of all the momentos she's crammed in there. At first I thought she was just being paranoid—after all, Tommy's legit creditors got their fair share a while back. But the incidents over the last month convince me that some truly unscrupulous types believe she's held onto some property worth their while and have her in their sights."

Tom Allbright had already briefed me on what he knew of this escalating persecution, and Larry added new details. There had been a series of threatening letters and phone calls, charging that Zithra had made off with a small fortune in Tommy's personal possessions that were rightly theirs in lieu of the huge sums of money owed them. The warnings repeated themselves from one message to the next: you better keep looking over your shoulder for muggers; watch out for speeding cars when you cross the street; don't eat something that lands you in the hospital. If I were in Zithra's shoes, I'd be worried too.

"Another letter arrived two days ago. It'd been left in the mailbox in the foyer, no post office mark or stamp, which means the messenger got inside." I remembered the slow, heavy swing of the front door as it closed the two times I'd visited Zithra. "Somebody's done his research, because this time the threat is specific—it says if she doesn't agree to hand over everything within days, get ready to be deported to the States to face outstanding criminal charges. Perhaps in an unguarded moment Tommy let something about her past slip to the wrong person. At any rate, the threat of exposure and extradition on top of everything else has frightened her out of her wits."

It dawned on me that this was much too dangerous a situation for Mr. Allbright, Larry, and me to be handling on our own; yet the authorities who by all rights *should* be involved were, given Zithra's tenuous legal situation, the last people in whom we could confide. I asked whether Mr. Allbright's investigator had learned anything useful.

"As far as who Tommy's enemies are, no—seems like Tommy's off-the-books deals could have made him any number of foes itching for payback. So, in answer to your question, we have no clues as to who's behind the harassment. But our investigator has verified that the apartment is being staked out: same Fiat circling the neighborhood far too many times. Sometimes it parks and waits. The license plate check was a dead-end—it was lifted off a totaled vehicle that was sold for parts last year."

The challenge, then, would be pirating Zithra out of the apartment undetected. In anticipation of this difficulty, Mr. Allbright and I had concocted an exit plan before I left Rocky Hill, which I now shared with Larry. First, did he have a hideaway outside of Paris in mind once we extracted Zithra from her present abode?

"That's the easy part. I've got a small property no one knows about in a quiet village outside Avignon, name of Pernes-Les-Fontaines. Been meaning to fix it up to use as a summer place for years. Now as for your and Mr. Allbright's plan..."

*

One hour later, I was patiently sharing our scheme with Zithra in the dim light of her crowded sitting room. Larry and I had agreed that I was less likely than he to attract attention entering or exiting her building since as one of Tommy's former associates he might be recognized, whereas the stakeout presumably had no idea of my existence. So it fell to me to convince Zithra that our plan, despite her deep aversion to change, was the only viable solution to her predicament. Shaken by the rapidity with which her already diminished world was shrinking, she put up less resistance than we'd expected, ultimately bowing to the verdict that she had to leave Paris. It was harder to convince her of the steps she immediately needed to set into motion. You need, I stressed in no uncertain terms, to establish a routine—starting *today*—one that's visible to the stakeout, leaving the building each morning on a series of errands that takes you a little bit further away with each trip: going to the bank, getting your hair done, stopping by travel agencies to check the cost of cruises to, say,

Brazil. Having been a recluse for so many weeks, her watchers would sit up, take notice, and tail her to see what she was up to, which is exactly what we wanted.

Zithra bemoaned, with a diva's flair for the melodramatic, that she'd as soon die. But once I set down my foot, she steeled herself with the same grandeur that had greeted me when she'd opened her door a week before.

"I'll be waiting here," I promised as I escorted her to the landing. "When you get back we'll begin sorting through your most valuable possessions, so we can start packing them. Shall I walk you down to the foyer?"

Zithra looked at me as if I came from another planet. "I don't do stairs!"

Fortunately, the elevator seemed to be working, for when Zithra pressed the button, the wrought-iron cage began its noisy rise to our level. Minutes later, concealed by the sitting room curtains, I watched Zithra step into the fresh air, don her oversized sequined sunglasses, and adjust the scarf around her stylish bouffant (one of many prized wigs, I soon discovered, for she got positively teary-eyed when I told her she could not bring all ten to Provence). Head held high, purse swinging at her hip, she strutted forward as if that uneven sidewalk were a runway and the world were watching. A dark Fiat pulled out of a space up the street and slowly followed in Zithra's wake. She turned the corner, and I turned to face the interior of the room.

That afternoon and the following day we began in earnest to sort through her valuables, deciding which to take away when the time was right. The guest bedroom, I discovered, was occupied by a fleet of Louis Vuitton luggage, enough to sink the Titanic all over again. "So we'll pack your treasures in these treasures," I said brightly, trying to coax Zithra out of her despair when she realized she actually had to *choose* among the possessions—valuable, worthless, sentimental—overflowing the apartment. I had suggested, earlier, that I begin carrying out smaller valuables, like her jewelry, in my pockets on a daily basis, but that's where she drew the line: "No toting, Newt Seward—not a single item leaves this apartment until I do too!"

Speaking of jewelry: two vanity table drawers held enough baubles to make Topkapi Palace's green emeralds grow even greener with
envy. "I never got around to properly sorting it out," she confessed
sheepishly, fishing out of the glittery jumble a ruby bracelet. "Fifth
anniversary he gave me this. I was always partial to red."

Meanwhile, I held up a live-to-goodness tiara.

"Wore that trinket to the premiere of the 'Firebird' in 1970. But,
honey, it's rhinestones—*this* is the real thing." She unearthed another
tiara, smaller but more brilliant, and laughed, with a hint of the craft-
iness I remembered from Furnace Creek. "Tommy bought this piece
for Héloïse to wear on her final concert tour, then he swiped it from
right under her nose during their break-up, claimed it was a rental and
gave it to *me*! Oh that man!"

My eyes, traveling across an array of combs and brushes and perfume bottles resting on a doily-lined silver tray on the vanity top, suddenly widened.

"Rubies are your favorite, you say?"

Sternly, I waved in front of Zithra the item that had riveted my
attention: a silver nail file with a ruby embedded in its handle.

She chuckled. "Caught me! René Coquinelle was a family friend
of the Beauchamps, in the art business like Tommy's daddy. When I
found out his museum work was taking him to Harvard and that he'd
be at the same party as you, I gave him this file on a whim. If there's a
chance, I said to him, make sure my boy Newt notices it! Lord knows
what I was thinking, I just was hoping it might make you recollect
pore ole Zithra filing her nails for a second."

We began making two stacks—valuable items that I felt we could
reasonably smuggle out of the house in her luggage, and items that
Zithra declared she could not live without. The first occupied the dining room table; the second a pair of matching Louis XIV-style love-
seats. Soon the piles on the sofas had grown taller than the one on
the table. It just wouldn't do. Pleading with Zithra to choose more
selectively among her mementos and wardrobe—her wigs and beauty products alone would have filled half the luggage—was enough to
try the patience of a saint. I was discovering I wasn't one. When she
added Tommy's tux to her collection, I laid down the law. "NO! None

of Tommy's clothing, not one cufflink!"

On the dining room table, Zithra's jewelry had been joined by several items of undeniable worth. Tommy had been something of a gatherer of fine objects from around the globe, and my years listening to Mr. Julian hold forth on his possessions had sharpened my sense of what was most valuable among this eclectic array. The man had favored two types of collectibles in particular. First, there was a coin collection that included ancient Greek, Roman, Syrian, and Indian coins, along with Napoleonic francs and Spanish doubloons.

Second, the mantel was lined with antique timepieces and ornate pocket-watches displayed under little glass domes. Two Aztec figurines would certainly weigh down the suitcases but were portable. The shimmering remnant of an eighth-century Persian tapestry hung in a frame on the wall; I carefully detached and folded it for transport. Inside a credenza I found, wrapped in felt, a collection of seventeenth-century Japanese horticultural manuscripts, all exquisitely illustrated in feathery pen and ink; a first edition of Blake's "Milton"; and, most amazingly, what a bill of sale in 1949 identified as a Gutenberg Bible in vellum.

Clearly, some of this "loot" had been in Tommy's hands longer than he had known Zithra, so I almost began to feel for those creditors suspecting that Zithra had absconded with belongings that, legally speaking, might have gone to them. But I also shared Mr. Allbright and Larry Fortinbras's feeling that Zithra had earned her share. In a pause in our ongoing debate about how many furs she needed during her Provençal exile, Zithra dug out some folders from a secretary choked full of papers and bills, folders Tommy had asked her to keep among her personal belongings years ago. As far as I could tell, they contained several stock options as well as shares in Ebony Essentials made out in her name. I was getting the feeling that Zithra was going to do just fine if we ever got her out of Paris.

As we packed suitcase after suitcase, a giddy euphoria seized us, as if we'd grown drunk on the riches themselves. But that mood evaporated in an instant when, opening the front door to leave for the day, I nearly tripped over a hot pink and black Fauchon's shopping bag on the landing. Inside was a white box, the kind bakeries use to transport their cakes. However, the odor emanating the container was anything but sweet or sugary. Zithra looked over my shoulder as I lifted up the box—sticky pink on its bottom—and carried it to the kitchen. Placing it on the counter, I raised the lid and almost gagged: lying on waxed paper, bloody animal entrails draped an indistinguishable object. Gingerly I extracted the latter and dropped it in the sink. It was the hand of a mannequin, fingertips painted vermillion red.

Zithra gasped. Looking back in the paper bag, I found an envelope. As I slit its seal, Zithra spoke shakily.

"It's Cleopatra's Crimson."

"What?"

"The nail polish, Ebony Essentials' most popular shade. That is one *mean* way to deliver a message. They're out to drive me mad!"

Grim too was the message in the "Get Well" card I extracted from the envelope.

A printed verse promised

BETTER DAYS TO COME!

after which the sender had scrawled a few lines informing Zithra she had two days to hand over Tommy's valuables, or else she would be reading her next Get Well card inside a federal penitentiary. To signal her compliance, she needed to tape this card to the upper sill of one of the front room windows, at which point "appropriate arrangements" would be made.

I stayed with Zithra another hour, calming her with a cup of tea and a few fingers of brandy. After the fright we'd been through, I didn't need to remind her to bolt the door. The shadows were closing in, and the time had come to act.

*

A fierce thunderstorm rattled my cubicle of a room that night, the rain pinging like a thousand gavels on the mansard shingles while the humidity neared 90 percent. I might as well have been back in Virginia in August, and I spent a restless night, dreaming of storm waters turning the Seine into a churning flood that toppled the city's bridges, and in my dream I saw my body bobbing on the crest of the tide as it rushed toward an end that was near yet invisible.

The bulky wreckage pulled into the wake of the flood metamorphosed into Zithra's pursuers, swiftly, silently, surely rushing forward in a bid to overtake us once and for all, and I awoke in sweat-drenched terror, uncertain who I was and unable to fall back to sleep.

The morning was dreary, and although it was only drizzling when I left my hotel, the gloomy sky was piled with mounds of steely clouds threatening to burst at the slightest provocation. I exited my bus and turned onto Zithra's block, glancing uneasily about—in the aftermath of my dreams I felt watched wherever I turned. So I kept the umbrella low over my head as I used Zithra's extra key to let myself in her building, and I made sure to push the door firmly shut behind me. The elevator light was on so I got in the cage and pressed the button for the third floor, but the contraption shuddered and groaned so frightfully that I stopped the car at the first landing and followed the winding stairs the rest of the way up.

Once I rang Zithra's doorbell and assured her that it was only me, Newt, I slipped into her foyer, wet as an otter that's just heaved itself onto a slimy riverbank to shake itself dry.

"You look awful," she remarked as she slid the bolt shut.

The circles under my eyes were a dead give-away.

"Terrible night. Yours?"

Her body convulsed in a shudder. "Three phone calls between midnight and three in the morning. I picked up in case it was you or Larry. Just heavy breathing till the last call. A man's voice started chanting *dying dying dead* till I hung up... it was horrible."

I took Zithra's trembling hands and led her to a seat. There was no time to waste, as I now explained to her: when, after leaving Zithra yesterday, I'd reported to Larry the latest gruesome scare tactic, he was as alarmed as I and agreed the hour had come to set the final stage of our exit strategy in motion.

"We leave *today*—it's too dangerous to stay any longer. That means we finish packing *now*. Larry's arriving in his limo in one hour. He's bringing the decoy who'll be carrying out your errands in your place if, God willing, the rain holds back."

Now that the actual moment of crisis was at hand, the jitters that had plagued Zithra all week and that had crested with yesterday's ominous delivery vanished, replaced by a look of determination reminding me of the convict I'd first laid eyes on at Furnace Creek. No more senseless arguments over how many more dresses, shoes, wigs, or knick-knacks to bring along—we wrapped the remaining objets d'art in whatever clothing in Zithra's stack did the job best and wedged them into her bags.

"Lord, I near forgot," Zithra exclaimed, pressing her hands to her lower back as she straightened up. "I need you to go through a stack of paintings I stored under the bed when I moved in. Mostly gloomy old things I never favored though Tommy seemed to like 'em well enough."

Moments later found me on my hands and knees, pulling out a pile of framed and unframed artwork, and I immediately realized I might well be looking at the cache that Tommy's unorthodox business partners were after—artwork that, if they'd ever been visitors in the old apartment, they might have seen hanging on the walls. Many of the age-darkened oils—tempestuous landscapes, dour portraits, and cavorting pagan gods—bore signatures I didn't recognize or were unsigned, but they looked late Renaissance and early Baroque— several had details of provenance listed on index cards affixed to their backs, which I skimmed with a low whistle. "Zithra, do you realize what you've got here? A mini-museum, maybe not the masters themselves, but works by their students and disciples." Among the oils were some drawings as well—a Rembrandt charcoal sketch of young woman, a Van Dyke pen-and-ink of a watermill, a Picasso that took my breath away.

Zithra was kneeling by me by now, looking at the paintings and drawings I'd singled out for special attention. "Well silly me! I thought most of this stuff was rubbish!"

There was one final painting, the largest and heaviest of all, to retrieve from its resting place. Although it was turned upside down, Zithra recognized it by its size and frame.

"Oh, *that*," she said with authority. "Sweet portrait of Tommy. It made me too sad, so I never hung it up."

I turned it around. I'd only seen framed photographs of an older Tommy arm-in-arm with Zithra, so I'm not sure I would have recognized him from the painting I now beheld. But I would have recognized Enzio Sorrento's work, even if it hadn't borne his signature. The painting was dated 1939.

"I *know* this artist." I placed the painting flat on the bed so that I could view it more fully. "Did Tommy tell you anything about this painting?"

"Just that he sat for it eons before he met me. Look how young he is—a full head of hair!"

Magically, the face that stared out of the frame captured what I'd learned of Tommy's paradoxical character—keen in creating schemes yet sloppy in the details, all business acumen yet sentimental to a fault, proper yet a playboy. The angular, slightly cubist shapes of Enzio's strokes, the open window in back of Tommy—in this case revealing a Parisian skyline—were stylistic signatures as familiar to me as my own reflection in a mirror. The room in which Tommy stood was filled with beautiful objects that, as in seventeenth century Dutch painting, attested to the subject's status. There, amid the rich clutter, I noticed something I'd never seen in a Sorrento portrait but that was also, utterly, uncannily, familiar: standing barely visible in the background was a statue—or rather, no, not a statue but a male torso rising from a perpendicular column of the same dark stone, a herm no less, with muscular arms raised, breasts that sagged from a massive masculine chest, and a gap from which its now missing erection had once jutted forth.

Zithra, leaning forward to see what held my attention, gaped. "Well, I'll be. I never noticed *that* before—naughty naughty naughty! Don't you bet Tommy enjoyed that!"

"This is it. The final piece of the puzzle," I murmured, as much to myself as Zithra. I propped the heavy painting against the bed's headboard to view it more clearly, feeling as if I had arrived at the end of a long journey. What had Enzio written about the keys? *Follow their lead to the other side?* I repeated the phrase, as if a mantra, while Tommy's jovial eyes twinkled from the portrait and Zithra's quizzical ones frowned up close.

"Ain't no time to be going weird on me. What on earth you are mumbling?"

"You sure Tommy didn't mention the artist?"

My fingers traced Enzio's signature.

"He was fond of the painting, that's all I recollect. It hung in his home office in the old apartment. This other stuff came to him by way of his daddy."

That rang a bell—Beauchamp Sr. who, as I'd learned from Mr. Allbright, had run a gallery on the Left Bank. "Did Tommy ever tell you the name of his dad's gallery?"

"You think I have a photographic memory? You're the scholar, not me!"

Zithra turned to the other paintings strewn at our feet. "I better fetch a suitcase to see how many of these we can fit in." She was right, we needed to keep moving. But I remained riveted in place, looking at Tommy's portrait.

"Can't remember the name," Zithra grumbled from the hallway. "But it was on Rue Guissarde, near Saint Sulpice, *that* I remember if you care to know!"

With those words, the pieces began to fall into place. The gallery that had sponsored Enzio's Paris show was located on Rue Guissarde, and its name, I now realized, was a word play on Beauchamp Senior's surname.

"Galerie des *Champ*ions des *Beaux* Artes," I announced, triumphantly.

"I could have come up with that if you'd given me another minute!"

So Enzio must have met Tommy through Tommy's father, which had resulted in this commission, completed just before the German invasion of France. By the looks of it, the portrait had been painted in Paris. *On the other side.*

And the painting's other side? On an impulse I flipped the oil over and laid it flat on the bed. Like most quality framings, the back had been tightly papered over with thick brown paper, discolored by age and dented by the other artwork that had been stacked on top of it for the past two years. I pressed my hands against the paper and was surprised that it felt so solid. I thrummed it with my fingers—no echo at all. Something filled what should have been the space between the rear of the canvas and the backing.

Zithra reentered the room, tugging a large suitcase.

"Curious," I said, motioning her to join me. There was a small rent in the backing. Inserting a finger, I felt something hard. I looked at Zithra, wedged my finger deeper into the cavity, and ripped through the paper.

Zithra gasped audibly. Cradled in the confines of the frame were two large binders, both made of acetone board, and a letter.

I turned to Zithra. "May I?"

She nodded.

I undid the ribbons of the thicker binder first, instinctively knowing what I would find inside.

One glance at the trace paper confirmed my intuition—dozens more of Enzio's designs for the furniture line that was never to be. "I'll explain later," I said, closing the folder and turning my attention to the second binder: thinner but longer and wider, exactly the dimensions of Tommy's portrait. My fingers touched fine linen as I reached within. The stiff object that I carefully extracted was swathed in the fabric. Folding back the linen strips, I had the oddest sensation of unwrapping a mummy, and I held my breath as a single piece of very old canvas revealed an oil painting dominated by dramatic contrasts of shadow and light. On a rocky bluff stood a prophet-like figure, unbroken by the miseries that marked his brow and ragged body while he exhorted the bowed figures below. Near the bottom of the bluff three words appeared, as if carved into the stone:

JOB PRIMA ELIPHAZ

Caravaggio. I recalled Mr. Julian's paraphrase of Enzio's letter to Julia, in which he mentioned Eliphaz and swore never to deliver "the work of innocents into the hands of the unworthy." In a moment of inspiration or desperation, using Tommy's portrait to hide both the Caravaggio and his designs had been Enzio's way of taking these works out of the hands of the unworthy and making them the legacy of the brother and sister who had represented a more innocent time, the world before the Fall. I gently laid the priceless oil down on the bed and picked up the envelope. I knew as surely as I had known the first folder would contain Enzio's designs that the letter enclosed within would explain the invisible chain linking Enzio, the Brewsters, Zithra, and myself in this strange discovery. I knew, in advance as well, that the writing in faded lilac ink on the envelope spelled out the letters "J.A.B." I pocketed the envelope—its narrative would wait.

Turning to Zithra, I placed my hands on her shoulders. "Understand that this painting is worth more than everything else put together in this apartment. I have every reason to believe that it's authentic. Its announcement will be an extraordinary event in the art world." I picked up the thicker but smaller portfolio of Enzio's furniture designs. "These aren't worth anything to anyone but myself—may I keep them?"

She was still looking at the Caravaggio as she nodded her assent.

"My my my, I've slept lots of interesting places in my life—but on top of a fortune? Oh my!" Then she looked at me shrewdly. "Did Tommy know it was hidden in this frame?"

"I doubt he knew *what* was here," I said. "I'll explain, later, but I'm certain it was meant for someone else to find. Neither they nor the artist who painted Tommy's portrait is living to claim it."

"So it's—"

We were interrupted by the downstairs entrance buzzer. Over the intercom Larry Fortinbras tersely announced his arrival and we buzzed him in. Opening Zithra's front door, I waited on the landing and watched the elevator cables creakily lift the cage into view, revealing Larry with a middle-aged black woman standing by his side. The elevator groaned to a stop ten inches short, forcing the two to step up to gain the landing. I ushered them inside and Zithra bolted the door. Larry introduced Luciette La Neige.

"We have a lot to do, and very little time," I told Larry, explaining the paintings we'd uncovered and still needed to pack.

"It's already time for Zithra's stroll," Larry said. "Zithra, do you have Luciette's outfit ready?"

The final stage of our plan was at hand. Luciette was an office manager Larry had known for years and trusted completely. Although she was perhaps ten years younger than Zithra, the two women were of a similar height and weight, so when Luciette emerged from the bathroom minutes later arrayed in one of Zithra's dresses and sporting one of her coiffed wigs, she was already starting to look the part she had been enlisted to play in our scheme.

Once she had knotted a Hermes scarf over her head, buttoned herself into Zithra's rain jacket, slipped Zithra's favorite alligator purse onto her arm, and—ultimate touch—put on Zithra's oversized sunglasses, the transformation was complete. I noted, with some satisfaction, that Luciette even had Zithra's shapely legs when I handed her down into the elevator, which was still paused ten inches short of the landing. The elevator jerked into service and Luciette disappeared from sight. With an umbrella shielding her face from the drizzle as she walked away from the building, no one would ever tell the difference between the two women. Her mission included several stops over the next hour that would take anyone on her trail far from the neighborhood. At the end of the hour she would disappear into a friend's apartment building from whose rear door she would emerge as her real self once the coast was clear.

Having dispatched our decoy, the three of us feverishly set to work in Zithra's bedroom, taking paintings out of their heavy frames, wrapping them in slips, towels, and pillowcases, and fitting them into the remaining suitcase. The folder protecting the Caravaggio proved too large, however, which caused me a moment of panic; I didn't dare damage the brittle canvas by rolling it up. Zithra solved the dilemma, suggesting that we fit it in the immense hanging bag in which she'd packed a mid-knee sable coat that she had insisted she couldn't live without and that I'd just as vigorously vetoed as unnecessary bulk. As we fitted the fur around the painting, she gave me one of those "I told you so" looks that, if I weren't so anxious to be gone, would have sent me roaring in aggravation.

"Would you like to bring Tommy's portrait, too?" I asked, since it was the same size as the Caravaggio.

Zithra thought for all of two seconds before dismissively tossing her head. "I think *not*... damn fool should have seen to a new will and saved me all this trouble!"

I hated leaving a Sorrento behind. But it couldn't be helped. I shoved it into its original hiding place under the bed and hoped for the best. Five minutes later, we succeeded in lugging all six heavy pieces of luggage plus clunky hanging coat bag onto the landing. As Zithra stood in the doorway, taking a final look at the remains of her home, my heart went out to her. Our speedy exit was forcing us to leave behind enough valuables—antique furniture, crystal, rugs, figurines—to make any collector ecstatic, so our flight was not going to leave Zithra's pursuers empty-handed. Whatever sentimental thoughts may have been passing through Zithra's mind as she silently paid her farewell to the life she was leaving behind, her last act when Larry declared it time to depart was to rip the "Get well" card that had arrived the previous day to shreds, its pieces littering the front door mat.

"Let 'em take *that* for my answer!" she declared, slamming the apartment door shut behind us.

Larry pushed the elevator button to summon the cage from the foyer. Just as the elevator machinery whirred into life, a series of loud crackles and pops followed, and the system shut down completely.

"It can't stop now!" Zithra moaned.

"We've got to hoof it," Larry said sternly. "Grab all you can." He clutched two bags and strapped a third over his back, heroically leading the way. Zithra followed, struggling to guide one enormous trunk, onto which she had balanced the valise containing all her jewelry, down the winding stairs. I took up the rear, the bulky fur coat bag over my shoulder and the largest suitcase in my other hand. The bags bumped against the banisters and bruised the walls and our legs as we descended the narrow stairs with all the speed they allowed.

It was hardly a quiet getaway.

But not so noisy as to disguise the distinct sound of the front door opening below as we gained the second landing. "A neighbor?" Larry whispered. As the door groaned on its hinges as it began to close, we heard it squeal open again and heavier steps rush into the foyer.

"*Vous ne pouvez pas faire irruption ici!*" a female voice protested. "*Allons-vous!*"

A loud smack was followed by a groan and the sound of a body dropping to the floor.

"What should we do?" I whispered.

Someone in the foyer must have pushed the elevator button, for the unpredictable piece of machinery decided now was the time to whir back to life. We watched in fascinated horror as the pulleys hanging in the open space between the winding stairs rotated and the cage commenced its jerky rise.

Larry hissed us back into action. "Now!"

Again he led the way as we charged down the narrow flight of stairs, no longer worried about the horrendous racket we were making. We'd just rounded the corner to the first floor landing when the elevator reached our level. For a split second, we found ourselves staring into the unpleasant eyes of the two men in the ascending cage. As it continued upwards, one of them yelled, "*C'est la femme! Arrête maintenant!*" and jabbed at the elevator buttons violently.

This elevator, however, had a mind of its own, and continued to groan upwards as we threw ourselves down the stairs, now within eyesight of the foyer. All of a sudden the contraption violently shuddered to a stop. I looked up, expecting it to descend any second. Instead there was no sound or movement at all and the electricity in the building went out with a deafening pop. Gazing up into the dim light afforded by a skylight in the roof, I saw that the cage had frozen to a stop between the second and third landings.

"*Merde! Cette putain d'ascenseur!*"

Stuck in their makeshift prison, its riders vented maledictions that echoed down the stairwell as we felt our way, sweaty and gasping for breath, into the foyer.

A man was kneeling in the dark by a woman who lay flat on the floor, feeling for the veins in her neck.

"Her pulse is fine, let's hope she just got the wind knocked out of her by those goons," he said, looking up at Larry. "Saw them follow her in, so I jumped out of the car and wedged my foot in the door just as they got into the elevator. I didn't know what to do, till I saw that box"—he pointed to a metal fuse box in the lobby wall—"and threw all the switches." He grinned. "Seems to have worked."

The man turned out to be Larry's driver. He tossed the keys to Larry. "Better drive yourself, I should take her to the hospital."

Already, we heard doors opening above and tenants calling out to each other in the darkness, so we knew we had no time to debate our course of action. With a final rush of adrenalin, we pulled open the massive door, heaved the baggage into the limousine, and piled onto its seats. Looking out of the rear window as we sped away, I saw that Larry's driver, with the young woman in his arms stirring to life, had just hailed a taxi. No figures had yet emerged from the door of Zithra's apartment building, and there was no sign of suspicious cars on our tail. Had we actually made a clean break? As we swerved around one corner and then another, I dared to hope that a new chapter was about to commence for each of us in that speeding car.

36

"LIFE IS BEAUTIFUL!"

By the time we reached Fontainebleau it was early afternoon and the fitful downpours that had chased us out of Paris had ceased, like a satisfied dog that's finally given up nipping at the wheels of the postman's van. As sporadic rays of sun glanced off the hood of the car, Zithra rolled down the window of the passenger seat and held her right arm out, the wind filling her sleeve like a balloon. "Oh happy day!" she laughed. "Life is beautiful right about now!"

Larry Fortinbras and I shared Zithra's jubilation, though we expressed it in different ways. Larry drumming his fingertips on the steering wheel in rhythm to acid rock booming from the radio was a sight to behold. Scrunched into a corner of the backseat by the luggage that hadn't fitted in the trunk, I felt a tremendous pressure—buoyant as a lifesaver in a cold mountain lake that's just broken the surface and popped into dazzling light—give way inside me. What a wonder that Zithra's summons had led me to discover Enzio's parting gift to Mr. Julian! If only he had lived long enough to hear this final installment of the quest on which his friend had sent us—but I was growing old enough to know there are no perfect endings.

In the speeding sedan, I explained to Larry and Zithra the story of Enzio's relation to Mr. Julian and his sister, the rupture caused by the partnership-gone-bad between the two fathers, the isolating effects of the war, Enzio's last attempt to communicate, and the chain of interlocking circumstances that prompted me, kneeling by Zithra's bed, to turn Tommy's portrait over. And as I opened Enzio's letter, reading its thirty-five-year-old message to my fellow passengers, I again felt a sense of wonderment at being the medium through which Enzio's words finally made themselves heard beyond the grave—read not by their intended addressee but, fittingly enough, by a youth who had known and esteemed that recipient despite his too human frailties. Yes, the letter announced, *if you are reading these words you have used your ingenuity, as I dared hope you might, to find the phone number I left for you in my studio. And it has connected you, as you now know, to one Thomas Ravenel Beauchamp, son of the owner of the gallery whose acquaintance you made back in '32 when you attended my Paris show. A few years ago Tommy asked me to paint his portrait. I traveled to Paris for several sittings over a six month period, during which time I learned that he was a man with a big heart and faith in his friends, and, if you are reading this letter, a man who has been as good as his word. Over time I confided to him my tortured relationship with my father, and I eventually made it known that I wished to smuggle some items for you, dear friend, out of Italy. So he allowed me to take this portrait back to Rome for its finishing touches, where I made its frame the haven in which to bring back to Paris these amends I offer you. I never got to share all the designs I created for our furniture line, and you are the only person, aside from Julia, who might appreciate them, shadows of what could have, should have, been. Keep them, ideal forms never realized in this world, in your thoughts and I will feel they have achieved some small bit of immortality.*

The painting is a Caravaggio—the real thing. Much better in your hands than my father's. A few months before I received Tommy's commission, Father ordered me to Napoli to authenticate the artwork belonging to an old aristocrat who had died intestate, the descendent, so the deceased had avowed, of one of the original knights of Malta and last of his line. My orders were to spirit away any paintings valuable enough for Father to sell on the black market before government officials confiscated the property. Some of Father's Neapolitan associates had alerted him about the impending seizure and paid the necessary bribes to get me onto the property in advance. I despised myself for being forced into the task. You can imagine my shame.

Then I spotted this painting, hanging quite obscurely on a wall covered with a dozen other poorly lit paintings. Instantly I knew what I was seeing, the lost work of a master, and just as instantly I knew I would do everything possible to keep it out of my father's hands. Luckily, the collection contained enough good art to give me something to deliver to Father, and I concealed the Caravaggio among the canvases in my studio. As I grew to know Tommy, I decided to take a chance. While I suspect he is a man who, like my father, doesn't always deal in official channels, unlike my father he is a kind man and, I sense, a man of his word. He never once asked me what I wished to convey into his safekeeping and has vowed that if he ever hears from you—I gave him your name—he would allow you, and only you, to extract the items affixed to the rear of his portrait.

I told him that they were remnants of a broken dream. I think that appealed to his romantic imagination, for he's a bit of a poet. So are you, if you'd allow yourself to follow the rhythms I've sounded in your heart and soul. Who knows if you'll ever read this letter? Probably not, and I'll no doubt have long since met my fate. But that doesn't mean I won't be watching and smiling.

Be well. E.S.

Enzio's words triggered Zithra's sniffles as he wrote of Tommy's integrity. My eyes welled, too, as I contemplated all the remnants of broken dreams that crowded my short life. And I am sure Enzio's words reminded Larry of the goodness that he had also sensed in Tommy, a goodness moving him to participate in our insane adventure to liberate Zithra.

Outside of Fontainebleau, Larry pulled into a rest stop where we revived ourselves with cafés crème and croissants while he checked in with his Paris sources via payphone. His driver reported that the female tenant he'd carried from Zithra's building was *très bien*, if a little unnerved, a condition he hoped to improve by taking her to dinner that evening. His Herculean efforts, Mr. Allbright chuckled, might just prove the beginning of a fine romance. Luciette informed Larry that she had made it home undetected ("Can she return my alligator bag?" was Zithra's comment). The private investigator didn't know what giveaway may have led to the attempted raid on Zithra's apartment, but tenants in the building excitedly told him that when the gendarmes arrived to see what the ruckus was all about, they discovered the concealed weapons that the two men trapped in the cage were carrying and promptly conveyed them, handcuffed, to the nearest precinct for questioning.

Six hours passed before we approached Pernes-les-Fontaines,

twilight turning the foundations of the medieval castle on whose precincts the village had been built a roseate pink; violet shadows outlined its crenellated arches and broken battlements. Larry's house, built into the inner walls of the former fortress, may not have been Zithra's dream of paradise but would have delighted any aspiring artist looking for a picturesque retreat. Life is indeed beautiful, I thought, half envying Zithra her hideaway. Larry had alerted a local to prepare the place for our arrival, and we'd barely eaten a cold dinner of crusty bread, pungent cheeses, and country sausages before we yawned our way into our bedrooms and fell, each of us, into deep sleeps between ironed and starched cotton sheets scented with fresh lavender. Our epic day had ended, and the sounds of the night spoke no more of criminality and mayhem, but of crickets and lowing cows and the occasional dog saluting its neighbor.

Next morning was back to business. On the trip down, Larry had explained that he would take charge of Zithra's valuables, making them available to reputable appraisers, opening a bank account in which to deposit the proceeds from their sale, and, in consultation with Zithra, looking into investments that should assure her income for the rest of her life. Zithra acceded with the grace of a well-bred lady who knows how to count her blessings. So the morning was spent separating Zithra's personal belongings from those that Larry would carry back for sale, and then repacking the latter in storage containers we'd purchased passing through Avignon. Several hours of daylight remained to wander the quaint village and introduce Zithra to the local residents and shopkeepers, several of whom Larry already knew. Over dinner at a local bistro, Larry assured Zithra that a year here, keeping a low profile, would give him sufficient time to sew up the financial side of things and then—we raised our flutes—she might choose to live wherever in the world she wished, provided it wasn't Paris or the States. In a few days Mr. Allbright, who'd been updated on the recent developments, would be arriving from the States, his plan to drive down to Provence first thing to make sure Zithra was settling in comfortably. As for myself, Larry would drop me off at the train station in Avignon on his way back north. From there I would transport myself to Marseilles and thence to Rome. I pictured Marky's awe as I told him the story of a lifetime that I'd compressed into the last twenty-four hours.

Saying goodbye to Zithra on the morrow was difficult. The woman who had once loomed in my youthful imagination as a frightful criminal and reminder of my own baseness had been replaced by a sophisticated woman of the world who had transformed, during our recent days of intimate intercourse, into a softer, more gentle person who, in turning to me for help, became someone I strove to love and respect. If she deserved my commiseration, her presence also taught me not to be so hard on myself, to put behind me my lost youth. If she deserved to live out her remaining days without fear, her presence also made me look forward to exploring the directions my own future might take.

Larry and I finished loading up the car, which we'd parked in the shadow of the old fortress wall. Zithra, dressed to the nines, lingered in the shade as she embraced Larry and then turned to me.

"Newt, honey." Her glossy lips broke into a wide smile. "Whoever would have guessed that summoning you to Paris was going to take us on this wild ride! You done right by your Zithra—don't think I don't know it! When Larry sorts out all this money business, we'll see about getting you back to Harvard. In the meantime, do right by *yourself*." She enfolded me in those still amazingly strong arms and planted wet kisses on both my cheeks.

"I'll visit," I promised. "First I need to prove to Carlo I'm still worth employing, but I'll return soon as I can. And I'll bring Marky—he'll be dying to meet you."

"I'll be here waiting." Zithra smiled a radiant smile. "Now it's high time you menfolk skeedaddle, if you intend to get back before dark. Don't worry about me—Zithra's going to be *just* fine. It's a beautiful life!"

I hugged her tight, forcing back tears battling to blur my vision. Zithra stepped back, and, lifting to my face those incredible, painted nails—miraculously undamaged in our mad struggle to convey that cumbersome luggage down so many stairs— wiped the corner of my eyes with her fingertips.

"Don't go gettin' sentimental on me, Newton Seward the Deacon's boy. Remember, I got the goods on you!"

She laughed deeply, her musical contralto reverberating against the medieval stone walls, and, turning away, she raised her right hand in a slow, majestic wave that looped through the air as she sashayed out of the shade and into the house while we settled into Larry's car. She never once looked back.

*

Marky welcomed me home with open arms, eager indeed to hear my tales. What I had to say astounded him. My life felt by comparison a slight narrative—but one I was ready to claim as my own. Zithra's story, though, was not quite finished, as I learned upon receiving a most remarkable call from Larry a few days after I'd resumed life in Rome. While packing the valuables that Larry would be taking with him, I'd created an inventory of all the items, making copies for Zithra as well as Larry. So Larry knew of which he spoke when he listed everything that had gone missing: the Caravaggio; the sketches by Rembrandt and van Dyke; the Picasso; the Guttenberg; the Persian tapestry. And when Larry opened the valise that held Zithra's fabled collection of jewelry, he found in the place of her baubles dusty pebbles from the front drive of the house in Provence.

At first, I couldn't make sense of what Larry was telling me. I was trying to figure out how her antagonists had tailed us to Pernes-les-Fontaines and when they'd made the switch. But, as I listened, Larry's laconic tone made the truth unbearably clear. Zithra had flown the coop. Long before we'd reached the village, she must have decided that monastic seclusion, however pastoral, was not to her taste and already been calculating which valuables would convert most easily to ready cash in the nether world in which they were doubtless in the process of being fenced. So eager was she to disappear that the loss of all the goods she left behind, as well as the forfeiture of the life-long security that Larry's investments surely would have yielded, were as nothing to her. I mourned that the Caravaggio would never end up, as it deserved, in a world-class museum, that instead it would find its way into the private collection of some billionaire who would pay a flat sum in cash less than its worth, off the books and no questions asked: lost for these centuries, it was once again dispatched to oblivion. You had to hand it to Zithra; she demonstrated excellent taste in deciding which loot to take with her.

The day after I talked to Larry, Mr. Allbright arrived in Paris only to learn from Larry that Zithra's actions had rendered his trip in vain. Although the two men harbored no great expectation of finding Zithra or any of the missing items, they decided to drive down to the house in Pernes-les-Fontaines anyway and check it out. Their instinct was correct. Zithra had left with nearly all her personal belongings and effects. In fact, she only left two personal items behind, one large, one small. The former was the fur coat that she'd so adamantly insisted was essential to her wellbeing—I had to suppose she was heading to warmer climes where it wouldn't be needed after all. The other item baffled Mr. Allbright and Larry Fortinbras when they found it on the dining room table. It was a silver fingernail file, a ruby embedded in its upper edge. Give credit where credit is due: Zithra knew I'd get the joke, since, frankly, it was on me.

I had no doubt that Zithra had left France and that she was traveling under the name of Loretta Fishbone, the alias on the passport she had used to enter the United States to check up on her prodigy at Phipps. By my calculations it was good for at least another four years. We could have attempted to trace the name on flight protocols. But where was the use? Bolting had been second nature to Zithra all of her life. If attaining freedom finally involved a bit of prevarication, a dash of the con-artist, and an element of financial risk, so be it: she had made her choice. As for me, I chose to believe that our involvement in her recent woes had helped her break free of a genuine paralysis and fear for her immediate future. I assumed we would never hear from her again.

Once again, she proved me wrong. Two years later a letter arrived, forwarded from my old Rome address to my new residence in Milan and postmarked Buenos Aires. Inside was a fine sheet of linen stationery, embossed with a Spanish coat of arms. I half-expected to see a brazen "Z" plastered across the page in nail polish when I unfolded the sheet. No, that was not the alphabetic choice of letters this time. Instead, Zithra had used the nail polish brush to paint a huge smiley face—below which ran an entire line of alternating x's and o's.

*

Meanwhile I got on in life. It goes without saying that Zithra's promise of making available the funds to send me back to Harvard went south with the lady herself. No matter; I had already resolved that that part of my education was behind me—I was ready to move forward, not backwards. Over the next year I designed and assembled more pieces that met Carlo's approval, and I would have been happy working for his small enterprise indefinitely. But Carlo strongly believed I needed to test my wings, and he pushed me out of the nest by securing me an internship with a design firm in Milan. I didn't want to leave Rome, but, as he lectured me, if I meant to take this profession seriously, I needed to educate myself in all its levels of operation. So I submitted to a trial run at the Milano firm, vowing to return to Rome as often as I could. That turned out to be less often than I intended, since Marky took the occasion of my absence to make the big leap—moving in with Fabrizio—which meant giving up the Ghetto apartment. Thus Marky Sumner beat us all in settling down, a fact that amused Mary Jo as greatly as it bemused myself.

Not long after I returned from my adventure with Zithra, Mary Jo decided to return to Paris permanently; the city offered her memories of a more pleasant epoch, one that she hoped she might revive in her future. Fred Offenbach's attempts to woo her back had lessened over the months; the last time he tried to plead his case in person by arriving in Andover unannounced, Miranda had met him at the door and answered his belligerence by giving him a black eye. He evidently enjoyed receiving physical pain less than he did administering it, and a year and a half later Mary Jo was granted the divorce she'd sought. In Paris she began seeing a French surgeon who admired her greatly, and whom she moderately admired in return. I wondered whether she would ever be truly happy—there was a pensiveness in her demeanor that never entirely disappeared.

"Oh, I've only grown wise," she would say, laughing away my concern. Did growing up, and growing wise, mean that she would never risk falling in love, that she would settle for a more muted happiness? I wanted to shake her and cry out "No!" but, in truth, these were the same questions I also asked of myself. Sometimes I felt too scarred to feel a deep passion ever again. Sometimes I felt engulfed in solitude. And yet, sometimes, as I surveyed what had become of my life, I felt myself in reach of something like true contentment, for which I was grateful. But those feelings had nothing to do romantic love.

The nearest I had to a constant companion in Milan stared at me from the wall of my new digs: Enzio's portrait of Mr. Julian, hanging over my drafting table. Tom Allbright had delivered the Sorrento to me in person, some weeks after Mr. Julian's will had been read—how like Mr. Allbright to fly across the Atlantic at a moment's notice and on a mission of mercy.

Yes, I keenly remembered Mr. Julian telling me that he intended for me to have the painting, but, no, he had failed to mention it in his will. Indeed, the reading of that document had been a shock to nearly all parties solemnly gathered to hear the old man's beneficence declared to the world. Those in attendance included Mr. Allbright, who only days before had learned that the will and testament he had drawn up, and occasionally amended, had been superseded by a more recent document, witnessed and signed in Mr. Julian's shaky but unmistakable hand less than a year before his passing. This new will had been executed by a lawyer from Richmond, one Luther Munroe, J. D., and in it Mr. Julian left the bulk of his estate to Bruno Epps and Hank Atwater, "indispensable companions to the bitter end." Those smug weasels must have been very proud of themselves for sticking it out all those years—it was easy to picture their hands all but guiding Mr. Julian's quavering one as he signed this last testament.

Every living relative, including Mark and Mary Jo, had been left exactly one hundred dollars, no more or less, along with an amulet to be filled with Mr. Julian's ashes, which they were admonished to wear around their necks for the rest of their lives if they truly revered him. Mother went on a minor rampage when she heard about the behests; she'd been convinced Mr. Julian intended to make a rich man of me at the end of the day. I didn't even merit an amulet. Mother's hopes were excusable, in that I'd never confessed to my parents that the actual source of my schooling lay elsewhere. It seemed too cruel—too confusing—to introduce the specter of Zithra Jackson Brown into their lives at this late stage in my faulty expectations.

Given this turn of events, I saw little reason to inform Bruno and

Hank that, along with the property, they had also come into a cache of museum-worthy furniture. Mr. Allbright agreed with my decision when I confided in him, and we were both recompensed for our silence when, as we expected, the two men sold the entire property, en masse, to a developer within the year. The buyer, smarter than Bruno and Hank, had an appraiser look at the furnishings and sold the best of the pieces to the Smithsonian, the Boston Museum of Fine Arts, and the St. Louis Museum of Art—realizing a profit that made the two men, when apprised of their loss, seethe and made Mr. Allbright and me smile.

The fact that I ended up with the Sorrento portrait I owed to the audacity of Tom Allbright, who, sitting with me and Marky at a trattoria around the corner from the Pantheon, related the whole incident with a glee that belied his staid demeanor. He'd been right ticked off to learn that Mr. Julian had supplanted his legal services with those of an outsider. Admittedly, Mr. Allbright would have refused to follow orders had Mr. Julian in his late, delusional state expressed to his wish to leave everything to Bruno and Hank, so perhaps Mr. Julian showed a remaining flicker of wisdom by leaving his adviser of thirty years in the dark when he changed his will. Nonetheless, it rankled. Sassafras, who had been working at Mr. Allbright's house on the day of the reading, saw that her employer was bent out of sorts when he returned home. A sworn foe of Bruno and Hank since they'd unceremoniously fired her, she proposed a remedy for the lawyer's drooping spirits. That very evening, while Bruno and Hank celebrated their good fortune at the finest restaurant in Rocky Hill—which isn't saying much—Sassafras and Mr. Allbright availed themselves of the master key to the Brewster house, which the cook had never relinquished, to let themselves into the mansion.

Marky laughed with glee. "You *broke* in?"

Mr. Allbright's pink cheeks turned pinker, and he dabbed at a trace of puttanesca sauce on his lips.

"I shouldn't call it *that!*"

It was Sassafras, bless her soul, recalling Mr. Julian's affection for me, who had suggested to Mr. Allbright that they make off with the Sorrento portrait and put it, as Mr. Julian always intended, in my

keeping. Once they had removed it from the wall, leaving a conspicuous white rectangle marking its absence from the spot where it had
hung for half a century, Mr. Allbright decided that he might rather
enjoy the portrait of Julia as his personal souvenir of the Brewster
dynasty. Sassafras couldn't be persuaded to take any memento, thoroughly satisfied with having helped carry out the heist. (Enzio's portrait of Tommy, I am happy to report, Larry Fortinbras had discreetly
retrieved from under Zithra's bed after our adventure; he'd toyed with
handing it to a museum but liked the old man so much he decided
he'd keep it—poor Enzio's portraits seemed destined for our private
viewing pleasures.)

So Sassafras and Mr. Allbright loaded both paintings in his Cadillac and made their furtive way home. Inevitably Bruno and Hank
would spot the absence of the portraits—but my erstwhile burglars
counted on the fact the two men would count their blessings and not
raise the alarm. After all, they'd burgled themselves into Mr. Julian's
affections and made out like bandits, so who were they to complain?
Raising a third glass of wine, Mr. Allbright solemnly declared the portrait of the man I had once believed my benefactor to be, on ethical
and moral if not precisely legal grounds, my possession to treasure—
and then, less solemnly, confessed that making off with the paintings
had rallied his spirits considerably.

I rather wished Sassafras and Mr. Allbright had thought of souvenirs for Mary Jo and Marky. But the twins had their share of fond
memories of the guardian who'd always doted on them, and neither
wanted for anything. Both, in fact, were tickled with their amulets,
which they happily wore around their necks, at least when it matched
the outfit of the day.

Marky was sporting his amulet when he visited me in Milan in
the spring of 1977.

He was wearing a black shirt, half unbuttoned, and the on-
yx-stoned amulet, strung on a thin silver chain, hung sexily between
lean pectoral muscles. Beautifully tailored gray slacks, thin belt, and
Prada loafers completed his outfit—his hipster rags had been relegated to the trashbins of yesteryear. His usually wavy hair was tightly
pulled back into a ponytail, accentuating the marvelous bone structure he shared with Mary Jo.

"You look like a prince, Marky. And now you're dressing like one."

"What can I say?" he chuckled. "My recent gigs have been paying really well."

He was on his way to a shoot for Bernardo's film—at long last in production—at a location north of Lake Como. The crew had stopped in Milan overnight, and Marky had called ahead to see if I were free. We sat in my apartment sipping grappa. Soon enough, he'd have to return to his hotel, as the crew would be departing early morning.

"You look... you look so *happy*," I said. "I swear I'm almost jealous!"

Marky laughed.

"I'm not only happy." We were sitting beside each other on my sofa—one I'd designed myself—and he leaned forward and gave me a fierce hug. "I'm in love. In love. Marky Sumner is head over heels for Fabrizio de Rosa! Yeah, yeah, it's perfectly bourgeois of me, but it's also pretty fucking awesome!" His laughter was infectious, and I hugged him back with all the years of feeling that I'd stored up for him.

"He's the best," I said. "I mean it, he's one in a million. Or at least in a thousand!"

"Now it's your turn," Marky said. "Mary Jo is dating her doctor, who seems a nice enough guy, I'm settled in for the long haul, so baby, we're counting on you!"

I thought about what Marky had just said, and I thought about how completely transformed he now was. And as I thought these thoughts, an electric shock coursed through me, along with a feeling I never anticipated. *This* was the Marky Sumner I could have fallen in love with, the Marky Sumner who might have succeeded in seducing me those many years ago had he been more like this. And now it was too late to do anything about it.

"What's the matter?" Marky asked.

Without thinking I bent towards Marky, taking the smooth curves of his face in my hands, and I kissed him with all the yearning and sadness that had so unexpectedly flared in my heart and body. For the longest time we held that kiss, Marky returning its pressure with a tentative hunger that soon matched my own as our hands roamed up and down each other with raw desire, clutching, feeling, kneading, molding flesh out of clay, breathing into the other shape and life.

Then, in one accord, we both drew back, flushed. Marky spoke first.

"What was *that* about?"

"I'm so sorry. Forget it."

"I'm confused, Newtie. What's the *it* here?"

"I don't know, I just feel"—I took a breath and looked at Marky—"I *want* you, the person you are now." I thought of Samson. "I guess I'm always too late."

If I'd been younger, I would have blushed beet-red making such a confession. Now, as Marky's gaze bore into my own, the blood had drained from my face, leaving it ashen.

"I love you, Newt—"

This time Marky made the first move, squeezing me in an embrace so tight I wanted to cry.

*

I'll never forget the last words he spoke that night, as he took both my hands and looked at me with an honesty that was part of this new Marky, this man who had just awakened my deepest desires.

"Give me some time. Wait till I finish the shoot. Nothing's impossible."

We were both shaking, overwhelmed by the moment. Once he had closed the door behind him, I felt ecstasy and despondency course through me with equal intensity.

Wait for me, Mary Jo had told us both, the evening of her wedding.

Marky's crew departed for Como the next morning, they wrapped shooting in two intense days—all this Bernardo told me afterward. It was the best footage yet. They partied hard after the shoot was finished, and, in the Alpine village where the film had really begun to come together, they got high on a synthetic drug that one of the crew had supplied. It was reckless of them, but they'd raced each other in their cars on mountain roads too precipitous for passing. But they made it through the curves and bends, as if blessed by some higher spirit, and they pulled off the road onto a lookout to watch the sun hoist itself over the snowcapped peaks. Some of the crew had broken into a spontaneous dance—a dance of liberation, if you will. Bernardo had remained seated in his car, door open, ecstatic that his dream project was one step closer to realization.

The view beyond the lookout, down the mountainside and into vales far below, was nothing short of sublime. Marky climbed on the low stone wall to salute the vistas beyond as the first rays of sunlight tinted them with color. Raising his arms, he shouted into the vast distance. "I'm in love! Life is beautiful!" Then he turned to the parked cars, to his friends, to his coworkers celebrating in the turn-out.

"Life is beautiful! I love you all!" he repeated, again lifting his arms in a rapture of triumph, and his footing slipped, and he gasped in disbelief as he fell backwards into empty space.

37

ANOTHER DAY

Eleven years passed, ten of them in self-imposed exile in Europe before I returned to live again in the land of my nativity. I gazed over my drawing table and out the open windows of my upstairs studio, my slant-roofed eyrie half concealed by the oaks and firs that still flanked the carriage house. As I toyed with the postcard in my hands, my eyes took in the undulating grounds visible beyond the late spring foliage—the swimming pool where children romped while their parents read the Saturday paper (no lap practice for me on weekends), the restored gardens whose vigorous annuals threatened to spill over the trim boxwood parterres, the putting green and driving range where the tennis courts used to be, and on the far side of the rush-filled creek a dozen new condo units that nestled into the landscape, their clean lines bearing no resemblance to the massy brick, stone, and timber of the old house looming nearby on my right.

So much changed, and so much the same: to my disappointment the developers had uprooted the towering shubbery that had shielded the pool from public view and leveled the pergola and old changing rooms; a clubhouse with all the modern facilities had replaced those richly tiled wonders. At least the memorial stone erected in honor of G.G. still graced the garden quadrant where he'd pampered his vegetables, and it was mirrored, in the adjacent quadrant, by an identical stone that, the year of Mr. Julian's death, Marky and Mary Jo had installed (no objections from Bruno or Hank, since they weren't footing the bill) in memory of the last scion of this House of Brewster. And the renovations subdividing the interior of the Brewster mansion into variously sized units had been tasteful—though no doubt Mr. Julian would have found plenty to grumble about, George Geronimo Washington even more. The drawing room and library remained intact as common areas, holding hints of their former grandeur despite the fact that the old furniture had vanished. The library, to my bemusement, still contained most of the books that I had filed on its shelves. The spaces on either side of the door, however, had given way to magazine racks displaying popular journals.

When I returned to Rocky Hill the previous year to help Mother after Dad's successive heart attack and stroke, I knew I needed to find a place of my own were I to survive reimmersion in a place I once assumed I'd left forever. Several years had passed since Bruno and Hank had sold the entire Brewster property—land, house, furnishings—to its enterprising developer for a hefty sum, after which they decamped from Rocky Hill in high spirits. According to the local wags, Bruno split his time between Atlanta and Hilton Head, as he was no longer obliged to ply his services as physical therapist. Hank hightailed it out of town in a brand-new Corvette convertible, his destination Las Vegas, where he squandered money on bets and showgirls.

The transformation of the huge mansion into apartment and condo units had been the first phase in the success story called "Elysium Estates," the name proudly announced in backlit letters attached to the stone wall by the entrance to the drive. The second phase of the makeover involved the addition of the condos on the slope adjacent to the driving range and renovation of the carriage house. The latter unit was for rent when I toured the property, and I took it on the spot. Living quarters were located on the ground floor, and the open space that comprised the second story, under the slanting beams, made a perfect studio.

Strange as it was to find myself dwelling in what had been Mr. Julian's domain, it was no more strange than being back in Rocky Hill, no more strange than finding myself about to launch a line of furniture based on Enzio Sorrento's designs that was already attracting advance notice, no more strange than finding my most valuable partner in this venture to be my mother, whose years of experience in interior design added considerably to the practical considerations of running a successful business. After father passed away in his sleep, six months after my return, Mother and I became business partners, and I renewed my apartment lease.

I looked down at the postcard I held. From Mary Jo, it had arrived in last week's mail. Mary Jo still lived in Paris but was vacationing in the States. After visiting her Connecticut relatives, she'd traveled to Philadelphia, where Miranda Fortinbras had moved after finishing her law degree, as predicted, at Georgetown. Miranda was a proud single mother—the turkey baster method, she'd laughingly confided—of a three-year-old son, and there was talk of a congressional run in her future. The thought of my two friends sharing quality time up north together, while I remained down here, alone, made me pensive.

And that pensiveness led to a sharper pang as I thought of Marky, of our shared years abroad. Not long after Marky's death, I finished my internship in Milan and returned to Rome, where I assumed a series of jobs to hone my skills in woodworking and furniture design. Feeling those pieces of tongue and groove take shape beneath my fingers was the only therapy that helped me through. In time Fabrizio reached out to me, and I tried to be a decent friend, empathizing as I did with the loss he so deeply felt. But I confess that I felt an impostor in his company, given the explosion of desire that Marky and I had shared three nights before his death. A residue of guilt and shame, I suspected, would always be part of my psychology.

I might have stayed in Rome forever, had not my father's failing health reminded me of other roots that needed tending. And in experiencing the gift of time freed from a daily work schedule, I had found the inspiration, working away in my upstairs studio, to recreate Sorrento's designs for a new era and, with Mother's business acumen, set in motion the wheels that would soon make our handcrafted line of furnishings available in select stores in the United States, France, and Italy. We named the line E/J (known as "edgy" to its fans) in homage to its creator Enzio and his miglior fabbro Julian.

Throughout my years in Europe after Marky's death, Mary Jo and I saw each other whenever we could. She had created a worthwhile life for herself in Paris, working as an advocate for a non-profit organization that took her on trips around the world. Her relationship with the neurosurgeon continued, and, although she confided in me that she never felt it was quite "love," she finally agreed to wed him. Her hopes for mitigated happiness in marriage, however, were squelched as history repeated itself—the doctor turned out to be psychologically manipulative, though not as overtly threatening as Fred Offenbach had been, and Mary Jo discovered he had been cheating on her for months on end. This time, at least, Mary Jo knew when to call it quits ahead of time. "I may have been beaten and battered," she told me, half seriously and half cajoling, the last time I'd seen her, "But I still have a heart."

As for my siblings, Katie and her husband lived in Houston and had three boys. None, unsurprisingly, were named Newt. Jubal, God bless him, was now Assistant Professor of Psychology at Penn State on the fast track to tenure. His first book, on dysfunctional families in the South, was creating quite a buzz in the field. And Mother? Not only did she serve as Rocky Hill's mayor for a very successful term, she threatened to live forever. Most surprising of all, our business partnership gradually made us appreciate each other in ways unimaginable in my youth, and as our intimacy grew, so did our confidences.

Mother's revelations were the most shocking; what I had to confess was of little to no surprise to her at all.

One afternoon after we finalized plans for some outsourcing details at my studio, we took our afternoon coffee out to the Adirondack chairs on the little lawn in front of the converted garage. Perhaps it was the sight of Mother looking so confident, so strong, that made me recall the utter dejection into which she had sunk a lifetime ago when she'd been raped. I wanted to express the sadness I had always felt for her misery that had always seemed forbidden to raise; I wanted to confess the guilt I'd always felt for not being home to protect her that day.

I had my say while she looked away, her eyes canvassing the far distance. After a long pause, she spoke. The culpability, she wanted me to know, was hers.

Yes, Mother had been sexually assaulted, but not by a stranger. She had been desparately unhappy in her marriage, for years I now learned, and for months she had been carrying on a passionate affair with a man she had met at her Wednesday art class in Ferrum. She'd fantasized about leaving us altogether but finally couldn't bring herself to take the step. When she broke off the relationship, her ex-lover had shown up at the house threatening to tell my father the truth, then grown violent and assaulted her.

As Mother lapsed into silence, a myriad of emotions coursed through my limbs: anger; sadness; amazement; and, finally, compassion.

For I understood. I too had always wanted a way out of Rocky Hill. I too had harbored guilty secrets. She had recreated a self that she could live with, remaining here in Rocky Hill with her compromised expectations.

What she couldn't understand, she admitted a month later, was why *I* had come home, how I could be happy back in Rocky Hill. You should be sharing your life with someone you care for, she'd challenged me, words uttered out of the blue one evening as she sat in the corner banquette of the kitchen watching me wash up Sunday dinner dishes. I smiled at her, over my shoulder.

"I am sharing my life with someone I care for."

"You know what I mean. Is it because you're gay, son? You don't have to hide it from me—*please*, I've been around designers long enough to have learned a thing or two. And you shouldn't be hiding away here in Rocky Hill—I mean, of all places, what are your chances of finding a partner worth your salt *here*?"

So, finally, I said it: "Yes, I'm gay." But, I hastened to reassure her, I hadn't come home to hide. Doing what we were doing together was what I *wanted* to do at this point in my life. When it was time to go, I promised I would.

"You need to trust me."

She looked at me sadly, shaking her head. Drawing on her own experience, she had doubts.

Mother, of course, wanted for me to live the romantic narrative that she'd denied herself; she *needed* to believe that a different ending was possible. I remembered how I used to fantasize that some day Hank's alibis for the afternoon of Mother's rape would prove false, that new evidence would reveal him as the villain *I* needed him to be. But some crimes, like some romances, don't have tidy endings. Sometimes we have to learn to live with the holes that our wounded pasts carve in us, building a life around those empty spaces. Mother had learned to do so; I was learning the same.

And this May afternoon, sitting at my drafting table, looking across Mr. Julian's lawn, I took stock of the home I had created here in Virginia. I looked again at the postcard Mary Jo had sent me, and I felt life passing. To shake off my mood, I decided to write in my journal; Carlo had given me the lovely, hand-tooled leather volume as a parting gift. The gesture called to mind the family good-luck charm that he'd pressed into my palm when I set out to Paris for that life-changing encounter with Zithra, all so many years ago, and I liked to think of the journal as another talisman, my special totem to ward off disaster. Since my return, I'd taken to recording on its creamy pages random observations, vivid dreams, memories that surfaced up out of nowhere, wish lists, self-abradings, imagined futures.

I inserted Mary Jo's postcard in the volume and carried it with me as I descended the spiral stair to the first floor. I poured myself a glass of Pinot Grigio, popped Lou Reed into the tape deck, and stepped out onto the lawn in front of the carriage house. Settling into my Adirondack chair, I took a sip of the chilled wine and, opening the volume on my lap, attempted to sketch Mary Jo and Marky as they had appeared to me when I had first set eyes on them. But I couldn't capture the line of their essence, not on paper, and so I closed my eyes to listen to the music wafting through the door, hoping that the twins might now emerge, in all their youthful glory, in my mind's eye.

> *Oh, it's such a perfect day*
> *I'm glad I spent it with you*

Within seconds, I felt asleep.

> *Oh, such a perfect day*
> *You just keep me hanging on*
> *You just keep me hanging on*

I dreamed that Miranda and Mary Jo had just driven down from Philadelphia to see me. They'd brought Miranda's son with them, and I saw a stranger in the back seat I couldn't recognize. I hoped it was Marky but instead the stranger was Samson, and he playfully jabbed me with both fists—he was whole again, his right hand magically restored, and we were happy to be together. Then, in the dream, we were somehow all at Furnace Creek, and Mary Jo had climbed the shot tower with me, where she took out the amulets that Mr. Julian had bequeathed her and Marky, and she crushed them with a rock. As a faint suspiration of ashes rose in the air, Mary Jo declared, tauntingly gleeful, that I was now free of the past. The sound of Miranda, Samson, and Miranda's son calling each other down by the creek reached us. I reached for Mary Jo, but she wasn't there, and I woke up, just hanging on.

Today hadn't been a perfect day, but, with the dream of seconds ago still hovering in my thoughts, I realized it hadn't been so bad a one either. I was alone, but I was alive.

Expecting nothing more, I closed my journal and stood to go inside.

37, REVISITED

A PERFECT DAY AT FURNACE CREEK

"Eleven years," I read.

Leaning over my drafting table, my journal spread open, I reviewed the pages I'd been writing, then once again took in the image on the vintage postcard I was using as a bookmark: Harvard Square before the work on the new subway entrance had begun. Mary Jo had sent it last week. If the message on the reverse side revived memories, it also roused anticipations:

> REMEMBER THE FIRST TIME WE MET BY THESE
> GATES? WE WENT TO CAFÉ ALGIERS, AND YOU LOOKED
> ADORABLE IN YOUR PREPPIE OUTFIT. PHIPPS BECOMES YOU,
> I REMEMBER SAYING. SOON, I LOOK FORWARD
> TO SEEING IF ROCKY HILL BECOMES YOU AS WELL.
> LOVE, MARY JO.

I raised my eyes to look out the open window of my upstairs studio, my slant-roofed eyrie half concealed by the oaks and firs that still flanked the carriage house. So much for the transformation of Harvard Square: what would Mary Jo have to say about the makeover of Mr. Julian's estate?

Every now and then, particularly when I drove onto the property late in the evening and passed the letters on the stone wall announcing "Elysium Estates," I found myself struck anew at the irony of the developers' choice of name. Lovely the manicured grounds were, indeed some might say heavenly. But the celestial designation hardly did justice to the sad lives that had once unfolded behind those stony walls and come to rueful ends. Nor did it hint at the existence of the mournful spirits still patrolling the premises, late at night while the new tenants slumbered on with untroubled dreams.

So much changed, and so much the same: the former carriage

house that was now my abode embodied both extremes. Such a thought had occurred to me the day I'd first toured the premises, shortly upon my return to Rocky Hill, and I'd immediately gravitated towards the just renovated outbuilding for this very reason. Taking the one available suite in the old mansion felt too close to invading Mr. Julian's sanctity. My father's reaction to the news of my new habitat when I visited the hospital later that afternoon was classic: he found it a most excellent omen that I would be occupying a space once sheltering vintage cars that, alas, he'd never been lucky enough to see, and he declared my smart decision had rallied his spirits considerably.

My gaze returned to the postcard in my hands.

Mary Jo still lived in Paris but was vacationing in the States. On her way to see the Connecticut Sumners—she was better than any of us at keeping in touch with extended family—she had stayed over in Boston to call on some old school friends: whence the inspired postcard. Her itinerary next took her to Philadelphia to visit Miranda, who had moved to the City of Brotherly Love upon finishing law school at Georgetown. Miranda may have missed making the Olympics in 1984, where Mary Lou Retton somersaulted her way to spectacular gold, but her legal career had soared just as spectacularly, and she was giving serious consideration to Democratic pols urging her to mount a run for Congress. The fact that she was the proud single mother of a three-year old son even more visibly biracial than she (the identity of the sperm donor father she kept a guarded secret) was seen as a plus rather than a negative in the forward-looking district where she resided.

This morning Mary Jo and Miranda had risen early to drive down to Virginia with Miranda's son, hoping to arrive in Rocky Hill mid-afternoon. I'd seen both women individually over the years, but all three of us had not been together since the slow hours we'd spent in Mr. Julian's drawing room as he lay dying in his bedroom a floor above. With a sharp pang I thought of Marky, who had been with us, sprawled in his favorite easy chair. How would Mary Jo react to the changes her uncle's property had undergone? I knew she wondered at the transformations that had brought me home.

The years I'd lived in Europe were a precious part of my existence; for all I knew, Italy might yet again be part of my future. After Marky's death, I returned to Rome, taking up a stint at a company that created fine fabrics, then working the production end of a contemporary brand, next joining an artisan guild to refine my skills as a woodworker—and all the while creating the occasional piece that Carlo put up for sale in his shop. In Rome, Fabrizio sought me out. Marky's death solemnized the comfort we found in each other, and the two of us became fast friends, discovering that we shared an array of similar interests and tastes that reached well beyond our common bond in having known—and loved—the same person.

Did I feel guilty, or at least ashamed, in Fabrizio's company, given the intense feelings I had shared with Marky three nights before his death? It would have been entirely within my psychology. But somehow, monumentously, no.

Every word of that final encounter with Marky will remain indelibly etched in my memory for as long as I breathe. When we'd drawn back from our spontaneous, groping embrace, flustered and breathless, and when I'd confessed to Marky my desire for the man he'd become, his answer was simple.

"I love you, Newt, only—"

"I know, I know. Only you are so in love with Fabrizio."

We were silent.

"My timing's entirely *fucked*," I'd said with a wry smile. "*Totally* fucked. I'm sorry I lost control like this."

"Don't apologize."

He'd hugged me again, in an embrace so heartfelt I wanted to cry.

"I'm not fucking things up for you and Fabrizio. Believe me when I say he's a lucky man."

"I can't explain, but unfaithful is the last thing I feel right now. I love Fabrizio, he's my life. But you are my history. That means so much to me. You don't know how much."

Wait, he'd said on parting, *wait till I finish the shoot.*

Nothing's impossible.

Wait.

I truly believe that whatever we'd contemplated in that stolen moment had since been sanctified by something deeper, by—as Marky put it—our shared history. That I could now look deeply into Fabrizio's eyes and know in my heart the loss he felt with neither shame nor guilt seemed a measure of how far I'd come since my traumatized youth. Perhaps that was Marky's ultimate gift to me.

Mary Jo and I saw each other whenever we could. Although she continued to live in Paris—where I always delighted in visiting her when time allowed—her humanitarian relief job took her to locations around the world I'd never even dreamed of visiting. Three years ago the organization was a finalist for the Nobel Peace Prize, and Mary Jo figured prominently in the press coverage. Wryly, I remembered Uncle Rafe telling my father that a most Noble prize awaited in his son's future—so much for predictions. It was through her NPO work that Mary Jo met the doctor with whom she remained involved for several years. Then the relationship arrived at the inevitable "do we finally commit or not?" stage. He was ready to settle down, have children, and although she cared for him, she did not, so Mary Jo confided in me, feel it was quite "love."

"But I do want to assure you," she told me one Christmas when I'd joined her in Paris because neither of us wanted to be alone for the holiday, "I still have a heart." She paused, smiled. "Knowing *you* has helped me grow a better heart."

In the last few years, she hadn't been dating anyone in particular. The same, too, could be said of me. I saw people, I desired to desire, but—since that final evening with Marky—I had not been struck by lightning. Perhaps the lightning had burned too close to my soul.

Over the years Mary Jo and I made several joint pilgrimages to the site of Marky's death. Italians have a poignant custom of building shrines on the side of the road where car accidents have taken away loved ones, and in breathtaking mountain passes where roads are barely wide enough to accommodate one car, these stony shrines dot the curves, sheltering weather-beaten statues of the Virgin, burnt votives, and desiccated flowers. On the anniversary of the first year of Marky's death, Mary Jo, Fabrizio, Bernardo, and I gathered above Como to attach our own little shrine to the retaining wall where Marky had slipped, so beautifully alive, into the beautiful vista below. Ours was a makeshift affair—quick-mix cement joining rounded stones that arched in the shape of a small kiln. On the inside, Mary Jo affixed a sealed and waterproofed photograph of Marky. I added the keys to Enzio's studio and the love beads Mary Jo had strung for both of us eons ago; Berto left the sunglasses he'd lifted from Godard; Fabrizio added a ring that had been a gift from Marky. Its inscription, *nel mezzo del cammin di nostra vita*, was a testament to their pledge to share their lives from this "middle point in the road" to the end. Little had they suspected the road would be so short. Mary Jo cut locks from each of our heads and braided them together, enclosing them in a locket that had been a gift from Mr. Julian. Then—in a departure from the Italian custom—we walled in our mementoes with more stone and cement, so that we might remember our relics as we left them, rather than abandoning them to theft or decay.

I suspected the next death to open on the road of my life would be my father's, and I pondered the memories I might enshrine in my heart when that day arrived. Mother had not asked me to come home to help with Dad's convalescence, but I discovered, spontaneously, that coming home was what I *wanted* to do. He'd emerged from his heart attack with his usual befuddlement and good humor but vastly weakened, and during his sojourn in the hospital his dark hair, always plastered to his head with Brilliantine, had turned snowy white. Under doctor's orders, he had retired from the car dealership, and once he was released from the hospital he spent the time he was allowed to be active in the carport under the hood of one of the family cars or in the toolshed in the backyard, inventing the strangest and most impractical gadgets: like other Sewards, he turned out to have a creative side. The gizmos kept him happy, and out of Mother's hair—now shagged and blow-dried, the French curl having never returned. He also enjoyed, immensely, playing with Katie's three young children when she and her husband traveled from their home in Houston for family visits—they appreciated Father's childlike delight as much as his childlike inventions. Jubal turned out to the true scholar in the family. After graduating from William and Mary, he'd earned an M.A. at UVA, then a Ph.D at Cornell in psychology with highest honors. Currently Assistant Professor at Penn State, his first book, on dysfunctional families in the South, was a success, making him a shoo-in for early tenure. Rueful as it sometimes made me to contemplate Jubal's success in the realm I had abandoned, I was sincerely elated that he, of us Sewards, had risen to the academic challenge and succeeded beyond expectations.

So too our mother, who, unlike our father, threatened to live forever. Her energy was unquenchable. Did I say that Mother actually served as Rocky Hill's mayor for a highly successful term? Miranda proclaimed her a feminist role model, though I privately thought that was going a mite too far. What wasn't going too far was my discovery, since relocating to Virginia, of the design tastes Mother and I shared—from colors and fabrics to shapes and volumes—and over these common interests we formed a bond such as had never existed when I was a boy living at home. With little explanation, she "got" Sorrento's drawings, indeed occasionally improved on my reconceptualizations with her no-nonsense eye for practicality as well as function, and she embraced the high concept E/J venture with the enthusiasm of a person half her age. If we succeeded, much of the credit would be hers.

Mother and I not only made a great business team; an intimacy unimaginable in my youth blossomed as we gradually learned to reveal parts of ourselves that, as adults, we only now felt comfortable enough to share.

We had just finished some outsourcing details and decided to take a coffee break outside the carriage house. Perhaps it was the way that late afternoon sun set her face aglow with such confidence, such serenity, that emboldened me to bring up that day, so long ago, when she'd been assaulted. For years it had remained a taboo subject in our family, an unspoken, unspeakable hurt that we all shared in different ways. I wanted to express the depth of sadness that I'd always felt for her misery but that, for fear of breaking the silence, I had repressed within myself; I too wanted to confess the culpability I'd always felt, but less successfully repressed, for not having been home to protect her that day.

"Oh, Newt," she sighed when I'd had my say. She turned slightly in her chair to look me squarely in the eye. "If I made you feel guilty, that's *my* sin to bear. The guilt is mine."

She was surprisingly frank, as she related the events of that day, and those leading up to it. Yes, Mother had been sexually assaulted, but not by a stranger, she now told me in an even, steady voice. For months she had been having a passionate affair with a man she had met at her Wednesday art class in Ferrum.

"I don't expect you to understand, or to forgive me, Newt, but I was so unhappy—with your father, poor soul; with the marriage; with the feeling that the house on Taliaferro Lane was a prison I'd never escape. Taking those art lessons was a first breath of freedom, and then I met Jack and let him sweep me off my feet. But over the months he became more and more demanding, insanely furious when I refused to leave you kids and your dad for him. So I finally ended it. That's when he broke the one rule I'd ever stipulated and showed up at the house, threatening to confront Harold with the truth, and we fought, and he grew violent."

As Mother lapsed into silence, a myriad of emotions coursed through my limbs and my mind: anger at the lifetime of shame I had needlessly harbored; sadness at the small-scale domestic disappointments that had led to such a large-scale tragedy; amazement at my own ignorance; and, oddly, more compassion for my mother than I had ever known I could feel.

For I understood. I too had always wanted a way out of Rocky Hill. I too had harbored guilty secrets. I reached out and took her hand, intertwined my fingers, one by one, with her own, and my heart swelled when she didn't resist my touch.

"So, you see, I *couldn't* tell the truth when they found me lying in the carport, when the doctors came and confirmed I'd been raped, when the police asked me all those questions and I pretended to remember nothing. I couldn't risk letting any of you find out how tempted I had been to abandon you. That winter I sank into a depression so deep I didn't feel or care for anything. I think I was too stunned by my own actions and their consequences to do anything but shut down. Then, when I woke up, months later, I was *mad* with energy, all I wanted to do was take charge of my life, and *do do do.*" She squeezed my hand. "Your poor father. I was unstoppable. But after that experience I couldn't go back to just being the old Jeanlyn; she was gone."

She had recreated a self that she could live with, remaining here in Rocky Hill with her compromised expectations. What she couldn't understand, she admitted a month later, was why *I* had come home.

"Why are you *here*?" she asked, out of the blue, one Sunday after I'd stopped by for noon dinner. Dad had fallen asleep in his recliner, Georgia Tech falling behind NC State in rhythm to his gentle snores. We were cleaning up in the kitchen. Sunday was one of Sassafras's days off, and Mother condescended to dry dishes while I washed.

"I'm thrilled that you're here, son, I love that we're working together on the furniture designs. But *why* on earth? After New England, after Europe, the world for God's sake!"

"It's what I want to do. For now."

She sat down in the corner banquette—the chipped yellow formica-top kitchen table had met its doom, as had the formica counters, when she'd redone the kitchen five years ago—and stared at me. "Are you truly *happy* here? You always yearned for *more*." She made me meet her gaze. "Do you remember me saying 'Go!' that evening Mr. Allbright surprised us on your sixteenth birthday? I meant it then, and I mean it now, Newt: Go, *now*—live the life you were born to live."

"I *am* living." I wiped my hands dry and joined her on the banquette cushions. "And sometimes I'm extraordinarily happy."

"You should be sharing your life with someone you adore, not us ancient folks. Don't let passion die in you!"

"I am sharing my life with people I care for."

"You know what I mean."

"Mom, believe me, I'm no stranger to love—"

"Is it because you're gay, son? You don't have to hide it from me—*please*, I've been around designers long enough to have learned a thing or two. And you don't need to hide away here in Rocky Hill—I mean, of all places, what are your chances of finding a partner worth your salt *here*?"

I started to explain how for a long time I had had sexual feelings for both women and men, but in face of her matter-of-fact question, I paused. Perhaps my truth of self, like the metaphorical ground under my feet, was shifting yet again.

"Yes, I am gay."

I'd said it: after all these years. Perhaps, after all, this was one reason I'd returned home.

"I'm sorry I haven't told you before. But that's not why I'm here—believe me, I didn't come here to hide. Being here with you and Dad, doing what we are doing, it's *right* for me now. When it's time to go, I promise I'll go. You need to trust me."

She looked at me sadly, shaking her head. Drawing on her own experience, she had her doubts.

I've said it once, and I must state it here again. Mother wanted for me to live the romantic narrative that she'd denied herself; she *needed* to believe that a different ending was possible. I've said, too, that I used to fantasize that some day Hank's alibis for the afternoon of Mother's rape would prove false, that new evidence would reveal him as the villain *I* needed him to be.

But I repeat: some crimes, like some romances, don't have tidy endings. Sometimes we have to learn to live with the holes that our wounded pasts carve in us, building a life around those empty spaces. Mother had learned to do so; I was learning the same.

*

And, yet again, sometimes poetic justice *does* seem to rule over our senseless universe: some mysteries give up their secrets at long last, betray the crime they've been designed to cover. Such was the case, it brings me great satisfaction to state here and now, regarding the status of Mr. Julian's final will and testament. "Case" is a bit strong, since no one (except the most avaricious Brewster relatives) questioned the legitimacy of the will at its reading; we accepted the fact that the contrary old man, daily growing more delusional and increasingly prey to the influence of his final caretakers, had left his estate to the two men in a self-conscious show of spite that was all too true to one side of his character. I had no doubt that Bruno and Hank had gone out of their way to convince Mr. Julian of the satisfaction that such an act would bring, alternately wheedling and coddling him till he saw things their way. But I didn't expect we'd ever learn more.

Not so Sassafras. Sometimes I ran into her at my parents' house where she cooked several days a week, sometimes when I visited Tom Allbright, and sometimes right outside my door, as it was not unusual for residents of Elysium Estates to call on her culinary skills for functions ranging from book-club teas on the terrace to children's birthday parties by the pool. No, Sassafras Beebe was convinced that someday the truth would out, revealing those two lowlifes for the scoundrels they were. On this topic she was relentless.

Which made it rather a pleasure that I arrived back in Virginia in time to witness a meltdown between Hank and Bruno. As part of his bargain with the estate developer, Bruno retained a small unit on the first floor of the old house that he occupied when he occasionally returned to Rocky Hill—no doubt when he needed to lie low, having seduced one too many a Hilton Head socialite with a vengeful husband and seeking solace with one of his local conquests. Seducing wives, rumor had it, had become his specialty now that he was no longer obliged to ply his services as physical therapist. Well, perhaps that's not quite accurate; according to Tom Allbright, Bruno had invested in a successful "massage" business near the Atlanta airport, Miss Kitty Fingers (for Discerning Gentlemen), so perhaps he taught his masseuses a trick or two from his old PT playbook. I dared not imagine how Mr. Allbright came upon this bit of information.

I was walking across the lawn the day Bruno drove up on one of his rare visits, so we couldn't help but give each other cool nods. No doubt my appearance startled him more than the reverse, as I'd been apprized of his periodic visits. He had no clue I'd returned from Europe. I discreetly turned around to watch him get out of his Cutlass Supreme. Sometime in the past decade the Man of Steel had grown a paunch, and his hair looked an unrealistic shade of black. With a smile I recalled Mr. Julian's dyed hair, and continued my walk.

That night I had dinner at my parents' house, the cooking courtesy of Sassafras. Taking the leftover lemon cake into the kitchen afterwards, I quipped that I'd seen her good pal Bruno Epps arriving at the estate. Sassafras, snapping the plastic lid on the cake container, hurrumphed. "Returning to the scene of the crime, is he?"

Two evenings later, around ten o'clock and in search of inspiration for a fabric design, I wandered over to the main house to check out the play of colors I recalled seeing in a volume on Matisse's North African paintings I'd shelved in the library in a past life. I entered through the patio's French doors into the empty drawing room. Across the way in the dim octagonal foyer, I caught the silhouette of someone moving to the front door. It turned out to be Sassafras.

"Who have you been cooking for tonight? Your bacon biscuits a hit?"

"Oh, just the usual, just the usual." B.B.'s eyes darted thither and yonder instead of looking at me as I approached. "A good night to you, Mr. Newt." All these years later, and I couldn't convince her to drop the "mister." As she let herself out, I noticed that the door to the powder room under the stairs was slightly ajar.

I returned the Matisse volume the next morning to discover that tables had been set up in the drawing room for the monthly luncheon of the Ladies' Auxiliary. When the old mansion had been renovated, the space that was formerly the massive kitchen had been closed off to create the studio that was now occupied by Bruno, and the adjoining pantry and china room had been converted into a food preparation area for events held in the drawing room or on the terrace such as this. Sassafras, arrayed in a frilly apron, was assembling Crab Louis appetizers where Mr. Julian's silver service had once gleamed.

"You just can't keep away!" I said.

"You'll never guess who *else* can't keep away. And I'm not talking about *him*."

She tilted her head in the direction of Bruno's apartment.

"I suppose I can't. Who?"

"Hank Atwater drove into town yesterday, lookin' the worse for wear when he checked into the TipTop, so my Sources say. Uh-huh." Sassafras lowered her eyebrows. "This is just between you and me, Mr. Newt. Last night Elvis Junior paid our fine Mr. Epps a call. And I happen to know he's returning tonight." Sassafras gave me a look. "Something's going down, you can be sure of that."

The intricate network by which Sassafras received and passed along her clandestine information remained a mystery to me. I recalled Zithra's similar intimations of a covert association of spies, spread ever so widely among the serving class of Rocky Hill, invisibly watching my every move and ready to blow the whistle if I stepped out of line. Perhaps Sassafras belonged to the same confederation. As she folded napkins into pyramids and placed them in the center of gold-rimmed plates, she informed me that she had it from good sources that two years ago Hank had run through his money and used his last dollar to drive cross-country to badger Bruno for a bailout. Afterwards, he removed himself to the Jersey shore. But now he was back again, like a bad dime. Having failed to reach Bruno in Atlanta or Hilton Head, he must have, for once in his life, made the educated guess that he'd find his ex-partner on hiatus in Rocky Hill.

When I begged Sassafras to reveal her sources, she responded by humming to herself and put me in charge of checking the iced tea goblets for water spots as if I'd never spoken. But she could only keep up her indifferent pose a few minutes, at which point she lobbed a seemingly innocuous question my direction. "Mr. Brewster ever show you the peep-holes in the powder room?"

In response to my affirmative, she could no longer resist telling me what she'd been up to. The custodial staff at the TipTop who'd tipped her off about Hank's arrival had also alerted her late last evening when he left the motel in his car. Suspecting he was on his way to plague Bruno, she'd hastened as quickly as her arthritic limbs would carry her to Elysium Estates, arriving in time to spy the two arguing heatedly as they moved in and out of the small circumference of vision that the peep-hole hidden behind the swinging mirror in the powder room allowed. The two other apertures had been covered over during the renovations, but this one still gave an unobstructed view into the studio apartment now occupied by Bruno.

The empty whiskey bottle on the table had no doubt helped inflame already sharp tempers. Bruno was clearly put out that Hank had tailed him to Rocky Hill—he had been ignoring the frantic messages his crony had been leaving on his answering machine for the past three weeks for good reason. Hank was demanding more money; Bruno protested that he had already gone the extra mile covering Hank's wastrel habits.

"As if I don't know the pricey honeypots you've been dippin' your dick into," Hank had sneered back. Although she was old enough to be my grandmother, Sassafras relished repeating verbatim the more salacious parts of the overheard conversation. "I could screw your scrawny ass to the wall in a heartbeat," Bruno replied, mangling his already mixed anatomical metaphors. Finally, he forced himself to calm down and suggested that Hank return at ten o'clock the next evening, at which point he would present a solution to their impasse.

"And tonight I'm getting their voices on tape!" Sassafras fetched her cavernous purse and pulled out a tape recorder.

Impressive: this model was as high-tech as 1987 had seen. "Voice activated," she said, proudly, promising to slip it into Bruno's flat the first chance she got. "And the sights the tape can't record we'll be witnessing with our own eyes from the powder room."

"We?"

"Don't tell me you want to miss out, Newton Seward!"

She was right, of course. Around one o'clock that afternoon Bruno strutted down to the pool to oil his now-overweight body in front of bored mothers whose babies were gurgling urine-flavored water in the new wading pool. His absence gave Sassafras, between main course and dessert, enough time to use her master key to slip into his apartment as fleetly as her swollen ankles allowed and position the recorder under a recliner. Its skirt hid the contraption from view. She was back in the drawing room before any of the lunching ladies started asking for their parfaits. An hour later, the luncheon debris cleared away, Sassafras was all too happy to decamp to my place and soak her feet in a bucket of Epsom salts as we waited for nightfall. "Keep a lookout for a white Ford Escort rental car," Sassafras informed me— again demonstrating her omnipotent knowledge of all things relevant regarding her foes—before settling into a cumbrous snooze.

Ten o'clock found us locked in the powder room under the staircase, taking turns at the spyhole. I'd brought along two water glasses to use as listening devices—which, placed against the wall, worked surprisingly well.

When Hank arrived a few minutes later, Bruno popped open beers before ponderously setting forth all the reasons that these handouts must cease. He ended with his final "offer": 10,000 dollars lent at 5% interest per annum and Hank's signature on a typed piece of paper attesting that he would never again ask for more money. Decent offer, I thought, considering it wasn't Bruno's fault that Hank had squandered who knows how much in just a decade. Hank didn't agree, however, as the livid visage visible through the peephole made quite clear.

"You think you're telling *me* what to do?" Hank's outdated pompadour quivered dangerously. Neither Sassafras nor I needed water-glass amplifiers to hear that declaration. "You don't get it, *pal*. I haven't come this far to be insulted with a fuckin' piece of paper, this *contract as* you call it. We're in this together, *pal*. You're going to give me everything I want, and I ain't disappearing if I don't want to. You seem to be forgetting I could wreck your fuckin' *sweet* life with all I know. You're the one who hired that two-bit lawyer to oversee the new will, I was *here* when you were doping the old man. You're up to your eyeballs in it, and I won't hesitate one fuckin' minute to bring you down."

Bruno spat back. "Bring me down and watch yourself sink in the same hole. See how long you last!"

"What ya going to do, shoot me like that damned fat cat?"

"You stupid piece of shit."

"Me, stupid? Not so stupid I didn't save some of those pill bottles—with your name on 'em—you was feeding him by the hour. And I xeroxed the checks and receipts for the antiques and silver you had me fencing while we waited for Mr. B to kick the bucket. Made out to you, remember? *Me* the stupid one? Asshole!"

Bruno sprang from his chair so quickly it crashed backwards with a bang. As he stomped back and forth, trying to contain himself, he halted right in front of our spyhole, obscuring the view. His voice had dropped a register but the menace in his tone was unmistakeable. Isolated phrases boomed out—"You sorry bastard... think you can blackmail me?... I'd sooner spend my money paying someone to wipe you off the face of the earth than give you another penny"—and alternated with Hank's shrill counter-threats.

Hank must have heaved something at Bruno, because we heard the thud of a projectile against the wall and Bruno yelling "What the hell!" As he stepped out of harm's way, I was again able to see into the room and witness Hank charging Bruno.

Spellbound, I ignored Sassafras's attempt to shoulder me aside and watched Bruno step to his left like a torero who knows his bull's weak points. Hank crashed into the recliner, sending it skidding backwards. In horror, I watched the edge of the tape recorder peek out from under the chair's dust ruffle and, turning too quickly to tell Sassafras of this pending disaster, I sent the water glass I'd set on the top of the toilet tumbling to the tile floor. It shattered with a burst that caused Sassafras to yelp aloud. She noisily slapped her hand over the peephole as if that might quell the sound.

There was no need to worry, however, because the two men's attention was immediately distracted by a loud hammering at their door. They'd failed to consider that the owners of the above unit, which incorporated Mr. Julian's old bedchamber, were the weary parents of a colicky newborn who woke wailing at the slightest noise—his screams often traversed the whole length of the back lawn to enter my studio windows. Nor had they considered that the father worked for the city police. So when he barked "Open up or I'm calling this in!" Hank and Bruno were forced to pay attention.

"What's going on, fellas?" We heard rather than saw the scowl in Upstairs Neighbor's voice as he elbowed his way into the room. "You're *this* close to disturbing the peace!"

From the new howls audible overhead, it appeared the peace had already been disturbed.

I peeled Sassafras's palm off the peephole for a glimpse of Bruno performing a contrite song and a dance before the officer, apologizing for "a friendly argument."

"Friendly? Sounds to me like you hotheads need some fresh air to cool you down while you tell me just how friendly you really are." Gesturing to the sliding door that led from the apartment to back terrace, Upstairs Neighbor grabbed each man by the shoulder and marched the two of them forward, past the recliner, and outside. I wasn't surprised to see Hank quaver before authority, but I'd never thought I'd live to see the day Bruno allowed himself to be manhandled by another dude.

Fortune smiled on us: the half-exposed recorder had gone unnoticed. And, just as fortunately, because Upstairs Neighbor was keen on walking the two men across the lawn till he was sure they'd truly chilled out, this was the perfect moment to retrieve it. I dashed into the apartment's open front door, scooped up the recorder and, with Sassafras leaning on my arm, we hurried out of the front entrance, cutting across the west lawn and through a thicket of dogwoods to reach the carriage house. We heard a low rumble of laughter coming from the back terrace—Bruno had no doubt struck the right macho tone to placate his upstairs neighbor.

Sassafras and I threw ourselves onto my sofa in giddy excitement, looking at each other as the gravity of the evidence we'd just gathered sank in.

"So they *were* scheming to get Mr. Julian's money."

"And makin' sure the poor man stayed high enough he couldn't think straight."

We imagined the elation Mr. Allbright would express when we presented our discoveries in the morning. He'd know best how to use this information to turn the screws on Bruno and Hank. But if I thought our recording was the primary proof of wrongdoing we'd be handing off to Allbright, B.B. now surprised me with another choice bit of intelligence. She had undertaken, some time ago, to locate the whereabouts of the lawyer who'd officiated at the execution of Mr. Brewster's final testament and, finally, she'd succeeded. How? By calling on none other than George Geronimo's son, Samson Washington—apparently yet one more in her legion of informants and contacts. I hadn't seen Samson in a decade, not since our confrontation in the changing room at the pool. I'd been too ashamed to reinitiate contact, and he probably felt the same. But Miranda reported that he was flourishing. Since their serendipitous meeting in Dupont Circle, they had become fast friends, graduating from Georgetown Law together in the class of 1981. Sam, as he was now called, stayed on in D.C., junior partner on the fast track in the firm of Tanner, Sisel, and Browne.

Just last week Sam had reported to Sassafras that one Luther Munroe, formerly J.D., had been disbarred three years ago for mismanaging client funds in a class action suit brought by senior citizens in retirement communities as far-flung as Fredericksburg, Lynchburg, and Newport News. It appeared that the lawyer with whom Bruno had contrived to replace Mr. Allbright in Mr. Julian's esteem made a speciality of catering to the needs of the elderly and infirm. And it turned out that earlier in his career Bruno had worked as a physical therapist at one of the old-folk homes where Mr. Munroe's services had also been proffered: theirs was a marriage of grifters made in heaven.

Unfortunately, we weren't going to be able to call upon Mr. Munroe as a material witness. Shortly after his disbarring, he had suffered a fatal blood clot more common to the octogenarians he was scamming than the hale man of forty-five he was. Regardless, as Mr. Allbright confirmed when B.B. and I shared our findings, the record of Munroe's prior activities, along with the taped conversation between Bruno and Hank, would be more than enough to put the legitimacy of Mr. Julian's final behest into question.

Nothing happened immediately, except for a happily humming Hank checking out of the TipTop the next day, which we took to mean that he and Bruno had finally reached a financial agreement that no doubt put more money in Hank's pocket than Bruno had first proposed. Bruno, a few days later, returned to Georgia, as unsuspecting as Hank of the mayhem to come once Mr. Allbright made our findings available to the Brewster clan. The last will and testament that Mr. Julian had drawn up with Allbright two years earlier differed considerably from the document Munroe had executed: in the former Mary Jo, Marky, and I each received quarter shares in the estate, George Geronimo's widow and Sassafras tenth shares, and Bruno and Hank ten thousand dollars each. The piddling remainder (along with his ash-filled amulets) the impish man had left—knowing full well the havoc that he was provoking—to the Brewsters to divide and fight over as they saw fit.

Since Mr. Allbright informed the Brewsters that the twins and I forswore our shares—Mary Jo and Marky didn't need it, and I didn't want mine, seeing as expectations had proved to be so equivocal a blessing in my life—the sweet smell of so much lucre so close to hand drove Mr. Julian's kin to near distraction as they set out to have the old man's final behest legally reversed. The factions bickering over which of its long-suffering members deserved the biggest slice of the Dearly Beloved Cousin's hoardings eventually had to agree to a truce while the claim worked its way through the legal system, though I had every confidence that the backbiting would reach operatic dimensions if and when the claim was recognized. In the meantime, both Bruno and Hank were suitably enough rattled by the heels of justice that had been set into motion to make themselves scarce—very scarce. What an eventual settlement in the Brewsters' favor might mean for the investment company that bought the property outright from Bruno and Hank, or for the residents of Elysium Heights, was beyond my powers of deduction. But I'd read enough Victorian fiction to know that it would be years before any such case was resolved legally, so I was tolerably satisfied that I wouldn't be forced from my abode before I chose to leave it of my own accord.

*

And this May afternoon, sitting at my drafting table and looking out the window at what had once been Mr. Julian's private kingdom—his purgatory as well as his elysium—I took stock of the home I had created here in Virginia as I awaited the arrival of Mary Jo and Miranda. Cooling off in the kitchen were the cheese and leek quiches I'd baked earlier in the day for the picnic I'd planned for us, and the savory odors, wafting up to my studio, drew me away from my journal. No more musing on paper today, no more revisiting the past or speculating about the shapes the future might assume; I descended to my living quarters, poured myself a glass of Pinot Grigio, popped Lou Reed into the tape deck, and stepped out onto the lawn in front of the carriage house.

Oh, it's such a perfect day
I'm glad I spent it with you

I settled into my Adirondack chair and listened.

> *Oh, such a perfect day*
> *You just keep me hanging on*
> *You just keep me hanging on*

As I sipped the chilled wine and looked across the lawn at the azalea bushes whose chorus of blooms exponentially multiplied the possibilities of hues of pink, I felt deeply content and drifted towards asleep.

> *Just a perfect day*
> *You made me forget myself*
>
> *I thought I was*
> *Someone else, someone good*
> *You just keep me hanging on*

When I awoke, forty minutes later, Miranda's car was pulling up right in front of me. In a waking daze, I saw Mary Jo emerge from the passenger side of the car and open the rear door to free my godson from his child's seat. Did I say that Miranda, touching the quick of my heart, had honored me immeasurably by naming her son Newton? Miranda emerged from the driver's seat looking as capable of executing a series of tumbles as ever. Behind her, I saw a fourth person surface from the rear seat—a striking black man I immediately, instinctively, knew to be Samson, although his paint-bespeckled overalls had been replaced by Izod shirt and cargo shorts. Was I still dreaming?

> *You're going to reap*
> *just what you sow*
> *You're going to reap*
> *just what you sow*

As I rose from my chair unsteadily, blinking myself awake, Newt ran in my direction, peeling laughter. Mary Jo reached me next, enclosing me in a deep embrace as little Newt tugged at my legs. Miranda and Sam brought up the rear, arm in arm.

"As long as we're having a reunion on your old stomping grounds," Miranda cheerily announced, "I thought you wouldn't mind my persuading Sam to join us. Seeing as it was once his stomping grounds too."

"I absolutely do not mind," I said, striding up to Sam and clasping his good hand. "It's been far too long."

"Good to see you, Scholar."

"You, too, Pockets."

Mary Jo laughed, gesturing around her. "Elysium Estates! Oh, Newt, what has come of the world where we once ruled!"

I ran my hand across little Newt's woolly head as I took in all of my guests, lingering on each face with a sense that this was a precious moment too long deferred. Mary Jo was as breathtaking as ever, the lines in her face and slight thickening of her once lithesome body only adding depth to her beauty. If Miranda's fiery mane of hair had been cropped to within an inch of her scalp, it only made the fiery determination in her eyes and smile all the more a sight to behold— and an implicit warning to any political opponents. I could see her on the campaign trail now. Then I looked down at little Newt, and up at Sam, and suddenly, clear as the sky above, I realized that Sam was Newt's father. His gay father. My godson, offspring of ferociously independent Miranda and the would-be boxer with whom I'd once gone fishing, the returned soldier who had shocked me into sexual self-recognition in the old swimming pool dressing room. And here, looking on, Mary Jo Sumner, whom, like her brother, I had once loved beyond life itself.

What a strange world, I thought to myself, what a strange and brave new world.

For the next hour, I showed my guests around the refurbished estate-turned-condo complex, including the common rooms in the main house that, at least for Mary Jo and me, reverberated with feelings of déjà vu and displacement, prospects and regrets. It did not go unnoted that, while the library's holdings remained by and large intact, the misbehaving cherubs in the frescoed ceiling now gaped in disbelief at Coca Cola and cigarette vending machines sulking below in opposite corners of the chamber.

Outside, we sauntered at a casual pace, trading companions every few minutes as we took in the landscape and caught up on each other's lives. When we reached the old pool, the Malibu tiles bordering the water as vibrant as ever, it was all we could do to keep little Newt from jumping in.

"I think we have a water-rat in the making, just like his namesake!" Miranda beamed at me. "Do you still swim, Newt? You look as fit as ever."

"Five mornings a week," I assured her. "But I have to be in the water before seven if I want the pool to myself."

"I understand why they took out the shrubs that screened the pool, but why, oh why, did they tear down the pergola and dressing rooms?" Mary Jo asked in a mournful tone. "They were exquisite, one of a kind."

Sam dared a glance in my direction. "Perhaps they harbored too many memories." The diamond stud in his left ear lobe sparkled in the sun.

We strolled on to the formal gardens, the narrow paths necessitating that we walk in pairs. Mary Jo hooked her arm in mine. "This, at least, is an improvement. I never thought I would live to see these beds flourishing with so much life!"

We passed the central fountain, where the lichen-covered nymph now poured sparkling water into the surrounding pool.

"She'll outlast us all," I muttered.

Not so the men memorialized by the marble slabs in the garden beds of the two adjacent quadrants.

"Dear Julian," Mary Jo sighed, as we paused before the stone she and Marky had commissioned for their cranky guardian a decade ago. She squeezed my arm. "He *did* mean well."

We turned to the slab that Mr. Julian had erected when the garden was still a wilderness. "I *miss* you, Dad," Sam said. He rested his good arm, so strong and sinewed with life, on my shoulder.

Later, as we strolled down the sloping lawn, Sam joined me at my side. We watched little Newt run ahead, straight for the rushes and irises bordering the creek. Mary Jo and Miranda ran after him, and, for a fleeting second, I had a vision of both as teenagers gamboling towards the promise of an unknown future.

Sam nodded ahead. "That's the tree where the swing hung. I remember repairing it—that summer." Then he pointed with his good arm to the fire-pit. "That can't be the remains of the well-house!"

I had a sudden intuition. "Don't tell me. Is the well-house where you and Marky—where you...?"

Sam laughed. "One of many places, you really don't want to know!" He stopped walking and looked at me, eye to eye. "How much you and Mary Jo must miss him, still."

I nodded. Marky's absence would always haunt us, a ghost with which we had learned to live. I turned to Sam.

"So *you* were Miranda's sperm donor?"

He laughed. "It's that obvious? It's supposed to be a well-kept secret!"

"Not the way Little Newt is starting to resemble his dad. Once he starts jabbing punching bags, no one will doubt it."

"For the record, Miranda consulted me about naming him Newt." Sam smiled. "It seemed just about right—to both of us."

"Well, if you decide Newt Junior needs a brother, perhaps you can name him Marky."

He grinned. "Maybe it will be twins, a boy and a girl. History repeating itself."

We strolled on in silence. Our arms brushed against each other, and the blonde hairs on my forearm tingled to the whispered touch of Sam's warm skin. I inhaled his scent, remembered the miraculous hailstorm that had united us on our first meeting.

"You're keeping yourself safe?" I asked.

"Safe as one knows how to be, these days. And you?"

"I'm clean, far as I know. Living here in Rocky Hill isn't exactly putting me at risk."

"Damn, Newt, we have so much to catch up on, you and I."

"Come back to the carriage house, later tonight, after the others have gone to bed. We'll talk."

"I'd like that. The perfect end to a perfect day."

Once we'd exhausted our tour of what had once been Mr. Julian's kingdom, I led our crew back to the carriage house to pack our late afternoon picnic.

With Miranda's permission, I took the wheel of the car. She got in beside me, while Sam and Mary Jo flanked little Newt in the back seat. In the rearview mirror I saw my namesake unselfconsciously clasp Sam's mangled hand with his own.

"Where are we going?" Mary Jo asked, never one to enjoy being kept in the dark.

She leaned forward and touched the nape of my neck like she used to do. A thrill of electricity no longer ran down my spine, instead a rush of warmer kinship.

"Wait and see."

Fifteen minutes later I pulled in to the small parking lot, newly paved, that abutted the piece of land that the county had recently denominated a historical landmark. The dense foliage of yesteryear was gone, and a swath of lawn, shaded here and there by the lofty oaks that had been allowed to remain, ran from the parking area downhill to the creek we could hear but not see. The grounds were overrun by wildflowers and rimmed by dense woods on either side. As we stepped onto the cedar-chipped path, carrying the baskets I'd packed, we passed a bronze plaque commemorating the Civil War furnace that had supplied General Jubal Early with ammunition that ultimately failed to win the cause.

Mary Jo took in the vista. "Look at this! Nothing stays the same."

"Nothing," I repeated.

She looked at me mischievously. "I'm afraid this makeover means that no more Newts will be using the furnace to practice their solitary vices."

We'd reached the shot tower. Three picnic tables dotted a green lawn extending from the dark stony heap to the creek, and in reach of each table was a charcoal grill—today's diminished version of the looming furnace. The sight of water once again mesmerized my namesake, and he made for the banks of the coursing creek as fast as his stubby legs would carry him. Miranda and Sam, chuckling, ran after him, catching his hands on either side. While they untied his shoelaces, slipping off his shoes so that they could suspend him over the stream and duck his feet in the fast-flowing cold water, Mary Jo and I strolled over to the old furnace. A metal chain surrounded its perimeter, and a sign warned of the penalties of climbing on or otherwise defacing this historical edifice.

"Since when was either of us a law-abiding citizen?" I asked, stepping over the barrier.

Mary Jo smiled and followed me. "*Il est interdit d'interdire*, Marky would have said."

We scaled the craggy rocks, scraping our nails and elbows as we reached for half-remembered handholds and wedged our feet in the enwrapping skein of ivy that, to this day, kept loose stones from tumbling earthward. I was now thirty-five, and Mary Jo thirty-seven, and, healthy as we were, both of us were as winded as Zithra had been by the time she'd reached the top of the stony mound. She hadn't been that much older than me now. Mary Jo and I lay back on the flat surface, gasping. A cascade of memories crowded our thoughts.

"We came here the Fourth of July," Mary Jo said.

"After the fireworks at Bonner Lake. You two *made* me take you to that circus!"

"And while we lay here, under the stars, stoned out of our minds, you told us about Zithra."

"That was a life ago."

"She's here, Newt. In these stones. In you. And that's all right."

"Is it?"

Mary Jo reached into the pocket of her slacks and withdrew two objects, amulets on thin chains. "These are the amulets Julian left Marky and me," she said. "My thought was to empty them on the old property. But I want to release them. Here. Now." She picked up a loose stone and, as I watched, she smashed both vials with a deft blow. A faint suspiration of ashes ascended from the rubble and dissipated, invisible within seconds.

"You, me, Marky, Uncle Julian—all of us here together where it all began for you, Newt. No shadows to haunt you, now. Let them all stay here when we leave."

She leaned over and kissed me, as tenderly as she'd ever kissed me. And, yet, it was the kiss of something greater than passion or romance.

From below, we heard laughing voices.

"Newt! Come see what your namesake is up to now!" Sam roared.

"And the sunset," Miranda enthused, "I've never seen a sky so grand! Come to the creek's edge, Mary Jo, Newt, and share the glory with us!"

Mary Jo and I smiled at each other, and we descended, careful step by careful step, that stony relic attesting to another world, another time, and, stepping out of its shadow, we linked arms as we walked forward across the lawn, drawn toward the mingled sounds of laughter and the trills of Furnace Creek coursing down its rocky bed as it sang, for another Newt, its insatiable siren song.

FINIS

ACKNOWLEDGMENTS

This novel would never have reached fruition without the support of friends and fellow writers spurring me to keep my expectations alive. Foremost, two wonderful Los-Angeles-based writers, Michelle Latiolais and Peter Gadol, were the first to endorse my creative aspirations with enthusiastic yet acute readings of early drafts—Michelle urging me to be even more outrageous and Peter asking exactly the right question about Newt's sexuality. I've saved a telephone message on my now-defunct answering machine from brilliant novelist Marianne Wiggins, who, a third of the way through an incomplete manuscript, called to exclaim that it should already be on an editor's desk. Two USC colleagues who are incomparable fiction writers and wordsmiths offered incisive readings: Dana Johnson, who laughed her way through multiple versions and affirmed my portrait of southern eccentricities, and Viet Nguyen, who with laser precision diagnosed how my channeling of Dickens' retrospective voice was limiting my engagement with the contemporary "here and now" of my retake on the author.

Dear friends Judith and Bill Holt fully entered the spirit of the project, reading multiple drafts with unabashed enthusiasm, empathy, and insight (apologies, Bill, if I didn't change the fate of your favorite character!). Likewise my brother Ben and his wife Alice Daniel were among my strongest supporters, helping me explore shades and nuances that have made this a much stronger story. Always engaged with my characters as if they were real breathing creatures, Moshe Sluhovsky raised provocative questions and offered fresh insights each time he read the novel. Juliet Fleming deserves be an editor for a major publishing house, given the quality of her line-by-line readings and emendations! Deborah Nord (a marvelous Victorianist who knows her Dickens inside out), Debra Shostak, and Deborah Holmes—my three Debs—offered unstinting support as they read and commented on the novel, as did Susan Winnett, Lisa Strauss, Kate

Collins, Kate Chandler, Doug Gleason, Carla Kaplan, Holly Brubach, and Jim Lock. Thanks to Jack Yeager, Tita Rosenthal, and Nany Vickers for graciously correcting my French and Italian, and to the gifted photographer Lara Porsak for relaxing me before her camera lens.

Other friends and family have offered encouragement and good cheer along the way—shoutouts to Dale, Rebecca, Phiroze, Emily, Bill, Rogers, Tom, Dara, Frank, Leo, Dorothy, Chris(es), Pam, Erika, Harry, Zan, John, Betsy, Atticus, Asher, Walt, Salo, Mel, David, Morgan, Brian, Lan, Dorinne, Bob, Ken, Michael, Kris, Meg(s), Alice(s), Kate, Susan, Tania, Joe, Stuart, Linda, Steve, Sue, Alun, Adem, the BBB book clubbers, all my NHC, SHC, and Bogliasco fellow adventurers, and a legion of students—for all their good wishes I remain indebted. I owe a great debt to my editor Todd Swift for taking on this project, Edwin Smet for his book design, and the rest of the team at BSGP, as well as to my US publicist, Steve Rohr, for their fine work. Many thanks too to the chair of the English department David St. John and the Deans of USC's Dornsife College of Letters, Arts, and Sciences for making the research and subvention funding available that has helped this novel realize its expectations.

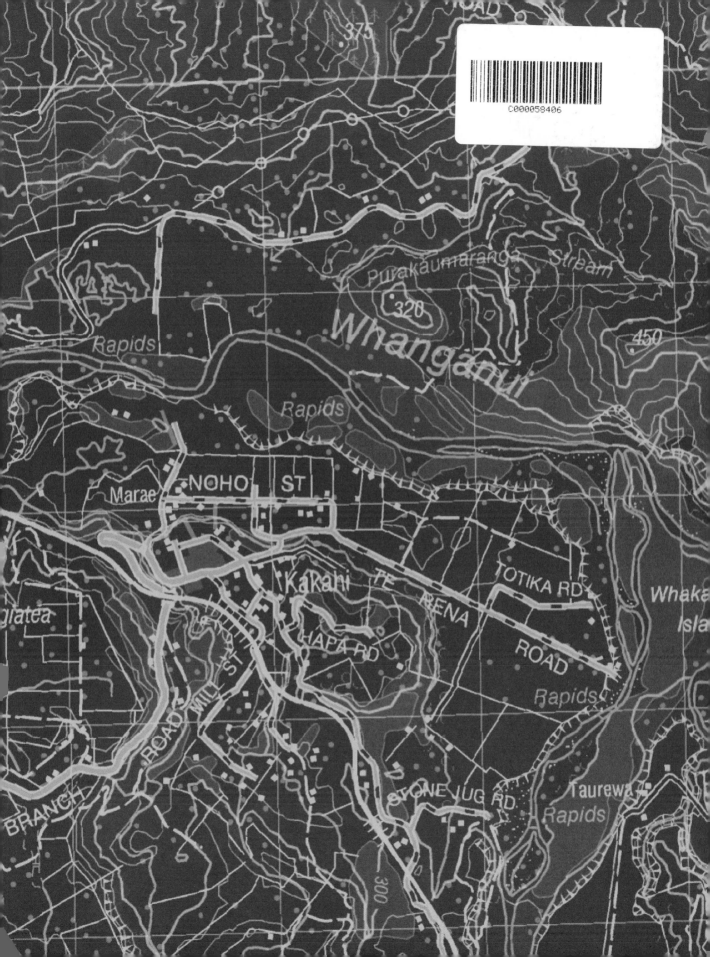

Observations
of a Rural Nurse

Observations
of a Rural Nurse

Sara McIntyre

MASSEY UNIVERSITY PRESS

To my parents,
Patti and Peter McIntyre

Pages 6–7:
Anzac Day, Miriama
Street, Taumarunui
2015

Pages 8–9:
Kākahi Town Hall
2017

Foreword

— Simon McIntyre

One of the marvels of photography is that you can look back at an old photograph and find, there in the detail, something prescient. In the image of my sister Sara and me, taken by our father at Kākahi around 1960, a close look reveals that Sara is holding an old camera. Now, on reflection, it is one of those 'oh yes' moments. Fast forward 18 years and I returned from my first spell overseas with a 35mm Pentax for her. This soon led to a bit of DIY processing and printing in the laundry cupboard of our old Wellington home.

Sara's interest in all things photographic has never waned, and Kākahi in the King Country became her testing ground — family picnics, the river, the locals. Her photographs of this subject matter were always vastly superior to my own so I soon realised I should stick to painting.

Less obvious in those days, but now recognised as a motivating spirit in her work, is the quiet but significant influence of the paintings of our father, Peter. He had devoted a large part of his painting life to depicting the people and landscape of the King Country and of Kākahi in particular. It is not just a shared interest in the subject matter that connects them but also a love of King Country light — golden in the late afternoon of summer, misty, solemn and grey on a cold winter's day. However, it was Sara's portraits and scenes of everyday life, as seen on her rounds as a district nurse in the King Country, that resonated so strongly.

The arrival of Instagram allowed Sara to get her remarkable photographs out to a much wider audience. Showing her photographs on this forum had an immediate and life-changing effect, even beyond the large number of people now experiencing her photographs for the first time. Anna Miles took Sara into her gallery stable, exhibitions followed and now the book.

Sara's story is one that warms the heart: someone who has both passion and talent, largely kept under wraps for most of her lifetime, then brought to life through a series of small but significant events. At this stage it is tempting to say, don't bother reading about it — just look at the pictures.

Left: Sara and Simon on the front lawn at Te Whare Ra, 1960.

13

Living and working in the King Country

— Sara McIntyre

Each year when I was a child my parents, Patti and Peter McIntyre, rented the Simpson cottage on the foreshore at Lake Taupō. That changed in the summer of 1960. After a stream of house guests and gin-drinking, we were off to stay in a remote place we'd never heard of. Ted and Cath Webber had invited us to stay at an old cottage, Te Whare Ra, in Kākahi in the King Country. Ted and Peter had become friends during the war. Ted had been editor of the *NZEF Times* when Peter was the war artist. They were both raconteurs and fishermen, but Patti and Cath were the more expert anglers. I was nine, my brother Simon was five.

My parents were exhausted and hadn't wanted to go to Te Whare Ra so it was a tense drive in the Vauxhall from Taupō, but as we came over the Waituhi Saddle and down the Punga Punga Road, the mood changed. Beyond us lay the rugged beauty of the King Country.

As it turned out, the week was a great success. Simon and I were soon in awe of the older Webber kids, Alison and Alastair, and Peter recorded in the visitors' book on Christmas Day that '26 trout were caught using tiny nymphs or small red-tipped Governors'. Within two years he and Patti had bought a section, and Peter designed and, with the help of a neighbour, built a two-room cottage overlooking the Whakapapa River. We children slept on the verandah and washed in the river. There was a long-drop with a river view among the kānuka. A studio was soon built, and later a bathroom was added to the back of the house.

My parents were fanatical anglers. Patti had taken to it when she first met Peter in Dunedin and soon outdid him. She would climb down ladders to the Huka Falls with us children, usually carrying the dog. There is a photo of her, pregnant with me, casting her line in the Tongariro. I was taken fishing for the first time when I was about six months old, and was probably parked up in an apple box on the riverbank while she fished. I became an avid reader as a child because of those riverbanks.

At Kākahi, Simon and I and our cousin Shona, or our neighbour, Coral, roamed the area. We never got lost, but even so no one knew quite where we were. Across the bridge, in the middle of the Whakapapa River, there was an island, still with its original native bush cover. We'd spend time there or riding bareback on Coral's very old, very slow horse. We became expert at shooting rapids, perhaps a little too confident of our expertise. On one expedition, Shona and

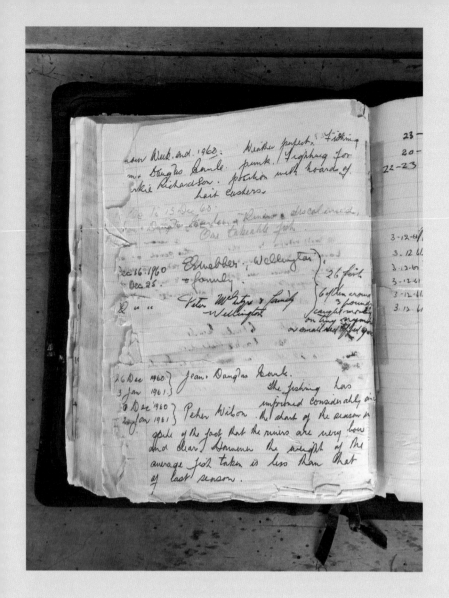

Te Whare Ra visitors' book. Entry for
December 1960. '26 fish. 6 of them around
3 pounds caught mostly on tiny nymphs or
small Red Tipped Governor.'

I attempted to cross the Whanganui River, holding Simon between us — he was too small to touch the bottom. We were halfway across when a grim-faced Patti and Peter emerged from the bush, looking for us. There were repercussions.

In the evenings, the time of the 'evening rise', we went fishing with the parents and my books. We had picnic tea. Hopefully there would be a trout. (Nowadays sausages get taken along.) Simon caught his first fish when he was seven or eight. He is a very good fisherman, and when he is here he talks about the yearning to get on the river; you can see the agitation start about 4pm.

Once we had left home for boarding school Patti and Peter would live at Kākahi for months at a time. Peter would hanker to get there earlier and earlier, but after six months they'd be keen to get back to Wellington and their social life. We'd all be there for the school holidays. People used to come to stay, relations and friends who were into fishing.

Almost every time Patti went to the store she'd go and visit one of her friends in the village, people like Mrs Lala, who had a big vegetable garden. Mrs Lala's husband, Dahya, and now their son Manu, have run the Kākahi General Store for over 60 years. Today Dahya Lala Drive and Peter McIntyre Street share a signpost in Kākahi. The store is one of the few general stores remaining in the country and is stocked with an extraordinary array of items: fishing flies, including the 'Kākahi Queen', gumboots, hockey sticks, jandals, cans of ballroom-dancing powder, secondhand copies of my father's books, and, in winter, chocolate éclairs and doughnuts from Johnny Nation's bakery in Ohakune. On Sundays the local postie does a run from Ohakune to Taumarunui via Kākahi and delivers an order of what the local kids call Johnny cakes. Our Sunday mornings in winter revolve around collecting doughnuts from the shop and eating them, with coffee.

Peter's idea of bliss was endless days of uninterrupted painting in his studio. To extract him from there Patti had a cowbell. Two rings meant coffee or drinks time. Visitors were banned from the studio. Three rings of the cowbell meant, visitors are here – come now. Sometimes she wouldn't ring the bell.

Peter went everywhere with a camera. I don't remember having an interest in them. Like his painting, I took his photography for granted. Simon began painting at an early age; I just lived amongst it.

Peter's book *Kakahi New Zealand* was published in 1972. On the cover is the painting of John Ham on horseback that now hangs in my living room. John's mother, Irene, was a friend of Patti's. Everyone called his grandfather Old Mr Ham. Patti loved the way he spoke; he was half Irish and used old-fashioned words. She described him as Shakespearean. She used to almost harass him: You have to get rid of the dead sheep! You need to fix your fence! He'd smile and say, Yes, Mrs McIntyre, and they'd end up having long conversations.

Mr Ham's sons and grandsons, including John, broke in wild horses. When the village needed to raise money to restore the Town Hall in the 1980s, they decided with Manu to organise a rodeo. They invited rodeo people from Raetihi and National Park. It was so well run that it became part of the national circuit and now the locals hardly enter it.

* * *

Patti and Peter travelled extensively through the 1950s, 60s and 70s. I saw them as glamorous and was in awe of their stories of travel and the people they had met. Undaunted by having twin sons, Sam and Matthew, at the age of 21, I announced I was going to Europe with two three-year-olds. Patti was mortified, 'worried sick'. Peter opened the champagne. He said, Go to Venice. You may be the last generation to see it. I did. In 1977 I set off to London via Disneyland.

I bought an old Bedford ambulance from the side of the road in Australia Square in London and set off to Ireland, France, Switzerland, Italy and Greece armed with an Instamatic 110 with drop-in film cartridges. I had the film processed at a Boots chemist back in London. The prints were small, square, ochre-tinged Kodak images with the date stamped on the side. They captured a small part of the world I was exploring for me to take home.

Simon soon realised the Instamatic wasn't in keeping with my enthusiasm for photography and bought me my first SLR, a Pentax. My travel obsession with the camera took hold: South East Asia, Central Asia, Antarctica, Europe, America, India… I became a hoarder of images. There grew to be shoeboxes full of them, expensive albums that no one ever looks at, except me.

By the time the boys were five I was married again. My third son, Henry, was born and I started going to mothers' coffee mornings.

18

I remember saying to Patti, I'll go nuts. I decided to go nursing. It interested me and I wanted to be employable.

Some time in my first year of nursing training, I had a placement at Wesley Hospital in Wellington for the elderly, where I worked with a nurse called Alan. One tea break together we chatted about the upcoming Easter holiday. Alan asked if I was going away and where to. Usually when I mentioned Kākahi people went blank but Alan nearly fell off his chair. I'm Alan Taumata from Kākahi!, he said. I'm Sara McIntyre!, I replied. We only knew each other's first names from our badges. No one else in the staffroom could understand our excitement. Alan had grown up in Kākahi, and went to school with Manu, but by the time our family bought the land he had left. Alan then told me he had first met Patti and Peter when he was working at Government House as a butler.

A nurse overheard me mention Kākahi during another staffroom conversation years later in the Wellington neonatal unit. She quietly announced, I'm Jane Johnson. I knew immediately. Jane had left Kākahi at 16, but her sister and brothers had been childhood friends. After chatting excitedly about Kākahi and our families I had to go to a meeting and Jane went to the milk room. I was with an entourage of doctors and nurses but stepped sideways into the milk room to speak to her. The day before I had been contemplating selling one of Peter's paintings from his *Kakahi* book of Jane's brother, David, in the sheep yards. I wanted to sell the painting so I could pay a builder to restore my house at Kākahi. I put the thought to Jane, explaining why I wanted to sell. Her response was immediate. Her family wanted a present for David. I had to catch up with the entourage but as I left she said, You realise David is a builder? When I got to the meeting they asked where I'd got to. Just selling a painting in the milk room, I said.

* * *

Peter died in 1995 and his memorial service at Taumaihiorongo Marae was organised by Alan Taumata. Soon after, the Whakapapa River began to change course. Some believe the river is coming for Peter. His ashes are buried in the garden under a golden tōtara. In 1998 a massive flood took the entire front lawn, leaving the house on the edge of a 30-metre cliff. Despite the risk of the house going into the river at any moment,

A painting from Peter's *Kakahi* book.
David Johnson and his neighbour are
dipping sheep.

in the dark and in torrential rain, Manu Lala rallied every able-bodied local with a vehicle to help empty the house. When Simon and I got there, all that remained in the house was the telephone and the phone book. In case you wanted to make a call, Manu said.

Since then the site of the house and entire garden have been taken by the river. Fortunately, some years beforehand, my parents had bought the adjoining 20 acres. Rumour had it that someone was interested in the site for a motor camp. Peter panicked and promptly bought the property, including the old house that would eventually become my home.

The *Penguin New Zealand Travel Guide* described Kākahi as 'a faded sawmilling settlement made famous by the paintings of Peter McIntyre… who had a house here (until it fell into the river gorge he liked so much to paint)'. Fortunately this last part is not correct. The house was unhooked from the concrete slab floor and set up on blocks in the paddock, where it sat for three years while negotiations went on over insurance. It was eventually re-established on new foundations in time for Patti to have her last Christmas and summer at Kākahi.

On a whim, I decided to take over the rat-infested, derelict house and overgrown garden next door. Simon and his wife, Sarah, kept Patti and Peter's house and we became neighbours. My house was originally a workman's cottage at the Egmont Box Company at Te Rena, which had been brought across the Whakapapa by horse and cart in the 1920s. After a life somewhere else in Kākahi, it was eventually moved to its current site in the 1940s by Greg Kelly, a forensic scientist, ranger and fisherman. His books, *Flies In My Hat* and *Gun In the Hills*, had cover designs by Peter. Greg named the house Mar Lodge, after a royal hunting and fishing lodge in Scotland. I never came to grips with the Mar Lodge thing, so today the house remains nameless.

For more than 20 years, the house was rented by Keith Chapple, a former president of the Royal Forest and Bird Society. Keith campaigned to protect the Whanganui and Whakapapa rivers and the whio or native duck before he died following a car accident. More tenants came and went, but the house went into decline and sat empty for a few years. I had it made liveable, insulated, and rodent-proof by David Johnson, and cleared the garden to let in some light.

Perched on a cliff, my house has views down the Whakapapa as it flows towards the white papa cliffs where it joins the Whanganui

River. The view to the west is down the valley towards the village. In the summer the late sun across the fields warms the heart. Each May I watch from the verandah as whio congregate to pair up. It can take days to sort out who's with who. As I write there are two in the pool below the house. From here I can see deer emerge from the bush into the clearings in the evening sun. Korimako, or bellbird, and tūī feed on the harakeke in front of the verandah and kererū soar theatrically as if to attract an audience.

Originally the plan was to make it a holiday house, but I made it so liveable that I became reluctant to return to Wellington. In any case, having two houses on a nurse's salary isn't really possible. I took six months leave without pay from my job in the Wellington Neonatal Intensive Care Unit to see if I could survive here. Selling my cottage on Wellington's south coast was hard, but there was that escapism. Kākahi locals also seemed pleased. McIntyres hadn't disappeared; I wasn't coming to a strange place. It felt like home.

* * *

I didn't intend to do more nursing, but one day I'd been at the supermarket and had run out of money. It was time to get a job. I walked into Taumarunui Hospital and talked to the woman on the front desk. Was there was someone I could see? Were there any positions for a casual nurse? They were about to advertise a position. Neonatal intensive care and coordinating the transport team had been fulfilling work, but it was specialised and not much help when applying for job in a small rural hospital. I'd have to relearn. The day I started they said, We'll put you with the district nurses. I was given the position of 'casual' district nurse based at Taumarunui Hospital. After years in an intensive care environment, to be given a bag and a car and sent out of the hospital was fantastic. I started off with the simple jobs and it built up rather quickly.

When I set out with Daphne, one of the four district nurses, on my first day, I could barely contain myself. This was going to be my job! Driving around the countryside! Half of the patients we saw that day I knew. On my first weekend working solo, I had to go to Whakahoro, over 60 kilometres away, 40 of which are on gravel roads along steep papa cliffs, across rugged farmland, through thick bush. After an hour's drive, the woman I was to see wasn't home. I was in despair. Two boys on a quad bike told me she was down the road at a café. Café? I was in the middle of nowhere. Woman located and her wound tended to, I was given coffee and chocolate cake. There were conversations about compost and whio.

Our work was largely wound care, everything from heel blisters and ulcers to amputations. There were all manner of medical issues and palliative care. I could at least adapt years of palliative experience from the children's ward and neonatal unit. In the community we liaised with the hospice nurses from the Waikato. The patients and their families, their attitudes and conversations, had a huge impact on my nursing and outlook.

One of my patients came in from the bush to see us after the new year. It's another year and I'm still here, he said. What's next? We loved his visits. He wanted to die at home in the bush and offered to leave a horse at the gate so we could ride the last couple of kilometres to his house when we next visited him. We declined the horse ride.

The district nurses travelled as far as National Park, Ōhura, Waimiha, Whakahoro, along many a gravel road. I had thought I knew the district reasonably well, but I got to know it in much more detail. I learnt how a small hospital works and how small communities work, the networking, the idiosyncrasies, the dramas, and humour. There's a bond with patients and their families that is not the same in the hospital environment. There is a better understanding and acceptance of people in their homes and, with time, some true friendships.

And there were so many things that made me want to get out my camera. At first I was fully occupied; after all, it was sort of like starting again. You couldn't get much more of a change. Driving the Ōpōtiki Road, for example, was quite daunting. I took a photograph of the really thick bush, deer, goats and ducks on the road that were part of my rounds.

Tess, from a big Taumarunui/Kākahi family, lived surrounded by a staggering array of tapestries — Jesus Christ, Aladdin, leaping tigers. She sat in a La-Z-Boy. Beside her another La-Z-Boy contained a huge toy tiger. The first time I sat down to talk to her, I moved the tiger. I was politely told to put him back and sit in another chair. Tess asked if I would make sure she had her lipstick on when she died. Within a week of her death her family had taken down all her stuff — all those tapestries.

An original painting in Oils of
the church,painted by Mrs Joan
Allen,a resident of Kakahi and
it was the centre-piece of the
Jubilee cake Mrs Allen iced for
the Diamond Jubilee of the church
Labour weekend,23rd Oct/1977.

Top: Goat in Para Street, 2014.

Above: Joan Allan's painting of the
Kākahi church, 2018. Joan and her sister
Mae from the Kākahi Bakery were the
only people Peter ever gave painting
lessons.

I really wanted to photograph Tess, but I felt I couldn't ask her. But being there made me very aware of these unique places I had access to. The husband of a district nurse friend who had retired soon after I started was an ex-cop who was also interested in photography. He and I discussed the opportunity of being able to photograph in the district. He understood the problem of having a camera when working. I decided I could observe while working and go back with the camera later. I used to drive along and notice people's curtains. Windows and doors are an attraction I cannot analyse.

When Simon first suggested I put my photos on Instagram, I didn't listen. I was half-hearted about it until my cousin Anna went ahead and set up an account for me. For a while Instagram was quite a special club — about six people followed me. Soon after I had parked my car in the middle of Taumarunui to write up my notes after visiting a patient I saw a goat on a doorstep. All I had was my iPhone. I took the photograph from the car window, through the drizzle, and posted it on my new Instagram account. Almost immediately I ordered a new phone. To lug a heavy Nikon camera on district nursing rounds was not feasible. The gallery owner Anna Miles saw my images on Instagram and it was from here the story of my photography began to emerge.

* * *

Taking photos inside without a tripod is almost impossible. I had become an expert at nearly fainting from not breathing using the Nikon. The iPhone cameras were improving dramatically while I was nursing and soon I upgraded again. Really, it was far too good at taking photos inside. On days off I'd return to places I had eyed up. Eventually I plucked up the courage to ask patients if I could photograph them or their homes, explaining that I was a photographer as well as a nurse. It opened up whole new conversations. People seemed intrigued by what I was doing — and that I was interested in their homes, their lives, in them.

Getting to photograph Erihi Adams in her home at Ngakonui took some time. I was unsure about asking. Knowing her, I knew her reply would be either a firm yes or no. She was delighted, it turned out, but it would take months for her to sort out her kākahu for the photograph, she said. I thought she was fixing one, but she had found a new one in a tourist shop in Ōtorohanga. Bring me my bag, she said. Out came the make-up bag and Erihi proceeded to pencil her eyebrows. We talked about the wall in her room, each of the deceased whānau and friends, her early kete weaving. What would she call the wall? There was no word for it. We decided on memorial wall, as a tribute to those whose portraits hung on it.

When I asked Manu if I could photograph him in his store, without a word he began fossicking around rearranging his shelf of secondhand Peter McIntyre books. Initially I thought the books made the scene contrived, but it was a photograph of Manu, in his shop, the way he wanted it. I have a few photographs of the store, but the one in this book is the one about Manu.

The photographs began to require an increasing amount of talking. Rowena, living in her caravan with various added tarpaulins and sheds, told me about being a Wiccan. I thought the skull and crossbones flag in her garden was part of this, but no. I'm really just a pirate, she said. Shane thought I was a bit odd wanting to photograph his clothesline, but he didn't seem to mind. In fact, the state of his backyard led to more conversation. Everyone was happy when doctors prescribed Valium and women baked and men mowed their lawns, he told me.

I had a lovely moment talking about this book with Shane. He knew that one of the district nurses lived at Kākahi but hadn't realised it was me. He started to tell me about another book about Kākahi, by the artist Peter McIntyre, and how he loved that book. I said Peter was my dad. He buried his face in his hands. Oh my god! The nurse from Kākahi! he said. I'm going to be in a McIntyre book just like my cousins! Half the kids in Peter's paintings are related to Shane.

I began photographing street scenes, boys on horses in the middle of town, houses, shops, the landscape, club rooms. I frequently returned to the Tea Cup Gallery in Manunui. The owner, Theona, was constantly rearranging the shelves. It was a shop but Theona was reluctant to part with her treasured collection.

In the early 1990s Alan Taumata returned to live in Kākahi with his partner, Ramon. When we get together he regales me with well-embellished local stories. I have the most photographed house in Kākahi, he says, as we move from room to room. Alan rearranges frequently, which lends to a constant stream of subject matter and conversation. He also takes care of arrangements in the wharekai of

26

Taumaihiorongo Marae at Kākahi and at St Peter's, the 100-year-old Catholic church opposite. His stamp is on all aspects of the floral decorations at the church and the marae and in the Chapel of the Holy Cross in a shed in his garden. I love photographing Alan's various outfits and tiki. He is a spiritual man, proud of his culture. He loves his whānau, and the royal whānau, both English and Māori.

Scenes, light and atmosphere were often discussed in my family. On car trips we frequently stopped so Peter could locate subject matter for painting. One day I moaned from the back of the car as we waited for him to trudge across yet another field with his camera. Patti snapped at me. This is your bread and butter. Think about it.

From time to time, my work as a nurse in the Wellington neonatal unit involved small photographic projects — a series for the Neonatal Trust, the New Zealand Nurses Organisation and for Life Flight — but it wasn't until I was back in the King Country that nursing and photography made sense. Every drive to work was laced with potential. I stopped often. On our family trips Peter would sometimes get back into the car and drive off elated. Now I know the feeling.

Kākahi Billiards Saloon
2017

Kākahi Town Hall
2014

No Smokes on Sale,
Kākahi Town Hall
2019

Kākahi Town Hall spread
2016

Kākahi working bee
2018

Kākahi pool shed
2017

Carrie-Ann's home
2008

Whakapapa picnic
2008

When I asked Manu if I could photograph him in his store, without a word he began fossicking around rearranging his shelf of secondhand Peter McIntyre books. Initially I thought the books made the scene contrived, but this was a photograph of Manu, in his shop, the way he wanted it. I have a few photographs of the store, but this is the one about Manu.

Following pages:
Manu Lala, Kākahi General Store
2008

Dax, 2015

Caravan and
foxglove, Kākahi
2014

Whakapapa River, my view
2019

Shirley, 2015

Shirley's wall
2015

Judy Rameka and
her garden shed
2016

Left, top:
Walshie's Khartoum
poster, 2015

Left, bottom:
Walshie's ceiling
2015

Right:
Jill's rescued dolls
and crocheted
blanket collection
2018

Te Rena Road
2018

The boys at the Kākahi Rodeo
2017

Kākahi Rodeo
2017

Totika Road
2019

78

In the early 1990s Alan Taumata returned to live in Kākahi with his partner, Ramon. When we get together he regales me with well-embellished local stories. I have the most photographed house in Kākahi, he says, as we move from room to room. Alan rearranges frequently, which lends to a constant stream of subject matter and conversation… I love photographing Alan's various outfits and tiki. He is a spiritual man, proud of his culture. He loves his whānau, and the royal whānau, both English and Māori.

Alan's Madonna
2015

Below:
Ramon and Alan
2008

Right:
Alan's hallway
2016

Right:
Alan's parlour
2017

Following pages:
Alan's parlour
2017

Alan's Chapel of
the Holy Cross
2016

Chapel of the Holy Cross
porch, 2016

Chapel of the Holy Cross
2008

Golden elm
2019

Previous pages:
Whakapapa cliffs, 2019

Above:
Simon and Sarah's
house. Originally built
by Peter but moved and
later re-established
2019

Whakapapa River where
the house used to be
2019

Alan also takes care of arrangements in the wharekai of Taumaihiorongo Marae at Kākahi and at St Peter's, the 100-year-old Catholic church opposite. His stamp is on all aspects of the floral decorations at the church and the marae and in the Chapel of the Holy Cross in a shed in his garden.

Following pages:
Taumaihiorongo Marae
at Kākahi, 2008

Gathering at the marae
2008

Gathering at the marae
2008

Wharenui at Kākahi
Marae, 2008

Top:
Wharekai at Kākahi
Marae, 2019

Bottom:
Hangi at Kākahi
Marae, 2019

119

Kākahi Marae, 2008

St Peter's Church,
Kākahi Marae, 2018

Previous pages:
St Peter's Church,
Kākahi Marae
2015

Right:
Kākahi urupā
2017

125

Ōwhango Market Day
2014

At Madonna's feet,
Kākahi Church, 2018

The Tree in winter
2017

Peter's book *Kakahi* was published
in 1972. On the cover is the painting
of John Ham on horseback that now
hangs in my living room. John's
mother, Irene, was a friend of Patti's.
Everyone called his grandfather
Old Mr Ham. Patti loved the way he
spoke; he was half Irish and used old-
fashioned words. She described him
as Shakespearean. She used to almost
harass him: You have to get rid of
the dead sheep! You need to fix your
fence! He'd smile and say, Yes, Mrs
McIntyre, and they'd end up having
long conversations.

The painting for the
cover of Peter's *Kakahi*
book, of John Ham
on horseback at the
Whakapapa River, 2017

142

Opportunity Shop
2016

Tea Cup Gallery, Manunui
2015

Te Rena, view from my
kitchen window, 2016

Early morning in the
backyard, 2018

Getting to photograph Erihi Adams in her home at Ngakonui took some time. I was unsure about asking. Knowing her, I knew her reply would be either a firm yes or no. She was delighted, it turned out, but it would take months for her to sort out her kākahu for the photograph, she said. I thought she was fixing one, but she had found a new one in a tourist shop in Ōtorohanga. Bring me my bag, she said. Out came the make-up bag and Erihi proceeded to pencil her eyebrows.

Below:
Erihi prepping for
photograph, 2016

Right:
Erihi, 2016

Following pages:
Erihi's memorial
wall, 2018

156

157

Barbecued lambs' tails
2016

BP station, Manunui
2018

Miro Street, 2017

167

Erihi's kākahu
2016

Manunui garden
2016

Rowena, living in her caravan with various added tarpaulins and sheds, told me about being a Wiccan. I thought the skull and crossbones flag in her garden was part of this, but no. I'm really just a pirate, she said.

Taumarunui tapestry
2017

Te Akau whānau wall
2017

Olive's needlework
2018

Shane thought I was a bit odd wanting to photograph his clothesline, but he didn't seem to mind. In fact, the state of the backyard led to more conversation. Everyone was happy when doctors prescribed Valium and women baked and men mowed their lawns, he told me.

Following pages:
Shane, 2015

191

International Zephyr Day
2016

Jubilee Dairy
2016

Ngatai Street
2017

Ōpōtiki Road
2016

The Tree, 2016

The Goat Farm
2015

Above:
Pātaka at Te Koura
Marae, 2016

Following pages:
Mrs Ruruku's house
2015

Previous pages:
Mrs Ruruku's porch
2015

Right:
Endean's native
timber mill, Waimiha
2015

Endean's timber mill office,
Waimiha, 2016

Ōhura CHAT
(Country Hospitality
and Tourism Shop)
2016

Janet's shop, Ōhura
2015

228

Janet's, 2015

Ōhura Museum, open by
appointment, 2015

Left:
Charlie and the
mannequin in Ōhura
Museum, 2015

Right:
Ōhura Museum
2015

Ōhura Museum
2015

240

Tui Street, Ōhura
2015

243

Ōhura fence
2017

The district nurses travelled as far as National Park, Ōhura, Waimiha, Whakahoro, along many a gravel road. I had thought I knew the district reasonably well, but I got to know it in much more detail. I learnt how a small hospital works and how small communities work, the networking, the idiosyncrasies, the dramas, and humour. There's a bond with patients and their families that is not the same in the hospital environment. There is a better understanding and acceptance of people in their homes and, with time, some true friendships.

250

Ōhura Church entrance
2015

Ōhura Church
2015

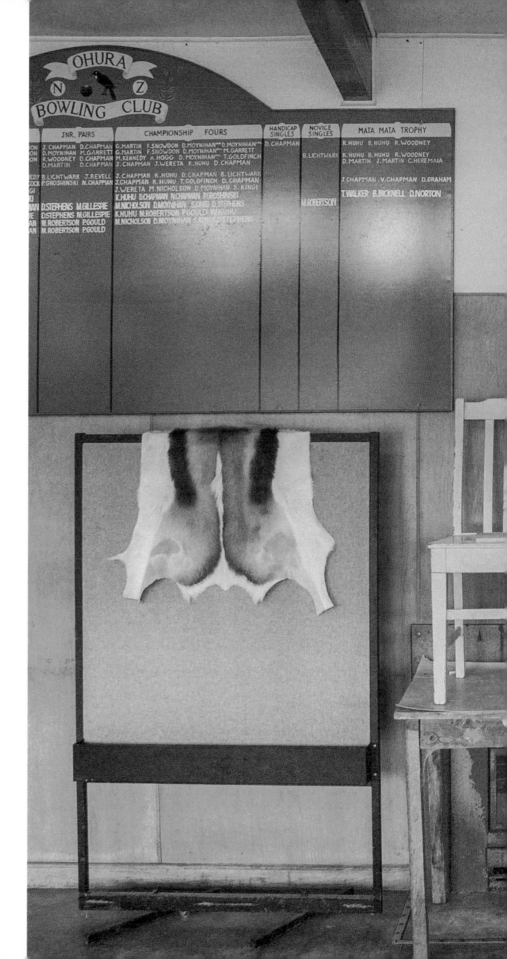

Ōpōtiki Road
2016

262

Evening sun on The Tree
2019

Matiere, 2015

View from the Punga
Punga Road descending
into the King Country
2019

Peter McIntyre Street
and Dahya Lala Drive,
Kākahi, 2016

Sara McIntyre at home

— Julia Waite

Sara McIntyre has photographed the old gum tree at the entrance to her driveway in all seasons and light conditions. The towering Australian native is a powerful indicator of place, and its presence in McIntyre's work is a marker of continuity and change in Kākahi.

Heading out of the driveway on a misty morning in the small King Country settlement, McIntyre stops close to the centre of the old village, at the junction of Peter McIntyre Street and Dahya Lala Drive. Lifting her iPhone, she shoots the road signs that bear the names of her father and the previous general store owner. For McIntyre, these otherwise everyday, uniform signposts represent intersecting familial connections that stretch back in time and remain alive to this day. The general store is nothing without the Lala family, who have been owner-operators of the business since 1937. McIntyre's portrait of Manu Lala, the current owner, conveys the closeness of the Lala family's relationship to the store in an image in which it's hard to tell where the shopkeeper's body ends and his stock begins.[1] Behind the counter, beneath the Milo and above the food colouring, a number of large hardbacks are proudly displayed with their covers facing out: *Peter McIntyre's New Zealand* (1964), *Peter McIntyre's Pacific* (1966) and *Peter McIntyre's West* (1970), the books that made Sara's father one of New Zealand's most well-known postwar artists.

A celebrated landscape painter, and winner of the Hays and Kelliher prizes, Peter McIntyre's book *Kakahi New Zealand* (1970) gave the village a kind of cult status when it was published almost 50 years ago. It was a visual elegy, with views of the mighty Whakapapa River winding through pages of paintings and drawings of a once bustling colonial settlement. Sara McIntyre's photographic project, which takes the viewer beyond Kākahi to Taumarunui and other small towns in the southern King Country, can be understood as a counterpoint to *Kakahi New Zealand*. While both artists were drawn to depict a place that is both personal and deeply familiar, McIntyre's photographs are part of a long-range project which involves going inside people's homes, into community spaces, and behind the crumbling heritage façades to present a layered essay on place and rural decline.

Peter McIntyre's *Kakahi New Zealand* is full of quiet painted scenes that dwell on absence: the old main street, an abandoned barn, an

1. Manu and his wife Kamu took over running the store in 1958.

273

empty hitching post and broken farm gates. What remained in the late 1960s were haunting reminders of a busier, more prosperous time and the logging boom of the early 1900s. While Peter McIntyre was aware of contemporary pressures facing the community, his book is largely nostalgic in tone. The early scenes of the 1969 New Zealand Broadcasting Corporation television series *Looking at New Zealand* — produced at the same time as the book was being made — show McIntyre walking along a long dusty country road in Kākahi with palette and easel under his arm, in search of something exciting to paint. The past appears powerfully present for the artist as he strolls through Taumaihiorongo Marae, with all the marae gatherings brought to mind.

Kākahi was a place of escape that Peter McIntyre viewed through a romantic lens. It was a country retreat and his 'hideout from an ever strident and ugly world'; 'a refuge from the inane persecution of the telephone'.[2] *Kakahi New Zealand* weaves an informative history of the area through the wistful meditation on a place that McIntyre believed was suspended in time. He feared the old ways were being quietly eroded by modern life, and was conscious of the limited opportunities for Māori; he lamented that 'sadly most of them drift away to the towns in their late teens'.[3] At the end of the book the painter alludes to the challenges facing the area, declaring that 'places such as Kākahi may seem to be going backwards, even to be dying', though his personal view differed.[4] When Peter McIntyre was filmed strolling into Kākahi he foresaw the future, proclaiming in his slow lilting way: 'Some say it's dying but I don't think so, I think in a way it's coming to life again.'[5]

Fifty years on, his photographer daughter Sara McIntyre picks up the story of the village in *Observations of a Rural Nurse* — a documentary photography project about the exact same place and the people who live there now.

* * *

2. Peter McIntyre, 'Foreword', *Kakahi New Zealand* (Wellington: A. H. & A. W. Reed, 1972).

3. McIntyre, *Kakahi*, caption for Plate 7.

4. McIntyre, *Kakahi*, np.

5. NZBC, *Looking At New Zealand*, 1969, www.nzonscreen.com/title/looking-at-new-zealand---peter-mcintyre-1969

6. The post was made on 13 July 2014. McIntyre titled it 'Morning coffee'.

Sara McIntyre's work came to public attention on Instagram five years ago when she made her first post with an image of Lake Camp, North Canterbury.[6] A slightly out of focus photograph of the river beneath her house appeared shortly afterwards, in early August 2014. Those early images, taken in and around her home, quickly grew into a major online photographic essay. It attracted an audience. McIntyre took her followers to see many of the same sites first recorded in oil and ink by her father: down through the cutting to the river; past the old shops, the Anglican church. The photographs may appear instantaneous, but they are informed by experiences of somewhere she first visited almost 60 years ago.

Her parents Peter and Patti came to Kākahi in the early 1960s for the river and its trout, and the area provided a rich source of subject matter for the painter. Sara recalls her parents' dedication to searching for subjects and views to paint. Patti was masterful at supporting Peter, at directing his eye, and together they instilled this skill in their daughter. Like Peter, Sara McIntyre is looking all the time, but the conditions of her looking have shifted dramatically. The framing device is the screen on her iPhone, and many of the images in this book were taken in between seeing the patients she visited while working as a rural nurse.

While memory informs much of the work, McIntyre's perception of Kākahi has been profoundly influenced by present-day experiences nursing there and in the surrounding area in towns, including Taumarunui, Ōhura and Ōwhango. Treating people in their homes has given her a unique understanding of the community's day-to-day realities. She has cared for people in the area and she lives there with them. Peter McIntyre was a landscape painter standing back from his subject to take in the surrounding view. Sara McIntyre's practice more closely recalls the participant observation used by cultural anthropologists. Her perspective is grounded, connected and empathetic of both the history of Kākahi and its state in the present.

However, her first photographs were not made with a view to creating a coherent body of work. Instead, McIntyre was slowly making her own way into Kākahi and getting to know the place on her terms. In the early photographs her eye was drawn to surprising details, and the overall approach could be described as random and opportunistic, best exemplified by the photograph of a goat sheltering from drizzle under a front porch in Taumarunui. McIntyre spied the creature standing as stiff as a piece of taxidermy, and shot it while balancing out of her car window.

What she came to discover through her photography was that Kākahi was full of unexpected juxtapositions and one-off scenes. *Whakapapa Picnic*, 2008, an early work in the series, is something of an outlier and was made before McIntyre took up permanent residence in Kākahi. The image reinforces the vision of Kākahi as a tranquil idyll, while also quietly disrupting that idea. The hillside bathed in golden light creates an almost lurid intensity of colour. The family group may initially convey a sense of togetherness, but look closer and a feeling of detachment becomes palpable. The picnic scene can also be read as an image about visiting, for the figures seem as if they have just landed in the King Country, and the overall mood is one of unreality. Focusing her attention on seemingly minor details results in a queering of any sense of the bucolic.

Sara McIntyre moved to Kākahi permanently in 2011, to a house perched above the river. It sits on land adjoining her parents' old property, and the modernist house they built is visible across a field of tall grass. The roar of riverwater over rocks is constant and audible from most rooms in the house where she now spends more time, having recently retired. During the six years of nursing in the region McIntyre acquired her own understanding of everyday life for the residents of Kākahi, and she established close friendships that continue to afford her privileged access to photograph the interiors of residents' houses.

Photographing in living rooms and halls, McIntyre has created tender visual symphonies to home, in which images of objects and textures speak of the personal and the familiar. In the 1970s décor of *Joan's Living Room*, 2016, books and *National Geographic* magazines press against each other on the left-hand side of the Huntly brick fireplace, and McIntyre paterfamilias is once more present in the spines of his books visible on the bookshelf. Sara McIntyre's interest in interiors mirrors that of Polish photographer Zofia Rydet (1911–1997), who set herself the task of recording every household in her native

7. Zofia Rydet, in Massimiliano Gioni and Natalie Bell (eds), *The Keeper* (New York: New Museum, 2016), 232.

8. Erihi Adams lives in Taumarunui.

9. Conversation with Sara McIntyre, 30 August 2019.

10. Orhan Pamuk, 'A modest manifesto for museums', in Gioni and Bell, *The Keeper*, 278.

11. Ibid.

12. McIntyre, *Kakahi*.

Poland. For Rydet, 'The house…is a reflection of the society, civilisation, and culture from which it originates; there are no two similar people or two similar houses.'[7]

What do McIntyre's empty interiors tell us about the inhabitants of Kākahi and the other neighbouring towns where she has nursed and photographed? The images of local elders' living rooms speak expressly of family and whakapapa. In *Erihi's Memorial Wall*, 2018, a patterned surface is festooned with photos of whānau.[8] Furry blankets, kete and fake flowers evoke tactility, and the four-bar heater and log burner, warmth. *Alan's Parlour 2*, 2017, shows a similarly active arrangement of family photos. The main wall above the mantelpiece in the front room is prime real estate — the objects displayed there tell us what is most important to McIntyre's friend. Alan Taumata is a kaumātua who was born and raised in Kākahi. Over the years, McIntyre has depicted him in a series of elegant portraits, often with his partner Ramon. She has also photographed his home and exquisite details of his private Chapel of the Holy Cross, which he has constructed on his back lawn. After Ramon died, McIntyre made a portrait of Alan in the kitchen holding his fox terrier Pee-wee. Of their friendship, she says, 'He's part of my life here.'[9] The kitchen portrait conveys the trust and gentleness that flow through this entire chapter of the project.

McIntyre's eye favours individuals over large groups, stories over histories, and the small and cheap over the expensive.[10] In this way, her work echoes the thinking of Turkish writer Orhan Pamuk who, in his discussion of museums, argues for the potency of intimate histories: rather than sweeping narratives, it is 'the stories of individuals,' writes Pamuk, that are 'much better suited to displaying the depths of our humanity'.[11] The intimacy with which McIntyre portrays Kākahi highlights a generational shift in approach when compared with that of her father. In *Kakahi New Zealand*, Peter McIntyre addressed the diversity of the residents in the village with an air of paternalism and detachment typical of its time. He observed 'something of a cosmopolitan touch to Kākahi with its European, Maori and Indian mixture'.[12] Sara McIntyre's angle is more 'show, don't tell'.

In the image *Walshie's*, 2015, she subtly grounds the local/global conversation in a room in which a paper map of the world is pinned up beside the faded poster of the 1966 classic *Khartoum*. The film dates from roughly the same time as Peter McIntyre's Kākahi book. White British actor Laurence Olivier famously played the Sudanese leader Muhammad Ahmed in the film — a culturally inappropriate miscasting. Sara McIntyre's photograph of the faded poster reminds us of the datedness of old Hollywood, and the pervasiveness of the ideologies of the recent past. *Walshie's* opens a conversation about globalisation, history and racial politics, telescoped down into a cosy Kākahi room, and reveals McIntyre's ability to ground her audience in the every day and undercut any sense of lofty grandeur.

The humility of the work could also be viewed as a challenge to her father. When Peter McIntyre travelled through the western states of America he recorded his experience in paintings that were later published in the aptly named *West* (1970). Echoing this heroic body of work, Sara McIntyre finds a pack of local cowboys at the summer rodeo in Kākahi and captures them in all their double-denim splendour in *Kākahi Rodeo*, 2014. Then she takes us one step further with *Taumarunui Tapestry*, 2016, an image of a herd of wild palomino ponies cantering across a kitsch wall-hanging beside a group of sleepy succulents and cats.

* * *

In Kākahi, a pervading twilight seems to hang over the village, which gives the place a precarious status, and many of McIntyre's images show the march of time, including *Vanguard*, 2008, a photograph of an old car in its final resting place beneath the sprawling branches of a tree. Once a thriving sawmill town with a population that could support three churches, a hotel, boarding house, cinema and pool hall, Kākahi has been in population decline for more than 60 years. When the school closed in 2016, some suggested it could be converted into a backpackers', but tourism in the area does not yet exist in sufficient numbers to support such a venture.[13]

Kākahi's streets are still home to crumbling colonial buildings and, just as her father did, McIntyre cannot resist recording the old architecture, returning to some of the same buildings first memorialised

13. https://www.stuff.co.nz/national/78606837/Kākahis-gradual-decline-is-history-in-the-making-for-blinks-smith

14. McIntyre, *Kakahi*, np.

in Peter McIntyre's paintings. In the text accompanying a painting of the shops on the main road, Peter McIntyre observes, 'with its haunting sense of time past it sits with a seedy charm like a western movie set awaiting the actors'.[14] Sara McIntyre also capitalises on the filmic quality of the old buildings. *Kākahi Bakery*, 2018, and *Kākahi Pool Hall 2*, 2017, are thick in mise en scène, with grey skies hanging over the boarded-up fronts and a lonely hound scampering past.

It might appear that there is nothing behind the flat weatherboard façades, but McIntyre has the keys to many of the community spaces and she lets herself in to see, ultimately taking us with her. A few public buildings, including the Kākahi Town Hall and the Ōhura Bowling Club, are still in use, but McIntyre chooses to explore these sites of community ritual and togetherness in images which are absent of people. In *Kākahi Town Hall*, 2016, it is the industrial-sized tomato sauce bottle, ready for drenching the mini bacon and egg pies, which punctuates the silence, not the people who will eat this food. It is the food that signals life and occupancy, and brings warmth to the scene. In *Ōhura Bowling Club*, 2015, McIntyre takes in all the textures and patina of the wooden surfaces with the honours boards and trestle tables, and the arrangement of stacked chairs. The composition evokes the slow accretion of stuff paid for by subs and fundraisers, and affirms collective community experience. Humour and tragedy share equal billing in McIntyre's image of an empty stage and abandoned table tennis match in the earlier work, *Kākahi Town Hall*, 2014. In the digital age, when children are glued to their screens and addicted to Minecraft, there is something especially poetic about a lone table-tennis table — a site of many teenage battles before virtual space invaded.

15. J. A. P. Alexander, *Perspectives on Place: Theory and practice in landscape photography* (London: Bloomsbury, 2014), 83.

16. The Kākahi General Store may close, which will take away from the settlement immediate access to commercially produced products and require residents to travel elsewhere to buy them. 'The town will go into deep mourning. It's not just the store. It's him, and Kamu.' Communication with Sara McIntyre, 4 September 2019.

17. The term 'edgeland' was first coined by Marion Shoard in 'Edgelands', in Jennifer Jenkins (ed.), *Remaking the Landscape: The changing face of Britain* (London: Profile Books, 2002).

In his discussion of the shaping of place in photography, J. A. P. Alexander organises land into distinct categories: 'inner city, suburban, rural countryside (cultivated land, villages, and hamlets), and the more expansive open spaces like national parks'.[15] Kākahi fits into the village subset — albeit a village with only one shop.[16] Alexander uses the term 'edgeland' to describe spaces that lack identity, such as business parks, conference centres and electricity substations; post-industrial wastelands also qualify.[17]

However, Alexander's British taxonomies cannot be neatly applied to the New Zealand context. The utilitarian nature of an 'edgeland' does not seem appropriate, for Kākahi is not without identity. What it lacks are some of the traditional markers of place — infrastructure, a steady population which replaces itself, jobs — but while McIntyre's project might highlight an uncertain future, images such as that of the slumping and weed-covered *Kākahi Pool Hall*, 2018, reveal how decline takes time. In this way, her photographs are like *very late* 'late photography', a term that defines the documenting of the aftermath of past events of historic proportions.[18] McIntyre's photographs, especially her images of old buildings, document the continuing effects of the colonial project. The promise of Kākahi's logging boom in the early decades of the twentieth century is fading.

This is not new territory in New Zealand art. Between 1953 and about 1966, photographer Les Cleveland explored the effects of the collapse of primary industries on the West Coast in one of the country's earliest photobooks: *The Silent Land* (1966).[19] Cleveland, like Peter McIntyre, established a precedent in his portrayal of stillness. About the painting of Kākahi's church and the old smithy, McIntyre writes, 'It is a place of peace, unconcerned with time.'[20] Compare this with one of Cleveland's descriptions:

Even shops, churches, halls
And places that seem inhabited
Remain smugly silent.[21]

Both artists identified an attitude of indifference in the old places they documented which lingered on, seemingly unaware of the progress all around them.

* * *

18. Photography specialist David Campany coined the term 'late photography' in the 2003 essay 'Safety in numbness: Some remarks on problems of "Late Photography"' in D. Green (ed.), *Where Is the Photograph?* (Brighton: Photoforum and Photoworks, 2003), 126.

19. Waiutu, Denniston and Barrytown all thrived when mining was good: www.stuff.co.nz/national/85447628/historic-new-zealand-towns-that-used-to-thrive-then-disappeared

20. McIntyre, *Kakahi*, np.

21. Les Cleveland, *The Silent Land: A pictorial record of the West Coast of the South Island of New Zealand* (Christchurch: Caxton Press, 1966), 42.

Not quite a town, with roughly fifty households, no public facilities and a falling population, Kākahi's future may appear uncertain, yet there is nothing silent about Sara McIntyre's project. Rather than dwell in the emptiness and quiet, she offers a constellation of imagery resonant in affection for, and a long-term connection with, the community of Kākahi. *Observations of a Rural Nurse* is at once a deeply personal project about memory and one that opens up a broader discussion about time, generational shifts, and the less than straightforward nature of rural decline in New Zealand. The body of work — diverse in approach and tone — complicates an easy narrative of falling away. In this book, images of decrepit buildings sit alongside social spaces that continue to draw the community together; quiet, seemingly forgotten parts of the village are presented with busy, highly tended interiors; we meet some of the permanent residents, while experiencing the ever-changing seasons. The landscape photographs interspersed throughout act like visual resting points. The land feels timeless, while the colonial past hangs on, remaining visible in the falling down architecture — and the life of the community continues.

Kākahi is experiencing something of a renaissance. In recent years, old houses have been bought as holiday homes, mostly by trout fishers. The community spirit remains strong, reflected in images like *Kākahi*, 2015, in which Dax and his dog confront the viewer like a pair of proud guards. *Kākahi Working Bee*, 2018, witnesses a group of young people gathered at the side of the Hemopo house for a rest after a morning's work tidying up Auntie Pipiana's house for whānau to use. Kākahi is a Māori place with a growing local population who whakapapa to the area. Like her father, Sara McIntyre is drawn to the marae, where she has photographed community events. Her images of the wharekai, opened in 2014, testify to the vision of Ngāti Manunui, who wanted to acknowledge the centenary of the marae with a new building.

Renovations continue in Kākahi and other parts of the southern King Country. For a long time, there was no electricity in Mrs Ruruku's old house and Sara McIntyre photographed the building blanketed in mist and lichen in 2015. When you drive south out of Taumarunui today, if you look up on the right you might see Mrs Ruruku's old house with its new roof and weatherboards.

Family album

— Sara McIntyre

These photographs are taken by family members, some are my father's paintings, some are my own early attempts at developing and printing in my parents' bathroom. A family album telling a further story — life at Kākahi.

Fig. 01 Te Whare Ra, the first little house we stayed at in Kākahi, today.
Fig. 02 Te Whare Ra.

Fig. 03 Alistair Webber, left, and Simon during that first summer at Kākahi.
Fig. 04 A drawing from Peter's *Kakahi New Zealand* book.

05

06

07

FEB · 65

08

Fig. 05 My parents' house-building in progress.
Fig. 06 Peter with Dick and Leslie Peacock.

Fig. 07 Tammy the horse, who moved very slowly but was a means of transport for our expeditions.
Fig. 08 Verandah living, 1965.

Fig. 09 A watercolour of the original front lawn from Peter's Kākahi book.
Fig. 10 Japanese maple and remnants of the floor of the house after the slip.

Fig. 11 The front lawn before the slip.
Fig. 12 My son Matthew and his daughter Mahina on the remains of the original house site.

Fig. 13 Two days after the flood. The house was moved back a week later. The river has since taken the entire site and garden.

285

14

15

16

17

18

Fig. 14 John and Billy Ham moving cattle up the cutting after crossing the river. This photo was taken by Patti, who only took photos when she was asked to hold a camera for safe-keeping.

Fig. 15 Patti and Emma McIntyre (Simon's daughter) on an evening stroll.
Fig. 16 This photo of Te Rena Road was one of my earliest attempts at processing and printing.

Fig. 17 Grandsons, cat and dog all tagged along on Peter's evening walks.
Fig. 18 David Allen, Simon and Manu Lala setting off on a hunting trip in David's Chevy, dubbed Green Acres.

19

20

21

22

23

Fig. 19 The Enchanted Forest, so named by my grandchildren before the blackberry took over.
Fig. 20 My granddaughter Mia.

Fig. 21 Mia and her brother Louis beside my garage when the garden was a wilderness.

Fig. 22 Our Valiant crossing the Whakapapa River bridge, which consisted of two logs and some planks. We usually got out to walk.

Fig. 23 Matthew and Sam painting the garage.

24

25

26

27

28

Fig. 24 An evening drink during Peter's last summer.
Fig. 25 Patti and Peter.
Fig. 26 Simon and Peter when Peter was gently declining but very content to be at Kākahi.

Fig. 27 Patti pickling walnuts. This was a long, drawn-out process. Patti and her brother-in-law, Douglas Fraser, were chief picklers.

Fig. 28 The pickling ritual continues through generations but now revolves around evening drinks time.

29

30

31

32

33

34

Fig. 29 Patti and cows.
Fig. 30 Renoir's Picnic. There's something about the light.

Fig. 31 Peter and my uncle, Douglas Fraser, spent hours talking about everything, neither listening to the other much.
Fig. 32 Simon thinking about fishing.

Fig. 33 My grandchildren, Mia and Louis, in the glow-worm cutting. It was made in the 1920s to put a railway through to Tokaanu but this is as far as it got.

Fig. 34 Matthew fishing the Whakapapa River below where the house used to be.

35

36

37

38

Fig. 35 A painting from *Kakahi New Zealand* of Simon and me on the front lawn looking towards 'the Junction', the point at which the Whakapapa joins the Whanganui River.

Fig. 36 At Alan Taumata's after Peter's memorial service at the marae.

Fig. 37 Rosie McIntosh on her back porch. This is another of my early processing and printing efforts.
Fig. 38 Kākahi in its heyday.

290

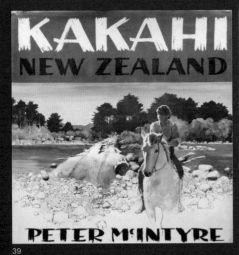

Fig. 39 The cover of Peter's book, showing John Ham on his horse and Patti, Simon and Curry the dog crossing the Whakapapa River bridge.

Fig. 40 Local children outside the original Kākahi General Store. Their families are still in the area.

Fig. 41 The Kākahi Postcentre at the back of the General Store is unchanged. Even the piupiu is still there.
Fig. 42 St Peter's Church at the Kākahi Marae, pre-1920s.

About the contributors

Sara McIntyre was born in Wellington and worked as a neonatal intensive care nurse for several years. In 2010 she moved to Kākahi in the King Country, where she had been visiting with her family since 1960. While working as a district nurse, based at Taumarunui Hospital, she had the opportunity to further explore the area as a photographer. This led to her first solo exhibition at the Anna Miles Gallery in 2016. The Sarjeant Gallery, Whanganui, will exhibit her work in May 2020.

Julia Waite is Curator, New Zealand Art at Auckland Art Gallery Toi o Tāmaki. Her research interests are focused on the development of modern art in New Zealand. In 2015 she curated the touring exhibition *Freedom and Structure: Cubism and New Zealand Art 1930–1960*. Most recently, she co-curated *Gordon Walters: New Vision* and contributed to the associated book which was shortlisted for the 2018 Ockham New Zealand Book Awards. In 2019 she co-curated the major survey *Louise Henderson: From Life*.

Acknowledgements

Anna Miles and Simon McIntyre for their extraordinary support, encouragement, and guidance. Without them none of this would have happened.

Sarah Gladwell, Julia Waite, Haru Sameshima, Mark Sweet, Sanji Karu, Greg Donson, Laurence Aberhart, Athol McCredie, Alistair Webber, Allie Webber, Alan Taumata, Manu and Kamu Lala, Mike Walsh and Maxine Adern.

Shirley Renata, Willie Rameka, Erihi Adams, Theona Turner, Rowena, and all who those generously allowed me to photograph them and or their homes, shops and gardens.

The people of Taumaihiorongo Marae and Kākahi.

The district nurses and staff at Taumarunui Hospital.

Jane Elliott and Edward Mee, Sarah McIntyre, Frances Walsh, Annabel Sinclair Thomson, Burton Silver, Al Brown.

My sons: Sam, Matthew and Henry.

Creative New Zealand.

Index
of works

MASSEY
UNIVERSITY
PRESS

First published in 2020 by
Massey University Press
Private Bag 102904,
North Shore Mail Centre
Auckland 0745, New Zealand
www.masseypress.ac.nz

Design by Sarah Gladwell
Cover image by Sara McIntyre

A catalogue record for this book is
available from the National Library
of New Zealand

Printed and bound in China by
Everbest Printing Investment Ltd

ISBN: 978-0-9951229-7-0

Developed with contributions
by Anna Miles Gallery and
Creative New Zealand

Anna Miles *Gallery*

creative nz
ARTS COUNCIL OF NEW ZEALAND TOI AOTEAROA

Cover:
Porou Street, 2015

Back cover:
Kākahi Town Hall, 2017

Pages 298–99:
My grand entrance
alongside the glow-worm
cutting, 2017

Pages 300–01:
Manunui clothesline
2017

Pages 302–03:
Ngarimu Street, Ōhura
2015